SOME MURDERS IN BERLIN

SOME MURDERS IN BERLIN

KAREN ROBARDS

mira

ISBN-13: 978-0-7783-0551-4

Some Murders in Berlin

Mira
22 Adelaide St. West, 41st Floor
Toronto, Ontario M5H 4E3, Canada

Printed in U.S.A.

To my boys, Peter, Christopher and Jack, with love. Eat dirt, children.

(Not to worry, dear readers. This is a mother/son joke.
My youngest said he'd laugh every time he saw the book if I put that in.)

1

POINTED DOWNWARD, THE BEAM FROM THE SLOTTED torch was a beacon in the darkness. Elin Lund picked her way toward it, shoes crunching through a carpet of debris from a recent Allied bombing. She knew it was recent from the reek of burning emanating from the waves of destroyed buildings on either side of the road.

Don't go, Mama. The memory of her son's imploring voice clutched at her just like six-year-old Niles's desperate hands had grabbed on to her skirt as she'd left him behind in Copenhagen some twelve hours before. Even as her heart contracted, Elin thrust the memory away. She'd had no choice, no possibility of refusing. All she could do was honor her promise to come home as soon as she could.

It was Thursday, September 9, 1943, and she was, most unwillingly, in Berlin. Though it was cooler now, the day had been stiflingly hot and dry and every step she took gave birth to a puff of dust. She could feel the grit settling inside her shoes, between her nylons and her sensible black pumps.

I don't want to visit Farmor. Niles's whisper, urgent and pleading, as Elin walked him to the door of his paternal grandmother's house, twisted through her mind despite her best efforts to block it. She hadn't said to him, *I'm afraid to leave you with anyone else*, although that was the truth. He was too young to be told that the faces people show the world are not necessarily who they are, and that you must always be on guard to protect yourself and those you love from what might lie hidden beneath.

Please, I want to come with you. Niles's words had ripped at her heart then, and they ripped at it now. Because of course that wasn't possible. A little more than a week ago, on Sunday, August 29, the entire Danish government had resigned in protest against the German occupiers' demand that they institute the death penalty for saboteurs. The Germans were now in complete control of Denmark. But if Denmark had just become infinitely more dangerous, Berlin was the beating heart of darkness that controlled all the evil in the world.

Sternly she told herself, *Niles is safe, and you're here to do a job. The sooner you get it done, the sooner you can go home again.*

The thought made her ache inside. More than anything in the world, she wanted to go home. Even more than she *didn't* want to be in Berlin.

But for now, like it or not, here she was.

Because of the mandated total blackout, the pale sickle moon and accompanying panorama of stars blazed diamond bright in the night sky. They provided sufficient light to reveal uneven mounds of rubble extending back to the damaged remains of structures jutting upward like jagged teeth. From what she could see, the destruction stretched for blocks. Farther on, more blocks of undamaged tenements crowded with the working-class residents of this southeastern suburb were silhouetted against the stars. About a dozen meters ahead, several men milled around in the deep, weed-clogged ditch that ran beside the road. The torch that drew her inexorably onward was held by one of the men.

What the light played over was, she saw as she drew closer, a woman. A *dead* woman. Naked, covered in what was almost certainly blood, tossed like garbage into the ditch. Probably from an automobile—although a quick glance around confirmed the presence of an elevated railway almost directly overhead, so an ejection from a train car was another possibility.

The torch flashed in her direction.

"Keep to the center of the road." The gruff order, barked by the man holding the torch, was directed at her and her two companions. Her *team*, for the purposes of this investigation. Pia Andersen and Jens Moller, weighted down with equipment as they walked a pace or so behind her, were fellow academics at the University of Copenhagen. Each was highly accomplished in fields far removed from her own. And right now, both had an urgent reason to flee Denmark.

We need your help. Pia's desperate plea, whispered as she'd dragged Jens into Elin's office minutes after Elin herself had arrived at work Wednesday morning, had been impossible to refuse. Not that she'd even thought of refusing. But afterward, as the minutes had ticked by, she'd grown increasingly afraid that her help wasn't going to be enough, that Pia and Jens would be discovered, that they all would be caught.

So when the opportunity had presented itself, she'd acted on a spur-of-the-desperate-moment flash of inspiration, and used the clout afforded by her unwanted celebrity to get Pia and Jens out of Copenhagen by bringing them with her. Their skills were indispensable, she'd insisted to the Nazi officials who'd shown up unannounced in her office to "request" her immediate departure from the university to assist in the investigation of what one described as "some murders in Berlin." If, that was, the Germans desired a quick resolution to the matter.

It seemed they did. The necessary travel papers had been issued, and the three of them had been whisked away from the university and given just enough time to make personal arrangements (which, for Elin, meant seeing to the safe disposition of Niles) and pack their bags before being shepherded onto an airplane and flown to the last place on earth she would have chosen to go.

Berlin. Being back here made her chest feel tight. But she wasn't going to let it throw her off balance. She was going to let the past stay in the past and concentrate on the here and now.

On this murder. On this terrifying situation.

The risky gamble she, Pia, and Jens were engaged in had worked—so far. With every breath she drew, Elin prayed their luck would continue to hold.

"Sorry," Jens called back as they moved to the center of the road. A lumbering blond giant of a man, Jens was gifted with an unflagging affability that didn't fail him even now.

The torch beam dropped. The man holding it—the *policeman* holding it—turned back to his task.

Will we be found out? Will they arrest us?

Elin's heart thudded as nerves threatened to get the better of her. If the Germans they'd eluded in Denmark even suspected where their quarry had disappeared to, all it would take would be a single telephone call to the authorities here in Berlin, and the jig would be up. Now that total power was theirs, the Nazi occupiers were cracking down hard on those caught participating in the Danish Resistance or aiding any participants in the Danish Resistance. And back in Copenhagen, acting on a tip from an informant, the Germans had already shut down the university while conducting a furious hunt through students and staff for members of the Holger Danske resistance group who were wanted in connection with the dynamiting of a factory some thirty-six hours before and the linked assassination of two of the thousands of German soldiers currently occupying Denmark.

One of the conspirators had been wounded fleeing the scene,

it was rumored, making him easy for authorities to identify once he was caught. The rumor was true, Elin knew, because that conspirator was Jens. She'd patched up his left shoulder not long after Pia, frantic with fear, had shown up in her office with him. The stitched-up wound was even now packed with wads of gauze and wrapped tightly to control any possible breakthrough bleeding.

The penalty for what they'd done, for all three of them, was death.

"Hello, welcome, glad you could join us." Pia's sarcastic mutter directed at the policeman who'd barked at them was just loud enough—and no louder, Elin devoutly hoped—to reach her ears.

"Hush." Elin hissed the warning over her shoulder. Pia hated the Nazis and made only minimal efforts to hide it. Up until the Sunday before last, in Copenhagen, in the university setting in which they all worked, her attitude had escaped official notice. Truth was, most of Copenhagen hated the Nazis, too.

But they weren't in Copenhagen now. And even there, everything had changed.

"What if you never come back?" Niles's tearful question as Elin hugged him goodbye had shattered her. They were both still haunted by the death of Niles's father some three years before. If, as Niles's grandmother claimed, the little boy clung too tightly to his mother, it was because he was terrified of losing his only remaining parent. Even entertaining the thought that such a thing could happen terrified Elin, too.

If I hadn't brought Jens and Pia along, I would be in no danger now.

Should she have left them to their fate? Did she owe that much to her child? But if she'd left them behind, they almost certainly would have been caught, arrested, and quite possibly, by now, summarily executed.

I couldn't have left them. Whatever happened, there was no disputing that, and the certainty of it made her feel better.

"I'm sick of kowtowing to the bastards," Pia hissed back.

"When your head is in the mouth of a bear, the only wise thing to do is say *Nice bear*," Elin replied in a grim undertone.

"She's right, you know." Jens's gentle intervention, directed at Pia, was rewarded with what sounded perilously like a growl.

"No more talking." Elin's warning had an edge to it as they neared the crime scene.

A surly grunt was the response. Petite, with a sleek cap of butter-colored hair, Pia was possessed of a mercurial temperament that the fraught events of the last few days had exacerbated. Or maybe—and this was being charitable—she was simply too exhausted to think clearly. It was, after all, past three in the morning, they'd arrived in Berlin only a few hours before, and while she didn't know how much sleep the other two had managed to snatch, Elin personally had been roused from her hotel room bed shortly after falling into it. As a result, she wasn't operating with her usual cool efficiency either. Otherwise, she would have already concluded that unless the body had been dropped from above, the rubble at the side of the road should hold signs of how it had arrived at its resting place. In other words, evidence that she and her "team" might be trampling.

Under less nerve-racking circumstances, it would have been mortifying to think that they were living up to the Kripo's disdain.

Which, along with their host's lack of enthusiasm for their presence, had already been made abundantly clear to them by the bracket-faced policewoman who'd collected them from the hotel, driven them to the scene, and now waited with the car behind the roadblock cordoning off the area.

"You ready for us to take her away?" one of the men in the ditch asked. Although the questioner didn't raise his voice and the question wasn't directed to her, Elin was now close enough to overhear.

A gesture of assent from the man with the torch, who seemed to be in charge, accompanied the reply. "Go ahead. We've done all we can here."

"Wait!" Elin's voice rang out as two of the men turned toward the body and bent over it with the clear intention of moving it to what she saw, as she reached the edge of the ditch, was a stretcher laid out nearby. "Leave her as she is. Please."

That last was tacked on as an afterthought as once more the torch swung in her direction. The men turned as one to look at her. There were four of them, two in uniform and two in civilian clothes, revealed as the light skimmed past. Throwing up her hand against the beam as it caught her full in the face, Elin clambered down the long, steep slope into the ditch.

"Professor Lund," the man holding the torch said, and the light dropped away from her face. "Or should I say, Dr. Murder." His deep, gravelly voice acquired the slightest hint of a sardonic edge on the last two words as he stepped forward to meet her. It wasn't a question. It was clear he knew who she was, and that he'd been expecting her. That in turn told her who he had to be: the CID detective in charge of the investigation, Kriminalinspektor Kurt Schneider. She'd been told that he would be waiting for her at the crime scene.

"Detective Schneider." Holding out her hand, she tried to keep the annoyance she felt at his use of her despised nickname out of her voice. "And Professor Lund is fine."

He took her hand, shook it. His was a big hand, thick palmed and long fingered, his grasp firm and quickly released. He wore a fedora, tipped low in front, and that plus the darkness veiled his features. But the impression he gave was that of a gangster, and she recalled that the Kripo had a reputation for thuggishness and brutality. He was tall—the top of her head reached to about his chin level and she was tall herself and wearing pumps—and leanly built, with wide shoulders. Besides the fedora, he had on a jacket and tie, civilian clothing, as was the norm for the detectives of the *kriminalpolizei*.

"I'd like to examine the body before it's moved."

His lids dropped, and she suspected his eyes were sliding over her just as the torch had done. Given the vagaries of the moon-light, he would be able to see no more of her than she could of him, she suspected. She was wearing a snugly belted black skirt with a white blouse, and was possessed of an unconventional kind of slim, angular beauty that combined sharp cheekbones and a well-defined jawline with ice-blue eyes and honey-blond hair that was twisted up just at present into a neat roll in back.

Still, there was something about the way he was looking her over that she found unsettling.

Could he know about Jens? As his lids lifted again she met the dark glint of his eyes—impossible to read them, or his expression—and panic bubbled up inside her. Taking a firm grip on her compo-sure, she dropped her own gaze to the corpse.

If these men knew, we would already be under arrest.

She half expected him to protest, but instead he said, "Be my guest," and made a gesture that invited her to proceed.

As she stepped past him, he swung the torch to illuminate something behind and above her. She didn't even have to glance around to know what he was looking at. The nervous flutter in her stomach told her.

"My team," she said with an airy wave, and introduced Pia and Jens, who stood together at the edge of the road above the ditch looking down on the grisly tableau. "Associate Professor Pia Andersen, Professor Jens Moller, from the University of Co-penhagen." Her manner was as briskly confident as if for her to appear with a team in Berlin—when she alone had been sent for—was to be expected. "Could I get some light here, please?" she concluded as she crouched beside the body.

The other man in civilian clothes was older, shorter, and heavy-set. Up until then he'd hovered like a shadow in the background. Now he switched on a torch, stepped forward, and handed it to her.

"Kriminalassistent Walter Trott," Schneider said.

Elin acknowledged him with a nod. The single, tightly focused light wasn't nearly sufficient, but with a quick thank-you to the donor she swept the beam over the victim.

2

THE HORROR OF WHAT ELIN SAW INSTANTLY WIPED ALL ELSE from her mind. Her every faculty coalesced on the woman on the ground. Her first impression was of multiple slashing wounds tearing ivory flesh. Throat ripped open, silvery cartilage rings that were what remained of her trachea glinted in the light. Copious amounts of blood, crusted now and brown. Exposed layers of yellow fat, red muscle, the white glint of bone. Flies, gnats, a line of ants crawling along the edge of a gaping wound in the uppermost shoulder blade.

Her heart pounded. *Poor thing.*

The unmistakable smell of death was sickly sweet, a nauseating perfume.

Carefully scooping the ants from the edge of the wound with a found leaf, she waved away the flies and gnats and pulled her professionalism around her like a cloak. No matter how many times she did it, confronting violent death never got easier.

But still she did it. Because as she had learned to her cost, there were monsters at large in the world, and she refused to let them win.

"Is it possible to get more light on her?" She didn't know what field equipment was available and had to assume, from the lack of any evidence, that it was minimal. "If we could get a vehicle over here with its headlights on…"

"More light would draw too much attention." Schneider crouched beside her. "We must work with what we have."

His tone was flat, final.

She made an impatient sound. "For fear of an air raid? Does Berlin not have warning sirens? In any case, outdoors as we are, we would surely hear any approaching bombers in plenty of time to douse our lights."

"It's not bombers that concern me. We're under strict orders not to let word of this get out to the public."

"Why is that?" Doing what she could with the woefully inadequate light, Elin continued her visual examination of the victim. She was no older than twenty, at a guess. Cheeks round with youth, expression surprisingly serene. Eyes closed, lips gently parted. As if she slept.

In life she would have been pretty. Now her face was settling into the death grimace that signified the onset of rigor mortis and her blond hair was matted with blood.

Elin touched the victim's cheek—her face had largely escaped the savagery that had been visited upon her—and found that while the skin felt rubbery, the body was still faintly warm. Traces of lipstick still clung to her lips. Her hair showed evidence of having been carefully curled.

"It's important not to cause panic," he said.

"You don't think it's important to warn Berlin's women that a murderer is roaming the city at night?" Elin ran the beam of light along the legs, the arms. Impossible to be certain without more light, but she thought she saw multiple contusions beneath the blood. The hands had already been encased in paper bags—paper as opposed to cellophane or a similar material allowed air circulation, preventing the formation of moisture that might contaminate evidence—and the feet as well, she noted with a mental nod to the Kripo for this evidence of efficiency. Not many police departments would have thought of the feet.

A glint of gold through the matted hair caught Elin's attention: an earring?

"The women must go to work to run the factories and do all the other jobs that were left behind when the men went off to war. The timing of the shifts means some must be out at night. If they should become too afraid to leave their homes, it will cause problems in the production of goods vital to the war effort. And the soldiers, if they think their women are in danger, will want to leave the front and come home to protect them. To reveal what is happening here would be bad for morale."

As he spoke Elin lifted the blood-stiffened hair and saw that the golden glint was indeed an earring, a heart-shaped button style still fastened in place. Gold rimmed, its clear celluloid center encased a tiny yellow flower. The earring was smeared with blood and the surrounding lobe was crusted with it.

Her pulse quickened. The smooth celluloid looked like the ideal surface from which to recover a fingerprint.

"I see," she said. These were not the circumstances for arguing with one who represented the iron fist of the Third Reich, but her response was perhaps more clipped than it should have been because she simply couldn't help it. She'd despised the Nazis even before they'd targeted Denmark, and ensuing events had only hardened her feelings into true hatred. But to let it show would not only be stupid; it could also prove fatal.

Directing her light toward the victim's other ear, she sensed rather than saw Schneider frown.

"The faster we catch whoever did this, the sooner our women will be safe. Which is why you've been brought in to help. The work you did on the Gerd Johansson case was impressive. Your investigative techniques are unorthodox, but they seem to pay off, at least in theory. We can only hope they will work as well in real life."

He didn't even trouble to hide that he had grave doubts that they would.

"They do," Elin said. If her reply was cold, he'd earned it.

"I'm excited to have the chance to observe them firsthand."

It wasn't so much his tone that was objectionable, she decided as she determined that the second earring was missing after running the light carefully over tangles of blond hair and the surrounding ground without finding it. It was his whole attitude. As if, having been thrust upon him, the hardened detective, she, the naive academic, was to be simultaneously humored and disregarded.

"In case it's escaped your notice, our victim is still wearing a single earring. The other is missing," she said.

"It didn't escape my notice."

"You chose not to remove the earring and bag it as evidence?"

"I thought it would be best to leave it in place to allow the coroner to see it in situ. Evidentiary-wise."

It was a defensible choice. Perhaps even a good one.

"From the pattern of blood on the earlobes, she was wearing both earrings when she was killed." She did *not* sound grudging. "If the other one's not here, it's possible the killer took it as a trophy."

"If we find the earring, we find our man, eh? Just like with the dog in the Johansson case."

He *had* been checking up on her. Her lips compressed. The abduction and murder of ten-year-old Swedish schoolgirl Gerd Johansson several years before still haunted her. The boy Gerd had been playing with when she'd disappeared was the primary suspect. But Elin, a psychiatrist with additional training in forensics and a particular interest in murder, had avidly followed the case and in her opinion the details didn't fit. She'd passed her observations on to the local police, for whom she'd consulted on a previous, far less sensational murder. They in turn had contacted the Stockholm police, who had requested her assistance, which she'd been pleased to provide. In the end, her profile of the killer had posited that he owned a particular type of dog, and that was the break the authorities had needed to identify the man who was later convicted of the murders.

A journalist who'd been following the investigation then wrote a book about it, casting her as the doctor/detective/heroine responsible for solving the case. The book was a huge bestseller, the journalist became famous, and Elin, without quite realizing what was happening, became famous as well.

With the publicity that had ensued, she'd been called in by her local police department to consult on additional cases, and somewhere along the way she'd been saddled with the sobriquet Dr. Murder.

"A psychological profile can be as revealing as a fingerprint," she said.

"I don't doubt it."

There it was again, the hint of skepticism beneath the blandness.

"I take it that it wasn't you who sent for me," she said.

"No."

That blunt answer was no more than she'd expected, though she would have thought he'd have couched it more tactfully. Perhaps trying to be polite to someone he had no desire to work with was wearing as thin for him as it was for her.

"I'll get started," Jens called. Not sorry to have her attention diverted, Elin lifted a hand to indicate that she'd heard.

"Get started with what?" Schneider asked as she reached for her black leather doctor's bag, which she'd put down beside her in the scraggly, debris-clogged weeds. Snapping it open, she thrust an unerring hand inside. Although the bag was large, she kept everything in its allotted place and thus no light was required to find what she sought. That would be her "murder kit"—a pouch containing plastic gloves, tweezers, a scalpel, glass slides and tubes, and evidence bags.

"Jens—Professor Moller—is a mathematician, among other things. He'll be taking measurements, and from them make calculations that will help identify the killer." At least in theory. She, Pia, and Jens had worked out a rudimentary plan for how their "team" would operate in the snatched moments they'd had alone since being escorted from the university. This was their first opportunity to put it into practice. What she schooled herself to remember was, it didn't matter if the plan worked. It only mattered if it appeared to this policeman—these policemen—to work. In reality, she could do everything that was necessary on her own.

"I didn't know I'd be getting so many assistants. I was prepared for only you," he said as she pulled on her gloves. Though she read nothing alarming in his face or voice, a cold prickle of unease slid over her skin. For him to conclude that the presence of Jens and Pia required further investigation could prove disastrous.

"I'm not your assistant, and neither are they. We're outside consultants brought in to contribute our expertise to the investigation. Your partners, not your subordinates." Her voice was crisp. If she'd learned anything in life, it was to never show fear. "I was told that it's imperative that the person who did this be caught quickly, so I would think you'd welcome the fresh perspective we bring."

"At this point, believe me, I welcome any help I can get." His voice was dry.

The near-blinding flash of a camera only slightly above their heads made them both start and look around.

"What the hell..." Schneider said.

Another flash. *Pia*, Elin realized, even as Schneider shot to his full height.

"No lights!" he snapped.

"If you want photographs, there must be light." It was too dark to see Pia's shrug, but it was there in her voice as she stepped around him. That was classic Pia, no respecter of authority even when said authority was not, as this one was, a hated Nazi.

"Then we'll do without photographs." Speaking of authority, Schneider now bristled with it.

"Photographs are essential in a murder investigation." Parroting what Elin had told her, Pia repositioned her bulky Leica, the better, Elin assumed, to get a fresh angle on the corpse. "We must—"

"No lights." It was a muted roar.

"Pia." Elin intervened before the situation could deteriorate. She was the one who'd told Pia to bring her camera, given her role of crime scene photographer, and emphasized how essential such photos were, so it was up to her to head off what could be building toward a disastrous confrontation. "You can make sketches instead. We'll use them, rather than photos, in this instance." Behind Pia, Jens, in the process of laying his metal measuring tape down the side of the ditch, had stopped what he was doing to straighten and look toward them. For all his good humor, Jens had lately developed a fierce protectiveness toward Pia, who he was in the process of trying to persuade to become his wife.

"Jens, when you finish what you're doing there, go ahead and look for footprints, tread marks, anything of that nature, along the road," Elin called to him.

"Will do." Jens's mild response told her that he at least had the full measure of the danger they were in. Pia, with a loud sniff that hopefully no one other than Elin knew reflected her opinion of Schneider, lowered her camera and headed in Jens's direction.

"No need. Herr Trott is seeing to that as we speak. Carry on with whatever else it is you would normally do," Schneider directed Jens. Sinking back down on his haunches beside Elin, he added for her ears alone, "We *have* investigated murders before, you know. Even solved a few."

She ignored the sarcasm. "I prefer to rely on my own findings whenever possible."

"I understand, but duplicating our efforts hardly makes sense. You have your areas of expertise, and that is why you were brought in. I would suggest you stick to them and leave the fundamental police work to us."

It took her only a few seconds' mental struggle to conclude that the sharp answer that sprang to the tip of her tongue was unwise. "I'll do my best to keep that in mind."

"Thank you." He watched in silence as she looked inside the uppermost ear for the internal bleeding that was one of the signifiers of a fractured skull. The ear canal was clogged with it. Probably the victim—

"Your female associate seems to be drawing *me*. Are her sketches going to be of any actual use?" Schneider asked.

Elin's head came up. She glanced at Pia, who had replaced the camera with her sketch pad and did indeed seem to be focusing her efforts in their direction. She frowned at him. "Pia's a gifted artist. Her sketches are extremely detailed and as accurate as any photo, and, yes, I expect them to be very helpful. If she's drawing you, as you say, it's because you're part of the crime scene. Although usually she likes to take photos of her subjects before she draws them, just as usually it's considered extremely important to have actual *photos* of a crime scene, particularly a murder, if for no other reason than for the record when the murderer is brought to trial."

"Then I await the results of her efforts with interest. And we must all adapt. When the occasion demands it."

"As we are doing." Elin passed her torch to him with a crisp, subject-changing "Hold this, please."

He took her torch as she extracted her notebook as well as the instruments she needed from the pouch.

"Keep the light pointed *here*." She indicated the desired area as she shifted into position. Setting one torch atop a boulder-sized piece of rubble, he turned it and the one he still held so that the light focused where she'd indicated. As the twin beams illuminated loose ribbons of bloodied skin and muscle hanging from what had once been softly rounded buttocks, he made an indecipherable sound.

"If you're squeamish, you might want to look away," Elin said. Without waiting to see if he followed her advice, she brushed another insect from mutilated flesh, then carefully inserted the thermometer into the victim's rectum.

"We have a coroner to do such things, you know," he said. A glance showed that, expression stony now as if to reject any suggestion he might be affected by what he saw, he continued to watch.

"As I said, I prefer to rely on my own findings when possible. And taking the body's temperature now, rather than waiting until the coroner gets a chance to do it, will help us more accurately pinpoint the time of death."

A moment later she had the reading: 93.7, which she recorded in her notebook along with the time.

"Do you know her name?" she asked as she jotted down a series of observations concerning the state of the corpse.

"No."

"Who found the body?"

"A man telephoned it in around 2:00 a.m. He didn't identify himself."

"You consider him a suspect." It wasn't a question. The person finding the body was always a suspect.

"Yes, but not necessarily a strong one. If he gave his name when he called in, he would be interrogated, and most people seek to avoid that. But we are doing what we can to identify him."

"Any other viable suspects?"

"Not at this time."

Elin finished her count: twenty-six stab wounds that she could see. Almost certainly there were more that would become apparent when the body, which lay on its left side in an ungainly position, was moved and more thoroughly examined. The concentration of the wounds was significant, as was the degree and location of lividity and pooling. She noted there didn't appear to be any defensive wounds.

One additional telling thing was that, while an oily-looking outline of blood marked the ground around the victim, there was no sign of spray from one at least partially severed artery and no puddle of blood beneath the corpse. She made more notes.

"I can see you're used to working alone," he said.

Alarmed, Elin looked at him sharply.

3

"I'D BE INTERESTED IN HEARING YOUR OBSERVATIONS," Schneider said. Sounding like an explanation, it was said patiently, and was probably offered, Elin realized, in response to the wide-eyed look she'd given him.

Nothing to do with Jens and Pia at all. Elin did *not* sigh with relief. But she felt like it.

"When I'm examining a victim, I tend to get caught up in my thoughts." As far as the letter of exculpatory explanations went, that was actually true. But she *was* used to working alone and that was the last thing she wanted him to suspect. Making a conscious effort, she continued in measured tones. "There are no observable defensive wounds, which in my opinion indicates she was probably unconscious or otherwise incapacitated when the fatal attack occurred. Her body temperature suggests she's been dead about four to six hours. And she was killed elsewhere."

"All of that fits with what we know."

What she read into that was, she'd given him nothing new.

Lips tightening, Elin moved up the body to examine the scalp. "On the way here, I was told that seven women have been murdered in a similar fashion in the city over the last four months." The quantity of blood matting the hair presupposed one or more serious wounds beneath it, she noted as she gently moved a stiffened strand aside. "Could you direct the light this way, please?"

He complied. "Eight now, with her. And the time frame is closer to five months."

"How far apart were the murders?"

"The first one, Inge Weber, was April 25. Astrid Lang, May 16. Roswitha Eckard, June 6. Pauline Fischer, June 27. Bella Richter, July 18. Anna Fromm, August 8. Greta Neuhaus, August 29. Eleven days ago."

He knew all the names, and dates, without having to check. She was reluctantly impressed.

"All Sundays," he added. "Except this one. And all exactly three weeks apart. Except this one."

She nodded acknowledgment of those important facts. "Cause of death the same?"

"Homicide."

She flicked an exasperated glance his way. "Could you be more specific?"

"Numbers one and two were strangled. Manually, as evidenced by broken hyoid bones plus the pattern of bruising on the neck. Three was beaten to death with what we believe was an iron pipe. Four, five, six, and seven had their throats cut. This victim appears to have met her end the same way, although I'll leave it to the coroner to determine the precise cause of death. Oh, and all were slashed multiple times by a very large and sharp fixed-blade knife, although according to our esteemed coroner, on numbers one through three those injuries were postmortem."

"These wounds were antemortem," she said. It was obvious

from the visible bruising around some of the wounds that this victim had been stabbed while still alive. Given the lack of light, it was difficult to be certain, but some of the bruises appeared to have been inflicted by a small, round object. "Before death."

"I know what *antemortem* means."

She ignored that. "Are the victims connected in any way? Do their jobs intersect, perhaps, or do they have something else in common?"

"No connection we've been able to find. Other than being young, attractive females. And their bodies were all nude, cut to ribbons, and found in Berlin."

"Are you certain you're dealing with a single killer?" Completing her examination of two separate scalp wounds, one of which was potentially serious enough to have constituted the fatal blow if the slit throat had not killed her, she sank back on her heels and looked at him.

"I'm not certain of anything. But I think so, yes."

"Why?"

"The letters."

Elin's brow furrowed. "Letters?"

"After each murder, he's sent a letter," Schneider said. "The first three were addressed to General Kaltenbrunner, head of the RSHA, which makes him my boss's boss. At that point someone in the department decided that these might be more than unconnected random acts, and I was put in charge of the investigation. The last four letters have been addressed to me."

Elin drew a breath as the ramifications pinged through her mind like the steel ball in an arcade game.

"There's been no publicity? No mention of the murders on the radio or in the newspapers? Or of you heading the investigation, or being the lead homicide detective, or anything of that nature?"

"No."

"Yet somehow he is following the investigation closely enough to know that you've been put in charge of it," she said.

"Yes."

"How many people know that?"

"A limited number. I would say the whole of Amt V, a few more up and down the chain of command."

"Amt V?"

"My department. Criminal Investigations."

"Oh." She frowned as she considered what that meant for the case. "It seems obvious that the killer must be one of those people. Or someone connected to one of them."

"It does." His tone said that once again she'd given him nothing new.

Despite his attitude, or, more accurately, her irritation at it, a quiver of excitement ran through her. She felt like a hunting dog getting a first scent of its quarry. Instead of the entire male population of Germany, which was basically the set of suspects she'd started with, she was now presented with a far more manageable subset. "With the pool of suspects winnowed to such an extent, solving this case should be achievable. There will be clues, markers—"

"Which is why you've been brought in. Your expertise is expected to succeed where our plodding investigative techniques have not."

If she hadn't already guessed what he thought about her addition to the case, that would have told her. At least it explained the attitude.

"What do they say? The letters?" she asked.

"You can read them tomorrow. In my office in the Alex. Our headquarters."

It was grudging acknowledgment that, however he felt about it, they would be working together.

"That would be very helpful." She turned back to the body. "Could you point the light here?" Gesturing to show him where she meant, Elin began the painstaking work of taking small scrapings from the dried blood around each of the scalp wounds.

"You know the coroner will do that as part of the autopsy."

"As I said—" She paused to concentrate as she carefully transferred one of the scrapings to a glass slide. The lack of sufficient light made the delicate task more difficult.

"You prefer to rely on your own findings," he finished for her.

"Yes." She prepared another slide.

"And as *I* said, it seems wasteful to duplicate what others can do."

"It's not a duplication. I'll be looking for things the coroner won't."

"Such as?"

"From the number and placement of the wounds, I feel relatively certain that in this case at least the final act, the murder itself, was committed in a violent rage or frenzy. With the killer in such a state, it's possible that his saliva or sweat found its way into the open wounds. I'll test the victim's blood for substances such as Pervitin. If it's there, it will be a strong indicator that the suspect is a military man."

Pervitin, as Schneider's expression told her he knew, was the secret fuel that kept the German army going. Passed out by the handful to soldiers from privates all the way up to commanders, the pills made them able to function for days at a time without sleep or food. It also made them incalculably cruel. The kind of cruel that might result in the vicious killings of innocent young women.

"Or simply able to obtain Pervitin."

She nodded. "As you say."

"And how do you test for Pervitin?"

"The presence of certain trace elements in the blood. It's not a screening a coroner usually performs."

His eyebrows went up. "Interesting. I withdraw my objection. Take as many samples as you want. Is there anything else the body can tell you that our highly esteemed coroner might not look for?"

"I'm not maligning your coroner. His specialty is not serial murder. Mine is. As you yourself pointed out, that's why I'm here."

"Fair enough. Now to get back to my original question—"

"Yes." She realized she'd paused with her scalpel suspended in midair and lowered it. "For example, a killer suffering from schizophrenia or delusional disorder tends to choose sharp instruments as a method of homicide. Depressed subjects or those suffering from mood disorders are more likely to kill by strangulation, asphyxiation, suffocation, or drowning. From what you've told me, we have both. Possibly the killer was experimenting at first and then settled upon a method that he feels works best. Or perhaps he suffers from both, probably at different times, which points us in the direction of someone who is disturbed to the point that he will exhibit maladaptive behavior unusual enough to be noticed. We should be searching personnel records of possible suspects for anything of that nature."

"Impressive."

"Psychiatry has its uses." Her reply had an edge to it. *Not wise.* She got back to work. And moderated her tone. "Also, the timing of this murder is important. Either something threw him off schedule, or he's escalating. By 'escalating,' I mean—"

"I know what you mean."

She glanced at him in surprise. The concept of escalation as applied to serial murderers was so new few had heard of it. It was too dark to read his expression, which applied to hers, too, she presumed, and was probably for the best because expressing astonishment that he should know this would do nothing, she suspected, to enhance their working relationship. But the mere act of turning her face in his direction must have given him some indication of her reaction, because he added, "I read your book. Both of them, actually."

"You did?" He *had* checked her out. "Since you found out I was coming?"

She supposed the decision to bring her in could have been made several days ago and the authorities had not bothered to tell her.

"I read fast. And the books aren't long."

Once again, that hint of dryness in his tone. This time it stung. As she finished sealing the last slide, she fought the urge to inform him that her books had been written as academic treatises, not entertainment for the masses.

Instead she tucked the container holding the slides into her bag, saying, "This killer won't quit until he's stopped. Which means we must assume he's escalating. If this is his new pattern and not an aberration of some sort, that gives us about ten days to catch him before he kills again."

"Yes."

The brevity of that single syllable said it all: he'd done the math and knew as well as she did that the clock was already ticking down on another young woman's life.

Somewhere out there, an innocent had days to live.

Elin felt the all-too-familiar, welcome-yet-dreaded rush of adrenaline that was her body's way of preparing for the coming hours and days and maybe even weeks and months of a grueling search.

Until the killer was caught she would be a heightened, edgier version of herself. She didn't like it, but there was nothing she could do about it.

She was a hunter now, and the hunt was on.

The sudden sound of an approaching train startled her, made her look up. Sleek and black, illuminated only by a thin streak of phosphorus paint that kept it from being totally invisible as it rushed through street crossings and an occasional glimmer of light from the edge of a heavily curtained window, it flew toward them on the elevated track.

Head turning to follow the train's progress as it rattled by, Elin pushed shoulder-length strands of hair blown loose by the slipstream of wind that trailed in its wake back from her face.

The body *could* have been thrown from such a train, she calculated, but—

Her attention was caught by two small figures unexpectedly popping into view atop a tram-sized pile of wreckage near the track. Solid shapes against the starry sky, they were jarringly out of place. One had long braids and wore a hugely oversize cardigan and a skirt that flapped as the train passed. The other wore baggy trousers and had close-cropped hair. They stopped short at the crest of the pile to stare down at the activity below.

Children. From their size, they were no more than eight to ten years old. Elin's breath caught. In this blacked-out, locked-down, heavily patrolled city in the wee small hours of the morning, what were children doing out?

The boy—she was almost certain the figure in trousers was a boy—pointed down at the corpse, which the torches partially illuminated. The girl stepped closer to him.

"Halt!" one of the uniformed policemen shouted from behind Elin, making her jump. Even as she threw an alarmed glance over her shoulder, his gun slapped out of its holster, snapped up toward the children. "Don't move!"

The boy grabbed the girl's hand.

"Halt! *Halt!*"

The children turned to flee. As they did a shot cracked like a thunderclap through the clatter of the departing train. It was followed in quick succession by another.

A child shrieked and dropped from view.

Elin's heart leaped into her throat.

4

"NO! THEY'RE *CHILDREN*," ELIN SCREAMED, JUMPING to her feet.

But they were already gone. Both of them. Disappeared. Fallen or running, shot or simply terrified into fleeing, Elin didn't know. Where they'd stood was now nothing but a black mound of debris against a starry sky.

"Hold your fire!" Schneider, too, was on his feet, shouting at his subordinate even as he grabbed Elin's arm to stop her when she would have dashed toward the spot where the children had been.

"Stay," he ordered her, then ignored her attempts to pull free as he turned his attention to the man who'd fired. "Holster your weapon!"

"What's happened?" Pia called from the road. "Elin—"

Schneider pointed at her. "You! Stay where you are!"

"I'm fine, Pia," Elin called back, before giving up the struggle against Schneider's viselike grip to turn on the policeman who'd fired. "How could you? How could you shoot at them?"

He shoved his gun back into its holster. "They're vermin! Street rats—"

"Quiet! The both of you!" Schneider's command was fierce.

"I won't be quiet! They're *children*."

The policeman sneered. "What would you know of it, lady doctor? You're not—"

"Enough!" Schneider's full-throated roar made Elin jump, and the policeman swallowed whatever else he'd been intending to say. With the train now rattling away into darkness, Schneider directed his torch toward the man who'd pulled the trigger. "Explain yourself, Herr Gunther! What the hell did you think you were doing?"

"We were instructed to shoot anyone who ran away upon being challenged!" Sounding frightened by Schneider's obvious wrath, Gunther seemed to shrink.

"I gave no such order!"

"Not—not you, Detective! Nebe himself gave the order!"

SS-Gruppenführer Arthur Nebe was head of the Kripo, Elin knew.

"It's true, Detective! We were all told, all of us, to shoot if they try to run." The second policeman jumped in to back up his partner.

Schneider cursed under his breath, then turned a steely gaze on his subordinates. "Do not fire your weapon again unless I tell you to. Is that understood?"

"Yes, sir!" Both policemen, clearly cowed, snapped off salutes.

Schneider made a sound of disgust even as he indicated the corpse. "Get her out of here. *Now.*"

"Idiots," Schneider muttered as the policemen scrambled to obey.

Elin tried to pull her arm free. "Let me go. I must—"

His gaze shifted to her. His fingers tightened. "No."

"One of those children screamed." Although Elin kept her

voice low, it was taut with urgency. "They might be badly hurt. I'm a physician. I need to find them, if for no other reason than to make sure they're all right."

"No." Once again, Schneider's response was jarring in its brevity.

Anger swamped caution. "What do you mean, no? You can't tell me no. I make my own decisions. And I can't just walk away. I *won't* just walk away. Not from children."

"You can and you will. I'm clearing the area. You included." Extinguishing and pocketing his torch, Schneider plucked her bag from the ground and shoved it at her. "Let's go."

"The only place I'm going is to check on those children." As Elin fumbled to secure her bag, he grabbed the second torch without releasing her arm.

"You mistake my position, and yours. *I'm* in charge here, and you will do as I say." He sounded like he was talking through his teeth as he shoved the torch in his pocket.

She practically vibrated with outrage. "I will never compromise my oath as a physician for—"

"You will do as I say." He loomed over her as they glared at one another. She gave another mighty jerk in an effort to free herself from his grip. Instead of letting go, his hand tightened. Then he let out an audible breath. The fingers wrapped around her arm relaxed and his tone moderated. "Professor Lund, I am asking you to be reasonable. You heard Gunther, and he isn't wrong. They're street rats, without a doubt. Part of a gang of feral youths that roam the city at night. Troublemakers. Criminals. No concern of yours."

"They're *children*."

"You keep saying that. It makes no difference. I respect your expertise in your field, *Dr. Murder*, but in turn you must respect mine. You know nothing of this city or its inhabitants, just as you know nothing of me or my department or the wider ramifications surrounding this investigation. I am asking that you defer to me in this matter. Now let's go."

He started walking, pulling her along with him. The little voice in her head once again cautioned her against antagonizing him. She ignored it. Digging in her heels, she stopped dead, causing him to stop, too, and swing around to frown at her.

"To make myself perfectly clear, Herr Detective, I will *not* defer to you in this matter. I don't need your permission to check on those *children*, and that's what I intend to do. Now let go of my arm!"

Just enough moonlight struck his face to let her watch his eyes narrow. In that moment he looked capable of anything, up to and including her murder.

She responded with a squaring of her shoulders and a jut of her chin.

His mouth tightened. "Is there a language barrier I'm not aware of? In Denmark, does 'no' not mean 'no'?"

"I'll go," a third party interjected before she could respond with any of the extremely impolitic things that sprang to the tip of her tongue. Trott, clearly having overheard at least some of their exchange, came up beside them. In response to the slashing, negative, *go away* gesture that was Schneider's reply, he added persuasively, "Kurt, think. If the goal is to avoid publicity, then we don't want a child's body turning up with a bullet in it on the other side of that hill. Let me go see what's there."

For a moment the issue hung in the balance. Then Schneider flicked a look at Trott and said, "Go. Make it fast." He handed over his torch. As the other man left, Schneider said to Elin, "There. You got what you wanted. Now come with me."

This time she did the only sensible thing. She went with him. Still, she couldn't completely contain herself.

"*Publicity* is what you're worried about?" The barbed question spilled out practically of its own accord as they started up the slope.

"Yes, it is, and I told you why."

"Oh, that's right, I remember now. If these murders are re-vealed it might hurt morale." She was still too angry and upset to be as careful as she knew she should be with him. "Which is the most important thing, after all, and never mind that a *child* may have been *shot*."

"I'm glad to discover that you have so fully grasped the situ-ation."

"Do you think your priorities might be a little skewed?"

The stretcher bearing the corpse, a policeman at each end, was ahead of them, tilted precariously as it was borne up toward the road. A sheet now covered the body, Elin was relieved to see. There was no dignity in death, but at least a small degree of decency had been accorded the victim.

"No," he said.

"Well, I do." Climbing up out of the ditch was harder than coming down, she discovered. The footing was loose and un-even, and her heels made it worse. He'd retrieved the second torch from his pocket and was lighting their way, the beam carefully directed at the ground, but still the going was difficult and darkness shrouded everything. She certainly didn't appreci-ate Schneider's continued hold on her arm, but the unwelcome truth was the support helped.

"That's because you haven't yet fully grasped what's at stake here. The High Command is on edge. In January, the Sixth Army fell to the Russians at Stalingrad. North Africa was lost to the Allies in May. In July, the counteroffensive against the Rus-sians at Kursk failed. Now Mussolini's under arrest and Ham-burg's been bombed to hell. People are growing sick of war, and not all of them are staying quiet about it. Those in charge are desperate to seem in control here at home, and that means domestic affairs must be seen to run like a well-oiled machine. Having a woman-killer running amok in Berlin makes the gov-ernment look bad. The government doesn't like to look bad. If the public learns of these murders through any fault of ours, the consequences to me and my people will be unpleasant, to say the least. You should be thanking me for doing my best to make sure that doesn't happen. I have little doubt those same unpleasant consequences would also extend to you and your team."

At the thought of what those "consequences" might entail, Elin felt a sudden chill. The Nazis were notorious for the brutality of their punishments. Over the last few weeks, as Denmark's occupiers had grown increasingly impatient with the burgeoning resistance movement, her citizens had seen ample evidence of it, culminating in a complete takeover of the government eleven days before.

When the Nazis had first steamrolled into Denmark, people had been hanged in the streets. Without trial. In quick, summary executions.

Elin shivered at the memory. She pushed the thought away. One more tie to the past that could only hinder.

"The public is bound to find out eventually," she said. "And you just might discover they're angry they weren't warned they had a murderer in their midst."

"The High Command's anger worries me far more than the public's. Ah, Walter's back. *So?*" Schneider threw the question over his shoulder. Elin looked back in time to catch Trott's shake of his head.

"Nothing," Trott said.

Schneider turned to Elin. "He found nothing. Satisfied?"

She wasn't, but short of insisting that a search be launched for the children, which she didn't have the authority to order and was completely certain he wouldn't agree to anyway, there was nothing more she could do.

They'd almost reached the top of the slope when she said, "What about securing the crime scene? We barely had time to—"

"No."

"Would you let me finish?" She glared at him, which she was perfectly sure he didn't get the full impact of because of the shadows enveloping them both. "We might be leaving important evidence behind. Something that could solve the case. There might be a button from the murderer's clothing. Or a cigarette butt he discarded. Or—"

He cut her off again. "A chance we must take. But if it comforts you, reflect that we have seven other murders' worth of evidence to fall back on."

It *didn't* comfort her. "Each murder is a separate piece of the puzzle. This one in particular, because of the difference in timing, can tell us something."

"Nevertheless, we must make do with what we have."

"Can you at least leave someone behind to guard the scene until morning to make sure it remains undisturbed?" Exasperation sharpened her voice. "We could come back then."

"No."

"Why not?"

"Because there are spying eyes and wagging tongues everywhere. You think a guard wouldn't be noticed? He would. As would a ground search for clues. Now that shots have been fired, there already will be too much attention turned in this direction."

"So we're just supposed to abandon the scene as if a body was never dumped here?"

"Your grasp of the situation astounds me."

By now they'd gained the top of the hill. Ahead of them, a meter or so farther along the road, the stretcher was being carried steadily toward the waiting cars. Almost directly in its path, Pia stood beside Jens, whose hand on her shoulder seemed to be restraining her. They both were looking toward Elin and Schneider, and Pia in particular seemed to vibrate with emotion. Of course she would be upset about what had happened, too, Elin realized. The stretcher reached her and Jens—

"Autsch." The policeman in front fell to one knee, losing his grip on his end of the stretcher in the process. In what could only have been an instinctive reaction, Jens lunged to catch

the falling poles before breaking off with a wordless cry and a jerky recoil. The front end of the stretcher hit the ground with a thump and the body tumbled off onto the pavement.

Elin barely noticed. Her horrified focus was squarely on Jens. Stumbling back, he clutched his injured shoulder.

"Jens!" Pia whirled and was instantly at Jens's side. At the same time, releasing Elin's arm at last, Schneider leaped forward to converge with the other policemen on the dislodged victim.

"I tripped!" The fallen policeman sprang up.

"Clumsy fool!" His partner still clutched the stretcher's rear poles even as he stared in dismay at the horribly sprawled corpse.

"Get her back on the stretcher." Schneider sounded like he was at the end of whatever patience he in theory possessed.

Fortunately, the policemen's flurry of activity covered their own. Having rushed to Jens's side and seen for herself that Pia's whispered "He's hurt himself" to her as she reached them was horribly true, Elin had time to do nothing more than stare at Jens in alarm before Schneider looked around at them, calling, "Everything all right?"

Elin's pulse jumped. Jens's hand dropped away from his shoulder but she feared it was too late. Schneider had to have seen. Jens was breathing too hard and although he stood perfectly still there was something in his stance that, to Elin at least, unmistakably screamed of pain.

"Yes, of course," she called back, and held her breath.

Schneider, however, did not appear to notice anything amiss. He merely waved at them to move on as, the corpse having been restored to it, the stretcher got underway again.

"We have to go. Can you manage it?" Elin asked Jens in an urgent undertone.

Jens nodded, tight-lipped.

"I'll see to him," Pia whispered, darting a glance past Elin at Schneider, who, clearly impatient, was waiting for them. "You go ahead."

Nodding, she walked away, hoping and praying all the while that no one would be able to tell how much distress Jens was in.

As she reached Schneider, she saw to her dismay that he was looking past her at Pia and Jens. *Frowning* past her at Pia and Jens.

"That fall will have transferred dust and dirt and all manner of foreign material from the road to the victim," Elin said crisply, hoping to redirect his attention. She kept moving as she talked, walking on past him, following the stretcher, and was rewarded by having him fall in beside her. "All trace evidence needs to be closely evaluated to determine its origin in case it came from the fall. Care must be taken so that it isn't identified as being germane to the case. The coroner needs to be informed about what happened so he can try to make those distinctions, and so he knows to make distinctions between ante- and post-mortem scrapes and abrasions."

"Everything that needs to be done will be done," Schneider said. "Once again, we *have* investigated murders before."

A furtive glance back told Elin that Jens, with Pia beside him, was walking after them with no sign that anything was wrong. The worst of her stress-induced tension eased a little even as she did her best to keep Schneider distracted by continuing to pontificate on the importance of uncontaminated trace evidence. But her relief was short-lived. As they reached the vehicles and she paused for a breath, Schneider took advantage of the break to look around at Jens.

"Hurt yourself back there?" he called.

Every cell in Elin's body froze.

"An old shoulder injury," Jens replied. "It acts up from time to time. I must have aggravated it by moving so quickly."

His tone was light and easy. Careful not to let out the breath she'd been holding in a telltale burst of exhalation, Elin silently blessed him for his sangfroid. Schneider seemed to accept his reply at face value, and as they moved on Elin hurried to fill Schneider's ears with more learned opinions that meant absolutely nothing but were designed to distract. Thankfully the darkness prevented him from subjecting Jens—or her—to any very close scrutiny.

The body was already being loaded into an ambulance as they reached the waiting vehicles and she was ready to chalk up her burst of alarm to a combination of guilt and nerves. But when the engines started up and the headlamps came on, Jens was caught full in the resulting blaze of light. A fresh stab of fear made Elin's heart skip a beat.

The shoulder of Jens's light gray jacket was dark with blood.

Wet, the spreading patch gleamed as the light hit it.

And Schneider was looking right at Jens.

5

ELIN EXITED THE AUTOPSY ROOM A FEW MINUTES AFTER EIGHT the following morning. Its bright lights and cold, antiseptic atmosphere followed her out into the overwarm stuffiness of the gloomy, windowless hallway of the Rudolf Virchow Hospital. A man leaned against the institutional-green wall just beyond the door, head bowed, arms folded across his chest, one foot raised to rest flat against the wall. As the door clicked shut behind her he looked up.

Schneider. Their eyes met, and he straightened away from the wall. Her pulse quickened as she realized he was waiting for her.

Last night he'd said nothing about the blood soaking Jens's coat although she was almost certain he'd seen it. How could he have not? He'd been standing right next to her, and from her perspective at least the shiny wet stain and what it meant was glaringly obvious. Why Schneider would have kept silent she didn't know, but her instinctive response to his presence now was to brace for questions and accusations.

"Professor Lund." His gaze swept her. He was unsmiling. The hardness in his eyes was unsettling.

"Detective." Quelling the urge to wet her lips, she acknowledged the greeting with a nod and kept walking right on past him. If he had something to say she didn't mean to make it easy for him. If he thought her rude, well, at least that gave him something besides Jens to think about.

And then there was the matter of the children.

She hadn't forgotten them, or his callousness in that regard. This was not a man she could be friends with.

"Cause of death?" His brusque question referred to the victim, she knew. As he asked it he swung into step beside her. There was an overtly masculine, too aggressive aura about him that made her shoulders tighten and she had to consciously relax them. She was rubbing lotion into her hands—constant washing plus the frequent use of plastic gloves made the skin dry—and the slight floral scent provided a welcome antidote to the disagreeable odors she'd just left behind. She kept on with it, feeling his gaze on her fingers as she massaged the soothing liquid into them, welcoming the distraction it provided them both.

"Homicide." Equally brusque, she echoed his response to her identical question from the night before and had the satisfaction of seeing his eyes narrow at her. Before he could say anything else, she shot a question of her own at him. Not because she expected him to know the answer—she was fairly certain there hadn't been time for any new information to come to light—but because the answer was in his purview and she hoped pointing a finger at what he didn't know would keep his mind on his own inadequacy and off of any interest he might have developed in Jens. "Victim's identity?"

"Still unknown."

"Ah."

"Care to elaborate on that cause of death?" he asked. If he even realized she'd been parroting him, he was not, it seemed, going to rise to the bait.

"Exsanguination due to multiple stab wounds," she replied.

"Ah," he said. *Was* he mocking her? She couldn't tell. "So it wasn't having her throat slit, or the blows to the head."

"No." Maybe he hadn't seen or hadn't recognized the blood on Jens's shoulder for what it was. Or maybe he was toying with her and meant to close in for the kill at any time. Her chest hurt at the thought. "Contrary to popular belief, having one's throat slit is not always a fatal injury, depending on the position of the cut. And I'd posit that the blows to the head happened before the sharp force trauma."

"He knocked her unconscious and then stabbed her to death?"

"Yes."

"Huh."

"What does that mean?"

"Just an observation."

Her lips compressed. "Not a very enlightening one."

"Unless I'm misremembering, he didn't knock his other victims unconscious before killing them."

They reached the elevator. He punched the button to call it and turned to face her. The unforgiving light of the overhead fixture gave Elin her first good look at him. Late thirties at a guess, and more handsome than she'd expected, with a wide forehead, broad cheekbones, a strong, straight nose, and a well-cut mouth above a square chin. His hair was black and thick, short on the sides, longer on top, and his eyebrows were straight black slashes above hooded dark brown eyes. But what caught and held her attention was a centimeters-wide scar, red and raised and angry-looking, that bisected his left eyebrow to angle up above his temple before disappearing into his hairline.

She knew a gunshot wound when she saw one.

At some point in the not so distant past, he'd been shot in the head.

"How much time do you estimate elapsed between the blows to the head and the stab wounds?" he asked.

She redirected her attention in a hurry. *Look at the eyes, not the scar.* "It's impossible to be certain, but at a guess I would say minutes. Although from the marks on her wrists and ankles, and the amount of generalized bruising, it appears she was bound and repeatedly beaten over several days before she was killed."

"He kept her prisoner?"

"It looks like it."

"Let me guess. She wasn't raped."

"Injuries to her genital region made it impossible to tell."

"Injuries?"

"Multiple penetrative stab wounds," she clarified, determined not to revisualize the horror that had been revealed on the autopsy table, then added, "The other victims didn't suffer genital injuries?"

"No."

"Were they raped?"

"No."

Considering, she was silent for a moment.

"The fact that the victims weren't raped doesn't rule out lust as a potential motivation. And the fact that this latest victim suffered severe genital wounds is just one more way this murder is different from the rest," she said as the elevator arrived and they stepped into it. "Third floor, please. Dr. Weimann has kindly offered to share his laboratory with me and I'm anxious to get to work on the samples I collected last night." Which she'd stored in the hotel icebox after a generous tip to a maid, then brought with her to the autopsy that morning in hopes that Dr. Weimann would allow her to use his laboratory.

Schneider shook his head and pressed the first-floor button instead.

"Your samples are being transferred to the lab in the Alex as we speak. Right now I need you to come with me. General Kaltenbrunner wants to see you. I'm to escort you to his office."

Elin's first paralyzing thought was that the general might have received a telephone call from Copenhagen. "But I have plans to—"

"It will have to wait." Schneider looked tired and irritable. She attributed the latter at least partially to her unwanted insertion into his life. As for him looking tired, well, she was tired, too. Or, more accurately, exhausted. After she, Pia, and Jens had arrived back at the hotel last night, she'd immediately gone to work cleaning, repacking, and resuturing Jens's wound, which had broken open as suspected, while Pia worked feverishly to remove all traces of blood from his clothes and their surroundings. By the time they'd finished, it was too late for her to even think of sleep if she meant to pay a solitary dawn visit to last night's crime scene before attending the early-morning autopsy of the latest victim, both of which she had done.

The crime scene had yielded nothing of value, no sign of the children, no overlooked clues. The autopsy had been instructive. The knife was a fixed-blade type, with the blade at least ten centimeters long. Most of the stab wounds had been furious slashes that had torn the flesh. The killing blow had been to the chest, penetrating the heart. And yes, it appeared that the victim had been rendered unconscious before the blow was delivered.

She told him all that, then added, carefully casual, "What does General Kaltenbrunner want to see me about?" Had she succeeded in keeping the hollowness out of her voice? She could only hope.

"I couldn't tell you. He doesn't confide in me."

Her stomach knotted. She said, "I was going to go over the previous victims' autopsy results with Dr. Weimann. But General Kaltenbrunner obviously takes precedence."

"He does."

"You shouldn't have had my samples moved without my permission." Her rebuke was sharper than she'd intended. Blame the anxiety that dried her mouth, made her throat feel tight.

"Weimann does most of the autopsies for the city. It's better that all evidence pertaining to this case be kept together and separate from everything else. Which means in the lab that's been specially set up to handle it in the Alex."

Elin couldn't disagree. "That makes sense."

"I'm glad you think so."

The elevator stopped. As the door opened, he gestured to her to precede him.

She said, "I should let Dr. Weimann know that our meeting will have to be postponed."

"I'll take care of it."

By then they were walking out through the lobby into the budding heat of an early September day. A pitted black car with a uniformed police officer behind the wheel waited out front. Having indicated that this was their ride, Schneider opened the passenger door and she slid in. Then he walked around to the driver's side and told the policeman, "I'll take it from here." As the man got out, Schneider added, "Go find Dr. Weimann and tell him Professor Lund has gone with me. She'll let him know when she's available to meet."

"Yes, sir."

A glance in the side-view mirror showed the policeman walking into the hospital as they pulled away from the curb. They were in the Wedding District, she knew, and seen by bright daylight rather than through the gray mists of dawn that had obscured much of the hospital's surroundings as she'd arrived, the poverty of this industrialized area was laid bare.

"Is this your first visit to Berlin?" Schneider asked. He was clearly making an effort, initiating small talk, trying to smooth things over between them.

Elin's chest tightened.

"No." She was not prone to idle chitchat at the best of times, and right now she was anxious and headachy enough without having to peer into the past. If he hadn't lifted his eyebrows at her in silent indication that he was waiting for more than that single monosyllable by way of an answer, she would have left it at that. But he did, and so she mentally girded her loins and thought, *All right, I can make an effort, too.*

"A long time ago, I came with my parents."

"A vacation?"

"A conference."

Again with the inquiring eyebrows. Her lips compressed.

"My father was a policeman. A detective like you. He came to Berlin to talk about a case and brought us—my mother and me—with him." If she'd known how disturbing the memories that came rushing back along with that were going to be, she would have stopped with the monosyllable. *My mother died on that trip.* But she wasn't going to think about that. Not now, not with him. And she certainly wasn't going to tell him. Baring her soul to a semihostile stranger was not in the cards. Pain equals weakness, and weakness was another of those things she'd learned was best kept to herself.

"You said *was.* I take it your father's retired?" he asked.

"He's dead." More unwelcome memories. He'd succumbed to a heart attack when she was twenty-four, having never recovered from her mother's death and leaving her, their only child, alone.

A quick frown, a glance at her. "I'm sorry."

"Yes," she said in acknowledgment, retreating to the monosyllables in sheer self-defense, and concentrating on shoving the bad memories away. Only when they were safely banished did she become aware that her hands had twined so tightly together in her lap that her knuckles showed white.

She shot a furtive glance at him. Had he noticed? He was a detective, after all.

If he had, there was no sign of it. His profile was turned to her as he drove, and it was impossible to read anything in his face. Slowly, she relaxed her fingers.

They stopped at an intersection. Apparently he'd had enough of the chitchat, too, because he didn't say anything more. Welcoming the silence, Elin looked out the window and took it all in: tall buildings adorned with enormous scarlet swastika banners that fluttered in the breeze; wide, tree-studded boulevards; a surprising paucity of vehicular traffic, which, come to think of it, was not so surprising considering that gasoline had been largely restricted to official use; bicycles everywhere; sidewalks crowded with hurrying pedestrians who were mostly women, from what she could see. Everything immaculately clean. This section of Berlin was decidedly more prosperous than the one they'd left, but the mood was just as somber—no laughter, few smiles, businesslike and burdened. The war was taking its toll.

Schneider still looked straight ahead, out through the windshield, though now his attention seemed to have been caught by a troop of teenage boys in brown shirts and black shorts crossing the street in front of them. He followed their progress as they goose-stepped in unison under the supervision of an officer, a tight little band in the midst of other assorted pedestrians moving through the crosswalk. Hitlerjugend, they were called. Young men in training for war.

Elin's mouth went dry at the sight. This was the Nazis readying the next generation of soldiers even after tens of thousands of their men had just been slaughtered in Russia, even as the Allies were bombing German cities into rubble, even as the horrors of what they had unleashed shook the world. Would they never stop? Would the war continue until nothing was left?

She was afraid it might.

"How are you finding your hotel?" Schneider asked as the signal changed and the car got underway. He was once again attempting conversation, making an effort, probably hoping that this new gambit was sufficiently prosaic to ward off any more uncomfortable moments.

I have to work with this man, she thought, and made another effort, too, responding as any polite guest should. "It's satisfactory, thank you."

"If we'd been notified in advance that you weren't coming alone, rooms would have been reserved for your team as well as yourself. I'll see that the situation is rectified today. I hope you weren't too uncomfortable in the available accommodations last night?"

"As we were whisked onto an airplane almost as soon as we learned we were coming, there wasn't time to notify anyone. But the hotel was able to provide an extra room for Jens when we arrived, and Pia and I shared, so we managed quite well."

"I'm glad to hear it. Still, I'll see that more appropriate arrangements are made."

"Thank you."

The conversation died again and she let it. Anxiety gnawed at her, and she welcomed the silence as a chance to calm herself and collect her thoughts before facing Kaltenbrunner. The windows were down, and disjointed bits of pedestrians' conversations merged with the rumble of traffic and the flapping sounds of the ubiquitous banners. The smell of gasoline and exhaust blew into the car along with the light, woody scent of the linden trees lining the streets. Her hair was twisted up off her neck and her simple blue dress had short sleeves, but still she felt much too warm. Summer had not yet released its grip on the city, and the day was setting up to be blazing hot. Accustomed to Copenhagen's cooler temperatures, she had not yet acclimated to the difference.

"We're here," Schneider said a few minutes later, indicating the massive pale brick building on Prinz Albrecht Strasse that served as the RSHA headquarters. As he pulled into the underground parking garage he added, "I'll take you up to General Kaltenbrunner's office, but you'll be going in to meet him alone."

"Why is that?" Elin was surprised by how much the idea bothered her. Schneider wasn't by any stretch of the imagination an ally, but— She supposed what it boiled down to was *better the devil you know.*

Schneider shrugged. "Orders."

"But—" She broke off as, having parked, he got out of the car and came around to open her door for her.

"Don't disagree with him, and you'll do fine," Schneider said as she got out. "Oh, and you should be aware that his face is heavily scarred. He responds poorly to being stared at, so I wouldn't if I were you. Wouldn't disagree and wouldn't stare." The briefest of hesitations. "Also, I feel it would be unwise to mention we were observed."

"What?" She frowned at him as they walked through the welcome shadowy coolness of the garage toward a metal door that was apparently their immediate destination.

"Last night." The look he threw her was impatient. "Don't tell him about those children."

Was he worried about his men getting in trouble for having shot at them? Was he worried about getting in trouble himself because he'd failed to keep witnesses away from the crime scene? Was he worried about—there were so many possibilities that she couldn't begin to consider them all. But whatever his reason, she found she agreed with the advice.

"No, I won't," she said.

His only reply was an acknowledging quirk of his lips. Neither of them said anything more, and it was left to their footsteps echoing through the cavernous space to fill the silence. They were at the door, and he'd reached past her to open it when he paused with a hand on the knob to look at her.

"One more thing. Once we're inside, you want to be careful what you say. Listening devices are everywhere. Amazing what people will talk about on their way to a meeting. Lots of interesting information gets picked up that way."

At what must have been her aghast expression, he smiled sardonically. Then he pulled open the door, and they went inside.

6

"YOU WILL, OF COURSE, DISCOVER THE MURDERER
among the less desirable elements of society." General Ernst
Kaltenbrunner looked down his long nose at Elin. He'd risen
from his chair and come out from behind his desk to offer her
an effusive greeting when his secretary had ushered her into his
vast white second-floor office, proclaiming himself a big fan of
"Dr. Murder" and one of the main architects of her summons
to Berlin. Then he'd quizzed her on last night's murder, the
broad outline of which had already been conveyed to him by
an unknown source. She'd confirmed the facts and answered
his questions, truthfully but carefully. That wasn't difficult to
do, because at this point she knew only the most basic elements
of the case. Since then, he'd paced back and forth from one end
of the room to the other while offering up his thoughts on the
investigation.

"The less desirable elements?" Unsure of his meaning, Elin frowned and shifted in her chair, which was one of two facing his massive desk. Kaltenbrunner stopped pacing to look down at her, his concentrated gaze reminding her of a hawk with a mouse in its sights. Around forty, his face disfigured by deep, slashing scars as Schneider had warned, Kaltenbrunner was a giant of a man with a thick, square chin and small, beady eyes. He dwarfed her even when she was standing and now, when at his invitation she was seated, he towered over her. His gray-green uniform with the silver swastika emblazoned on a black armband was intimidating. *He* was intimidating, and she would have thought so even if Schneider hadn't told her that he regularly presided over activities in the torture rooms in the building's basement.

Breaking eye contact, she glanced down at the delicate porcelain cup in her hand and took a sip of the real and indescribably delicious coffee he'd had his secretary bring them. The hot, strong brew was, quite possibly, the best thing she'd ever tasted, and she savored it. His own cup sat untouched on his desk. To ignore such a luxury as real coffee was, Elin thought, a sign of how little the deprivations of war affected the Nazi elite. For everyone else, real coffee was simply unobtainable. For years now, she and everyone she knew had been reduced to drinking hot water infused with chicory and herbs, which made for a bitter and unsatisfying brew.

"Homosexuals. Jehovah's Witnesses. Slavs. Gypsies. Jews. The *untermenschen*." His tone was impatient, as though the answer was obvious.

Untermenschen, Elin knew, meant subhumans. The Nazis called them "life unworthy of life" and at the description she barely managed to repress a shiver. Behind him, the pair of large golden imperial eagle statues—ubiquitous symbols of the Reich—that perched on either end of his desk seemed to glare at her. On another wall, a portrait of Hitler took pride of place.

"We have an abundance of foreign factory workers in the city.

Poles, Eastern Europeans. They should also be looked at. One thing you may be sure of is, the man we seek is not an Aryan. No Aryan would ever commit such depraved acts."

Elin remembered Schneider's advice. *Don't disagree with him.*

"A valuable observation," she said.

He gave a decisive nod. "It also seems likely that he will have come, not from a respectable family, but from a family of criminals. Asocial acts, along with the base instincts that lead to them, are hereditary, as you know."

The hereditary principle, which stated that criminal tendencies and behavior were inherited and ran in families, had been well researched, and was widely accepted in certain scientific circles. The Nazis, especially, were firm believers. Elin was not. In fact, her stomach knotted at his allusion to the concept. To condemn whole families for one individual's misdeeds seemed to her barbaric. As well as factually, empirically, wrong.

"We'll certainly check the family background of any potential suspect," she said.

"There is *we*, and there is *you*." He fixed her with a penetrating gaze. "It's important that this case be solved quickly, and *quietly*. The Führer himself demands it."

Hitler was personally interested in the investigation? The knowledge made her fingers tighten on the handle of her cup. Too much attention from such a source could pose a problem. For her and all those connected with her, as well as for the case.

"I understand," she said.

"I'm not sure you do. The Führer wants this threat to our innocent women eliminated with all possible dispatch and has entrusted me with overseeing the effort. I have *personally* chosen you to bring your expertise to bear on the task."

She understood the veiled warning in that statement. Or, perhaps, a threat? Elin's chest constricted.

"I'm flattered by your confidence in me, Herr General." The intensity with which he was regarding her was unsettling. Though apparently favored for the moment, she suspected she would suffer a swift fall from grace if she should fail to meet his expectations, or he should discover one of any number of uncomfortable truths about her. Not wanting to hold his gaze longer than she had to for fear of what he might read in her eyes, she looked down at the cup in her hand, then lifted it—carefully so that her fraying nerves wouldn't cause it to rattle against the saucer as she picked it up—to sip more coffee. The coffee was the only good thing about the meeting, she reflected. Everything else, including the man in front of her, was profoundly disturbing.

"No flattery involved. Your credentials are outstanding and your abilities are well-documented. You would not be here otherwise. I know I can count on you to achieve your usual stellar results. The correct perpetrator will be identified and the threat he poses eliminated with the utmost efficiency."

"I will do everything within my power to find the person responsible," she said. To *promise* results, much less fast and "stellar" ones, in a murder investigation of this nature was something she wasn't prepared to do. Too many variables, too much still unknown. And the intimation that the killer should be sought among certain despised groups worried her. What would happen if he was not, after all, what Kaltenbrunner and his ilk were expecting?

Killers of this type usually sought victims from among their own kind.

"There is something else. Something of a more personal nature we must discuss." The sudden harshness of his voice caused her to very nearly choke on her coffee as she swallowed too much too fast. His expression—the change was unmistakable there, too. His mouth had thinned. His eyes bored into hers.

What does he know? Guilt sent her pulse racing. Her mind instantly flew to Jens. But there were other matters he might be getting ready to question her about, too.

Never show fear. And never mind that she'd almost choked on the last mouthful. She dropped her gaze to her cup and drank more coffee.

What did it say about the state of her nerves that now she couldn't even taste it?

"This fellow—Herr Schneider," Kaltenbrunner said. "He has been slow to provide results. Given his background, I would not have chosen him for this investigation, but Nebe insists he is the best detective he has. What is your opinion of him? Are you finding him competent to carry out this most important assignment?"

Not what she had feared. A niggle of relief was followed by wary confusion. She had no idea what "background" Kaltenbrunner was referring to, and she wasn't about to ask. If this was a choice, a fork in the road so to speak, she once again felt safer sticking with the devil she knew.

They had not exactly established a rapport, she and Schneider, but as the man looming over her illustrated, she might find herself partnered with someone far worse.

"Yes." She successfully restored her cup to its saucer with nary a rattle. "Quite competent."

He gave a slow, almost reluctant nod. "If your opinion should change, you have only to let me know. Herr Schneider can be replaced like *that*." He snapped his fingers. His eyes—gray, she saw as the sunlight slanting in through the half-closed blinds touched them—had grown so hard they glinted as silver as the pips on his collar. She got the impression that he would be glad to have an excuse to be done with Schneider.

"I'll remember that."

"Please do so. May I offer you more coffee?" He gestured at her cup. It was empty, she saw with some surprise.

"Oh, no. Thank you. But the coffee was wonderful."

"Melitta Gold," he named the brand, sounding gratified at her praise. "It's a favorite of mine as well."

With a quick nod at her cup and a murmured "May I?" he

took her cup and saucer and set it down on his desk beside his own still-untouched coffee before turning back to her.

"Now, in your estimation, how long will it take to uncover the murderer's identity and deliver him to justice?"

The question caught Elin by surprise. "I...couldn't say. I haven't yet had a chance to fully review the evidence, or—"

A tap on the door was followed by his secretary, an attractive brunette, poking her head into the room. Voice low, she said, "Herr General, General Haupt is here to speak with you."

Her tone made it clear that the visit was significant. Underlining that, Kaltenbrunner suddenly looked uneasy. It was the most fleeting of expressions, formed by a flicker of his eyes, a twist of his lips, but Elin caught it and wondered.

He said, "Yes, very well, give me one moment to finish up here and then you may show him in."

"Yes, sir." The secretary left.

Kaltenbrunner looked back at Elin, who, thankful for the interruption, was already rising to her feet. "I was forgetting you only joined us last night. Expecting an answer so soon is not realistic, is it? Suppose I check with you again on, let us say, next Friday. At this same time, here in my office. You can fill me in on your progress and provide me with a timeline then. Unless, of course, by that time you have solved the case." The thin smile that accompanied that was supposed to indicate he was joking, she thought, but she got the feeling he really wasn't. "I'll have Fräulein Kubler—" the secretary, Elin presumed "—set it up."

"I'll look forward to it." What else could she say? Certainly not the truth. With a crisp "*Heil* Hitler!" he ushered her out the door. She felt like a prisoner granted a reprieve.

Besides Fräulein Kubler, two men waited in the outer office. Both were hard-faced and handsome and had an air of authority. Having been seated, they rose, hats in hand, to their feet as she appeared. One was fair-haired, muscular, unsmiling, and resplendent in a field-gray SS uniform glittering with medals.

The other was dark haired, muscular, unsmiling, a great deal less than resplendent in a lived-in-looking civilian jacket and tie—and, most unexpectedly, a welcome sight.

The devil you know.

The other man—General Haupt, she presumed—gave her an assessing look and then a brusque nod as he passed her on his way into Kaltenbrunner's office. There was something in his expression as their eyes met—curiosity, perhaps? Did he know who she was, why she was there? She thought he might.

"To what do I owe—" Kaltenbrunner greeted him, only to be cut off by Haupt's abrupt "The Führer wishes to see the results of your experiments at Mauthausen. The efficiency of gas versus hanging versus shooting as a means of large-scale extermination interests him greatly. I have come to collect the report you have compiled on the results and take it to him."

"Now? Give it to you? But I had planned to present it to the Führer myself." Kaltenbrunner sounded taken aback.

"You are not questioning the Führer's orders, I hope." Haupt walked on past Kaltenbrunner into the inner office as if he, and not the man whose office it was, was in command.

Experiments? From the context, it sounded as if they were talking about experiments in methods of mass murder. Elin's palms felt suddenly damp, and of their own volition her hands pressed flat against her skirt as if in an instinctive effort to hide the fact.

One thing she was sure of: this was something she would have been better off not to have overheard. In this insane new world, the wrong kind of knowledge could prove disastrous.

Mauthausen was a forced labor camp designed to imprison and punish enemies of the Reich. Even in Denmark, they had heard of it, and of other, similar, camps as well. Gusen, Neuengamme, Gross-Rosen, Sobibor, Auschwitz—all those were known concentration camps built to intern deported populations of Jews and other asocials, as the Nazis called them. But whispers that they were more than forced labor camps were growing louder.

Whispers of inhuman conditions, of starvation and cruelty and disease, of deaths. Thousands of deaths. Thousands of intentional *murders*. But they were just that—whispers—easy to question, to disbelieve. Please God they were just that.

But now, with her own ears, had she just heard the whispers confirmed?

She felt cold all over. Her knees turned to jelly.

Elin had no idea what her expression conveyed as Kaltenbrunner, following Haupt back into his office, closed the door, but Schneider took one look at her face as she reached him and his brows snapped together.

"Don't say a word," he said, so quietly only she could hear. "And for God's sake, smile."

Curling a hand around her elbow, he exchanged the obligatory "*Heil* Hitler" with Fräulein Kubler even as he guided Elin toward the door.

7

CONSCIOUS OF THE SECRETARY'S EYES AND, NO DOUBT, ears following them, and of Schneider's warning that others might be listening in on any conversation as well, Elin obediently pasted a smile on her lips and stayed silent as he escorted her from the building.

Once they were back in the car, she relaxed facial muscles that felt like they'd been frozen in place by that smile and stared blindly through the windshield.

There's nothing I can do, she told herself. Then she thought of Niles, and as a shiver of fear ran like a cold finger down her spine added fiercely, *Except get home as fast as I can.*

She could feel Schneider's gaze on her.

"So you want to tell me what happened in there that has you looking like a ghost?"

The sudden brightness of the day made her blink as the car

left the gloom of the parking garage to nose into the queue of traffic behind an exhaust-spewing double-decker bus. Sunlight sparkled off its windows, made its dark green paint look almost cheery. The gray cloud of exhaust it emitted stank. The smell, like just about everything else in her life lately, had to be endured. It was too hot to roll up the windows.

Anyway, she didn't want to. Despite the smell, she welcomed the heat.

The encounter with Kaltenbrunner—and with Haupt—had left her bone cold.

"Well?" Schneider said, and she looked at him in time to catch his frowning sideways glance.

Taking a firm grip on her composure, she started to answer, to tell him everything from beginning to end, only to hesitate. Since the Danish Army had laid down its weapons and King Christian and the country's leadership had agreed to a "peaceful occupation" to end the so-called Six Hour War in which Germany had conquered Denmark, the Danes had been careful not to provoke the occupiers into taking harsh measures against them. As a people, they had for three years now collectively walked a tightrope—mouths shut, eyes straight ahead, no stepping out of line. Whatever they might privately think or feel, the consensus was that outward compliance was their best chance at survival.

Hear no evil, see no evil, speak no evil. That was the principle by which she and most everyone she knew lived.

Until a little more than a week ago, it had served them well. The Danish government, including the king, had remained in place. Life went on almost as it had before the occupation. The relationship with their Nazi occupiers was uneasy, but despite the German soldiers stationed on street corners and the Reich plenipotentiary who had supervisory control of most everything, the citizens of Denmark, including the Jews and other "undesirables," had stayed safe.

But now—she couldn't let herself think about what might

happen now. Now that the Germans had seized total control, everything had changed.

I have to go home.

The knowledge that she couldn't panicked her.

What she needed to remember was, Schneider was not someone in whom she could confide. He was a Kripo detective, a Nazi, one of *them*. If she questioned what she had overheard, if she expressed her horror at it, or her dismay at being instructed to look among certain targeted populations for the killer they sought, or uttered any criticism at all of Kaltenbrunner or the government, Schneider might report it. He might report her. People turned in neighbors, friends, relatives all the time. The authorities encouraged it, had set up tip lines to facilitate it and gave out generous rewards for what Elin could only think of as the basest of betrayals. Merely expressing an anti-Nazi sentiment was enough to get someone arrested, or worse. And the last thing she needed was to have the gimlet eye of the Reich turn her way.

She had too much to lose. Too much to hide.

But he clearly knew she'd found the appointment distressing and was waiting for an answer as to why. She reached for something innocuous to pacify him with.

"General Kaltenbrunner asked me about last night's murder."

"I would have been surprised if he hadn't. Herr General stays well-informed." His voice was dry. "What did you tell him?"

"Only what I know. Which at this point isn't much. He wants me to return to his office next Friday to further brief him on the case. Unless, as he said, the case has been solved by then. His secretary is to set up an appointment."

He made an unamused sound. "Before then, we'll go over everything together so that you'll know exactly what to say."

Remembering his warning about the children, she slanted a look at him. "And what not to say?"

"That, too."

Neither said anything more for a few minutes, during which

Elin digested the many implications of that and Schneider negotiated his way past a knot of military vehicles that were clustered outside the ethnological museum.

After they were clear, he said, "You want to tell me the rest? Because I'm fairly certain that wasn't what upset you."

He wasn't stupid; she had to give him that. Cautiously she offered up a little bit more. "That man—General Haupt—who is he? He gave me a strange look, like he knows why I'm here, which would mean that he, too, must know about the murders."

"Maybe you misinterpreted it." He gave her a quick, wry smile. "Maybe the look he gave you is the look he gives all pretty women. I've heard he's quite the ladies' man."

Elin was too preoccupied with trying to grope her way through what was starting to seem like a minefield of potential pitfalls to do more than vaguely register that he'd called her pretty. It was something she tucked away for further consideration even as she resolved the question *How much should I tell him* with the answer *Nothing that could cause me trouble.*

She shook her head. "It was more than that."

"Then perhaps you're right, although if he's aware of the murders, word of them has reached higher even than I thought. All the way to the Führer, in fact."

"General Kaltenbrunner said that Herr Hitler is aware of them. He said that he's following the investigation."

Schneider grimaced. A moment later all signs of his reaction had disappeared. It was impossible to read anything at all in his face.

"We naturally welcome the Führer's interest," he said smoothly. But she knew he didn't, and he didn't trust her, either.

"Who is he?" Elin asked again. "General Haupt?"

He glanced at her. "Erhard Haupt is the Führer's eyes and ears into all manner of things. They call him Hitler's attack dog. He's one of the Führer's closest advisers, having been with him from almost the beginning. He used to work as his bodyguard, but he's advanced far beyond that. He keeps the Führer's secrets, does his dirty work. If he does indeed know who you are and why you're here—"

"He does, I'm almost certain," Elin said.

"Then so does the Führer." His tone was unmistakably grim. "In which case I doubt that Haupt's arrival in Kaltenbrunner's office at that particular time was an accident. He was sent to get a look at you."

"And that's a problem," she said. It wasn't a question. His attitude left no doubt.

"It increases the pressure on us to solve these murders fast—and correctly. And it puts the spotlight squarely on you."

"That's *terrifying*." Her instant, appalled reaction escaped before she could stop it.

He didn't nod. His reaction was much more subtle: a tightening of the skin around his eyes, a firming of his lips. But the effect was total agreement.

"You should be aware, Haupt will probably come nosing around you, trying to find out what you know, doing his best to worm any details from you that he can take straight back to the Führer while bypassing official channels."

"Oh, no."

"It does pose something of a problem. If the Führer is indeed interested in the progress we're making, I'm guessing Kaltenbrunner was hoping to be the one to keep him updated. He must be gnashing his teeth now that Haupt's in the picture. Ordinarily it would be interesting to see how that rivalry plays out, but not if our case is going to be the bone Kaltenbrunner and Haupt fight over."

"I won't tell him—either of them—anything we haven't agreed on first." Her swift response sounded almost like she was pledging loyalty to Schneider. Which, given the treacherous political seas in which she found herself, she supposed she was.

Another subtle change in his expression made her think he

was weighing that. Did he accept it? She wasn't sure. A slant of his eyes in her direction ended with no more than "Tell me what Kaltenbrunner said."

Elin obediently recounted as much of the conversation as she thought she should reveal. What she kept back was Kaltenbrunner's remarks about Schneider himself. She didn't know Schneider well, she cautioned herself, and she didn't know what circumstances had prompted Kaltenbrunner's remarks, or how Schneider would react if he learned that Kaltenbrunner harbored doubts about him, or that she had been given the option to replace him. First and foremost, she had to look out for herself. For Niles's sake.

But there was a matter she couldn't ignore.

"And then Herr Haupt spoke of Mauthausen." She said it casually, almost as a throwaway, while keeping a covert watch on Schneider's face. His lips thinned. His jaw tightened. Even on such short acquaintance, she was beginning to be able to read the signs: clearly the subject was unwelcome. "You must have heard for yourself what he said."

An abbreviated nod was the answer. She waited, but he said nothing, and after a minute or two she realized that curt nod was the only reply she was going to get. His attention seemed totally given over to the traffic that had worsened around them to the point where it was now hemming them in. Their surroundings were starting to seem familiar—streets lined with leafy lindens, red flags flapping, the Tiergarten—and she thought they were heading back the way they had come, with the Alex as their most likely destination. But she didn't ask because it seemed unimportant compared to the topic looming ever larger in her mind.

Letting it go was the smart, obvious choice. But she couldn't. It would haunt her, she knew.

"Haupt said something about extermination—*mass* extermination—by means of gas or shooting or hanging. At Mauthausen. What was he talking about?" Her pulse raced by the time she finished. He'd heard Haupt, too, so it wasn't like she was poking her nose in out of the blue, but still even asking about such a thing felt risky.

Her eyes stayed fixed on his face.

But there was nothing to read in it. No reaction at all. He was slowing the car to match the rest of the traffic, braking for an intersection, and to all appearances he was entirely intent on those actions.

Then the car stopped and he looked at her.

"A word of advice, Professor Lund." There was nothing to be made of his voice, either. He could have been speaking of the weather. "Keep your focus on the murders you were brought here to assist with. Let everything else pass you by. Then when the job is done you may go safely home again, back to your own life, having taken no hurt from your time with us."

Despite the evenness of his tone, it was such a stark warning that she was shaken, too shaken to even attempt a reply. As traffic started to move again and he returned his attention to his driving, she forced herself to glance away from him, out at the street, at their surroundings, at the bicycles speeding past and the shop windows just beyond the pedestrians crowding the sidewalk and—

"*Der Schweinekerl!*" Schneider's harsh exclamation—*Bastard!* she translated the German—exploded out of nowhere, making Elin jump.

"What...?" Her startled gaze flew to him as he whipped the car to the curb then braked so hard that she had to catch herself with a hand on the dashboard to keep from smacking into the windshield.

"*Wait here.*" He leaped from the car.

Sinking back in her seat, Elin watched wide-eyed through the open window as he stormed onto the concrete plaza he'd stopped beside. Situated between tall buildings and lined by more of the ubiquitous lindens, the center area was presently being used by a troop of Hitlerjugend for what appeared to be a marching exercise.

"Do something like that again and I'll beat you into the ground!" he roared at a stocky, square-jawed officer, one of several observing the group, who turned sharply toward him.

"You! You have no right to be here!" Drawing himself up, the officer pointed an accusatory finger at Schneider as Schneider, radiating aggression, bore down on him. The confrontation was loud enough, and close enough to Elin, that she heard every word. So apparently did everyone else in the vicinity. Even the marching boys stopped in mid–goose step to turn and look.

"I have every right!" A couple of quick, final strides brought Schneider practically nose to nose with the other man, who stood his ground. Schneider was taller and at least as broad shouldered, but his opponent was a barrel-chested bulldog of a man and Elin feared for the outcome if the clash should become physical.

"The law says—"

"To hell with the law." Schneider's fists clenched. "And to hell with you, you—"

"No! It's all right! I deserved it!" A thin boy of perhaps twelve or thirteen scrambled up from where he'd been sprawled full-length on the concrete near the officer's feet and grabbed Schneider's arm. Dressed in a brown shirt and black shorts that revealed long shanks and knobby knees, he was unmistakably one of the Hitlerjugend. "I was in the wrong place! It was my fault!"

Schneider spared no more than a lightning glance for the boy before refocusing on the officer. But the grip on his arm seemed to have checked him physically. He practically vibrated with anger but did not lay hands on the other man.

"Two weeks ago he had a split lip. Before that, it was bruised ribs. Before that, it was a sprained wrist. A swollen cheek. A sore arm. All accidents, he said. Boys fighting, his mother said. But this time, by God, I saw you! *I saw you.* You shoved him to the ground, you fat bastard."

"You can thank me for training him up in the right way so that he doesn't turn out to be a *dummer narr* like you."

Elin caught her breath as the other man called Schneider a stupid fool.

Schneider's brows snapped together. "*Thank* you—"

"No! I don't need your help! It was nothing. Nothing!" The boy tugged urgently at Schneider's arm. "Go away! Please!"

Glancing from the boy to Schneider, the officer smirked. "You heard him. Go away. Stay away. Or shall I contact the court— or your superiors—and report this violation?"

"You can contact anyone you damned well—"

"Vater, stop! I'm all right, everything's all right. Just leave." Even as Elin registered with surprise that this was Schneider's son, the boy cast a swift glance toward the rest of the troop, now milling around near the confrontation while obviously drinking in every word. His distress was palpable. "You're making everything worse. Just leave. *Please.*"

Schneider's mouth twisted. Casting a quick glance at his son's anguished face and from there to the gaping onlookers, he then said something to the officer that was too low for Elin to hear but that made the other man's face flame red. Schneider looked at his son—Elin couldn't read his expression—then pulled his arm free of the boy's grip, turned on his heel, and strode back to the car.

The other man, face still flaming, followed Schneider's progress with angry eyes, and then as Schneider reached the car, seemed to see Elin there in the window for the first time. He raked her with a furious glare.

8

ELIN'S ATTENTION WAS IMMEDIATELY DIVERTED AS Schneider threw himself into the driver's seat and slammed the transmission into gear without a word to her. Taking one look at his set face, Elin said nothing. His anger was palpable, filling the available space with a dangerous-feeling charge. As the car peeled away from the curb, she saw that the Hitlerjugend troop was once again marching.

Except for Schneider's son, who stood, head hanging, beside the red-faced officer, who appeared to be furiously berating him. Now that she knew, she could see a distinct resemblance in the close-cropped dark hair and narrow face of the boy to the man beside her.

Elin sensed that it took every ounce of self-control Schneider possessed to simply drive away.

He sped through the heavy traffic with a barely leashed savagery that more than once made Elin catch her breath—and clutch at the armrest. Neither of them had yet said a word. His grim silence was more telling than a steady stream of curses would have been. The Alex was in sight before the granite lock of his jaw eased, and he threw a glance her way.

"I'm sorry you had to see that. It was nothing, a family matter," he said.

Unable to think of an appropriate reply, she simply nodded. After the slightest of pauses he sent another glance her way and added, "I'd appreciate it if you could keep what you saw to yourself."

The gruffness with which he spoke told her how much he hated having to ask it of her.

She felt an unexpected stirring of sympathy for him. Family troubles she knew. "Of course I will."

He nodded a curt thanks. Then they reached the Alex, and he parked and they went inside.

The hand-lettered sign on the heavy metal door said Special Project Unit. Inside, a war room of sorts had been set up. Or, rather, war rooms. Located in a neglected corner of the Alex's vast basement, they appeared to hold everything the Kripo knew or had collected about the case. Individual desks outfitted with telephones were occupied by men in jackets and ties who Elin presumed were detectives. They looked up curiously as Elin and Schneider walked through. Rows of file cabinets populated the first room. Opening off the second room was a small lab that, as far as Elin could tell, was equipped with at least the basics. Brightening, she turned into it saying, "I'll just check that everything is properly stored," only to have Schneider curl a hand around her elbow.

"It is, trust me. And you can take all the lab time you want later, but for now you need to come with me." He pulled her on with him. He pointed out a darkroom for developing photos as they passed it. A small private office that belonged to him—another hand-lettered sign affixed to the door read simply Schneider—was not discussed. A room with a closed door was identified in passing as the evidence room, and a conference room complete with multiple freestanding blackboards with photos and facts about the victims on them was their immediate destination.

"Good morning, Chief." A gray-haired woman with a grandmotherly demeanor finished affixing something to a blackboard and turned to face them as they entered. Elin saw it was a photo of last night's victim, clearly taken as part of this morning's autopsy and, from the faint but unmistakable smell that still clung to it, was just as clearly recently developed. She also saw, from the corner of her eye, that as she looked at the photo the woman gave her a thorough inspection, looking her up and down with barely concealed disapproval.

"Good morning, Marta. Professor Lund, this is Frau Skelton." Schneider made the introduction as he walked over to the new photo. The women exchanged polite greetings, the other woman headed for the door, and Elin joined Schneider in front of the picture. Death was never pretty, and this black-and-white image of the deceased on the autopsy table was no exception. The one small mercy was that it was a headshot only. The dark stiffness of the dried blood caking much of the blond hair was the worst visible evidence of her injuries.

"Now that you're here, shall I call everyone into the meeting?" Frau Skelton asked from the doorway.

"We have two more still to arrive. We'll wait for them," Schneider replied, and the woman nodded and left. Elin was still studying the photo. The harsh light above the autopsy table highlighted the rubbery texture of the victim's skin, the closed, sunken eyes, the gray of the lips, as well as a small, semicircular, perimortem bruise on the left cheekbone that she hadn't noticed previously. Elin felt the now-familiar pit in her stomach as Schneider added, "Your team is on the way. I arranged to have

Fräulein Kubler notify Frau Skelton when we left Kaltenbrunner's office, and she had a car sent for them."

When last seen, Jens had been pale, sweating, and in considerable pain. Elin could only hope that the trauma of having his wound break open and then re-treated had faded in the ensuing hours.

All she could do was proceed as if everything was fine. Doing her best to keep her face expressionless, she nodded.

"These are the victims. Let me walk you through them before the others get here." His sweeping gesture encompassed the photos. The strong emotion he'd been laboring under scant minutes before was nowhere in evidence. If she hadn't witnessed that violent confrontation over his son, she wouldn't have suspected there was anything on his mind other than the case. "It starts with her."

She followed him to the far end of the room. Three photos of each victim—a headshot and a full body shot taken in life that had almost certainly been acquired from a family member or friend, and another headshot taken, like that of the latest victim, on the autopsy table—were lined up above scrawled lists specifying particulars such as name, cause, date and approximate time of death, age, occupation, marital status, existence and number of children, last known address, and more.

"Inge Weber. Astrid Lang. Roswitha Eckard. Pauline Fischer. Bella Richter. Anna Fromm. Greta Neuhaus." Schneider gestured at each victim's pictures as they passed them, while Elin tried to absorb as much as she could. Most were blondes. Pauline Fischer's hair was a golden brown. All were young, all possessed similar body types, and all would be considered above average in looks.

Elin didn't have time to do more than give a cursory scan to the information below the photos as Schneider walked her down the row of blackboards. What she was able to do was put a face to the names.

The heaviness that settled in her chest as she looked from the pictures of the living faces to the corresponding dead ones was as familiar as it was unwelcome. *I'll find out who did this to you*, she promised, then pushed emotion away.

Emotion did no one any good. The only thing she could do for them now was her job.

Elin stopped in front of a map of Berlin marked with the circled numbers 1 through 8. Schneider, stopping behind her, said, "The numbers mark where the bodies were found."

"I see." Frowning, she studied the map.

"The first two bodies were discovered in Mitte." He touched the numbers one and two, which were perhaps a kilometer and a half apart. "Three and four were in Horst Wessel. The fifth was in Kreuzberg. The sixth was in Tiergarten, and number seven and last night's victim, number eight, were in Wedding."

"Do you have any information indicating where the first victim was killed?" Elin asked.

"Not yet, although that could change at any time."

"The reason I ask is, the location of the first victim's murder is particularly important. Predators of this sort tend to take their first victim in an area they know well, usually within a few kilometers of their home."

"I'll tell my men to make finding out where Inge Weber was killed a top priority. Although we haven't had a great deal of luck with that so far."

Elin studied the map. "If you notice, there's a pattern here, a reverse C shape. At a guess, I'd say he lives or works somewhere inside that area."

"How sure are you of that?"

"About ninety-five percent."

A corner of his mouth quirked up. "Not one hundred percent? Tsk, tsk, Professor."

"I'm about ninety-five percent sure," she said evenly, "because it's virtually impossible to be one hundred percent sure about anything. There are always anomalies, and not to leave room for them can lead to valuable information being missed. I've found that, regardless of motivation, spatial behavior tends to be predictable across the spectrum of serial murderer behavior. In other words, his actions are to some degree shaped by his physical environment. Places where he spends a great deal of time—his home or workplace, for example, as well as the homes of any friends or relatives he sees regularly, the shops he frequents, the social activities he engages in—form a kind of 'home range,' if you will, and will typically be within the parameters of the places where the bodies are disposed of, because his choice will be influenced by his familiarity with his surroundings and his desire to avoid detection. Also, on a practical basis, transporting a dead body is both difficult and dangerous. That's why many serial murderers kill on their own premises and dispose of the bodies somewhere on their own property. In cases where the bodies are transported, the distance is usually within ten to thirty kilometers of where the murder took place."

"So you're saying he either lives or works in Berlin." At the dryness of that, she gave him a look. His tone said, *Tell me something I didn't already know* and her look, at which he grimaced appreciatively, answered with, *You really think I should have assumed you knew that?* He continued, "And probably somewhere in here."

Grabbing a pencil from a nearby chalk tray, he circled the area she'd indicated.

"Yes," she said. "Perhaps if you sent people door-to-door in that area they might be able to identify possible suspects. Checking their backgrounds could—"

He was already shaking his head before he broke in, "We're talking a population of thousands. And the attention such an action would attract would be massive."

After her meeting with Kaltenbrunner, Elin didn't even bother to argue that concerns about publicity shouldn't be allowed to hamper their investigation. The reality was, the top brass had spoken and whoever disobeyed did so at their peril.

"The first seven victims were killed on Sundays," Elin said, moving on. It was a tacit admission that she now understood his desire to keep their investigation out of the public eye. "When were they reported missing?"

"Astrid Lang, Bella Richter, Anna Fromm, and Greta Neuhaus weren't reported missing until they didn't show up to work on Monday, after their bodies were already found. Inge Weber and Pauline Fischer were reported missing on Sunday hours before their bodies were found. Roswitha Eckard was never reported missing. Her family either never noticed or were afraid to contact the authorities. And as far as we know, this latest victim hasn't been reported missing, either."

"Hmm. Do we know what they were doing right before they went missing?"

"They all went out on the Saturday night before they died. Three of them are known to have returned home safely afterward and were presumed to have gone to bed. With the other four—Astrid Lang, Roswitha Eckard, Pauline Fischer, and Greta Neuhaus—it's impossible to know if they made it home, as they either lived alone or were, as far as we know, staying alone that night."

"So did the three that returned home go missing out of their bedrooms?"

"We don't know. All three had dates, and returned from their dates. In only one case do we have an eyewitness—Inge Weber, and the eyewitness is her flatmate—who actually saw her go into her bedroom, presumably to go to bed. Did the killer snatch them out of their bedrooms? There's no evidence for it. Did any or all of them go out again? There's no evidence for that, either. At this point, we simply don't know what happened between the time they were last seen alive and the time their bodies were found."

"Besides the fact that they were all young and attractive, what else do we know that they had in common?"

"They all lived in Berlin, the first two—Inge Weber and Astrid Lang—in Mitte, the others in different sectors. They were all single, although Pauline Fischer was a widow while the others were never married. Astrid Lang was a student at Friedrich Wilhelm University. The other six had paying jobs, although at different places and in different occupations, and Roswitha Eckard worked some nights. But to all intents and purposes we can say that they each were employed outside the home. Most had boyfriends—Pauline Fischer did not—and all those boyfriends have alibis that would seem to eliminate them as suspects. They all had family, friends, an active social life. They ran the usual errands, went to restaurants, clubs, the cinema. They all rode the S-Bahn, the buses, the trams, on a regular basis. They were all found nude, but none of them were raped. None of them were robbed as far as we could tell. They were all killed in an unidentified location and their bodies were transported by unknown means to where they were found. And they were all found outdoors during blackout hours, on a Sunday night into the early hours of the next Monday morning."

"Except for her." With a gesture Elin indicated the photo of last night's victim, still unidentified.

"Yes."

"From the pattern and depth of bruising on her wrists and ankles, she was bound for several days before she was killed."

"Since Sunday, perhaps?"

"It's possible."

It was obvious that Schneider, too, was aware of the significance. If the latest victim had been taken on Sunday, then that would place the time frame of her disappearance more comfortably within the pattern, even if it wasn't exact and the other aspects of her murder didn't conform.

Schneider said, "So he took her and kept her alive for a while."

"It seems like it."

"The question is, why? All the others were killed within twelve to twenty-four hours of them last being seen alive, so why would he keep this one for so long?" He was thinking out loud. "What is it about her that's different?"

"Maybe he knew her. Or—" She shook her head. "It's too early even to speculate. But there's a reason, and once we figure out what it is we'll be a whole lot closer to solving these crimes." She looked down the row of photos. "Was there any point at which all the others' lives intersected? Did they shop at the same stores, visit the same dentist, walk in the same park?"

"We haven't found anything. And we've looked, believe me."

"There has to be something. They had to have met the killer somewhere, while they were doing something. Somewhere they all went, something they all did. There has to be a common element."

He said, "None of them reported being the recipients of any type of harassing behavior. None of them reported being afraid of anyone. Maybe he simply chose them at random. Maybe they were simply at the wrong place at the wrong time and caught his eye."

Random murders were the hardest to solve, as he clearly also knew. But— She shook her head. "It wasn't random. These women were targeted. He chose them for a reason. They'd had some sort of interaction that, to him at least, was significant."

"How can you be sure?"

"The violence of the murders indicates rage and hate for the victims. It's unlikely he'd feel that strongly toward random strangers. They were targeted. These killings were *personal*."

"So he knew them."

"In some way. Perhaps very tangentially, such as regularly shopping at the same store or riding the same tram."

"That would be difficult considering that they all lived in different parts of the city."

"Whoever he is, he's free on Saturday nights into sometime on Sunday with enough time and privacy to take a victim to a secret location and kill her."

"That applies to thousands of men. We've already tried narrowing it down by job, hours worked, that kind of thing, and gotten nowhere."

"We need to focus on *her*." Elin tapped the photo of the latest victim. "Something about her threw him off his routine. Identify her, talk to her family, friends, associates, scour her background and trace her movements over the last few days before she went missing. Perhaps she knew him and saw him with one of the victims. Perhaps—" She broke off, threw up her hands in mystification. "Who knows? However it occurred, she encountered him at some point, in circumstances that provoked him into taking her and then not killing her for days, thus deviating from his usual pattern. *She* is the key. If we can just figure out how to use that key, we might be able to stop another murder before it happens."

That last underlined what she knew they both understood: even as they spoke, the predator was out there somewhere hunting his next victim.

"I've had two secretaries checking the Register of Persons for candidates who fit her description since dawn, and another one combing through Green Cards. Someone else has been going through missing persons reports from Berlin and surrounding towns in the hope she's been reported missing. So far no luck with any of that, but eventually we'll find her. And we'll find him." He sounded so grim she knew he felt the weight of that life hanging in the balance as fully as she did. What remained unspoken between them was that neither of those things might happen in time.

"I'm not familiar with the Register of Persons or Green Cards," she said.

"The Register of Persons contains the name, birth date, birthplace, marital status, religion, race, occupation, citizenship, military status, and criminal record, as well as the same information for spouse, children, and parents, of every single person in Germany. A valuable resource, it's flawed for our purposes in that it's in alphabetical order. To make quick use of it, it's necessary to know the name of the person being sought. Green Cards are part of the People's Card Index. It classifies people by group, including sex and age, with green cards for females and brown ones for males. In theory, that should go a little faster, given that we know she's a female of a certain age. According to Fräulein Engel, who's searching through the Green Cards, she only has fifty thousand or so to go. And a stack of about a thousand already that meet her general description."

"Can't you get her more help?"

Schneider shook his head. "We have the personnel we have. Nebe's made it clear he can't spare more. To do so would mean pulling people off their regular assignments, and that might attract attention."

"And publicity."

"The bête noire of our case."

Elin made a face. Unless someone got very lucky, those searches weren't likely to pay off in time to save the next target's life. There had to be something else they could do. "You said you'd show me the letters the killer wrote."

"Chief—" Frau Skelton appeared in the doorway before he could reply. "Everyone's here."

"Send them in," he told her. He turned to Elin. "After the meeting I'll show you the letters. I want to get my men back out there as fast as possible."

"Yes," she agreed. In this race against time, every minute counted.

A short while later, the meeting was in full swing. Sitting around the conference table that was the centerpiece of the room were three middle-aged men who Schneider introduced as Detectives Beckman, Albrecht, and Vogel. In their nondescript civilian clothes, they all looked to be in their midforties to early fifties and enough alike that the best way Elin found to differentiate them from each other in her mind was tall, short, round: Beckman was tall and spare; Albrecht was short and muscular;

and Vogel was round as a children's toy ball with the red, bulbous nose of a heavy drinker. Clearly older than the others—Elin guessed he was sixty at least—Walter Trott was present as well. The unforgiving overhead light glinted off his nearly bald head and highlighted the bloodhound-like bags under his eyes. Unlike the others, who exuded intensity, he leaned back in his chair, looking half asleep. In addition to the plainclothes detectives, there were also two uniformed police officers: Herr Roth and the man who'd shot at the children, Herr Gunther, who seemed to be making a deliberate effort not to catch her eye.

"Professor Lund and her team..." That was how Schneider made her, Pia, and Jens known to their new associates. From the way he said it Elin realized that the entire group had been aware that she, if not Pia and Jens, would be joining them. She was relieved to see that Jens looked pale and tired but nothing more damning than that, and that his shirt, vest, and loose black jacket—never mind about the heat—served very well to conceal the bandages that she'd done her best to keep as compact as possible. Beside him, Pia mostly kept her eyes on the small notebook she'd pulled out of her bag soon after sitting down. Having started by jotting down a few lines of information, she was now busy making what Elin, from her vantage point beside her, could see were quick drawings of everyone around the table.

After explaining Elin's theory that the killer would be found within the area delineated by where the bodies had been discovered and that he'd circled on the map, Schneider called on each policeman in turn to report his progress. Detective Beckman was the only one to offer any significant new information, namely that a coworker at Greta Neuhaus's place of employment, Wertheim Department Store, recalled that on the Friday before she was killed a man had lingered in the department where they both worked for a long time before finally buying something, and then asking Greta out as she rang up the sale and becoming irate when she turned him down.

"Wertheim's has turned over the store receipt for that transaction, but there's no information on it that identifies the customer. I'm doing everything possible to track him down," Beckman concluded.

"If the clerk remembers what he looks like, I could draw him for you," Pia volunteered. Her pencil stilled on the sketch pad as she looked across the table at the detective.

"I, uh—" Beckman glanced at Schneider, clearly unsure how to respond.

"That would be a huge help," Elin said to Pia, and looked at Schneider, too, in the expectation that he would endorse her words. When he didn't immediately reply, she frowned. Knowing the need to prove her ability would rankle Pia, who was accustomed to having her talent widely known and acknowledged, she nevertheless reached for Pia's sketch pad and held it up so everyone around the table including Schneider could see it, then flipped the pages so that the near perfect likenesses she'd made of each of them were visible to all.

Their expressions told her that they were impressed. The charged look Pia gave her as she handed the sketch pad back told her what she already knew: Pia was unimpressed.

"Can you do that from a verbal description?" Schneider asked Pia.

"Yes." Pia's absolute confidence rang out in her voice. "Although the sketch will only be as accurate as the verbal description."

"Understood." Schneider looked at Beckman. "Go back to Wertheim's when you leave here and take Associate Professor Andersen here with you. Find the clerk in question and set the two of them up so that Associate Professor Andersen can make her sketch."

Beckman nodded. "Yes, Chief."

"If I can get the height and weight of each body and a picture or diagram of the area where it was found, I think I can come up with a rough estimate of the killer's size. It would help if I had the location where the body was removed from the vehicle transporting it, but if that's not available I can make a best guess according to the terrain," Jens said when Schneider asked him if he had anything to contribute.

Schneider nodded, said to the officer, "See that he has the information he needs," then looked at Elin. "Do you have any additional observations you'd like to make, Professor Lund?" Glancing around the table, he added, "As a psychiatrist, Professor Lund comes at the investigation from a different angle than we do. Her observations and recommendations are valuable to the investigation, so pay attention."

9

SCHNEIDER'S POINTED TONE DIDN'T ESCAPE ELIN'S notice, and as she, too, glanced around the table she saw the reason for it. The men's eyes had taken on the slightly glazed look of experienced police officers anticipating being confronted by what they considered the "mumbo jumbo" of unproven scientific theories with no relevance to the real world in which they operated, which was how most people outside academia felt about psychiatrists and their insights.

"These murders are almost certainly the work of one man, acting alone. He's angry. These are rage-fueled killings." Elin stood up as she spoke, the better, as she'd learned, to compel respect from a roomful of skeptical men. "The person we're looking for is a psychopath, and such psychopathy doesn't spring upon a fully formed, adult personality out of nowhere but rather has its roots in childhood. The killer will typically have been a victim of violence in his youth, most likely physical abuse by a parent or parental figure, probably his mother or someone who stands in the place of his mother, which we can assume because of the gender of his victims. He will have responded early on by exhibiting cruelty toward animals or others, perhaps even other children, that he will have singled out because he perceived them to be weaker than himself. He will feel no remorse for even the most horrendous acts of cruelty, which he will justify in his own mind by telling himself 'the victim deserved it.' It's likely that he will engage in role reversal, where he perceives himself as the victim of the individual or group he has attacked, and for that reason absolves himself of responsibility for his actions. It's also likely that Inge Weber was not his first murder. We should look for unsolved slayings of girls or young women, possibly outside of Berlin, because the killer may have moved here from somewhere else. These may stretch all the way back into his youth. In fact, they probably do. There will be a history of maladaptation in school or in social groups such as might have brought him to the attention of authorities at an early age. It's too soon to make other than general recommendations, but if you should come across a male under the age of forty-five with a history of aggression or bullying others as a child or youth, of cruelty toward animals, of voyeurism or unacceptable behavior toward girls or women, that suspect should be flagged for a closer look."

It was clear from the expressions of some of the listening men, notably Detectives Albrecht and Vogel and Officer Gunther, that they remained unimpressed by what she was saying or unimpressed by her in general, not only because she was a psychiatrist but, just as damning in their view, because she was a woman. Well, she'd dealt with such attitudes before and as the saying went, the proof was in the pudding. Their minds would change once the investigation started proving her right. "I'll have a more targeted list of markers to look for once I've had a chance to examine the facts of each murder."

Schneider said, "Thank you, Professor Lund." As she sat back down, he looked at his men. "Any of the rest of you have anything to add? No? Then let's get going. If this new timetable holds, we may have only ten days or so until he kills again. Our job is to catch him first."

To the accompaniment of murmurs of agreement and the scraping sound of chairs being pushed back, Pia, having stood up along with Elin, said, "You might want this," and pulled a roll of papers secured with a rubber band from her bag.

Taking the roll, Elin looked a question at her as she slid the rubber band off.

"The drawings from last night." After a quick glance around, presumably to make sure no one was in a position to observe, Pia shot a significant look at Jens as he headed out the door behind Officer Roth before looking back at Elin. Her message was clear. *Watch out for him while I'm gone.* Elin replied with a barely perceptible nod. Pia then left with Detective Beckman, who was waiting for her.

"Think there's any real chance your male colleague will be able to figure out the height and weight of our killer based on the location of the bodies?" Schneider joined her as Elin unrolled the drawings.

"Based on the distance the killer had to personally, physically carry or toss or drag the bodies to the locations in which they were found?" Elin shrugged. "If Jens thinks he can, he probably can."

"I bow to your superior knowledge of your team's abilities." He studied the drawings as Elin leafed through them. Select moments from the crime scene had been recorded in exacting detail. The dead woman and her surroundings; Schneider and Elin crouched beside the corpse; Trott and the other policemen, busy at their jobs. Jens, measuring distances. The children, clasping hands atop the hill of debris as they turned to run.

Elin's gaze lingered on the children.

Caught in the middle of their turn away from Gunther's warning shouts, they were rendered in three-quarter view with the moonlight pouring over them. Their hair was dark, their arms and legs painfully thin, and their clothes hung on their bodies. Of course, that could be no more than a sign of the deprivation many were suffering as the war dragged on, she cautioned herself. Even with a parent to provide, obtaining sufficient food and clothing for growing children was difficult, as she was personally aware. But what really jumped out at her was the impression they gave of frightened desperation. She suspected that Gunther, while offensive, had not been wrong in his suggestion that they lived on the streets.

Pia with her keen artist's eye had managed to catch other details that had escaped Elin in real life, and as she studied the drawing more closely she picked up on them. The boy appeared to be missing the lower part of his left ear—the flesh there looked ragged, as though a portion of the lobe had been torn off—and his left arm seemed to crook in an unnatural way between his elbow and wrist, making her think it had been broken and never properly healed.

The girl was hollow-cheeked in a way that was jarringly out of place in a child so young, and her way-too-big cardigan was adorned with embroidered flowers and butterflies and looked like the kind of garment an old woman might wear. A grandmother, perhaps—Elin found herself hoping she had a grandmother. That she and the boy were *safe* with a grandmother.

"This we keep." Schneider took the drawing of the children out of her hands, rolled it back up, and stuck it in his jacket pocket.

Why? She opened her mouth to ask and then—didn't. Had he seen something she hadn't? Or earlier he'd warned her to say nothing of the children to Kaltenbrunner. *That* was what gave her pause now.

That and his warning that the walls had ears; was it possible someone unseen was listening?

The thought made her skin prickle.

Ignoring Elin's frown—she knew he saw it and was choosing not to respond—Schneider tapped the final drawing, a sketch of the victim as she might have appeared in life. In Pia's version, she was smiling and rosy-cheeked and looked young and happy.

"This is actually very useful."

"You'll find that *Pia* is very useful," Elin replied. "As is Jens. Which is why I brought them with me."

"I never doubted it." Bland expression, bland tone. Too bland? Or was she so on edge she was reading a sinister meaning into everything?

Calling Frau Skelton to come photograph the sketch and then affix the photo to the appropriate blackboard, Schneider handed the other sketches, with the exception of the one of the children, which remained rolled up in his pocket, to Detective Albrecht, who had not yet left the room, with instructions to file them with the crime scene photographs.

Then he turned to Elin and said, "Come along."

To look at the letters, she thought. She went with him into his office. It was small, windowless, airless, and had obviously not been intended to serve as an office. A storage closet pressed by necessity into alternate service? Possibly. An advantage to being in the cellar was that it was pleasantly cool, if a little musty smelling. A glance around as he gestured her toward an aluminum table that took up part of one wall reinforced her initial impression. The furnishings had been hastily cobbled together: a big, scarred wooden desk with a box and some folders on its top and a utilitarian wooden chair behind it; a quartet of mismatched file cabinets; a pair of dented metal lamps, one on the desk and one on the table in front of which she now sat, complementing the single ceiling bulb that bathed the room in a harsh white light.

"I warn you, you might find these disturbing." He gave her a measuring look as he pulled a folder out of one of the file cabinets. She got the impression that he was remembering that she was a woman and that fact was giving him second thoughts.

"Whether I find them disturbing or not doesn't matter. My job is to catch the killer, the same as yours." The composure with which she spoke did nothing to clear his frown as he put the folder on the table in front of her.

"I'm assuming this means the letters have been tested for fingerprints?" She pulled on the gloves he handed her.

He nodded. "None found. So far, he's been careful. But sooner or later he'll make a mistake. They all do."

He swung his desk chair over to the table and sat down beside her.

"All except the ones we don't catch," Elin said.

"Now there's an encouraging thought." Schneider thrust his hands into a pair of gloves before opening the folder. "They're in order." He tapped the uppermost page. "We received this eleven days after discovering Inge Weber's body."

A sheet of ordinary white writing paper was about two-thirds covered in a spidery, cramped scrawl that Elin squinted at for several seconds before admitting to herself that her initial impression was correct: she could make no sense of it. The letter was handwritten in black ink in what she recognized as a distinctly German style called Kurrent, which the Third Reich had once prized and praised as evocative of German uniqueness and then banned in favor of more modern, Latin-type script. Unfortunately, that uniqueness made the text in front of her all but indecipherable, at least to her.

She looked up, chagrined. "My ability to translate isn't up to this, I'm afraid. I'm having trouble reading it."

"I'll read it to you." He picked up the letter, gave her a look that seemed to assess her fortitude, and then began to read.

"My dear General Kaltenbrunner,
Did you know? Beautiful women are not so beautiful once you begin to hurt them. This one was naked, begging me on her knees, thinking to make me take pity when she looked like a troll with red swollen eyes squirting tears, snotty nose running, loose wet lips screaming please no, please I'll do anything, please let me go, please please please when I told her she was going to die and she should say her prayers. She offered up her breasts and spread her legs for me as if that would make me soften, then squealed like a pig being slaughtered as she felt my knife, squealed so loud she made my head hurt and all I wanted from her was to stop her noise. By then she wasn't beautiful, but ugly, re-pulsive. So repulsive no man could want her. Do you think she thought until the very last second that the authorities would come, that she would be saved? I think she did. But you failed at your job. You didn't save her. Perhaps you'll have better luck with the next one."

"Poor woman." The words squeezed out before Elin could stop them. Reflected in her voice was the horror of the image that had formed in her mind as she'd realized that what Schnei-der was reading was the killer's own description of the terrified victim's last moments of life. Her gaze collided with his.

"Yes." No emotion in his answer. None in his expression, ei-ther. Of course, he'd worked many murders, and he'd read the letter before, so its contents would be blunted for him now. "Then he signed it."

"Signed it?"

"Look here." He put the letter down on the table and pointed to a large, stylized vertical *Z* crossed midway with a bar that stood alone in the center of the page beneath the text of the letter, taking up most of the bottom third of the sheet of paper.

"He uses this as his signature on all the letters." He fanned them out so she could see that, indeed, each letter—all seven were single sheets covered with the same black-ink Kurrent scrawl—was signed the same way. "A *wolfsangel*." At Elin's questioning look, he continued, "It's used as a symbol by a number of Wehrmacht and SS units. Thousands of men strong, most of them not in Berlin, but we're reviewing personnel and leave records in case something relevant should turn up." Elin was just reflecting that that was likely to prove as time prohibitive as the other record searches already underway when he added, "The symbol is also said by some to possess magical powers and is associated with wolves, including werewolves."

"Werewolves." Elin digested that. "So is our killer bold enough to use as his signature a symbol of a military unit he's associated with, or does he think he's a werewolf?"

"Could be either, or something else entirely. Maybe he simply likes the look of it. Maybe he chose it to send us off on a wild-goose chase, knowing we'd explore every possible angle. I should probably mention that Kurrent is no longer being taught in the schools. It was phased out in 1935 and banned entirely in 1941."

"I see you've been thorough."

He almost smiled. "Like I said, we have solved—"

"Murders before. Yes, I know," she finished the sentence for him.

"The reason I mention the timeline for Kurrent is that it means we most likely have a twenty-six-year window—from 1915 to 1941—in which the killer attended school. Handwriting is typically taught in the fourth year, and the style rarely changes once it's learned. That would make him thirty-six, thirty-seven years old or thereabouts."

"I said he would be younger than forty-five."

He gave an acknowledging nod. "It also means that he's most likely a German citizen educated in a German school."

"I think given the evidence we can safely stipulate that." She hesitated to say out loud the rest of what she was thinking: that serial murderers tended to prey on those who were like themselves. In other words, since the victims were, from everything she had seen, all Aryans, the killer was most likely Aryan, too.

But that might be a dangerous point to make.

"And thus little by little we continue to narrow the suspect pool." He tapped a single line of writing located all by itself at the very bottom of the page. "And finally we have this."

Even given her unfamiliarity with Kurrent, Elin could see that the "this" he referred to was different, a mix of letters, numbers, and symbols. An absolutely senseless mix, as far as she could tell.

She frowned at it.

"He ends each letter like this—with a line of what we're almost certain is some kind of code," Schneider said. "Is he sending us a message? Giving us a clue to his identity? Pointing us toward the next victim? Or playing us for fools because it's meaningless and we're wasting valuable time trying to make sense of it? At this point I couldn't tell you. We don't know."

Elin studied the line: composed of single letters, numbers, two triangles, one of which was upside down, a circle, a plus sign, a tiny simplistic drawing of a fish, and a squiggle that could be a backward S or a snake or any number of things, it contained no breaks that would make one think the figures represented words. Yet if the purpose was to send a message, what else could they represent?

Glancing at the remaining six letters, now spread out so that she could look them over side by side, she saw that they, too, ended with a single continuously running line of letters, numbers, and symbols.

Each line was different, although some of the letters and numbers repeated.

"It means something," she said with conviction.

"Probably," he agreed. "Albrecht is checking it against known codes, runic alphabets, hieroglyphics, everything he can think of, but so far no luck."

Elin looked at the other letters. The stylized *Z* signature—a *wolfsangel*, she committed the term to memory—the line of code at the bottom, the all-but-unreadable (to her) text that made up the body of the letter, were almost certainly the work of one man, and that man was their serial murderer. The profile she was building in her mind started to take on shape and detail.

"Read the rest of them to me, please," she said.

"Sure you want me to? They get worse, and you've heard enough to get the gist."

"I don't need only the gist, I need the details," she said, and so after another long look at her he began to read.

As he'd warned, each letter was worse, more graphic, more sadistic, than the last. The killer's glee in recounting his victims' suffering shone through ever more strongly, and his delight in hurting the women, humiliating them, watching them cry and beg before they died, palpably increased with each killing. Elin shuddered inwardly at the horrible acts described with such obvious relish, but by the time Schneider finished she was steely cold inside with determination.

"We have to find him," she said. "He'll keep killing until we do. More frequently, and more viciously. He's escalating at an alarming rate."

"The letters give you any more brilliant insights that might help us out?"

"I think these are most probably lust-based as well as rage-based murders. The killer is, or feels he is, in some way sexually inadequate, and that fills him with rage." That was her immediate analysis. "The man we're looking for is a loner, with a secret life, who presents quite a different face to the world. Outwardly he blends in, has a job, a routine, a wife or girlfriend, maybe even a family. The most ordinary of men, no one you would pick out of a crowd. Neighbors would probably describe him as polite, helpful, a good neighbor. But he has another side— a mirror image, sort of, that takes over when he kills. Think of it as a Mr. Hyde to his Dr. Jekyll, if you're familiar with—"

"I've read the book."

"Well, then, that's the kind of personality we're looking for. I'll be able to tell you more after I've had a chance to go over the case files. Which I'd like to do now, if possible, while the letters are still fresh in my mind."

Before Schneider could reply, a muffled sound brought him to his feet and had him striding toward his desk. Elin watched in bemusement as he lifted the box from his desk to reveal that it lacked a bottom and had been used to cover his telephone.

"Schneider," he said into the receiver. He listened for a minute, said "Yes, *sir*" with a definite edge, hung up, and carefully placed the box back over his phone. From his expression, she deduced that the conversation had not been pleasant. She wondered if it had anything to do with the scene with his son, but she wasn't about to ask.

He was frowning as he returned to stand beside her.

"I have to go out for a while. You can use my office to go over the files while I'm gone. I'll have Frau Skelton bring them in and provide you with anything else you need. You have only to ask her. I've already arranged for a car and driver to be at your disposal, so whenever you're ready for it just tell her and she'll see that it's brought round. Oh, and there's a great little diner just down the street if you should want a meal."

Their eyes met. His told her nothing.

"Thank you. I'll remember that."

He nodded. "If you've finished with the letters, I'll—"

"Leave them, please. I can't easily read them, but the handwriting itself and the way they're composed help me get a sense of who he is."

"Have Frau Skelton file them away when you're finished with them."

"I will." As he turned to leave she had to ask. "You cover your telephone with a box?"

"Like I told you, the walls have ears. And telephones sometimes have listening devices inserted into them." A hint of a smile just touched his mouth. "The box is filled with cotton padding. I don't like being spied on."

10

SCHNEIDER LEFT BEFORE ELIN COULD SHAKE THE CHILL that gripped her at his words. While she waited for Frau Skelton to bring the case files, she stepped into the lab to make sure that her samples were stored properly and that everything was in order for her to do the tests she needed to do.

"The chief said you wanted these," Frau Skelton said from the doorway, and Elin turned to see that she was carrying a box full of file folders. Her tone wasn't overly friendly, but Elin was more interested in what she'd said. She'd been struck by it before but hadn't liked to ask. With Schneider gone, she seized the chance.

"Thank you. I do." She reached for the box Frau Skelton held. "I've noticed that you and some of the officers working this case call Detective Schneider 'Chief.' Why is that? Is that something I should be doing?"

"Because we worked for him when he *was* the chief here at

the Kripo. He was the chief of criminal investigations for years until he was sent to the front. When he was brought back and put in charge of this case, we fell into the way of it again. And that's all I have to say about *that*." She relinquished the box to Elin. "As for what you should call him, I'd say that's up to you."

With that Frau Skelton turned and left, and Elin lugged the surprisingly heavy box back to Schneider's office. Minutes later she was once again seated at the table against the wall, frowning unseeingly at the box's contents as she tried to make sense of what she'd learned. Chief of criminal investigations was a high-level post, directly under Kripo head Arthur Nebe. That Schneider had held it and been sent to the front only to be brought back and placed in charge of this investigation raised a thousand questions. Unfortunately, she had no way to obtain the answers so put the matter aside in favor of getting to work. It took her a few minutes to accomplish, but once the files were open in front of her, she was totally absorbed in the minutiae of the murders.

She worked, combing through victim histories, comparing crime scene evidence and witness statements, making notes, trying to see a pattern in the similarities and find clues in the differences, until the sense of a nearby presence broke the spell. She glanced up.

Jens stood beside her chair. She'd been so intent on what she was doing that she hadn't even heard him come in. His usually ruddy face was pale, his skin was pinched-looking around the eyes, his lips were more gray than pink, but all that was only to be expected given what he had been through with his wound. To her knowing eye, his left arm looked stiff and he kept it close against his side—it should have been in a sling but they didn't dare. What truly alarmed her was his fists were clenched so tightly that the knuckles showed white.

"What?" she asked. If his pain was that bad, he…

"I took a break and went outside for some air. There's a telephone booth across the street. I called my brother to see what was happening at home. He said that the search of the university has ended." He paused, and Elin's stomach tightened. Clearly, from Jens's expression, what should have been good news was not. "But not until after two were arrested. One is Wilhelm Kessel. The other is Borge Meitner."

Elin suddenly couldn't breathe as the reason for Jens's reaction became clear.

Chancellor Wilhelm Kessel was well loved by everyone at the university. Borge Meitner, chairman of the Physics Department, was not so well loved. He was acerbic, outspoken, and impatient of fools. He was also her former father-in-law and her son's grandfather.

The news hit her like a thunderbolt.

"Borge is no saboteur." As fear gripped her, Elin gave voice to none of the reactions exploding through her. Instead, she chose her words carefully. Besides being an administrator at the university, Jens's brother Pieter was a regular contributor to the *Land og Folk*, the newspaper that was the mouthpiece of the Communist Party of Denmark, and as such stayed well-informed. "Neither, I'm sure, is Chancellor Kessel."

Her chest felt like it was being crushed. Her heart had no room to beat. Niles—what of Niles? And Hilde, Borge's wife, Niles's grandmother? Niles was in their care. In their house. If Borge had been arrested—

I have to go home. A surge of adrenaline set her pulse to pounding, had her gripping the arms of her chair as a means of restraining herself. Her immediate impulse to jump up, run to the airport, beg a seat on the first available airplane, and race to her son's side, had to be quelled in favor of a more careful, more measured response.

One that wouldn't do more harm than good.

The Nazis were notorious for retaliation against the families of those they arrested. And Borge's family had more reason than most to be afraid.

What will they do to him?

A kaleidoscope of terrifying images spun through her mind. She felt lightheaded. The walls around her seemed to recede.

"Not to my knowledge," Jens said. "But it may be that—"

"Hush." Though she mouthed the word, the slashing gesture with which she accompanied it was fierce enough to stop him from finishing what he'd been going to say as panic acted like a jolt of cold water restoring the acuity of her senses. Schneider's warning about the walls having ears assumed electrifying urgency. And then there was Frau Skelton, at her desk just beyond Schneider's door, and the secretaries at their desks behind Frau Skelton, as well as whoever else happened to be about.

Anyone could be listening. Anyone could overhear.

His brows rose in a silent question, but when she shook her head Jens said no more.

"No doubt it's simply a misunderstanding." Her untroubled tone was belied by the shakiness of her knees as she stood and the fumbling of her gloved fingers as she began gathering up the papers in front of her to restore them to their files. "Let's hope they discover their mistake soon and the university is left in peace. In the meantime, you should join me for lunch. Herr Schneider told me of a restaurant—"

"It's nearer dinner than lunch." Jens reached past her to help with the papers. He wasn't wearing gloves; despite her inner turmoil, she retained just enough awareness to shake her head again. *Don't touch.*

"Is it?" The windowless basement made it difficult to judge the time. She wasn't hungry; the day had been too fraught. "Is Pia back?"

"Not yet." Jens's voice changed. "So what's the God Equation got to do with this?"

"The God Equation?" She looked up to find he was frowning down at one of the papers she held. It was, she saw as she looked down at it herself, the last letter, the one about Greta Neuhaus's murder.

"Euler's Identity," Jens said, as if that explained everything. Elin realized she must still have looked uncomprehending because he added with a hint of impatience, "Leonhard Euler is a famous mathematician. It's a mathematical equation. Right here." He pointed to a series of numbers in the line of presumed code at the bottom of the letter.

"Really." Too worried at the moment about the ramifications of Borge's arrest to wrestle with the significance of a mathematical equation in a madman's letter, she vowed to share that information with Schneider when next she saw him. "We'll puzzle it out later." Tucking the papers back into their respective files, she said, "I'm finished here. Let's go."

Having been warned, Jens didn't speak as she handed the files over to Frau Skelton and they left the building. Once out on the busy street, Elin initiated a line of mundane conversation for the benefit of any interested passersby until they reached a small park in the next block. The attraction as she pulled Jens into it wasn't the neat rows of trees shading the paths from the baking sun; it was that unlike the teeming sidewalks, the park was relatively empty. The path she chose curved away from the street through an obscuring grove of immaculately manicured greenery. A few meters in, she abruptly abandoned their increasingly inane conversation, cast a comprehensive look around to make sure no one was near enough to overhear, and in an undertone asked, "When did it happen?"

He knew instantly what she was referring to. "First thing this morning. Right after the chancellor and Meitner arrived on campus."

Less than a day after they'd managed to get Jens safely away. She would have felt lucky but—

"Niles is staying with his grandparents." No need to say anything more—or to try to hide the tension that made her voice taut as a stretched wire. Because of Pia, who'd been one of Elin's closest friends since they'd met as children, Jens knew all about Elin's situation.

"I wouldn't worry too much," Jens said. But the tiny pause before he spoke conveyed the opposite. Elin's stomach pitted even as he continued with more certainty. "If anything had happened to the families, my brother would be aware and would have told me."

"If anything had happened *yet*."

Jens's silence in response to that stark pronouncement said it all.

"*Is* Borge involved in—" It was the merest breath of a question, broken off as a woman carrying a string bag of groceries and holding a child by the hand appeared around a bend in the path. She was followed by a young couple who, ignoring their lush surroundings, had eyes only for each other. Pretending to be absorbed in admiring the beauty of the flower beds interspersed among the trees, Elin could think of nothing but Niles as the groups passed. Was he frightened? Was he safe? If the Nazis came for Hilde…

"Not that I know of." As soon as they were alone again, Jens immediately picked up the conversation where they had left off. Pulled from the midst of a thousand frantic thoughts, Elin remembered that she had asked about Borge's involvement in the Resistance. Jens's answer should have been comforting, but she didn't even have time to feel a quiver of relief before he added, in a voice that was so low she had to strain to hear it, "But there are many layers to what is being undertaken, and many moving parts. I only know the ones that I know."

Cells. The small but growing Resistance operated in cells. Besides Holger Danske and the communist Borgerlige Partisaner, other organized groups included the Churchill Club and the Samsing Group. But a host of emerging cells, more fluid than those, were popping up to engage in specific acts such as the dynamiting of a factory or the derailment of a train, then dissolving and re-forming with interchangeable members to re-spond to different challenges. The more the iron fist of the Reich tightened around Denmark, the more her people were rising up and fighting back.

Elin was proud—and frightened. For them, her family and friends, herself. Her son.

"Borge has been so angry about Lars." Even now, remember-ing sent a shaft of pain through Elin's heart. Lars—her husband, Niles's father, Borge and Hilde's son, had been killed in the first hours of Germany's invasion of Denmark. Not in battle, but hanged as a saboteur in the aftermath, his body left to rot until friends sneaked in under cover of darkness to cut him down, his family left in ignorance of what had happened for days after-ward. The memory still had the power to make her sick. She wasn't sure the invading Germans had even known his name. She knew the family had faced no retaliation for his action.

Yet.

Jens said, "And with good reason. But Borge Meitner is no fool. He would not have—" a bicyclist pedaled past, and Jens paused until he was safely out of earshot before continuing "—done anything to endanger his family now after holding back all this time."

"I'm not so sure." Her relationship with her in-laws had never been particularly close—wealthy and influential, they had not approved of their beloved only child's marriage to a woman of what they delicately referred to as her "background"—but Lars's death had cemented them as family. From what she had observed, Borge's hatred toward the German occupiers who had taken his son's life had only grown over the years. Borge was enough like Lars that he would never relinquish his anger, or his need for revenge. Once his passions were roused, he would plunge ahead with what he felt was right without regard for the cost to anyone, including himself.

With the clarity of hindsight, she could see that that trait had been a factor in Lars's choice to marry her.

And in his death as well.

"Another possibility is that the Germans have no real proof against them, but swept them up anyway," Jens said.

"Why would they do that?"

Jens's grimace gave her the answer without the need for him to say anything else.

"Because they're Jews." Her words sounded hollow to her own ears. The terror that had lived within her since the Germans had rolled into their peaceful country had blazed to renewed life on Sunday. Now it flared as brightly hot as an eruption on the surface of the sun. She'd long feared that the Nazis would do as they had done in every other territory they'd invaded and target the country's Jews. The Meitners, Borge, Hilde, and Lars, were part of Denmark's 8,000-strong Jewish population. And that made Niles, her Niles, as the child of a Jewish father, part of it, too.

11

JENS GAVE A SLOW NOD. "I FEAR SO."

Elin could feel the thudding of her heart. Never mind that she herself was Aryan. The threat to her son was terrifyingly real. *Mischling* was what the Nazis called Niles and those like him: the product of a union between a Jewish parent and an Aryan one. Mixed race; mongrel; half-breed. It was a legal term, and an insult, and now a danger. While at first the *mischlinge* had been spared the worst of the regime's racial intolerance, now they were hated along with the rest of the Jews. In Germany and everywhere else the Germans ruled, *mischlinge* were increasingly subject to the same fate as any other Jew.

He's just a little boy. The thought was nearly a prayer. Hastily, she made it into one and sent it winging skyward. *Protect him, please.*

Since the occupation, the Nazi overlords had allowed Denmark to function more or less as usual and had made no overt moves against its Jewish population, which was well integrated into society. There was no forced registration, no mandated wearing of yellow stars, no confiscating of homes or bank accounts, no loss of jobs or friends. The Jews were simply Danish citizens, indistinguishable from the rest. Most, like the Meitners, were long established and well respected in their communities. Denmark, the Nazis felt, was an Aryan country with the same basic values as Germany. There was no need to stir up bad feelings between the two by going after such a small percentage of the population as long as the occupation went smoothly and the mandates of the newly co-opted government were obeyed.

But over the last several months, growing resistance to the occupation had strained relations between the countries. Labor strikes and acts of sabotage had inflamed the situation until a palpable tension between occupiers and the occupied hung like a cloud over the land. In Copenhagen, where most of Denmark's Jews lived, German soldiers had begun what amounted to a campaign of harassment, stopping those they suspected of being Jews on the flimsiest of excuses, demanding papers, searching briefcases and backpacks. The Great Synagogue, the main place of worship for Copenhagen's Jews, was felt to be under surveillance by sinister forces that, at a minimum, made note of everyone who entered. The Jewish community had grown increasingly wary even as most continued to go about their daily business.

Everywhere else the Nazis ruled, Jews by the thousands were being swept up into ghettos, deported to forced labor camps, removed from society.

Murdered? So the whispers claimed—and what she had overheard that morning seemed to confirm it.

She went cold all over at the thought. Such evil seemed impossible. But in February, right here in Berlin in a drive so comprehensive it had made the front page of a German newspaper popular enough to be sold in Denmark, the Gestapo had spearheaded the Fabrik-Aktion, a major roundup and deportation of some of the last remaining Jews in the city. And just this past May 19, Joseph Goebbels, the Reich Minister of Propaganda, had gloatingly declared that Berlin was *Judenrein*. That alone should have awakened any remaining skeptics to the reality that the eradication of the Jews was one of the primary goals of Hitler and his brutal regime.

Was the very term Goebbels had used a clue? *Judenfrei* was what they'd called it once, meaning that an area had been freed of its Jewish population, ostensibly by forced evacuation and re-settlement. *Judenrein* had a more sinister connotation. It meant that Berlin had been *cleansed* of every last drop of Jewish blood.

The collective thinking of the majority of the Danes had continued to be, *It won't happen here.*

But Elin was deathly afraid that the ruthless purging of the Jews from other Nazi-dominated countries served as a bellwether. The worst simply hadn't happened in Denmark yet.

And there was that word, that heart-stopping word, again: *yet.* It kept echoing through her mind like the chiming of some terrible doomsday clock.

"Have we really come to that?" Her question, addressed as much to herself as to Jens, emerged as an anguished whisper.

"We have to look at the facts," Jens said. "The war is not going well for Germany, and with each defeat their mood grows uglier. They're tightening their grip on the territories they've swallowed up. Now they've seized total control of Denmark. And in every instance, one of their first acts on taking total control is the rounding up of the Jews."

"You think that's what they're preparing to do." Panic fluttered in her stomach.

"I think it's a strong possibility," Jens said. "That's why we—"

He broke off, but Elin understood. That's why the Resistance was ramping up like it was. That's why Jens had done what he'd done, which had led to him standing with her in Berlin now rather than going about his normal daily life in Copenhagen.

The signs were all there, as anyone who dared to look could see. The German beast was finally baring its teeth and claws.

Terror for the safety of Niles solidified into what felt like a rock lodged beneath her breastbone.

"I shouldn't have left him with his grandparents." She realized she was speaking her thoughts aloud when she hadn't meant to and broke off. The Meitners were well-known within the Jewish community. Borge was already under arrest. If Niles was with Hilde when the Nazis came… She shuddered. But who else could she have left him with, for an indeterminate and possibly extended stay? Any non-Jewish family might not have dared to keep him if his presence put them at risk. Leaving him with the Meitners had seemed like the best, safest thing to do. They loved him; and despite her own complicated relationship with them, where Niles's welfare was concerned she trusted them completely. They would protect him with their lives, if it came to that.

"I shouldn't have left him at all. I shouldn't have agreed to come." Rising distress quickened her breathing.

Jens patted her shoulder. The gentle gesture from a man roughly the size of a polar bear was meant to comfort, she knew. The fact that her agitation was apparent enough to prompt him to offer comfort was what was concerning. Letting anyone see that she was upset would only focus attention on the cause. That knowledge helped her wrest her outward composure back into place and cram her burgeoning terror for her child back down into the nightmarish compartment where such paralyzing emotions lived.

Jens said, "As far as I know, you didn't *agree* to come. You were summoned and had no choice but to obey. As for Niles, you did what you thought was best."

"I know. You're right." She managed the smallest of smiles for him. Her heart still pounded and the knot in her chest was still there, but giving in to fear did no one any good. Then it hit her. *Jens* was the one who should be panicking. He was the saboteur the Nazis searched for. The one who faced certain death if he was caught.

Her eyes widened on his face. If those arrested talked—

"Does Borge—or Chancellor Kessel—know about you?"

"I don't know," Jens said. "I don't think so. The cells are kept separate for a reason."

But she could tell from his tone that the prospect of a security breach had occurred to him, too.

All it would take was one tortured confession followed by one telephone call to the authorities in Berlin, and Jens would be detained. He would be searched, his wound would be discovered, and that would get him arrested. And she and Pia would be arrested right along with him.

What would happen to Niles then?

The knot in her chest expanded until she could scarcely breathe.

"I should return to Copenhagen," Jens said. "At least then, if anything were to be revealed, it won't involve you—or Pia."

Elin managed a deep breath and then slowly, slowly let it out.

"You can't." She was clearheaded now, her thoughts sharp and focused. As they had to be, for her child's sake. "For you to leave now would draw too much attention. That applies to me as well. None of us can go home. The smartest thing we can do is keep our heads down and do our jobs and solve these murders as quickly as we can. *Then* we can go home."

In the meantime, she could only pray that the small safeguards she'd put in place on her son's behalf would do what they had been designed to do. They wouldn't, she feared, stand up to any in-depth scrutiny, which would certainly reveal his ancestry, but they might keep the authorities from looking too closely at him to begin with.

After what had happened to Lars, she'd insisted that Niles be known by her last name, Lund, instead of Meitner, for fear of retaliation against the family, much to her former in-laws', particularly her mother-in-law's, distress.

"You would strip Lars's son of his name? Every father has the right to give his son his name. Every son has the right to bear his father's name," Hilde had raged.

"It's to protect him." Elin had done her best to explain. "I don't want Niles to have to pay a price for what Lars did. The Nazis—"

"*This* for the Nazis." Hilde, elegant Hilde, had spit on the grass outside her palatial front door. "We won't live our lives to suit them."

Hilde had spoken in the weeks just after the invasion, when the shock of what had happened was still fresh and grief clouded their judgment. As the weeks had turned into months and then years, the acuteness of Elin's fear that the Nazis might come looking for Lars's relatives had waned. But her fear that they might target Jews had grown, as had her determination to protect her son at all costs.

Once rumors of possible surveillance had arisen, she'd kept him away from the Great Synagogue. She'd limited his participation in any public celebration of Jewish holidays. She'd made sure that his activities, his friends, his routines, were the same as those of any other Danish boy his age. Her goal was for him to blend in, to be indistinguishable from the rest. Not easily identifiable as *mischling*.

Would it be enough?

"I need to talk to Hilde, and to Niles," she said. "What time is it?"

Hilde's daily maid left at four. She wanted to speak directly to her former mother-in-law rather than go through the maid, who usually answered the telephone when she was on duty. Her cautionary instincts were on high alert, and they were screaming that the fewer witnesses there were to her call to the Meitner home, the better.

Then it occurred to her—the maid might be the least of her worries. Given Borge's arrest, it was possible that government agents could even now be listening in on calls to his home.

The prospect was appalling, but it was a chance she was going to have to take. She didn't think she could survive another hour, let alone the next days or weeks or however long it was going to be until she could get home again, without talking to Hilde and to her son.

It was a quarter past four when Elin reached Hilde. At Jens's urging they'd eaten a quick meal at the diner Schneider had recommended, not that she'd been able to swallow more than a few bites. Then they'd returned to the telephone booth opposite the Alex, where she placed her call while Jens hovered protectively outside. With the door closed, the bright yellow, glass-sided structure was hot and airless as an oven. She kept her back to the street as she dialed, but still she knew she was perfectly visible to the constant stream of passersby on the sidewalk and the traffic-heavy street. Her shoulders tensed at the thought that, as a high-profile visitor to the country or because of General Kaltenbrunner's or someone else's interest in what she was doing or even because suspicion might already be attached to Jens, she could be under observation by the Gestapo or the SS, but if so there was nothing to be done about it. And so she pressed on.

"I heard what happened," Elin said when Hilde answered. Knowing Hilde would instantly recognize her voice, she didn't identify herself. And she was careful in her choice of words. "Are you all right?"

"We are fine." The brevity of Hilde's response told Elin that she, too, was aware of the possibility that someone might be listening in, while the brittleness of her usually beautifully modulated voice spoke of stress. "The authorities have made a mistake. I expect Borge to be released and to return home at any time."

That was either pure bravado or posturing for the sake of any listeners, or both, Elin knew. Even over the distance between them, she could feel Hilde's fear, palpable as a cold wind.

"I'm sure he will be. But while you wait for him perhaps you might want to pay a visit to the Rasks," Elin said. *That* was the message she desperately wanted to convey. "It would be such a comfort to me to know that you had the support of your good friends at this time."

The Rasks were the caretakers of a holiday home her in-laws owned in Charlottenlund, a popular summer retreat just north of Copenhagen. Elin deliberately didn't mention the name of the house—Smukkeso, which meant Beautiful Lake—or its location. She was sure Hilde would understand that she was suggesting Hilde take Niles and go out of Copenhagen to their vacation home. Just in case the Nazis decided to come for Borge's family, too.

"I will wait here at home for Borge," Hilde said.

Elin's stomach twisted. Always rigid in her thinking, Hilde was staying true to form. There was so much she wanted to say— *Borge may not be coming home, it might not be safe for you to stay there, the Nazis could arrive at any time and sweep up you and Niles*—but she dared not give voice to any of that. A series of telltale clicks on the line made the hair rise on the back of her neck and convinced her that the call *was* being listened in on. From somewhere. Perhaps the Gestapo eavesdropped on all country-to-country calls? Or perhaps the pay telephone outside the Alex was routinely monitored? Or was Borge's line truly tapped?

"I know the Rasks would love to see you," she said, rattled by the sounds and desperately trying to convey all she couldn't put into words. "The last time I saw them they asked me to tell you to please come by as soon as you possibly could. With extra emphasis on the *please*."

"It *is* always comforting to be with friends," Hilde said slowly. Had she heard the clicks, too? Or was she responding to the urgency in Elin's voice? "Perhaps a quick visit—"

"Yes," Elin said as she hesitated. "That's just what I would recommend."

"Is that Mama?" Niles piped up in the background. Elin closed her eyes. Her heart flew across the distance between them. Her beloved boy, with his slight build and shock of blond hair that was from her, and his warm brown eyes that owed everything to Lars. "May I please talk to her?"

"You may say hello, but that's all," Hilde told him as Elin opened her eyes again to stare unseeingly out at the giant Kakao Schokolade advertisement on the building beyond the glass wall. "She is very busy, you know, and can only spare us a few minutes."

That edict, Elin knew, was not simply Hilde being severe, as she sometimes was. It was her way of trying to limit the chance of any unguarded words of Niles's causing damage. Even a reference by Niles to his grandfather could possibly be used against Borge, if his captors chose to threaten Borge with harm to his grandson unless he cooperated with them.

Her mind reeled at all the horrifying possibilities even as her son got on the line.

"Are you coming home soon?" His voice, his beloved voice, brought a lump to her throat.

"As soon as I can. I have to finish my job here first. But I'm working really fast, and it shouldn't be too long." She only hoped he wouldn't recognize the huskiness in her voice for what it was.

"I have school."

"I know. I wish I could be there. But you'll be fine. After all, you're six now." His birthday was in July, and he'd been so proud of turning six. *My big boy*, she'd called him, wrapping him in a hug, and he'd hugged her back and beamed even though she'd done it in front of his friends. At the memory, her fingers tightened around the receiver until she could feel the hard plastic digging into her skin.

"Farmor doesn't know what to pack in my satchel. I have to *tell* her. And Farfar isn't even here. He—"

At that mention of his grandfather the clicks in the background sounded again, followed by an indistinct whir. Elin went on instant alert. Were the authorities not only listening to but *recording* the conversation?

Her blood ran cold.

"Say goodbye now, Niles." Hilde's voice came through loud and clear. Elin pictured her hovering over Niles as she reached for the receiver. Although she knew that given the real dangers of the situation it was best that they end the call, still she yearned for more time, for more than just a tense and hurried chat, for her *son*.

"I miss you." Probably she shouldn't have said it. Probably it just made the separation harder for them both.

"I miss you, too. Farmor says I have to go now. I love you, Mama."

Elin's heart broke at the forlorn note in his voice. "I love you, too, *musling*. I'll be home as soon as I can. It won't be long, you'll see."

"I'll take care of him, Elin." Hilde was back on the line.

"I know you will." She could hear the clicking and whirring again. Her pulse raced. "He loves the Rasks, by the way. He'll love seeing them again."

"I think you're right, visiting my old friends will do me good," Hilde said, and Elin was sure she could hear the clicking, too. "But now I must go. Britta left *knepkager* in the oven and it's ready to come out. We'll be glad to see you when you get home. Say goodbye, Niles."

"Goodbye, Mama," Niles called, and Elin pictured him, probably still in his school uniform because he always forgot to change, standing behind Hilde in her always-tidy kitchen that right at that moment would be filled with the warm, spicy smell of the crunchy biscuits that he loved—while the Gestapo interrogated his grandfather and malignant government agents listened in on their telephone calls for what could only be an ominous purpose.

"Goodbye," Elin called back around the lump in her throat.

Then Hilde hung up, and Elin was left clinging to the receiver like a lifeline.

She was sweating as she left the telephone booth, and not only—or even primarily—from the confined space's concentrated heat. Here it was, the danger she had foreseen, terrifyingly close and growing closer, and she couldn't go home, couldn't get to her son, couldn't protect him.

"So?" Jens materialized in front of her. The concern in his bright blue eyes steadied her.

"They're all right," she said, and was just giving him a brief summary of the call when a taxi pulled up in front of the Alex and Pia stepped out.

"Pia!" Jens called in his booming voice. Pia looked around, spotted them, and waved. Jens waved back and hustled Elin across the street in the teeth of the streaming traffic.

"The customer was a policeman." As they joined her on the sidewalk, Pia greeted them with obvious excitement. Dressed in pale yellow with a tiny white hat perched jauntily on her smooth blond hair, her white platform peep-toes giving her the height she lacked, she looked cool as a glass of water despite the heat. "The clerk described him, and I drew him, and when the detective saw the sketch he recognized the man! He made a telephone call and Herr Schneider and another detective came and looked at the drawing and talked to the clerk. They're on the way to pick the man up for questioning right now."

12

SOME SEVEN HOURS LATER, ELIN WAS IN THE LAB IN
the basement of the Alex, grainy eyed with exhaustion. Except
for the brightly lit area right around her table, the rest of the lab
was dark and shadowy. A sliver of light showing beneath the
closed door made her think that she was not the only one still
working, but she'd seen no one in hours and could hear nothing
beyond the clink of her instruments as she finished what she was
doing and gathered them up. Stepping away from the microscope, she blinked rapidly as her eyes struggled to recover from
the strain of staring at dozens of slides. If the man they sought
truly had been found—and how she hoped, no, prayed, that it
was so—she wanted to be able to close out her part of the case
as quickly as possible so she could get home to Niles. Along with
creating a psychological profile of the killer, she had to check
the collected material for evidence that could be used to con-

vict a suspect. Having completed the former to the extent she could with the available facts, she was still working on the latter.

She was just returning the slide she'd been examining to its place in cold storage when the door to the lab opened. To her surprise, Schneider walked in. She hadn't seen him since he'd left her in his office earlier in the day.

Silhouetted by a dim light from somewhere farther along the hallway, he looked formidably tall and broad shouldered as he stopped short just inside the door. He didn't say anything, which she found unnerving. Had news come from Copenhagen? Was their cover blown?

"What are you doing here?" His question was abrupt, and came as he moved, shutting the door behind him. To say he didn't sound glad to see her would be an understatement.

"I might ask the same of you." She turned away from the refrigeration unit to arrange her instruments in the sterilization tray. Looking over her shoulder at him, she said with as much collegiality as she could muster, "Don't you have a family you need to get home to?"

"No." That uncompromising answer made her frown. She'd seen his son. He walked farther into the room. The light hit him. His hat was pushed to the back of his head. His eyes were bloodshot, he needed a shave, and he was unsmiling as he met her gaze.

She only hoped the fear he provoked didn't show on her face.

She tried for a friendlier tone. "I suppose they're used to you working all available hours. I know my father did."

"I live alone. My wife divorced me years ago and our son lives with her. His name is Markus and he's two months short of being thirteen. And just to give you the full picture since you're apparently so interested in my background, that buffoon I butted heads with on the parade ground earlier is her second husband, Major General Artur Pohl. Anything else about my personal life you want to know?" He was practically growling at her by the time he finished.

She abandoned friendly. "Only how your ex-wife managed to let such a charmer get away."

Their eyes clashed and held. Then the ghost of a smile touched his lips and the tension in his jaw eased.

"I apologize. I've had an unpleasant few hours explaining to my boss why I accosted my son's stepfather, and then justifying the amount of time that has been put into this case without solving it. How about we move on from my bad manners and talk about the case?"

"Good idea. I understand we have a suspect." She was too relieved to know that his bad mood had nothing to do with Jens to hold a grudge.

"A suspect," he agreed. "But the killer? We'll see. You find anything that could help us identify our guy?"

"Type A blood in one of the scalp wounds. And traces of Pervitin." She felt the same warm rush of satisfaction she'd experienced earlier when, after mixing the blood and sera on the slide and reading the reactions, she'd made the discovery. That helped settle her nerves as she determinedly dismissed everything else to concentrate on the case. "The deceased was type O. Which means the killer's blood is probably type A. And, since no hint of Pervitin was found in the victim's blood, he probably takes Pervitin."

"Good work. I'll pass that along." He moved to a telephone in the corner of the lab and placed a call. It was quick and to the point, and she listened shamelessly. When he returned, he perched on one of the tall stools beside the table where she'd been working and sat watching her in brooding silence while she carefully dampened a cloth with alcohol. The resultant sharp odor was merely one more added to the mix. Chemical smells permeated the room, and were, she thought, largely responsible for the slight headache that had been troubling her for the last hour.

He regarded her with demoralizing intensity.

"Want to talk about it?" She just managed to keep her tone polite. His frowning preoccupation was driving her mad. "I am a psychiatrist, you know."

She would have found his answering snort insulting at any other time. But she was too worried about what he might be thinking to be offended.

Focus on the case. "Pia said that your detective identified the man from her sketch."

"He did. Paul Dalsing, an officer of the Orpo, believe it or not. Order Police," he clarified when her lack of comprehension must have become obvious. "You know, wears a uniform, responsible for traffic control, public safety, that kind of thing. Forty-one years old, married, one child. Says he was in Wertheim's to buy a gift for his wife. His only memory of Fräulein Neuhaus was of her as a salesclerk who overcharged him, which was why he was irate. He swears he never asked her out. And, more importantly, he didn't kill her."

"Do you believe him?" She wiped down the table she'd used as she spoke. Carefully, because even the tiniest amount of blood or fluid left behind could contaminate the next item of potential evidence placed there. He sat at the end of that table and lifted his hat, which he had removed, and his arms, both of which rested on the table, obligingly out of her way. He was still frowning, and she was still nervous about it, but it didn't seem as though his bad mood had anything to do with her, or the events in Copenhagen.

"I think he was lying about not asking her out. Was he lying about not killing her? Like I said, we'll see. But we did a physical exam, and he didn't have any partly healed wounds or injuries. Given that our last victim was killed so recently, I would've expected to see some. Blood is slippery. In my experience, it would be almost impossible for a subject to stab someone the way she was stabbed and not suffer any cuts to his own hands or arms in the process."

"He might have been wearing protective clothing," Elin said. "Gloves, and a coat or something of that nature that covered his arms. But if he wasn't bleeding, how would his blood get on our victim?"

"Good question," Schneider said. "And one that I already considered. Which is why I just told the officer in charge of his detention to conduct another full body check for any hidden injuries as well as a blood test."

"He should also be checked for a background or interest in mathematics." She finished wiping down the table and tossed the cloth in the bin meant for such used items as he gave her an inquiring look. "Jens found a mathematical equation in the line of code at the bottom of the killer's letter about Greta Neuhaus. The God Equation, he called it. Although he has no idea what it means in the broader context of what the killer may have been trying to convey. At some point, though, that will hopefully change."

"The God Equation." Schneider seemed to mull that over for a few seconds. "I've never heard of it, but that doesn't mean much. I'm no mathematician." He gave Elin a frowning look. "How reliable is your friend Jens?"

"Extremely reliable. And he *is* a mathematician. If Jens says that equation is in the code at the bottom of the letter, then it is."

"I thought he was busy trying to determine the killer's height and weight by whatever magic formula he's supposedly using."

"It's not a magic formula, it's mathematics." In response to the barely perceptible skepticism he exhibited toward Jens's ability, her voice once again had bite. "And after he found the equation in the code, well, that seemed like it was of more immediate value to the investigation so I told him to concentrate on that."

"Where is he? I'd like him to show me, and hear his explanation for myself."

"I sent him and Pia back to the hotel." Elin wasn't sure how Schneider was going to feel about what else she'd done, but getting Jens away from the direct observation of the parade of policemen coming in and out of their war offices in the Alex was what she'd felt she had to do, given Borge's and the chancellor's arrests and what might be coming their way as a result. Besides providing what seemed to her to be their best hope for breaking the code in an expeditious manner, setting Jens to working on it and stipulating that he needed complete privacy to do so had been the perfect excuse to keep him out of the way for a few days. *Out of sight, out of mind* was the principle she was operating by. She only hoped it would be enough.

"With an eye toward not compromising the originals, I had Pia take photos of the letters and sent the photos back to the hotel with Jens, so he could try to figure out the code in the peace and quiet of his room. There were too many distractions here for him to be able to work efficiently."

Schneider's brows snapped together. Brooding gave way to scowling. "You should have asked me first. Those letters have purposely only been shown to a small, select group of people, and shouldn't have been shared with your friend, or photographed, or had those photographs taken out of the Alex without my permission."

Indignation at his rebuke stiffened her spine and had her scowling right back at him. "My *friend* is a professor at the University of Copenhagen, has a doctorate in mathematics, and found the God Equation in the code when none of your people, who you said have gone over those letters many times without success, did. And he is a consultant on this case, and a member of my team. As such, I am perfectly within my rights to set him to any task I consider important. Also, just so we're clear—" and that was a deliberate echo of words he'd said to her previously "—I don't have to ask your permission to do anything I feel is germane to solving this case, which, if I may remind you, is what your government brought me here to do."

"You were brought in to *help* solve the case. The operative word there is *help*." His eyes had narrowed at her and his jaw had hardened. It was once again clear from his expression that he wasn't used to having his authority questioned, and she remembered what Frau Skelton had told her about him previously having been the chief of criminal investigations.

"And who will bear the blame if those letters leak, as you just made it much easier for them to do?" He held up a hand to stop her before she could reply. "No, don't even say it. I guarantee it won't be you."

Since she'd been about to say *I will*, that took the wind out of her sails.

"They won't leak," she said instead.

The telephone rang before he could reply, which was probably just as well, she thought. With a hard look at her he got up to answer it. Quarreling with the man was unwise. The last thing she needed was to turn him into an enemy. But for her, solving the case had taken on an even greater urgency, and she meant to leave no stone unturned whether he liked the way she went about it or not.

While he was on the telephone she washed her hands. She could hear his side of the conversation even over the running water, but it was largely monosyllabic and she was able to glean just enough to ascertain that the call was about the suspect and nothing else. Hanging up the apron she'd been wearing on a hook beside the sink, she turned to look at him as he rang off. This time when he walked to the table he didn't sit, but stayed standing beside it, drumming his fingers on the surface, frowning at her.

"Well?" she asked when he didn't say anything.

"Type AB blood, no injuries beyond a few bruises." He seemed to have gotten over, or thought better of, his annoyance with her.

"Oh." Disappointment increased her exhaustion tenfold. She could almost feel her body sag. Of course her prospective deliverance had come too fast, and been too simple. When was life ever that easy? "So what now? Will you release him?"

He shook his head. "We'll keep him on ice for a few days. At least until we can verify his whereabouts at the time of the murders. His alibis for most of them are basically 'I was home asleep.' Possible, maybe even probable, but we still need to take a closer look at him. Among other things, find out if he's some kind of secret mathematician."

If that was an attempt at a peace offering, she was going to ignore it. "The blood type alone should rule him out."

"Unless it wasn't his blood. Maybe he has a partner."

"I feel confident in saying this killer works alone."

"You may be right."

"I usually am. Anyway, how would he get blood on the victim if he has no injuries?"

"Maybe he had a nosebleed."

Her lips compressed. Was he *trying* to be funny? She gave him a censorious look. There was no place for joking in a murder investigation. Especially *this* murder investigation, when there was so much at stake. "Of the wrong blood type? You seem very invested in keeping this man locked up."

"In my experience, it pays to be thorough. And you seem very invested in letting him go."

"Focusing on the wrong man will hurt the investigation. It will slow us down, waste precious time and resources, and leave the real killer out there free to slaughter another young woman. Which he may do in a matter of days."

"If his alibis hold up and we're able to confirm he's not our man, he'll be released. But at this point, we don't know that. Not for sure. And I wouldn't want to release him and be wrong."

Something about the way he said it made her look at him more closely. His eyes were impossible to read. His mouth was set in an unrevealing straight line. *He's keeping something from me.*

She experienced a moment of unease.

"You're using him, aren't you? To get Kaltenbrunner and the rest off our backs."

"To give us some breathing room to work, you mean? Maybe. But I promise you Herr Dalsing will be released if he's cleared, which he hasn't been."

"Does he know Kurrent? Mathematics? Have any kind of criminal history? Does he know any details of the murders, or that you're in charge of the investigation?" She rapid-fired the questions at him. Any *no* answers were disqualifying, and the more *no*es there were, the more unlikely it became that Herr Dalsing was the killer.

"All still to be determined. His life is being gone through with a fine-tooth comb right now, believe me."

"You said yourself you don't think he's the killer."

"What I think and what I know are two entirely different things." He glanced around the lab. "Are you finished here? I'll drive you back to your hotel."

She shook her head. The thought of collapsing into bed was almost irresistible, but there was so much to do and so little time. "I'm finished in the lab, but there are still some things in the evidence room I want to go over. It's important that—"

"It's important that you get some sleep," he interrupted her. "Your eyes are puffy, you're snappish, and you're all but swaying on your feet." He nodded at her doctor's bag, which stood open on another stool. "Get what you need, close that up, and let's go. You're no good to anybody if you can't think straight, and you know it." She stood there for a moment, indignant—*had he really called her snappish?* Then he added with a touch of exasperation, "Are you always this stubborn, or am I just getting lucky here?"

That earned him a glare, and then, slowly, a small, reluctant smile. "All right, I admit it, I need sleep. I'll go. Thank you for offering to drive me." Retrieving her notebook, she tucked it into her bag. "It's just I feel like we're racing the clock."

"I know. But at this point it's a marathon, not a sprint. You have to pace yourself. We all do."

He followed her out the door.

★ ★ ★

"Any luck identifying our latest victim?" Even to her own ears, Elin sounded groggy. The soporific sound of wheels on pavement coupled with the lulling motion of the ride had provided the coup de grâce. Her head dropped back against the rolled top of the leather seat even as she addressed the question to Schneider. If she wasn't careful, she would fall asleep right there in his car. She was having to work to keep her eyes open. It was all she could do to suppress a yawn. They were driving through the moonlit darkness of the nightly total blackout, heading southwest along Berlin's wide boulevards toward where her small hotel was located not far from the immense green oasis-in-the-city that was Grunewald Forest. Only a few vehicles were on the road, their slotted headlights rendering them almost invisible until they were upon them. On the sidewalks and the paths that wove between the buildings and crisscrossed the squares and public gardens, the glowing coin-sized green phosphorus pins pedestrians wore on their clothing to avoid collisions bobbed through the night. Moving gray shadows of those who, for whatever, probably nefarious reason, chose not to wear the pins made the darkness seem alive.

"If anyone's filed a missing person report on her, we haven't found it. And showing the picture your friend drew around places young women are likely to frequent hasn't yielded anything, either." A corner of his mouth quirked up. "I gave Walter that job. His story is she's his daughter, and she ran away from home, and he just wants to find her to make sure she's all right. He's getting a lot of sympathy, and a lot of invitations to dinner by lonely women, but so far no one's recognized her."

"Killers often return to the scene of the crime. You should set someone to watching the field where he dumped her body."

"Something to think about."

"Maybe there were witnesses to the body being dumped. Like

those children your man *shot at.* We should try to find them, ask what they saw."

She thought his mouth tightened, although the darkness made it difficult to tell. "Something else to think about. And for the record, those children weren't hit and they're long gone. Any other suggestions?"

"We only have a few days to find this guy. We must do everything we possibly can."

He sent an assessing glance her way. "Sounds like you're in a hurry to get home. Missing the husband and kids?"

Jolted into full wakefulness by the turn the conversation had taken, she sat up. "I'm a widow."

That sounded abrupt, but she couldn't help it. Thoughts of Lars stirred up so many conflicting emotions these days. She was ashamed to realize that anger was almost the predominant one now. Anger that he'd carried on a whole secret life in the months leading up to his death, that he hadn't put her and Niles first instead of joining in with the saboteurs. And fear was right up there, too. She was afraid for anyone, such as, for example, *Detective* Schneider, to look too closely into his death. Or, now, his life. All it could do was bring trouble and danger to her and, most especially, to Niles.

"I'm sorry to hear that." There was a note of genuine sympathy in Schneider's voice. It touched her and, paradoxically, served to harden her heart against feeling any emotion at all. Looking back was always a mistake. She had to keep putting one foot in front of the other and focus on what lay ahead. His tone was apologetic as he added, "I read that you were married and had a son on the back of one of your books."

Ah, yes. She'd forgotten about the brief bio that had been limited to a few lines under her picture. No real details, no names other than her own, professional one. No mention that her husband was a Jew.

"It's an old book. And I do have a son." In an effort to shift his thoughts away from her personal life, she added, "And just so you know, it's not so much that I'm in a hurry to get home. It's that I'm in a hurry to catch a killer before he can kill again."

"We'll catch him," he said. "All it will take is one mistake on his part, one piece of evidence, one detail or witness coming to our attention, and we'll have him." He sped up noticeably as they left the tall buildings of central Berlin behind and the small amount of traffic on the roads dwindled to none at all. "Speaking of, was anything found on that one remaining earring on our unidentified victim?"

"No," she said, and they proceeded to discuss various details of the case.

The night became noticeably darker as they neared their destination and the towering pines that dominated the 7400-acre forest formed jagged peaks that blocked the moon from view. Situated near a small lake that gleamed blue-black where stray moonbeams sifted down through the trees to touch it, the Hotel Waldschloss was formerly a sixteenth-century manor house that had been converted into a hotel. With its heavy blackout curtains and lack of any outdoor lighting, it appeared as no more than a series of boxy shapes against the night sky as the car swept into the brick forecourt, where Schneider parked.

Elin had to make a real effort to peel herself off the seat and slide out as he came around and opened her door for her. The drive had sapped the last of her energy. She was so tired she felt boneless. To steady herself, she caught the top of the door frame and took a great gulp of the pine-scented night air before starting off across what she knew from experience was a sea of uneven bricks.

Behind her, the car door slammed shut.

"Careful, you don't want to turn an ankle." Schneider sounded amused as he came up behind her and gripped her elbow for support, and she knew her exhaustion had been noted.

"It was a long ride." She frowned at the corollary thought. "Why put us in a hotel so far from the Alex, anyway?"

"You don't like this place? We can always make a change." He was a tall presence beside her, nearly invisible in the darkness. His hand felt warm and strong around her bare arm. *Trust* was a strong word, and she wasn't prepared to go that far, but she was starting to feel cautiously comfortable with him, she realized. As if he were more friend than enemy.

"I do like it. But—" she threw out a hand in a questioning gesture "—why here? I would have expected to stay somewhere closer in."

"It was chosen to keep you as safe as possible from the air raids. They usually hit nearer to the center of the city. You're lucky to have been spared any so far." He pulled open the massive front door. Muted lamplight and a faint floral scent spilled out, and she stepped inside onto a highly polished marble floor. Richly paneled walls and a soaring ceiling were paired with slightly faded if still elegant furnishings. The desk clerk, a pink-cheeked young woman in a dirndl, looked up as she entered.

"*Guten Abend*, Professor Lund," the girl said, and Elin returned the greeting.

"I'll leave you now. Get some sleep," Schneider said, turning away.

Elin barely had time to say good-night before he was out the door.

She was heading for the elevator when she remembered she'd left her doctor's bag in his car.

For a vexed moment she thought about simply leaving it, which was a measure of just how tired she was. But she meant to be back in the lab early in the morning, and she would need it then.

Hurrying was almost beyond her, but hurry she did, because she was afraid she would miss him and, thus, her bag.

Stepping out into the darkness of the forecourt, she saw with relief that his car was still there. Then, walking toward it, she frowned. As far as she could tell, the car was empty.

Schneider wasn't inside it. Or outside it, either, at least not anywhere near the car. Had he stepped away for some reason, maybe to have a cigarette? Although she hadn't seen him smoke. Or maybe he was answering nature's call outdoors, as men sometimes disgustingly did.

Looking around, she spotted him as he stepped into a dappled patch of moonlight. His back was to her, and he was striding across the road they'd driven in on. There was no mistaking his tall frame, his gait, or the tilt of his fedora.

As she watched he walked out of the patch of moonlight and kept on going, right into the enveloping darkness of Grunewald Forest.

13

"WHAT TIME DID YOU FINALLY GET IN LAST NIGHT? I stopped by your room around ten, and you were nowhere to be found." Pia, looking smart in a tan shirtdress with a red kerchief knotted around her neck, kept her voice carefully low as they walked out the front door and on across the forecourt of the Waldschloss early the next morning. Before they'd parted the afternoon before, Elin had told Pia and Jens about Schneider's warning concerning listening devices, and as a result they'd given up all thought of speaking freely about sensitive topics unless they were alone together outdoors.

"Late," Elin said. "How's Jens?" A quick glance confirmed that Schneider's car was gone. So, presumably, was Schneider. The air was heavy and stagnant, with no hint of a breeze. It was already blisteringly hot. Across the road, even the tall pines looked limp.

An image of Schneider disappearing into those pines flashed

into her mind. Wherever he'd been headed, whatever his purpose had been, she was better off not knowing, she told herself. She wasn't going to think about it again, or certainly tell anyone, including Pia or Jens. She was going to put it out of her head and pretend she'd never seen him.

"He's better. Everything's holding together."

"Is he making any progress on the code? Has he said anything about it to you?" Elin asked.

"Just that it makes no sense."

"Wonderful."

Pia nodded, while at the same time giving her an assessing look.

Elin frowned. "What, is my lipstick on crooked?" The soft red crème that defined her mouth plus a dab of powder on her nose were the only cosmetics she wore. It was too hot for anything else. That was also why her hair was rolled up off her neck in a soft chignon.

Making an aren't-you-funny face, Pia said in an even quieter voice, "I know you're worried about *everything*, but you need to be sure to get enough sleep, and enough to eat. You're looking pale as a ghost and you have dark circles under your eyes."

"Gee, thanks."

"Jens told me that yesterday you ate about three bites of your meal."

Elin eyed her friend. An only child like herself, Pia had been mothering her, or trying to boss her, depending on how you looked at it, since she and Elin had met as eight-year-olds in *folkeskole*. "I'm fine. I don't need more sleep, and I don't need more food. What I need is—" *to get home as fast as possible to be with my son*, was what she wanted to say, but their driver got out of the waiting car just then to open the rear door for them. Assigned to them by Schneider, said driver was Officer Sonja Lutts, a sturdy woman with a coronet of honey-colored braids above an unsmiling face. She was part of the Female Criminal Police, the Weibliche Kriminalpolizei, also known as the WKP. Not coincidentally, she was the same unsympathetic policewoman who had driven them from the hotel to the murder scene the night of their arrival in Berlin.

Afraid of being overheard and thus drawing unneeded attention to her son, Elin substituted "—for you and everyone else to quit worrying about me while we all do our jobs."

Behind Officer Lutts's back, she and Pia exchanged measuring looks before Pia slid into the car. Elin got in next, smoothing the skirt of her own slim, olive green dress beneath her legs to protect them from the leather seat that was already starting to feel hot. Moments later they were on their way.

"The desk clerk said that a storm's coming," Pia said. Elin recognized and appreciated the effort at idle conversation for the sake of their minder.

"I thought I smelled rain."

Pia was riding to the Alex with her because victim Astrid Lang's family had reported that a strange man had been seen loitering around their house in the days immediately after the murder, and Pia had been asked to attempt to draw that strange man. The original police investigation had failed to follow up on the information, which they'd had for a while, because, first of all, the man hadn't appeared until *after* the victim had been killed, so wasn't considered a viable suspect. Second, they had no way to identify him, much less track him down, even if they *had* felt he deserved scrutiny.

But upon coming across that information in the files, Elin had pointed out that serial murderers often put themselves in a position where they could observe the reaction of a victim's loved ones in the aftermath of a crime and thus continue to revel in the pleasure of what they had done.

And, after the success of her drawing of the arrested suspect, Paul Dalsing, there was a real hope that Pia could accurately draw this man from the eyewitness descriptions. If this drawing, too, should happen to resemble Dalsing, then the case against him would be considerably strengthened. Detective Beckman, who Pia was meeting at the Alex, would be escorting her to visit Astrid Lang's family, and everyone involved awaited the results with interest.

"I'm planning to telephone my mother later," Pia said. "I haven't talked to her since we got here, and you know how she worries."

Elin nodded acknowledgment of what Pia was really telling her: she would telephone her mother, who was a near neighbor and friend of the Meitners, and find out everything she knew about what was happening with Niles, Hilde, and Borge. Elin didn't want to telephone herself, for the second day running, for fear that it might convey a suspicious degree of anxiety to anyone listening in, and the same reservation applied to Jens and his brother.

The truth was, merely thinking about Niles and what he might be facing was so anxiety producing that her stomach had turned into what felt like a constant yawning pit. Not knowing what was happening was excruciating.

"Tell your mother I said hello," Elin said for the benefit of the stolid policewoman behind the wheel, who gave no indication that she was listening or had heard anything they'd said. But obviously she *had* heard and could be expected to report anything that struck her as suspicious to her superiors.

"I will," Pia replied, and, with thoughts of the rearview mirror in mind, Elin managed a smile for her.

Elin didn't know what her eyes revealed, but Pia must have read something concerning in them because she reached over to give Elin's hand a quick squeeze.

She and Pia continued to exchange mundane conversation until Andreasplatz with its sparkling fountain came into view. Then she leaned forward to say to Officer Lutts, "Same route as yesterday, please."

Yesterday her instruction to Officer Lutts to drive past the place where their latest victim had been found on the way into the Alex had provoked the policewoman into giving her a long glance through the rearview mirror. Today the woman's only reaction was to nod and turn down the appropriate street. Elin had to assume that she'd reported the prior deviation from the expected route to someone, probably Schneider, but obviously whoever it was had not instructed Officer Lutts not to obey, and if Schneider knew and had a problem with it he'd said nothing to Elin.

But then, she'd already learned he liked to play things close to the vest.

"Thank God nothing like this has happened in Copenhagen," Pia murmured devoutly as the bombed-out area, which the dawn revealed in all its burned and tumbledown horror, came into view.

Yet—that was the response that immediately popped into Elin's head, but she didn't say it and nodded agreement instead.

Pia's eyes were wide with distress as she took in the blocks of rubble that the bombing had left behind. Elin remembered that, unlike herself, Pia was seeing it by daylight for the first time. That first night, so much had been cloaked by darkness and their concentration on the murder that the full scope of the devastation had been lost on them. Now there was no escaping the extent of the damage. Behind the destroyed buildings more blocks of narrow, rundown tenement houses crowded close to pitted streets. Few cars were out at such an early hour, but a parade of men who looked like they might be factory workers or day laborers trudged glumly along. They appeared to be on their way to work, with their most likely immediate destination being the nearby Silesian train station, which, Elin had learned, was the closest one. It was at that station where the train that had passed overhead when she'd been at the crime scene would have stopped next.

One thing she was no longer in any doubt about: the body had not been thrown from the train. The autopsy had made that clear. A fall from such a height, even postmortem, would have left telltale signs.

"Keep an eye out for anyone who looks out of place, or seems to be loitering about," Elin said, including Officer Lutts in the instruction. The possibility that the killer might return to the site where he'd dumped the body was reason enough for them to be there, although the chance that they would spot him on a random drive-by was admittedly small. But she was also looking for the children. Not that she was likely to have any luck in either case, but still she could not *not* try.

"If he *is* here, he could be anywhere," Pia said as the car bumped through one more crater in the pavement. The only good thing about the pockmarked street was that they *had* to drive slowly; doing anything else would likely lead to a flat tire or broken axle. "If it were me, and I wanted to keep watch, I'd be inside one of those buildings where no one could see me, looking out a window or something."

"That's a thought." Glancing around at the stockade of grim, gray concrete and faded brick walls formed by the nearby buildings, she concluded glumly that it would take dozens of police to conduct an effective, around-the-clock surveillance. And even that might not yield anything, as there was only a slim chance that the killer would actually return to the scene of the crime.

"Could you slow down, please?" she asked Officer Lutts as they neared the section of ditch where the body had been found.

Big drops of rain started to fall, splattering on the windshield, streaking down the side windows, tapping a quickening rhythm on the roof. One mighty clap of thunder later, and they were caught in a downpour. Through the rain's silvery curtain Elin could see the steep slope, the tall weeds, the flattened area in the ditch where the body had lain, the mounds of bombed-out rubble where the children had appeared. Once they reached the place farther along the street where the cars and ambulance had waited, Elin gave up the quest, telling Officer Lutts, "We can go on to the Alex now."

The policewoman nodded.

Slumping back in her seat, Elin looked dispiritedly out the window as the car sped up again. Even before the bombs had hit, she'd learned, this had been an economically depressed high crime area with a large population of transients. Now, with the rain turning the ground to mud and thunderclouds blotting out the sun, it looked like an unrelenting gray sea of misery.

Out of nowhere, Pia grabbed her wrist. Lost in her own thoughts, Elin jumped and shot her a startled glance.

Pia pointed urgently out the window on her side.

Elin saw two children, a girl with long brown braids that flapped behind her and a boy with a strangely bent arm. The girl's too big, gaily embroidered sweater, limp and clinging now as the rain soaked it, sealed their identity. Bent almost double in a bid to defeat the downpour, they ran along the edge of a ditch about half a block away, then turned and disappeared into a fissure in the mountain of debris.

"Have you ever seen any of these women before?" Schneider slapped images of the victims down on the table in front of Orpo officer Paul Dalsing one by one.

"No. Except for this one. The clerk from Wertheim's." He indicated Greta Neuhaus's photograph.

"She's the only one you've ever seen, and the occasion that we've already talked about in Wertheim's is the only time you've ever seen her?"

"Yes."

Schneider glanced at Elin, who was seated off to the side observing his interrogation of their prime suspect in this small room on the fifth floor of the Alex while Schneider sat directly across the table from him. The three of them were alone in the room, while the two uniformed policemen who'd brought Dalsing in to be questioned waited outside the door. Pale and plumpish, Dalsing had been in custody since the previous day. Still wearing his green Orpo uniform, he was a disheveled mess. He'd clearly had no chance to shave or comb his dark hair, which was stiff with pomade and sticking up from his scalp like porcupine quills.

Elin shook her head at Schneider. He looked back at Dalsing.

"You are saying that this woman—" Schneider tapped Greta Neuhaus's photo "—is the only one of this group you've ever seen, do I have that right?"

"Yes," Dalsing said.

Elin nodded.

Schneider continued, "You are also saying that you've only ever seen her that once, during the incident at Wertheim's. Is that right?"

"Yes," Dalsing said.

The overhead light cast a brilliant white glow that revealed every line and crevice in Dalsing's moon-shaped face. His changing expressions fit the circumstances, switching for the most part between panicked and angry depending on the question, but it wasn't his face Elin was watching so much as his hands.

Pudgy and pale like the rest of him, his palms were flattened down on the surface of the table. A classic position indicating deception.

She shook her head at Schneider. *He's not telling the truth.*

She was there to listen in on Schneider's grilling of the subject for the purpose of interpreting the suspect's nonverbal behavior for him. In her book about the psychology of multiple murderers she'd explained how the guilty would often give themselves away by certain physical actions when being questioned. Having read the book, Schneider had decided to make use of her expertise and had sent an aide to fetch her from the evidence room. She'd interpreted *his* nonverbal behavior upon greeting her just outside the interrogation room door and explaining the reason behind his summons to mean, *On the slim chance that what you wrote in your book actually works.*

Until she'd joined him for this interview, she hadn't seen Schneider since he'd disappeared into the forest the previous night. She'd thought then about waiting for him beside the car—she'd really needed her bag and the car was locked—but had decided against it. His warning to her about confining her activities to their murder investigation if she wanted to get home safely had replayed itself in her mind, and she'd gone inside and done what her body longed to do, which was sleep. Later, when she'd awakened, she'd vowed to put his nocturnal walk into the forest out of her mind.

Whatever he'd been up to, it was nothing to do with her. She really, truly didn't want to know.

Her bag had been waiting for her in the lab when she'd arrived at the Alex. She could only suppose Schneider had dropped it off either last night or early this morning.

"And you are absolutely certain you've only ever seen the victim that once?" Schneider switched his attention back to Dalsing.

"Yes," Dalsing said.

Elin shook her head at Schneider again.

His eyes narrowed.

"Let's move on to those nights we've talked about. What were you doing then? I have a calendar marked with the dates right here, if it helps to refresh your memory." He put a one-page, mimeographed calendar with the dates the victims went missing circled in red in front of Dalsing.

"I don't need my memory refreshed. I already told you. On each of those nights I was home in bed. Asleep." Dalsing rolled his eyes in exasperation. "Where else would I be? These last months, I've been pulling double duty. I need my sleep."

"Can anyone verify that?" Schneider asked. Outside, the rain still poured down. Inside, it was stuffy to the point of suffocation. The smell of the pomade, coupled with the overwarm closeness of the room, was enough to make Elin long to fling open the only window, which was currently heavily curtained although it was midafternoon. The purpose was to give the suspect nothing to focus on except what was put before him, which was also the reason the walls were bare and the L-shaped table and folding chairs were the only furniture.

"You've asked me that before, and I'll give you the same answer! My wife! My wife can verify it!"

Sometime before Elin had arrived, Schneider had removed his jacket and rolled up his shirtsleeves in deference to the heat. His jacket hung from the back of the metal folding chair in which he sat. His shoulders looked very broad in his white shirt. His forearms, brawny and sprinkled with a liberal amount of black hair, rested on the table in front of him. His expression was for the most part unreadable, but the hard planes and angles of his face were forbidding in and of themselves. He drummed his fingers on the wooden surface as he looked at Dalsing.

"Your wife says you don't always share the same bed."

"I—it's because I snore! She doesn't like it. But I'm there. At home. In the spare room, sometimes, sure, but there asleep. She can verify that, I tell you!"

Elin shook her head.

Looking back at Dalsing, Schneider said, "All right. Suppose you tell me exactly where you were and what you were doing the Saturday night before last. The twenty-eighth. In detail. Let's start with your evening meal. What did you eat?"

"I've told you. I've *told you*." Dalsing threw his hands in the air, then clasped his head in a gesture of angry frustration.

"Tell me again."

Elin watched and listened as Dalsing recounted the particulars of his evening. Nothing he did indicated deception—until, under Schneider's continued prodding, he said that after listening to a radio program with his children, he went to bed, and to sleep.

He shuffled his feet as he said that last. He pressed his hands palm down, flat against the table. Finishing, he folded his lips into a practically undetectable line.

Elin shook her head at Schneider. *Not true.*

Like Schneider, she hadn't really believed this was their man. But as he continued to exhibit classic signs of deception, she began to seriously consider the possibility.

Looking back at Dalsing, Schneider frowned. Heavily. Dalsing met his gaze and seemed to shrink in his chair.

Elin didn't blame him.

"Herr Dalsing, you're not telling the truth," Schneider said. "If you continue to lie to me, believe me when I tell you things will go badly for you."

Dalsing brought his hands down on the table with a force that made Elin jump, and he shot to his feet.

"I am not lying!"

"Sit down." Schneider was on his feet, too. The barked order, coupled with his physicality, was so intimidating that even Elin was conscious of it. Chin quivering, Dalsing sank back in his chair.

"If you do something like that again, I'll have you handcuffed to the chair." Schneider spoke quietly. He tapped the photo of the drawing of the latest victim that rested on the table near Dalsing. "Do you know this woman?"

"No." Dalsing's denial was almost a howl. "I've *told* you I don't. I've never seen her before in my life. I've never seen any of them except *her.*" He stabbed Greta Neuhaus's photo with a stubby forefinger.

Before Elin had a chance to indicate her opinion of the truthfulness of that, a knock on the door caused them all to glance toward it.

"Enter," Schneider said.

Detective Albrecht stepped into the room. "Can I talk to you? Outside?"

With a curt nod, Schneider headed for the door. As he reached Elin's chair he paused, glancing from her to Dalsing and back as if suddenly having second thoughts.

"You'll be all right in here with him?" His voice was low, meant for her ears alone.

"Yes."

"I'll be right outside the door. Yell if you need me." Then he raised his voice, directing his next words at Dalsing. "Don't get out of that chair." It was an order, and Dalsing nodded nervously. As Schneider left the room, Dalsing's gaze followed him. Then he glanced at Elin and quickly glanced away again before resting his elbows on the table and dropping his head into his hands.

It was a posture of utter despair.

Schneider was back within minutes. She'd seen that carved-from-stone look of his before and knew it didn't bode well for Dalsing.

Whatever Albrecht had told him had changed the situation in some way.

Schneider crossed the room without saying a word. Dalsing, whose head had come up when the door opened, watched with obvious dread. Schneider stopped behind the chair he'd been sitting in and leaned forward, gripping the seat back. Silent, he simply stood there looking at the other man. Even though it wasn't directed at her, Elin felt the force of that look clear down to her toes. Dalsing met his gaze, glanced away, fidgeted, flushed, looked at him again, and finally burst out, "Is…is something wrong?"

"We have a witness," Schneider said.

Dalsing's indrawn breath was loud in that small room. "A witness?"

"That's right. You're a policeman yourself, Herr Dalsing. You know how serious it is to lie when being questioned."

"I didn't lie." There was a squeak in Dalsing's voice now.

"A witness has seen you leaving your house through a side window in the middle of the night. On more than one occasion."

Dalsing's split second of hesitation, the blink-and-you'd-miss-it widening of his eyes, the sudden lizard-flick visibility of his tongue between his lips, told Elin everything she needed to know.

She nodded at Schneider. What he'd accused Dalsing of was true.

"What witness? You can't pull your bluffs on me!" Beads of sweat popped out on Dalsing's brow.

"I think we both know I'm not bluffing. A neighbor of yours who works an evening shift apparently comes home at the same time as you slip out. The last time you were seen doing this was— Well, you tell me, Herr Dalsing. Now. I'm waiting."

"There is no such neighbor! Or if there is, they're lying, or have made a mistake!" His face had crimsoned. His forehead was shiny with sweat. The whites of his eyes were visible. Beneath the table, his feet shifted back and forth.

Elin shook her head. *He's lying.*

Schneider nodded, the first time he had openly acknowledged her guidance. Then he pointed at her.

"Do you see that lady, Herr Dalsing? Do you wonder why she is sitting with us? She's a famous doctor, a professor, and do you know what her special skill is? She can tell when people are lying." He looked at Elin. Dalsing, clearly horror-struck, did the same. "Is Herr Dalsing lying, Professor? Did he sneak out a window in his house in the middle of the night when his family thought he was in bed asleep?"

"Yes," she said.

Dalsing made a sound under his breath.

Schneider said, "I'm giving you one last chance to tell me the truth, Herr Dalsing. The entire truth. Otherwise—"

He didn't have time to finish. Now drenched in sweat, Dalsing broke. "All right. All right. I sometimes go to a club. Eden. I didn't tell you because…because it's illegal and I didn't want to get in trouble. I just go to listen to the music, you know? To relax and have a few drinks. *You* know how hard the job is, and I have a wife, a family. They wouldn't understand, so I wait until they're asleep and I go out. It's just a little harmless fun."

"And did you encounter this lady?" Schneider pointed to

Greta Neuhaus's picture. Then, interrupting himself, he added, "Do you even know her name, Herr Dalsing?"

"Greta. I think it's Greta."

"That's right. Did you encounter Greta during one of your secret excursions? And remember, my associate can tell if you're lying." He nodded at Elin. "So you want to be very careful with what you say."

"Yes! *Yes.*" Dalsing wet his lips. "I *saw* her there. At Eden. That's all."

Elin gave a slow nod. Dalsing was now so agitated it was difficult to be sure, but she thought he was telling the truth.

"What about the other women? Did you see them at Eden, or anywhere else?"

"No, no, I swear I didn't. I never saw any of the others. Never once. Not anywhere."

Elin nodded. This time she was sure he was telling the truth.

"All right, let's move on. When did you last leave your house through the window in the middle of the night?" Schneider's question was soft, almost gentle. Elin could tell he already knew the answer.

Dalsing looked ashen. There was no doubting that he was guilty, in Elin's judgment. But guilty of what?

"You already know, don't you?" Dalsing asked in a wretched-sounding whisper. "It was Saturday before last. The twenty-eighth."

"Ah." It was a sound of satisfaction. "And you went to this club? Eden?"

"Yes."

"Did you see Greta there? At Eden, when you were there last?"

"Y-yes." Dalsing's face contorted, his lips trembled, and then the words came pouring out. "I know that sounds bad! But I only *saw* her. After what had happened at Wertheim's, I didn't even speak to her. I swear to you I didn't."

"So you saw Greta Neuhaus at Eden on the Saturday night she

went missing, not long after your quarrel with her at her work-place."

"I... I guess. I mean, yes, I did." His eyes were wild. "But I didn't do anything to her! I certainly didn't kill her! I didn't kill anyone! I swear to you I didn't! You have to believe me!"

14

SCHNEIDER AND ELIN WERE BOTH STILL IN THE INTER-
rogation room after Dalsing had been escorted away. Schneider
stood with his back to the closed door, arms crossed over his
chest, frowning thoughtfully as he seemed to replay the interview in his mind. Elin, seated at the table, finished jotting down
one last note, closed her notebook, and looked up at him.

"Do you believe him?" Schneider asked,

"I don't know," she said. "His blood type is wrong. He doesn't
have any evidence of cuts or wounds, as he presumably would if
he's the killer. It's yet to be determined if his handwriting matches
the handwriting in the letters, or if he's familiar with Kurrent,
or knows anything about mathematics. On the other hand, he
lied, he has no verifiable alibi, he's a police officer so presumably
he might have known that you were put in charge of the investigation, he's about the right age, he works within the area we'd

expect, he's Aryan, he was seen arguing with one of our victims *and* admits to having seen her the night she disappeared—"

"Wait a minute. What does him being Aryan have to do
with it?"

She should have left that part out, she thought with an inner
grimace, remembering Kaltenbrunner's insistence that no Aryan
would commit such crimes. *That's what comes from thinking out
loud.* Did Schneider have the same prejudice? It seemed likely.
But if they were to stop a killer, research had to be respected
and facts faced. And for good or ill, he was her partner in solving this case.

She said, "Studies have shown that murderers of this type tend
to prey on those who are like them." From the furrowing of
his brow, she inferred that she wasn't being entirely clear. Lifting her chin, she spelled it out. "The victims are all Aryan." She
knew that by now. "That means the killer is almost certainly
Aryan, too."

He looked at her without saying anything for a moment.

"Interesting." His one-word comment left her with no idea
what he really thought about her pronouncement.

Before she could say anything else, he followed up with a
question. "What do you think about the possibility that he might
have an accomplice? That would explain why his blood type is
wrong, and why he doesn't have any wounds."

He was still frowning, with his jaw set and his mouth tight.
The bright overhead light revealed every detail of the chiseled
contours of his face. He looked tired and faintly irritable. But it
was his eyes, intent with what she realized was a warning, that
finally got his message across.

The room was bugged.

The knowledge burst on her like a bomb. She couldn't believe she hadn't realized it sooner. It was an interrogation room
in Kripo headquarters. Of course someone was listening in.

What if she'd told him about seeing the children earlier? Because it had occurred to her to do so. The only thing that had held her back was that he'd been so dismissive of her desire to find them, so adamant that she say nothing to anyone about them. She didn't understand why, and that made her wary. She still hadn't made up her mind whether she would tell him, but she could have. And whoever was listening would have heard.

She didn't know what the consequences would have been, but the thought was enough to make her heart beat faster.

"I've told you before, I think he works alone," she said, and was proud of how calm and collected she sounded.

The tight line of his mouth eased. His eyes encouraged her.

"But you can't be sure," he said.

"I'm ninety-five percent sure." There was the slightest edge to her voice because she really was sure even though it was impossible to be one hundred percent sure of anything and so she'd qualified it, and to her surprise he smiled. His smile held an unexpected amount of appeal. She found her recognition of that appeal both annoying and the tiniest bit disturbing, and so she frowned.

"You know, I think we may have just had a breakthrough." His tone was pensive. Not quite certain of his meaning, she raised questioning, and perhaps even slightly haughty, eyebrows at him. "Dalsing said he saw Greta Neuhaus at an illegal club. I still don't think he's our killer, but he may have pointed us in the right direction. Maybe the killer saw her there, too. Maybe that's what our victims were doing. Sneaking out after they were presumed to be in bed. Maybe, like Herr Dalsing, they were going to an illegal club."

He'd been talking about a breakthrough in the case. Of course he had. She remembered the traces of lipstick on the latest victim's mouth, the carefully curled hair, the single earring. It all fit.

"It's possible," she said.

"We know where Herr Dalsing said he was." He tapped the paper on which Dalsing, at his command, had written down the name of the club he'd visited on the twenty-eighth, along with the address and other pertinent information.

"If this doesn't check out," Schneider had warned as Dalsing was writing, "I'll presume you're lying again and your alibis are nonexistent and proceed accordingly."

"I'm not lying." Dalsing had stopped writing long enough to shoot Schneider a sullen look. Then, as he presumably remembered that up until he'd been forced to come clean he had been lying, he turned bright red and hastily added, "Not about this. You can ask Erich about me. Erich Frank. The head bartender at Eden. He'll tell you I'm often there, and I was there that Saturday night. And that I didn't speak to anyone. I just had a few drinks and listened to the music."

"I will ask him, believe me. And you'd better hope you were there, and he remembers." Schneider gestured at him to continue writing, which he did, only to ask in a small, shamed voice as he finished, "Do you have to tell my wife about this?"

"It depends on you. If I find you're lying, or withholding information—"

"I'm not. I'm not!"

"Then we'll see."

That vague promise had been enough to prompt Dalsing to add another line to his note, saying as he wrote, "This is the password. You give it at the door. No one is admitted without it."

"We can use this to check his handwriting against the killer's," Elin said now as she looked down at what he'd written. From what she could tell, it wasn't a match, but it was possible Dalsing had altered his handwriting either on the note or in the letters to keep from being identified by it. A definitive answer would have to wait until a more in-depth comparison could be made.

"We can, can't we?" The way he said it told Elin that he'd already thought of that.

She made a face at him. "You know, even if his alibi checks out and he *was* at that club when he said he was and he *didn't* interact with Greta Neuhaus and he left alone, that still doesn't necessarily rule him out as our killer. He could have picked her up later."

A quick rap on the door interrupted. In response to Schneider's "Enter," Frau Skelton poked her head into the room.

"You have a telephone call, Chief." Her tone conveyed that the call was urgent, and problematic. The quick glance she shot Elin gave her to understand that whatever it was about was not for her to know.

Elin's thoughts automatically flew to Jens, and her stomach tightened. But there were many other reasons why Schneider might be receiving such a telephone call, and her anxiety over Jens being apprehended was not as sharp as it had been. Possibly, she thought wryly, because she had so many other things to be anxious about.

Schneider nodded his thanks and Frau Skelton withdrew.

"You make a good point. Maybe he killed her and disposed of the body later that day," he said, as if their conversation had never been interrupted. But his mouth had gone hard again and his eyes were expressionless. She knew that was because of the telephone call. That told her, too, that he had a good idea who it was from and what it was about and was expecting it to be unpleasant. "I have to take this call, and then I have some matters to attend to. Later tonight I'm going to Dalsing's club. Do you want to come with me?"

"Yes, I certainly do."

"Then I suggest you head back to your hotel by four or five o'clock and get some rest. I'll pick you up there at eleven. Be prepared for a late night."

"She said they're not there. She said the maid didn't come, and the house is locked and empty." Pia's low-voiced, worried update, given as they exited the Alex together, remained lodged in the back of Elin's mind even as the taxi they were riding in turned down the night-dark street that would take them into the blighted neighborhood where the last body had been found. "She" was Pia's mother, and "they" were Niles and Hilde. The most likely explanation for their absence and the empty house was that Hilde had gone with Niles to Smukkeso, as Elin had suggested. But until she could confirm that, the fear that they'd been taken in for questioning, or worse, chilled her to the bone.

I can't do anything about it now, Elin told herself, and did her best to put it out of her mind as their destination came into view.

"Stop here," Elin said to the taxi driver, who grudgingly pulled to the side of the road. They were on Koppenstrafe—she'd made a mental note of the street name earlier—in front of the gap in the rubble through which the children had disappeared. Except for the barely-there illumination provided by the taxi's slotted headlights, the area was so dark thanks to the blackout that she could scarcely see an arm's length in any direction. The rising moon shone with a silvery light that was randomly blotted out by a moving blanket of clouds. On the ground, the effect was to cast distorting shadows everywhere. The rain had stopped, but from the heaviness in the air it could start up again at any time. A mugginess lay like fog over the city.

"Turn off the lights, please," Elin said to the driver. Attracting attention to their presence, or to what might turn out to be the children's bolt hole, was the last thing she wanted to do. She was already lifting the door handle as he responded with a grunt, then did as she asked.

"You positive you don't want me to come with you?" Voice low, Pia, who was in the back seat with her, cast a nervous glance around as Elin slid out of the car. It was a little after 9:00 p.m., and they were on their way back to the hotel. Having been informed by Frau Skelton that Officer Lutts and her car were not immediately available, they'd chosen not to wait but to take a taxi.

Then Elin had been struck by the anonymity afforded by a

taxi, and, with Pia's agreement, had decided to seize this window of unwatched opportunity to try to find the children.

"No." They'd talked about this, she and Pia, before getting into the taxi. One of them had to stay with the vehicle for fear it might leave them. At such an hour in such a neighborhood, that could prove disastrous.

"Be careful," Pia breathed.

Elin nodded. "I won't be long," she said, and closed the door. A quick glance around should have been reassuring in that her immediate surroundings seemed to be deserted, but the night was so full of sound and the darkness so full of movement from the interplay between the moon and the shifting cloud cover she couldn't be sure.

Careful to keep it pointed at the ground, Elin clicked on the small torch she'd brought.

Up front, the wizened old man who was the driver, bribed to stop and wait in this area he hadn't even wanted to drive through, shook his head at her as he said through the open window, "You don't want to be going far, Fräulein."

"I won't," she promised, and felt him watching her as she started to pick her way across the uneven field of debris that fronted the wall of rubble into which the children had disappeared. As she neared it, she saw that the wall was actually an unsteady-looking tower of dislodged bricks buttressed by the gutted skeleton of the apartment building for which they'd once served as a facade. Although it was partially blocked by the fallen ceiling behind it, the door frame to what had been the building's entrance still stood, and appeared to provide access to an inner, protected area.

She shone the light through the door frame. The interior area was a hallway, and still seemed to be reasonably intact.

With the torch beam probing ahead of her, illuminating scattered islands of rubble strewed across a scarred wooden floor,

Elin disregarded the prickle of unease that argued against it and ducked into the opening.

She would just take a quick look around.

Only a few steps later, darkness swallowed her. The last of the moonbeams drifting in from the door were lost as she continued steadily on and the wreckage seemed to curl in on itself while shrinking around her. What she was in was not so much a hallway anymore as a tunnel formed by broken plaster and collapsed beams, she saw as her torch played over them. It seemed stable enough, but there was always the chance it was not.

This was the space she and Pia had seen the children dart into earlier; she was as close to certain as it was possible to be. Whether or not they were inside it now—and they very well could be, since it had been raining off and on all day—there was no way to know. If they were, if she did find them… Well, what would happen after that was uncertain. But at the very least, if she found them, she could assess whether they were hurt and if they needed urgent help. One thing she knew: she was unlikely to get a better chance to look for them than this.

Alternatively, she could leave now, tell Schneider, who would be picking her up at the hotel in a little under two hours, about this place and what she and Pia had seen, and turn the whole matter over to him. But there was no way to know how he would react, or what he would do regarding the children, or if indeed he would do anything at all. Again, she didn't know him that well.

Her sensible pumps and slim-fitting dress were not the best clothing choices for venturing into a bombed-out ruin, she realized ruefully as she did exactly that, but then she didn't mean to go far. Moving carefully, ducking as needed, she reached out through the enveloping darkness with every sense she possessed. The soft crunch of her shoes on the debris underfoot seemed to echo back at her. A series of steady drips spoke of rain leaking in. Overhead creaks warned that the wreckage was still settling.

The air smelled of damp and rotting things. She didn't want to think about what might lie crushed beneath the debris, but there was no mistaking the putrid-sweet stench of death.

Goose bumps slid over her skin.

I should turn back, she thought, and was about to do just that when the torch beam touched on something that made her breath catch.

The broken building around her had bled out in the form of plaster dust. The powdery white substance coated the walls, revealing signs of having been brushed against by others passing through before her. But what riveted her attention was a child-sized handprint in the dust. It was intact, unsmeared, and showed conclusively that a child had recently been in that space. The equally powdery floor bore a distinct trail from where someone—multiple someones?—had shuffled over it.

She felt a rush of satisfaction. The children *were* there. Or at least, they had been there not long before.

Except for the handprint, anyone could have made those marks. Anyone could have visited this passage at any time since the bombing. Anyone could be anywhere in these ruins right now.

That sobering reality stopped her in her tracks. Handprint or no handprint, the sensible thing to do would be turn back now and pass the whole business along to Schneider.

But in the end, she couldn't. She simply *could not* turn and walk away. The mother in her wouldn't allow it.

The thought that kept her there was, *What if it were Niles, hiding and frightened and in danger?*

They were *children*.

Cautiously, she started off again, negotiating her way around a bend in the hallway that took her far away from any outside source of light.

The pitch darkness, the closeness of the walls and ceiling, the sense of being cut off from the outside world, felt claustrophobic and a little dangerous now. Steeling herself against a rising tide of misgivings, she kept on going until, she discovered as the torch beam hit it, the passage was blocked by an apparently impassable barrier formed by a landslide of debris from the upper floors. A deeper blackness to the left of that barrier suggested the existence of another passage or room of some sort.

The air seemed thicker as the dust her feet kicked up floated around her like a fine mist. The plaster had been sheered away from the wooden battens beneath in numerous places, leaving gaps in the wall that afforded glimpses of dangling electrical wires and lead pipes and more darkness beyond. Her torch flashed on shards of glass, on splintered boards and exposed nails, on jagged edges of broken furniture, crushed in the collapse. She had to be careful where she put her feet, her shoulders, her hands, her head.

The possibility of injury was very real.

She reached the barrier, shone her light into the darkness on the left. It *was* a cavity, fronted by the passage she was in and barricaded on three sides by materials that had cascaded down through the collapsed ceiling from the upper floors. It was the size of a small washroom, it was empty, and it was a dead end.

Even if she'd wanted to keep going, she couldn't. The way forward was blocked. There was nowhere to go but back.

At the realization, she felt a wave of relief so strong it left her ashamed.

Truth was, the cramped darkness was giving her the willies. She was glad of the excuse to turn around.

She'd taken no more than a couple of steps back the way she had come when a muffled sound—she was sure it was a sneeze!—made her start with surprise.

"Shh."

The hissed response to the sneeze, like the sneeze itself, unmistakably came from a child.

They're here. They're close.

A stab of excitement sent her pulse racing. Senses on high alert, she swiveled in the direction of the sounds, sweeping the

torch beam everywhere it could reach, scanning nooks and cran-
nies as thoroughly as the dim light would allow.

Nothing. Not a glimpse of the children, or of an opening that
might lead to them. Not another sound.

But she knew what she'd heard.

*Can they see the light? Do they know I'm here? Is that what the
"shh" was about?*

She turned off the torch. A darkness blacker than the blackest
night rendered her instantly blind. Gritting her teeth, she willed
herself to ignore a stab of what she recognized was a primordial
fear. It was a natural human instinct to be afraid of the dark. *Nothing's there that wasn't there when the torch was on*, she told herself. Silent
and unmoving, she ignored the shivery feeling to listen intently.

The absence of light, she discovered, amplified every sound.

But she heard nothing more from the children.

Where were they? Answer: somewhere deeper in the darkness.

Alarmed by the noise they'd made, perhaps aware of her presence, were they lying low? She pictured them crouched motionless like small rabbits when the hawk flies over.

She almost called out to them, then decided against it. She was
as sure as was possible that they weren't going to come running at
the sound of her voice. From what she'd seen of them, the children weren't much older than Niles. They were almost certainly
terrified. She'd seen how thin and bedraggled they were, seen
the desperation in their faces, seen that the boy at least had suffered previous injuries. Whatever had happened to turn them out
into a life on the streets must have been traumatic. A few nights
ago, they'd viewed a naked and bloody corpse, and then they'd
been shot at by a uniformed policeman. For all anyone knew,
one of them might even have been wounded. No, they would
not come running if she called to them. They would hide or flee.

Standing there in the dark, scarcely breathing so that she
wouldn't miss any child-connected sounds, she debated what
to do.

A flash of light made her blink. It was small, scarcely bigger than a match flame, and distant, but definitely there. As she watched, transfixed, it grew larger, glimmering off and on: a torch.

She realized within seconds that it appeared to glimmer off and on because the wall was shared with another passage, and the torch was in the other passage shining through the chinks in the wall. It was growing larger because whoever was holding it was coming closer.

When the light hit her, she stood frozen for an instant, caught by surprise. Even as she dodged sideways, it moved on. The light was in the other passage shining through a chink in the wall. She hadn't been targeted deliberately, and from the way the light continued on along its previous path she didn't think she'd been seen.

Her jangled nerves nevertheless stayed on edge.

"There he is! *Der Schwarzer Mann!* Christoph, *run!*" A little girl's shriek erupting from what sounded like right beside her made Elin jump, sent her heart catapulting into her throat. An explosion of sound—a thud, multiple pounding feet, a man's guttural curse—was accompanied by the glimmer blurring into a lightning-fast streak as whoever held the torch raced toward her.

15

ACCOMPANIED BY THE CRASHING SOUNDS OF SEVERAL people in full flight, the light flashed toward Elin and then past. Like the children, like the man holding it, the torch was right there on the other side of the broken wall.

Elin whirled to follow it with her eyes.

"Halt! This is the police! Halt!" The man's voice, while deep and menacing, was not a full-blown shout, not pitched to be heard beyond the confines of the fallen building. "*Wertlos kinder!* Halt, or I'll shoot!"

There was no answer, and, like the light, the sounds of panicked flight and relentless pursuit were gone in a moment.

The adjacent passage must have veered in a different direction.

I have to do something. I have to try to help them.

But what could she do? The passage she was in was a dead end; there wasn't any way that she'd seen to get through to the other side. And shouting after them would be worse than useless. It could be dangerous.

Heart pounding, breath held, Elin stared into the darkness where she'd last seen the light, straining to hear, to see.

Nothing. Just a suffocating, echoing blackness.

Finally she had to breathe.

The children were being chased by a policeman? What policeman and why?

None of the possibilities she could come up with were good.

The policeman hadn't fired his weapon. Why not? Gunther had not hesitated to shoot at the children. Was this officer simply more cautious? Had the darkness precluded a good shot? Or did he not want the attention that firing a shot would attract?

Just as she had with Gunther, she could have shouted at this man to stop. She'd remained quiet as a stone instead.

Why?

She'd been caught by surprise. It had all happened so fast…

Yet that wasn't it, she acknowledged to herself. She'd stayed silent because every instinct she possessed had kept her so. And that would be because she'd been gripped by fear the minute the light had appeared. The knowledge filled her with chagrin, and yet her heart still pounded.

One thing she'd learned in the course of her work was to trust her intuition. That wave of fear was her body warning her that the threat she sensed was real.

If she couldn't help the children, then she needed to help herself.

I should leave. Now.

She was already moving in the direction of the exit as she had the thought, but her foot caught on something. She stumbled and almost went to her knees. Her pumps had sensible heels, but they hadn't been made for walking blindly through such rough, uneven terrain. To find her way out without injuring herself she needed to turn on her torch.

Her thumb found the switch but once again instinct, honed by her experiences with the most depraved of predators, kicked in to stop her from pressing it. Her sense of being in imminent peril increased a hundredfold as she realized that she was *afraid* to risk turning on the light.

Go.

Listening to that inner voice, she continued blindly on. Head ducked, shoulders hunched, arms tucked in close to her sides except for the hand touching the wall to her right that served as her guide, she made herself as small as possible to avoid the dangerous areas that she remembered but couldn't see. She tried to picture the passage she had come through in her mind, but with little success. It took a turn not too far ahead that, once she rounded it, would at least allow her to see the doorway that was the way out. That knowledge sustained her. Feeling her way along, she stumbled several times on loose debris but managed not to turn an ankle or fall. The crunch of her footsteps was unavoidable, and she winced inwardly at their noise. The rasp of her breathing came loud and harsh.

Too loud and harsh.

The hair stood up on the back of her neck.

It wasn't *her own* breathing that she heard.

Someone else was there in the dark with her, someone who was breathing as if he'd been running. Someone *on the other side of the wall.*

Her pulse leaped. Her head turned sharply toward the wall to her left, the one she wasn't touching, even as she shrank back against the one she was. Then she froze. Held her breath. Stared fearfully into the dark without being able to see anything at all.

She could hear him, though. Hear his breathing, his movements, the rustle of his clothing, the shifting of his feet.

A terrifying thought gripped her. Can *he* hear *me*?

The possibility made her blood run cold.

Every instinct she possessed screamed a warning. *Don't let him know you're here.*

Taking tiny sips of air now only because she had to, she stayed still as a statue, leaning back against the wall to steady herself, her every faculty focused on the man—from the position and sound of the breathing she was certain it was a man—in front of her, hidden in the dark on the other side of the wall.

She tried to think rationally. If it was the policeman, having given up the chase and turned back, she had nothing to fear. She could call out to him, ask for help, explain herself—

If it was the policeman, then where was his light? *Why was he standing there so silently in the dark?*

Like he was listening, too.

What felt like an icy finger ran down her spine.

The only thing she knew for sure was her mouth was dry and her heart pounded and she had an overwhelming desire to break cover and run.

Don't move. Don't make a sound.

How long she stood there, frozen in place, scarcely daring to breathe, she didn't know. It felt like a lifetime, but it might have been no more than a minute or two.

On the other side of the wall, his breathing normalized until she could scarcely hear it. Finally he gave what sounded like a tired sigh, and then she heard him move, heard the grittiness of his feet shuffling amid the rubble—

A splintering crash right in front of her made her jump and squeak as a man's gloved hand, rough and preternaturally strong, grabbed her arm just above the elbow and dug in.

Caught by surprise, she screamed like a steam whistle.

A torch's beam came at her through the chinks in the wall.

"Got you!" The triumphant growl came as she was yanked forward. He'd punched a fist-sized hole right through the wall, she saw with horror in the split second before the light went out again. Flinging up a hand against the light only to be almost instantly plunged back into spine-chilling darkness, she connected palm first with rough plaster just in time to save herself from smacking into the crumbling wall.

"Who are you? Let me go!" Pushing hard against the wall for leverage, she jerked back against the painfully tightening grip in a futile effort to wrest free.

Wordlessly he yanked her toward him again. Adrenaline shot through her, galvanizing her, as the knowledge that this was not a mix-up, not a policeman mistaking his target, burst upon her.

This is evil.

The miasma of it, cloud or fog or whatever evil was made of, touched her with its icy tendrils. She recognized it from that place in the depths of her soul that had become familiar with it long ago. Screaming, she fought with all her strength to get free.

"Shut up! Shut up!"

"Let go! *Help!*"

Smashing sounds punctuated her screams as he rammed his shoulder, his whole body, against the barrier that still existed between them. The wall shook. Bits of plaster fell like rain. He was doing everything he could to break through the wall, to get to her while she struggled like a mad thing and he kept her from escaping with his iron grip on her arm.

"Help! Help me!"

The bottom of the wall ruptured in a shower of wreckage that hit her legs as he kicked through it.

Her heart went haywire.

"Say your prayers." His near whisper was more petrifying than any shout.

His voice, previously deep and guttural, had turned in a moment into a high-pitched, sibilant hiss. It made her heart explode with terror and her skin crawl.

"No!" she screamed. *"Help! Help me!"*

Even as he yanked her arm toward him, jamming it up against the hole he'd punched in the wall, trying to pull it through, pull *her* through, she bent her head and bit him. Her teeth found the flesh at the edge of the glove, clamped down.

Viciously. For her life.

He howled and his grip loosened. She jerked free, screaming, and ran for the exit, for the way out that she knew was there just beyond the bend. She'd dropped the torch. It was lost, gone, leaving her in a stygian blackness that could have belonged to Hell itself. All she could do was guide herself with one hand against the wall while trying to shield herself from injury with the other, keeping her head low as she careened over obstacles she couldn't see. She tripped, almost went down, regained her footing and lurched on. Her heart thundered as a tremendous crash behind her convinced her that, finally, he'd broken through the wall.

Oh, no. No. No.

A torch beam flashed after her, casting giant monstrous shadows on broken walls, ruptured ceiling. He *was* through. She wasn't wrong about that. Would he shoot her? Her back muscles tensed in horrified expectation. If this was the policeman, he'd said he had a gun. Running footsteps, harsh breathing—she could hear him. He was coming after her, catching up; even if he didn't shoot her he would catch her before she ever reached the bend.

The ear-shattering scream that tore out of her throat then filled the passage bounced off walls and ceiling and floor.

"Professor!" A shout—Schneider's voice—cut through her shrieks. Another beam of light appeared, small and dim but ahead of her now, illuminating the bend in the passage. Not much farther—

"Detective!" she cried. It was a strangled-sounding croak as she used what felt like the last reserves of her strength to bolt toward this new light, toward him.

"Professor!" Schneider roared.

"I'm here!" She reached the bend in the passage just as Schneider came around it. Colliding with him, literally running right into the solid mass of his body hard enough to knock herself off balance, she grabbed hold of him like she never meant to let go.

"What—"

"He's behind me. He's coming," she gasped, throwing a fearful glance over her shoulder. It was only then that she realized that the passage behind her was once again dark as a cave. The light that had been chasing her was gone.

"Who?"

"I don't know. A policeman. Somebody. He's back there!"

"A policeman?"

"I don't know!"

As his torch shone briefly past her, back down the way she had come, he wrapped an arm around her waist and lifted her off her feet, swinging her around to deposit her in the part of the passage that led to the exit, putting himself and a wall between her and danger. She could see the small patch of moonlight beyond the door frame, see the way out. The sight made her go weak at the knees.

"Go. Get out of here." He turned away, clearly intent on rushing down the passage toward the man whose light she could no longer see, who she could no longer hear, but who was *still there.* She knew it, felt it in her bones.

"No!" She grabbed at him to stop him. "He's armed!"

"So am I." With that grim pronouncement he pulled free and was gone, and she was left shivering in the dark. Leaning against the wall to steady herself, she listened with her heart in her throat to Schneider's rapid footsteps receding until she could no longer hear them. Then nothing. No shouts, no gunshots, no sounds of a struggle.

The thought that the man who'd grabbed her might have found another way around, another way to get to her, took terrifying possession of her mind. The rectangle of moonlight that was the way out beckoned. Pushing away from the wall, she stumbled toward it. The darkness lightened, was no longer absolute; she could see shapes and outlines and was grateful for that. Her knees were jelly. Her heart pounded like it would beat its way out of her chest.

Moments later footsteps coming up fast behind her made her dart a panicky glance over her shoulder. The steady beam of the slotted torch, the broad-shouldered shape of the man holding it, told her who it was even before he spoke. She sagged with relief.

"He was gone. Big hole in the wall that he must have ducked through. I thought it was better to come back here and check on you than go chasing after a phantom in the dark," Schneider said as he caught up with her.

"What if he comes back?" It was all she could do to keep her teeth from chattering.

"He won't. He bolted after he realized you weren't alone anymore. Coming after you by yourself is a whole different enterprise than coming after you when you're with me."

She must have sounded as shaken as she felt, or maybe he could tell she was unsteady on her feet, because he thrust the torch into his pocket and wrapped an arm around her. In his other hand, she thought from the way he was holding his arm straight down at his side, was his gun. Despite his reassurance, she was glad of that gun, just as she was glad to lean against him, to let him take some of her weight. Enormous bursts of adrenaline such as she had just experienced often left people weak and trembling in their wake, she knew, and to her chagrin that was proving true in her case.

He said, "You want to tell me what happened?"

Wedged close against his side as they made their way toward the pale charcoal rectangle that was the doorway, she gave him a general summary in quick, disjointed sentences.

"So it was a policeman who grabbed you?"

"I don't know. A man yelled, 'This is the police.' But he might have been lying. And he might not be the one who grabbed me. There might have been a second man."

"What the hell were you thinking, to go into a bombed-out building on your own at night?"

"I told you. Pia and I saw those children go in. And whether you like it or not, I can't just forget about them. They're *children*. And they might have seen something that can help us. Help the investigation."

"You're lucky you're not dead."

"Yes." She didn't merely say it aloud. She felt the truth of it in her soul. Slanting a look up at him, she said, "Thank you, by the way. I think you might have saved my life."

"I think so, too. And you're welcome." He sounded grim.

"What are you doing here, anyway? How did you even know I was here?"

"I didn't. I just happened to be driving by. I saw a taxi stopped on the nearest cross street from our latest crime scene with its headlamps off and a woman walking away from it. Bad neighborhood for a woman alone, I thought, so I pulled up and got out to see what she was doing. Turns out it was your friend, and she was worried because you'd gone into a pitch-black hole in a collapsing building and hadn't come out. I sent her back to the taxi, went to the hole, and heard you screaming. Which makes you one very lucky lady." He sounded even grimmer than before. "Which brings us to the question of what *you're* doing here. In a taxi. You have an assigned car and driver, and when I saw you last you were supposed to be going back to your hotel, where I was supposed to pick you up about an hour from now."

"Officer Lutts wasn't available when we were ready to leave. And I can't just go back to the hotel and rest. There's no *time*."

On that note they reached the entrance and stepped out into a murky darkness dappled with moonlight. The air was hot and muggy and smelled of rain, of mud, but after the claustrophobic airlessness of the passageway Elin sucked it in with gratitude. Her heart still pounded, her pulse still raced, and her legs still felt weak, but she would survive.

They reached a patch of moonlight and he stopped, which meant she stopped, too, because he had his arm around her and she was hanging on to him like she suspected her knees would collapse if she let go, which she did.

"Are you hurt?" he asked.

"No," she replied, because shaken and bruised didn't really count.

"Look at me."

She looked up, met his gaze. She could feel the moonlight on her face. Bent over hers, his was in shadow. All she could really see of him was a dark silhouette, the outline of which consisted of thick black hair and a sturdy neck and those shoulders, along with the hard angle of his jaw and the narrowed gleam of his eyes.

"I thought so. You've got blood on your mouth." His voice was rougher than before.

Frowning, Elin touched her lips.

16

"BLOOD?" THERE *WAS* A KIND OF STICKY DAMPNESS ON her mouth, Elin discovered. As she drew her fingers away and frowned down at the dark smears on her fingertips, she remembered. "Oh. I bit him. It's not my blood."

Then it hit home. If there was blood on her face, *it was not her blood.*

Schneider's hold on her tightened still more. "You *bit* him?"

"I need my bag. From the taxi," she said urgently. Her legs felt stronger now. *She* felt stronger now. A jolt of adrenaline rushed through her bloodstream. It was the prospect of verifying what could be a solid lead that accounted for it, she knew.

"What? Why?"

She pulled free of him. He let her go.

"The blood on my face. It's *his* blood. The man in the tunnel. I think there's a possibility he might be the killer." She was working it through in her mind even as she headed determinedly toward where the taxi, a shapeless oblong in the dark, waited.

"What makes you think that?" He stayed beside her, a welcome presence given the shifting shadows that could have concealed anything or anyone.

She hesitated before replying, unable to face the prospect of attempting to explain the aura of evil that she'd felt radiating toward her in that passageway. The aura of evil that she recognized because she knew it and had known it for so long and so well that there was no possibility of mistaking it for anything else.

"He said something to me," she said. "'Say your prayers.' It was— I'm almost certain something like that was in one of the letters the killer wrote. 'I told her to say her prayers.'"

As the eerie voice in which he'd said it replayed itself in her head, it was all she could do not to give in to the dread that seized her and start shivering again.

"Inge Weber. You're right, it was." Schneider was back to sounding like what he was, a policeman on the job. "Did he say anything else?"

The taxi's rear door flew open before she could answer. Pia, a slim wisp of a moving shadow among a multitude of moving shadows, jumped out. "Elin! Thank God!"

As Pia hurried toward her Elin saw that another car was parked near the taxi: Schneider's.

Replying to Schneider before Pia could reach them, Elin said, "Nothing important."

Pia was there and would have wrapped her in a hug if Elin had not thrown up a hand and taken a quick sideways step of avoidance.

"Careful," she warned, skirting her, and kept walking. "I'm covered with evidence. I need my bag."

"Thank God you're all right." Keeping pace, Pia looked her over anxiously. It was, Elin knew, difficult to see much in the way of detail in the dark, but Pia was trying. "You *are* all right, aren't you? You seem a little wobbly."

"I'm all right. Did you see anything?"

"Anything?" Pia frowned. "Oh, you mean like the chil—"

She broke off abruptly to cast a self-conscious glance at Schneider, who loomed on Elin's other side.

"Nice to know you can be discreet when necessary. I hope you were equally discreet with the taxi driver." Schneider's voice was dry. "Both of you. No talk of women being murdered in front of him, for example."

Pia sputtered with indignation.

"Of course we didn't talk about anything to do with the case in front of the driver, or anyone else who isn't connected to it," Elin intervened with a chastening frown for Schneider before Pia could find her tongue. To Pia, she added, "Herr Schneider knows why we came. I told him about seeing the children this morning."

"Oh," Pia said. "Then, no. After you went into that hole, there was no sign of the children or anyone else. It was like being marooned on a deserted island in the dead of night. Spooky." She jerked a thumb at Schneider. "By the time *he* pulled up I was going crazy with worry for you. Then I heard you scream. What happened in there? Did you find them?"

"Tell you later." Reaching the taxi, Elin opened the rear door. Shifting around in his seat, the driver shook his head at her as she got in.

"I told you, Fräulein, we shouldn't have stopped. We shouldn't even have come this way." His tone made it a lament. "It's too dangerous around here at night."

"Yes, I see you were right." Elin slid across the seat toward her bag, which waited in the footwell behind him.

At the same time she heard Pia, standing near the open door, say quietly but with steel in her voice to Schneider, "It may surprise you to learn that we're not customarily indiscreet, but I assure you we're not. We know how to keep our mouths shut."

"It does surprise me," Schneider said. "Get in the car."

Pia did, and he closed the door behind her with a solid-sounding thump.

"Pikansjos," Pia muttered sourly in Schneider's direction as he walked away.

Elin was only peripherally aware of their exchange, but she did register Pia's final crude insult, which hopefully Schneider hadn't heard. She ignored it and everything else to concentrate on what she was doing. With her bag open beside her and the powder compact from the small stash of cosmetics she kept in the bag's side pocket angled on her lap so that she could see herself in its mirror, she worked carefully to transfer the blood on her mouth into one of the sterile glass vials she kept for such purposes. There wasn't much blood, and what remained was already drying, but she thought it would be enough. Best practices dictated that it be tested soon, before it completely dried up. With that done, she wiped her mouth until she was as sure as it was possible to be that no traces remained. The thought of having what was possibly the killer's blood on her skin was revolting.

Schneider had just reached her side of the car; for what purpose she had no idea. It didn't matter. She slid out of the car, responded to Pia's surprised "Where are you going?" with a give-me-a-minute wave, caught Schneider by the arm, and dragged him away from the taxi so they couldn't be overheard.

"I need you to take me to the Alex," she said as he looked at her in surprise. "Right now."

"Why?"

"I need to test the blood I've collected. I think it's important that we know as soon as possible if my theory about the man who attacked me is correct," she said. "If the blood's type A, then we can proceed on the strong presumption that he's our killer."

"A lot of people have type A blood."

"Which is why it's a strong presumption and not a one hundred percent certainty."

A corner of his mouth twitched up unexpectedly. "Just ninety-five percent?"

She narrowed her eyes at him. "Something like that. Given all the factors involved." She began to enumerate them, but he stopped her with a raised hand.

"After what you just went through, don't you think you should go back to the hotel for the night?"

"Like you, I have a killer to catch. I need to test the blood while it's relatively fresh. Take me to the Alex so I can do my job."

His brows twitched together. "Fine. You want to go to the Alex, we'll go to the Alex."

"Thank you," Elin said, and turned back to give Pia some idea of what was happening.

Schneider, meanwhile, had moved to the driver's window, where he flashed his warrant badge at the old man.

"Herr Erling?" With the light-limiting properties of its slotted cover enhanced by his hand curled protectively around it, Schneider's torch was out and focused on the papers that the driver was showing him, which presumably included his name. The driver must have made a gesture affirming his identity, because Schneider continued, "Take the lady in the back to the Hotel Waldschloss. Don't stop until you get there no matter what she or anyone else says or does, and make sure she gets inside safely. This is a police matter, do you understand?"

The driver nodded vigorously in response.

"Very well. I'll hold you personally responsible for her safety." Schneider stepped back, gesturing for the taxi to go.

"Wait," Elin said to the driver as Pia handed her bag through the open window. Face etched with worry, Pia caught her hand.

"You sure you're going to be all right?" Voice low, Pia cast a meaningful look at Schneider, who waited nearby. Rather than observing their interaction, he appeared to be intently scanning the ruins.

"I'm sure." Elin squeezed her friend's hand reassuringly, released it, and stepped back. "I'll see you later."

Pia lifted a hand in reluctant goodbye and the taxi pulled away.

Now that she'd been left alone in the dark with him, Elin instinctively moved closer to Schneider. The thought that the man who'd attacked her might be lurking somewhere in the shadows made her appreciate the detective and his gun far more than she'd ever expected to.

She scanned the ruins just as he was doing. He glanced at her.

"You need to have the area searched for those children," she said. "If it was the killer who attacked me, he's obviously here after them. We have to find them before he does."

Taking her bag, he shepherded her toward his car. She noticed he placed himself between her and the ruins, and she felt a cold trickle of fear slide down her spine.

"Or maybe he was here after you," he said. "*You're* the one he attacked. Maybe he followed you here, and when you went into a dark hole where no one could see or hear you, he could hardly believe his luck and decided to seize the day."

She hadn't thought of that.

"That's not very likely." Elin turned the possibility over in her mind. "To begin with, why would he be following *me*? I've only been on the case for a few days. And I can't see how I pose a bigger threat to him at this point than, say, you do. And Pia and I only took that taxi because Officer Lutts was unavailable, and we only stopped here because we were in the taxi, so he couldn't have known where we were going in advance and been lying in wait. He would have had to follow us from the Alex."

She frowned, then shook her head. "The man who chased the children claimed to be a policeman, so for him to be coming from the Alex might make sense, but if he was really here after me he was in the wrong passage. Both men, if there were two, were in the wrong passage. He had to have been hunting the children. And we have to find them before he does. They must have seen something, or know something, that can identify him, and he knows it." Her voice turned urgent. "And he'll kill them to prevent it from getting out."

"Or maybe *you've* seen something, or know something, that can identify him," Schneider said. "And he'll kill *you* to prevent it from getting out. And maybe he was in the other passage because the entrance you used could be seen by anyone waiting in the taxi, which he would have known was there because he followed it."

A flash memory of the attack, and the attacker, made her chest feel tight. *Say your prayers.* He would have killed her if he could have; she was convinced. Summoning every bit of resolution she possessed, she warded off another long shiver.

"I haven't seen anything, and I don't know anything, that could identify him. At least not as far as I'm aware." She frowned. "Unless he thinks I can recognize his voice. Until I was attacked, the only adult voice I heard was the policeman, or the man claiming to be a policeman, yelling after the children. My attacker didn't speak until he grabbed me. Does that mean that the policeman is the one who attacked me? Or were there two men in the passageway? I don't know, and in any case I didn't recognize anybody's voice. But I do think that it was the killer who attacked me."

"Then I suggest you get in the car." Schneider opened the passenger door for her as they reached it. "I don't think the guy is still around, but I wouldn't want to be proved wrong by, say, having him take a potshot at you."

That was something else she hadn't thought of. Elin quickly got in the car. Handing her bag over, he shut the door, came around, and slid behind the wheel. Having the windows down—it was too steaming hot for anything else—made her feel way too vulnerable, but short of huddling in the footwell there wasn't anywhere she could hide.

"We have to find those children," she said as they got underway. The interior of the car was so dark she could barely see her bag where it rested on her lap, but the moonlight streaming past the windows silhouetted the clean lines of his profile and revealed his hands curled around the wheel. His gun was back in its holster, concealed by the drape of his jacket. "Whether there were two men in that passageway or one, someone is hunting them."

"I don't think we stand a chance of finding anybody tonight. It's too damned dark, and there are too many places someone could hide."

"We have to *try*."

"No, we don't. Not tonight." At the indignant huff that was her response to that, his mouth tightened impatiently. "Look, even if the man who attacked you *is* the killer and he's looking for them, those children have already gotten away. After a scare like that I doubt they're coming back anywhere near here. The man ran away, too, after I showed up, and their paths are unlikely to cross. Wherever they've gone, the children should be safe enough for the next few hours. When it's light outside I'll order a search of the ruins."

"Won't that attract too much attention?" As gibes went, it was a mild one. "We wouldn't want anyone to think we're hunting a killer."

"Not if it's done with an excuse like, say, we've received reports of some unexploded ordnance in the vicinity." If he'd even noticed the barb, he didn't react to it. "I'd say the chances of us finding anybody we're looking for even then are slim, but we might. And we might find something, some evidence, we can use to find or identify them."

She started to protest, to insist that for the children's sake the search needed to happen immediately, but then as the full scope of what she was looking at hit her she reluctantly concluded that he was right. Spread out over many blocks, the degree of destruction was staggering. Any sweep of the ruins would be riddled with danger for searchers, who would need to make their way through bombed-out buildings and a sea of debris, to say nothing of a possible encounter with a ruthless killer. To attempt it during the hours of the blackout would be foolish.

"All right," she said, defeated.

"Tell me what happened one more time from the beginning, and don't leave anything out," he said.

She talked while he drove and looked around. The slotted headlamps illuminated no more than the pitted concrete directly in front of the car. Seen by uncertain moonlight, the broken buildings and mounds of rubble rising around them looked almost haunted. Remembering the smell of death that had lingered in the passageway, Elin found herself wondering how many had been caught inside when the bombs hit. Moving shadows and will-o'-the-wisp flickers of light owed more to the rolling cloud cover and the reflective properties of broken glass than anything supernatural, she told herself stoutly. But then, as they reached an intersection near the edge of the bombed-out area, she saw a beam of moonlight strike something that wasn't a shadow at all.

"Someone's over there." Pulse quickening, she pointed to a figure—no, several figures in a loose group—slinking around a fallen building. Then, as the cloud cover shifted so that entire shafts of gossamer moonlight hit the ground, she discovered more furtive shapes skulking through the darkness. None that she could see looked the right size to be children, but— "There are people here. We should stop."

"No, we shouldn't." He barely glanced where she pointed.

"You're very good at saying *no*, aren't you?" she said, nettled. "We should talk to them. They're potential witnesses. They might know something that could lead us to the children. Or the killer." With her eyes grown accustomed to the dark, she thought she could pick out perhaps twelve, fifteen, maybe more, furtive figures. All seemed intent on their own business. None wore the phosphorus pins that marked honest pedestrians out after blackout.

His short laugh held a brutal quality. "Lucky for you, I'm in charge and I ultimately call the shots. You have no idea what you'd be wading into here. Believe me when I tell you they're not going to talk to us. What you're seeing out there is part of the dark underbelly of the city. Looters. The homeless. The worst off of the refugees from Hamburg who fled to Berlin only to wind up wandering the streets with no money and nowhere to go. Unruly youths such as the Edelweiss Pirates who take advantage of the blackout to vandalize and spread fear. Prostitutes and their customers, drug dealers and their customers, smugglers of black market goods, human traffickers, weapons traffickers, gang members, petty criminals, the insane, U-boats and catchers—"

"U-boats?" She'd heard the term used by a policeman at the Alex, in passing, in a way that had made it clear that it was a derogatory reference to Jews. While the precise definition remained murky, hearing it again made her stomach sink.

"For all that Berlin has been declared free of Jews, the dirty little secret is that some remain. They're in hiding and most dare to venture out only after blackout. U-boats, they're called. Catchers have been employed to find them and bring them in. They hunt them through the dark." She must have made a sound, because he glanced at her. "Remember what I said about keeping your focus on the murders and ignoring everything else? That applies here."

She didn't answer. The reminder of the perilous state of any Jew forced to try to survive under the iron fist of the Reich made her heart thump, and instantly brought Niles to mind.

Please, God, let him be safe with Hilde at Smukkeso.

Whatever it took to get home to him as soon as possible, she was prepared to do.

She just had to make sure she stayed alive long enough to get home.

17

PUSHING HER SAFETY GLASSES TO THE TOP OF HER
head, Elin observed the results of the test she'd just concluded
with satisfaction.

"Let me guess. It's type A. And contains traces of Pervitin,"
Schneider said.

He'd settled onto a lab stool behind her as she worked. Glancing around at him, she still tingled with the excitement of it.
"Yes. How could you tell?"

"Oh, I don't know. Maybe it has something to do with the
fact that you're grinning like the cat who got the cream."

"I am not." Suddenly self-conscious, she wiped anything that
could possibly be construed as a smile from her face as she turned
to face him. "And even if I were, it would be totally appropriate
because those are important pieces of information. I now feel
confident in saying that our killer has type A blood and takes
Pervitin. And also that the man who attacked me is the killer."

"One hundred percent confident?"

Most unexpectedly, it seemed he was teasing her. She frowned at him.

He smiled.

"There remains a small possibility of error," she conceded.

"So ninety-five percent confident. Quit frowning at me, that's more than good enough. We'll—how did you put it?—*posit* that our killer has type A blood and takes Pervitin."

"And was the man who attacked me in the passageway," she repeated, stripping off her gloves and removing the safety glasses.

"That, too."

"Although I still don't know if he and the policeman were one and the same."

"An enduring mystery."

"You realize that those facts combined mean Herr Dalsing isn't our killer. You need to have him released."

Schneider shook his head. "Not until I'm a lot more certain than I am now that our killer didn't have an accomplice."

"He acted alone." Elin put her instruments in the sterilization tray and dampened a cloth with alcohol, wrinkling her nose against the familiar but still too pungent smell as she started wiping down her work area.

"You're ninety-five percent certain?"

Tossing her used cloth into the bin, Elin gave him a withering look. "Statistically, that's quite certain enough."

"Not for me. Not yet." He slid off the stool. "If you're all done here, I'll take you back to the hotel."

"You're forgetting about Eden." A check of her watch revealed that it was not quite eleven. According to what Dalsing had told them, the real action in the club didn't begin until after midnight.

"That can wait for another time. You've had a rough day."

He was right, in more ways even than he knew. But the clock was ticking down. They desperately, desperately needed to find the killer. An unknown woman's life hung in the balance. And she needed to get home to her son.

"We can't slow down now. We're closing in, making the killer uncomfortable as is evidenced by the fact that he attacked me tonight. We have to keep going full steam ahead until we catch him. If he's finding his victims in this club on Saturday nights, then we need to be in there looking for him."

"We don't know that this club is where he's finding his victims. It's a possibility. And, like you, our killer's had a busy night. He's probably gone home to bed."

"I don't think so. You must understand, he's energized by the act of hunting his victims."

"Kind of like you seem to be energized by the act of hunting him?"

That extremely perceptive observation stopped her in her tracks. No one else had ever before picked up on the similarity.

"In a way, I suppose. A *lesser* way." Did she sound defensive? Maybe a little.

"If you say so."

"By this point the process has become an *addiction* for him and he craves the adrenaline rush it gives him exactly as if it were a narcotic drug. He's too wound up to need much sleep, he won't be eating regular meals, and he'll be prone to irritability and aggression."

"A lesser way. I see."

Ignoring the sarcasm, she continued, "This state will build until it culminates in the taking and killing of a victim. And if we don't find him before then, that will happen next Saturday night."

His mouth tightened. "You realize that you're probably the one in the most danger here, right? Tonight the guy attacked *you*."

That stark truth caused her chest to constrict. "I know, and I haven't yet figured out why, exactly. I admit, that bothers me."

"It bothers me, too. Which is why I'm taking you back to the hotel."

She shook her head at him. "You're not seeing the full picture here. I'm convinced of it now after going through the autopsy reports. This last killing wasn't a change in his pattern. It was an anomaly. She was killed for a different reason than the others, as is evidenced by the fact that he kept her captive for several days first. He had to work himself up to killing her. Which means he's almost certainly still on schedule. He'll take another victim next Saturday night. We have to use tonight, the only Saturday night we have left before he kills again, to try to identify him, or at least identify his hunting grounds. If we can do that, we stand a good chance of catching him and, not coincidentally, saving a life. And Herr Dalsing's lead about this club is the best one we've got."

Giving her a long look, he crossed his arms over his chest. "I *posit* that it's you who's not seeing the full picture here. See, if he'd killed you, you'd be dead."

"But *you'd* still have a serial killer on the loose who'd be taking another victim next Saturday night. Even if he'd succeeded in killing me, that wouldn't prevent him from sticking to his schedule. It wouldn't satisfy his compulsion. He's rigid, methodical, and purpose driven, and I'm not his chosen prey. I'm just someone he's singled out as being in his way."

"You don't know that. You said yourself that you don't know why he attacked you, or even, with one hundred percent certainty, that it was our killer who did. And until we have some answers, I'm not prepared to put you in a situation where you could be in danger." He stood up. "For the remainder of the time you're with us, day or night, you're not to go anywhere outside of this building or your hotel without a police escort. And you're sitting the rest of tonight out. I'll take you back to the hotel, get Walter out there to stand guard duty in case the guy decides to take a second run at you, then go to the clubs by myself. End of discussion. Get your bag, we're leaving."

Stiffening with indignation, she drew herself up to her full height. "No." It was a flat refusal. "And for the record, you can't just say 'end of discussion' and expect me to fall in line. From here on out, that's not how this collaboration of ours is going to work."

"Oh, is that what we're calling this now, a collaboration?"

"That's what it is. Whether you like it or not, we're partners. *Equal* partners, each with our own areas of expertise, working together to achieve our common goal of *catching a murderous psychopath before he kills again*. And that means we go to Herr Dalsing's club. Together."

"I agree about going to the club. But since my area of expertise seems to include keeping you alive, I disagree about us going together. I'm going. You're not. Has it occurred to you that he apparently knows what you look like? If he's in this club you're hell-bent to go to, he'll see you."

"Has it occurred to you that he apparently knows what *you* look like, too? After all, I'm not the one he's sending letters to."

"But you're the one he tried to kill tonight. That being the case, I'd say the chances are at least fair that he'll try again."

"That's where you come in. I'm counting on you to keep me alive. And it gives us one more thing to look for. Someone paying too much attention to me. Or you."

"Maybe we should consider that seeing either one of us in the place where he's hunting women will cause him to choose another place, thus rendering our best lead useless. That leaves you out, and I could stay back and send any of the other detectives in my place, but I'm guessing that if he knows me he knows them, too."

"Yes," Elin agreed. "I think we're getting to the stage where we can be confident that the killer has a connection to the police. A close enough connection that he's aware of the broad strokes at least of this investigation, and the identities of the key players."

"Confident," Schneider echoed.

Narrowing her eyes at him, Elin waited for another crack about ninety-five percent, which to his credit didn't come. When he continued, it sounded as if he was not so much talking to her as thinking the situation through out loud.

"So would it be better to send someone totally unknown? I could try to get another detective out of Nebe, and maybe even wrangle a policewoman to go with him. The problem with that is, they wouldn't know what to look for beyond 'suspicious behavior,' so I don't think they'd be of much use."

Whether he was talking to her or not, Elin responded. "They wouldn't. I have to be the one to go, and since you've taken on the job of keeping me alive you should probably come with me. Seeing me won't disrupt his routine. The compulsion that drives him is too strong. Anyway, by now he knows that I didn't recognize him in that passageway and clearly can't identify him, because if I could he'd either already be under arrest or you'd be coming after him full bore. And if you knew his identity, the same thing would apply. So he won't feel threatened if he sees either one of us. He'll be excited and even more energized to know we're close on his trail. The thrill of the chase, you know? And that might even be enough to cause him to make a mistake. Which might help us catch him."

He grimaced. "Or maybe all your theories are wrong, and there is no compulsion driving him beyond the fact that he just likes killing women. Maybe now that the pretty doctor chasing him has somehow got herself on his radar, he's decided she's next."

"My theories aren't wrong."

"You willing to bet your life on that? Because I'm not. Which is why I'm *not* taking you out to a club and possibly dangling you under his nose tonight. You're going back to the hotel, and I'm going alone. And that's the way it's going to be until I've had a chance to work this thing that happened to you tonight through in my head."

"We don't have time for you to work anything through in your head. Tonight's our best chance to gather information, and we can't afford not to use it." Her eyes flashed dangerously at him. "Can *you* read the messages in nonverbal behavior? Would *you* be able to spot a man sizing up a woman as a potential target by analyzing his posture, the tilt of his head, what he does with his hands? Or a woman's vulnerability to a predator by the way she walks or sits or stands?"

She didn't give him time to answer. "No, you can't. But I can. That's *my* area of expertise. Catching this killer is my job just as much as it is yours. And getting it done probably matters even more to me, because I can't go home to my son until I do."

His face tightened. "You can't go home to your son if you're dead."

That was the part she knew. The part that made her stomach clench. "The best way to make sure that doesn't happen is for us to catch the killer. Until he's under arrest, no matter what we do, I'm at risk. And you know it."

He gave her a long, considering look.

"You make a good point," he said, then swung around and headed for the door. Opening it, he gestured for her to precede him through it. "Fine. You win. Let's go."

When Elin had visited Berlin with her parents some fifteen years before, the city at night was a beautiful, sparkling jewel to rival Paris and the atmosphere crackled with energy. The restaurants and cabarets, the elegant fashions, the sheer vitality of the bustling crowds that seemed to fill the streets at all hours were exciting, even dazzling. At night, there was such a variety of entertainments to choose from. Whole neighborhoods were packed with glittering marquees advertising spectacular musical revues. Sidewalks teemed with pleasure-seeking bons vivants flitting in and out of the dozens of nightclubs. Dance halls where music spilled over into the streets and couples of all descriptions indulged in everything from the staid foxtrot to the new, boisterous Charleston could be found on practically every corner.

Now the decadence of those pre-Nazi years was gone, along with any semblance of gaiety or glamor. While restaurants still operated, and trips to the orchestra, the theater, and the cinema remained popular, all entertainment offerings had to be approved by the government, and the Reichmusikkamer controlled every aspect of the music scene. Public and private dance events were banned along with "degenerate" music and styles of dance. The prohibition covered swing and jazz and any music by non-Aryan artists or with connections to enemy countries, which included most of the popular songs and artists of the day. The Gestapo was vigilant in its enforcement, zealously seeking out and raiding venues where the forbidden music was played.

As a result, the glittering nightclubs and dance halls and musical revues Elin remembered were no more. When Goebbels had declared "total war" in February, all the unapproved establishments had been completely shut down. Anyone caught breaking the prohibition was subject to arrest and possible severe punishment, including torture and deportation to a camp.

That didn't mean the clubs were gone, however. The ban had simply driven the rebellious holdouts into hiding. And it was in one of those hidden clubs that Dalsing had apparently encountered Greta Neuhaus, and that club was their current destination.

As Schneider drove past Potsdamer Platz, Elin spotted the very theater she and her parents had visited so many years ago, gone dark now like all of Berlin, and felt her heart break a little. Looking back now with the knowledge of what was to come, with both parents gone and herself the sole, battered survivor of their little family of three, she found that she cherished the memory of that simple outing more than she'd ever thought possible. Other, terrible memories from the tragic denouement of that trip crowded in almost immediately, bringing pain with them, but she was able to push away both the memories and the accompanying welling sorrow with Schneider's unwitting assistance. Having slid into a parking spot while she was lost in the past, he gave her thoughts a welcome new direction by opening her door and ushering her out of the car and into the mist the rain had left behind.

"Tired yet?" Schneider asked as they started to walk along the dark and dangerously pitted sidewalk.

"No. Are you?"

"I'm way past tired. Tired was a couple of weeks ago. But I'll try to keep going."

"If you can't, don't worry. I'll pick up the slack."

The sound he made could have been a laugh, but when she glanced at him he wasn't looking at her. Instead, he was squinting at something. Following his gaze, she saw that he was watching a man who, in a possible reaction to their presence, disappeared into an inky black cellar stairwell as they approached. The man's action seemed furtive, and Elin tensed. But nothing happened, and as they passed the spot and continued on without incident she relaxed a little—until she spotted other furtive figures skulking through the darkness.

18

"YOU'RE STILL ARMED, RIGHT?" ELIN ASKED SCHNEIDER under her breath.

"Nervous, Professor?"

"Not if you're armed, Detective."

"Would it make you feel better if I said, *Always*?"

"Infinitely," she said, and this time the sound he made was definitely a laugh.

Still, she saw that he was keeping a careful watch out without seeming to be on alert at all.

The street was shrouded in gloom, and thick shadows hung around the buildings, but the cloud cover that had made the night so dark had largely blown away. Thanks to the moonlight the mist shimmying up around them held a silvery tint, and the puddles filling the craters in the street gleamed like mirrors. Their shadows stretched out in front of them, and the image of him in his fedora and suit jacket looked large and masculine next to her slender shape in the formfitting dress.

They turned down a street crammed with long, multistory buildings that looked like they were or had once been factories, but if they were still in use as such she couldn't tell from the dark, silent exteriors. A few people walked openly now on the sidewalks, and they, along with the line of cars parked at the curb, were the only indication that any of the buildings might be occupied.

"Don't all these cars kind of give away the presence of a secret club?" Elin asked as Schneider hurried her across the street while keeping one eye on a vehicle sending up sprays of water from the puddles as it traveled too fast toward them.

"There are other establishments here that find more favor with the authorities." He nodded toward a four-story brick building that, from the outside, looked as dark and empty as all the others. "A restaurant, a billiards hall, and, above that perfectly legitimate barber shop—" he nodded at another deserted-looking building "—a brothel." He smiled a little at the expression on her face. "Since the brothel serves mainly high-level Wehrmacht officers, this street is for the most part left alone. Not even the Gestapo wants to take the risk of bursting in on the wrong general."

She frowned. "When Herr Dalsing was telling us about this club we're heading to, you never mentioned you were familiar with the area."

"I'm a cop. I'm familiar with all the bad places." He shot a frowning glance toward the base of a mulberry bush near the sidewalk. Elin shivered a little as, following his gaze, she caught a glimpse of a long, naked tail as something scurried away. "But it's been a while, and I didn't know there was an illegal club here."

The car that had been speeding their way slowed, pulled over beside the line of parked cars nearest them, and jerked to a stop.

Elin looked on in surprise as Schneider took the two strides into the street necessary to speak with the driver through the open window. Elin had no sooner recognized Herr Trott as the driver than Schneider slapped the roof in dismissal and returned to her side while the car sped away.

"What was that about?" Elin asked as they started walking again.

"In about twenty minutes, Walter's going to follow us inside. He'll stay to himself, act like he doesn't know us, but he'll be providing backup in case something should go wrong. If we come across anyone of interest, I'll make sure Walter is aware. Walter will follow the suspect when he leaves, and alert Gunther and Roth, who are already in a car parked over there." He nodded toward the cars across the street, and Elin automatically looked in that direction without being able to tell which car he meant. "They'll arrest him under the pretext that he was visiting an illegal club, and we'll take it from there."

"All they need to do is check his wrists to see if he has a recent bite mark. If not, they don't need to arrest him because he's not our killer," she said, and frowned. "When did you arrange all this?"

"When you were in the ladies' room freshening up." He gave her an impatient look. "And I'd rather they arrest anyone we identify as a potential suspect whether he has a bite mark or not, just in case it *wasn't* the killer who attacked you."

"Is this it?" Elin asked doubtfully as Schneider stopped in front of one of the long brick buildings. If there was light anywhere inside, no hint of it showed. The many windows glinted black where the moonlight hit them, making Elin think of row upon row of malevolent eyes glaring out at the street. What was even more surprising was that, although Dalsing had said he came for the music, she heard nothing beyond the usual street sounds.

"Supposed to be." Having finished his quick survey of the exterior, he picked up her hand and tucked it into the crook of his arm. "Stay close," he said, confirming her suspicion that he, too, had some doubts about what they were getting into, and started up a set of wide brick steps that led to what, thanks to the metal overhang, was the nearly pitch-black stoop.

"Expecting trouble, Detective?" Elin asked. The wet steps didn't feature a handrail on either side. Wary of slipping, she clung to his arm, and was close enough to feel his shrug.

"Anything's possible. And by the way, my name's Kurt and that's what you want to call me. It'll only take one of your 'Detectives' to ruin us."

"Or one of your 'Professors.'"

"I'm aware, *Elin*."

"Glad to hear it, *Kurt*."

Then they were on the stoop. He knocked, and after a moment she heard a sliding sound that, remembering Dalsing's description, she attributed to a peephole in the door. Ah, there it was. She could see the faint gleam of an eyeball looking out at them.

"Who's there?" The male voice spoke to them through the thick wood panel.

Schneider responded with the fake name that was the password, and the door swung open.

"Welcome to Eden," the doorkeeper said.

As they walked past him into a long, narrow hallway the door closed behind them. It was darker and cooler inside than out, and instead of smelling of damp earth a faint sweetish scent hung in the air. A pulsing, muffled beat that was clearly musical in nature drew Elin's gaze upward before a distinctive clang that she was sure was the door being locked behind them distracted her. Instinctive wariness sent her sidling closer to Schneider. Then a small overhead light came on in time to reveal a second man walking toward them out of the darkness at the back of the house.

"Herr Konigsberg," the man who'd admitted them said, repeating the password that had gotten them inside as the other man reached them. Elin inferred from the way in which it was said that the password was also a directive signifying where to take them.

"This way." The second man motioned to them to follow him. The complete absence of light and sound reaching the street was explained as they were led past boarded-up windows and bales of straw packed tightly against the outer walls, and then up a flight of stairs.

On the second floor, a series of rooms opened off either side of a narrow, dimly lit corridor. Most of the doors stayed closed as they passed, but as people she could barely see in the gloom moved in and out of the smoke-filled rooms, Elin caught a glimpse, in one, of a man injecting himself with some substance in a syringe while another lay, apparently passed out, on a cot nearby. In a second room a naked man hung by bound wrists from the ceiling while a woman lashed him with a riding crop. The sharp sounds as the whip landed would have made her jump if she had not been tightly controlling her reactions. Adding to her discomfort were the accompanying ecstatic-sounding moans from the man, and she was thankful when both were cut off as a second woman, in dominatrix gear, closed the door. In a third room, two nearly naked women danced for a circle of admirers reclining on sofas and puffing away at what she identified by the sweetish smell as opium.

Her takeaway from what she'd seen was that vice, so openly rampant under the Weimar Republic and so energetically de-plored by the Nazis, clearly still survived in the Third Reich.

They went up another flight of stairs, and the pulsing beat she'd been listening to all along resolved itself into a throbbing jazz rendition of "In the Mood." In different circumstances, she would have been delighted to hear it. She loved that song. But now all she could think of was the victims—and the killer. Was the lure of forbidden music what was drawing young women to their deaths? Considered in that context, the sprightly tune suddenly felt sinister.

A moment later, their guide stopped in front of another heavy wooden door and knocked—a special knock, three quick, two slow. A moment after that, the door swung open.

Cigarette smoke, alcohol, cheap perfume—the smell engulfed them in a pungent cloud. A husky, wailing female voice accompanied by a blaring of horns had Elin turning her head to look for its source as, releasing Schneider's arm, she walked inside ahead of him. He followed, and the door closed behind them with a solid thud. Without looking around, she instinctively shifted her focus to what was happening behind them, but if the door locked this time she didn't hear it.

"Looks like this is the place," Schneider said in her ear, and she nodded.

Loud and raucous, the music filled the cavernous room. Backed by a live band, a sequin-clad singer swayed in front of a standing microphone on a raised stage against the far wall. Dancers, sweating and energetic, triple stepped and jived and twirled on a dance floor in front of the band. The walls were lined with red-draped tables, and many of the laughing, drinking patrons seated at them nodded their heads and tapped their toes in time to the music. The pendant lighting hung low and emitted a pale white glow that was dimmed even more by the thick haze of cigarette smoke that cast a wafting gray veil over everything. Glowing red tips of dozens of cigarettes bobbed through the haze. The walls were raw brick, the floor well-worn wood.

"Erich Frank working the bar tonight?" Schneider asked the scantily dressed hostess who hurried up to greet them. He had to raise his voice to make himself heard over the music.

She shook her head. "Not tonight."

"I thought he usually worked Saturday nights."

"He does. But tonight he didn't come in." The shrug was there in her voice. "Do you want the bar? Or can I show you to a table?"

"A table. In the back, if you have one."

The hostess responded with a comprehensive look at Elin and a knowing smile. Elin was left to wonder exactly what kind of hanky-panky was being got up to in the shadows as the hostess beckoned them to follow. By the time they were seated at a table against the wall, Elin had witnessed enough necking going on in the crowd to have her answer.

"What would you like to drink?" A pretty brunette waitress stopped in front of their table.

"I'll have a beer and the lady will have—what?" Schneider glanced at Elin. The corners of his mouth quirked up as their eyes met. Almost imperceptibly, but she saw. "Fanta, maybe?"

He was teasing her, she realized. The look she gave him in response said, *Aren't you funny.* If she'd had any doubt before, she was sure then that her reaction to the scenes in the rooms off the hallway and all the necking going on at the tables around them hadn't gone unnoticed.

"Schnapps, please," she said with dignity to the waitress. "Apricot if you have it."

Schneider's smile widened as the waitress nodded and left. He put his hat down on the table and leaned back in his chair, steepling his hands on his chest and stretching his long legs out under the table. He looked tired and tough and, yes, all kinds of handsome, which she hated that she noticed. Pointedly ignoring him, *and* the couple locking lips at the next table, Elin looked around. Men and girls alike were piled three deep in front of the long bar on the opposite wall. Everywhere couples were on the move as one after the other they either jumped up and made their way to join the dancers frenetically gyrating in front of the band, or left the dance floor to sit down again. Waitresses in tiny sparkly outfits wove their way in and out of the tables while deftly balancing drink-filled trays. Nearly every table was occupied, some with couples, some with groups of animated young women crowded around a table clearly meant for two, a few with two or three men. More unaccompanied men were propped against the walls and openly ogled the young women. Elin watched one of those men push away from the wall and walk over to a table.

He said something to one of the young women seated there, and then as she smiled and stood up he grabbed her hand and pulled her onto the dance floor. A second man did the same thing with a girl at another table, and Elin had a burst of insight.

"They're here to meet men. The girls, I mean," she said to Schneider. He was right beside her, so close she could feel the brush of his arm or leg whenever either of them moved, but still she had to lean closer and practically whisper in his ear to make sure he, and no one else, could hear. "That's probably what our victims were doing, and how he was able to connect with them. With so many men off fighting, it makes perfect sense."

"Just like Dalsing wasn't here for the music. He was here for the girls, same as all these other guys." Schneider, too, had to lean closer to make himself heard. So close that his mouth was just a whisper away from her ear and she could feel the warmth of his breath feathering across her skin. She registered the sensation, registered the unexpected thrill it gave her, registered her sudden, acute awareness of him as a man, then immediately shut that down. She was there to do a job that had been forced upon her, working in an alien environment with a colleague who'd been thrust upon her, and anything that wasn't part of getting that job done was a dangerous distraction that she didn't need.

"Do you believe him? That he was here?" She didn't lean as close, this time, and was careful to direct her words so that, she hoped, he wouldn't be able to feel her breath on his skin as she'd felt his.

Schneider nodded. If he was aware of any wayward thrills, it wasn't showing. "I do. I also think it's interesting that Erich the bartender isn't here tonight."

Elin's surprise as his meaning hit home drove all other thoughts from her mind. He was suggesting that the bartender might have been warned not to come in or had been prevented from doing so, and in her opinion both options were worth considering. "If someone was listening in on the interrogation—who listens in on the interrogations?"

"A transcriptionist, for sure. Depending on the interview, maybe a cop or two, or someone higher up." That he'd been able to follow her train of thought without effort showed how attuned they, as investigators, were becoming. Good for the case, maybe bad for her firm resolve to keep anything beyond a professional collaboration strictly off the table. "The transcribed interview is placed in the case file, but that's not to say that there aren't copies floating around, or that someone couldn't access it."

"So anyone could have learned Erich Frank's name, and that he's part of Dalsing's alibi."

"I'd probably limit that to anyone in Amt V." He grimaced. "Or anyone connected to anyone in Amt V. Which, admittedly, is a fairly large pool. I'll have someone locate Erich the bartender tomorrow. Shouldn't be hard to get an address."

Elin frowned. "Dalsing would have no reason to prevent him from coming to work—unless Erich can't verify that Dalsing was here when he said he was. Anyway, Dalsing's in custody, so unless he sent someone else *he* didn't interfere with Erich. Our killer, on the other hand, might not want Dalsing's alibi to check out so that he's not eliminated from the pool of suspects. Which presumes he knows Dalsing's *on* the list of suspects."

"Exactly."

"Which brings us back to the killer being a policeman or connected to the police."

"It does."

"So if something's happened to Erich, you think our killer's behind it."

"I'd say the probability is about, oh, ninety-five percent." The smile that accompanied that was slow and charming.

The full effect of the look she gave him in return was probably lost on him as the waitress arrived with their drinks. Schneider paid, and the waitress was off again.

"See anybody promising?" Schneider asked as Elin took a cautious sip of her drink. The apricot flavor was pleasant but weak, and she suspected that, like so much of the alcohol sold since rationing had become so strict, it was watered down.

"It's not like they're giving off sparks. I have to observe and evaluate nuances of behavior. It takes a little time."

"I see." He took a large quaff from the heavy stein that held his beer while she looked around. The smoky atmosphere stung her eyes. She had to blink several times as she tried to focus on, first of all, the men observing or approaching the tables full of girls. A few of those men appeared very young, early twenties at most, and those she quickly ruled out. A dapper man who looked to be fortysomething got her undivided attention as he bowed over a girl's hand, then picked it up and kissed it. The girl pulled her hand away and shook her head vehemently, and he frowned, obviously affronted. He'd asked her to dance and been rejected, Elin surmised, and watched him with interest as he walked stiffly away. But a moment later he was performing the same hand-kiss routine on another girl at another table, and this time he was successful.

She was making a mental note to check on him again when her eye was caught by a door opening in what she'd thought was a solid brick wall near the stage. Getting the merest glimpse of what looked like a back stairway behind him, she observed a tall, thin man step through the door and then close it. He was arresting enough in appearance that her gaze lingered on him: white blond hair, slicked back; aquiline features accented with a toothbrush mustache; a modish suit with exaggerated shoulders and a nipped-in waist that was unusual on a man of his age, which she estimated to be early forties. He made his way across the room toward the bar. The hostess, spotting him, rushed to greet him. He paused to say something to her, and she nodded deferentially and hurried off.

"Storch," Schneider said on a note of grim satisfaction. Elin glanced at him to see that he was looking at the same man and raised her eyebrows at him questioningly.

"Baron Armin von Storch. A gangster from way back. Aristocratic lineage without wealth to back it up, sought to remedy that lack as a youth by turning to crime, one of the primary players in Sport Club *Immertrau*." One look at Elin's face must have conveyed her ignorance of the name, because he went on to explain, "It started out as a boxing club but soon turned into a criminal enterprise disguised as a sports club under the umbrella of the Ringvereine." Another flick of his eyes over her face was followed by another explanation. "That is an organization of gangs that ran illegal gambling, drugs, prostitution, all kinds of street crime, you name it, they ran it. Did I say 'ran'? The word is 'run,' because whatever the propagandists like to put out, the Ringvereine is still around, and you can bet your life Storch is still part of it. He was smart enough to throw in with Hitler and the National Socialists when they first came to power, so he's been protected to a degree. An illegal club like this is right up his alley. I wouldn't be surprised to discover that the Ringvereine—or Storch himself—owns it, paying protection to somebody for the privilege, of course."

Elin shot another glance at Storch, who'd moved on to talk to a couple at a table near the bar.

"He looks deceptively respectable," she said.

"That's how they see themselves. Respectable criminals. They pal around with all the right people, buy expensive property, drive expensive cars, wear expensive clothes, flash fine jewelry around. Including the signet rings that signify membership in the organization, which they earn once they reach a certain level."

A quick stab of possibility made her eyes widen. "Are the rings set with a circular stone?"

"Depends."

"Depends on what?"

"Which branch of the organization you belong to."

"What about this Storch? Does he wear one? Have you seen it?"

"I have. Heavy silver with a setting of a round ruby."

"Some of the bruises on our unnamed victim could have been made by a ring with a round stone." Making such a link sent a quiver of excitement through her.

"Could they indeed?" Schneider's eyes narrowed as he looked at Storch, who'd turned to accept a drink from the waitress. Dismissing her with a nod, he raised the glass to his mouth as his eyes swept the room.

"Will he recognize you?" she asked. The thought with all its implications was alarming.

"If he gets a good look." Picking up his hat, Schneider put it on, tilting it forward in a way that shaded his features. "He always did like brandy," he added absently, and Elin, who'd been observing Storch closely enough to see that what he held was indeed a snifter of brandy, looked back at him.

Schneider was watching Storch.

How well do you know him? was the question that hovered on the tip of her tongue.

Before she could ask it there was a distant boom and they were instantly plunged into pitch darkness as every light in the place went out.

19

ELIN'S PULSE LEAPED AS A MULTITUDE OF HIGH-PITCHED screams pierced the air. Being rendered effectively blind between one moment and the next sent adrenaline racing through her, put her on high alert. Somewhere nearby a tray hit the floor with a nerve-rattling clatter and the sound of smashing glass. Drums crashed and trumpets bleated in a truncated finale that underlined the singer's over-the-microphone yelp, "For God's sake, somebody turn on the damned lights!"

Schneider grabbed her right wrist. From the position of his hand she could tell it was his left, and she had the comforting thought that he was keeping his right hand free in case he had to draw his gun and fire. Then she realized with a tingle of alarm that his gun was useless if he couldn't *see*.

"Get under the table." His voice was an urgent growl in her ear. "If the killer's here and he's seen you..." He didn't have to finish, because she made the connection in a horrifying flash of comprehension. If he knew her location, the killer could use the darkness to launch a lightning attack. One quick stab in the dark and she would be done for and he could escape unseen. Elin thought of the savagery of his attack on her earlier, of his fixed-blade knife and what he had done to his victims with it, and instantly slid off her seat and crawled under the table. Schneider dropped down beside her. She could feel him crouched next to her, protecting her with his body, putting himself between her and any possible danger.

"What's happening?" she whispered.

"Air raid. Hear that siren?"

Over all the noise and confusion around them she could indeed hear, now that she was alerted to it, a spine-tingling mechanical wail. It was in the distant background emanating from somewhere outside the building, but it was there and growing louder and more insistent with every repetition.

"What do we do?" She'd never experienced an air raid, since Denmark hadn't been bombed, and the thought of going through one was terrifying. He was not, she realized, all the way under the table with her. There wasn't room for them both. She pressed close against his hard-muscled thigh. His hand was still wrapped around her wrist, and she welcomed the warm strength of it. Maintaining physical contact was essential. It would be too easy to lose one another in this, the complete absence of light.

"For now, we stay put," he said.

Her heart thumped. Nobody else seemed to be doing that. There was chaos in the form of babbling voices, furniture scraping over floors, thumps and crashes and an explosion of cries and curses as people jumped to their feet or tried to find someone or navigate through the darkness. Except for glowing cigarette tips, most of which were violently arcing downward now in a way that made Elin think they were either being tossed into ashtrays or dropped and hopefully ground out as whoever was holding them surged toward the exit, the room was inky black.

Now that she was attuned to it, she couldn't unhear it. The siren waxed and waned, a keening banshee warning of approaching death. The vivid imagery *that* conjured up sent shivers down her spine.

"Shouldn't we try to leave?"

"Don't move."

A light, dim and tiny as a distant star, appeared. It was a slotted torch, and from its position she realized that whoever was holding it was standing on the stage. At almost the same time another torch sprang to life on the other side of the room.

"Gentlemen, ladies, please, there is no need to panic," a man yelled over the noise. He held the first torch and played it over the crowd that was now pushing and shoving into an amorphous blob in the center of the room. "If you will proceed in an orderly fashion toward my associate holding the torch over there by the door, you will be escorted down to the cellar, where we'll all stay until the danger has passed. There's plenty of room for everyone, don't be afraid. And please, don't push. We have ample time—"

A short, sharp burst of what sounded like distant fireworks erupted, eliciting agitated cries and a surge toward the door from the crowd. It was followed by another staccato burst and another until in just a matter of moments the night outside was alive with a barrage of tooth-rattling explosions. Above it all, the siren—multiple sirens now, from their volume—continued to howl.

"What is that?" Fear dried Elin's mouth.

"Flak," Schneider said. "Antiaircraft fire. That means the bombers are close. They must have snuck in behind the cloud cover. Come on, let's go."

Oh, God, bombs. An instant memory of the destroyed neighborhood where she'd been earlier flashed into her mind even as Schneider tugged at her wrist. Obediently she scrambled out from under the table. The smell of death that had permeated the fallen layers of the building where the children had hidden served as a stark warning of what bombs could do, and her heart started to pound. Then there was no more time to think, or to do anything but *move* as he pulled her along with him in the exact opposite direction everybody else was trying to go in. She stumbled over a discarded item and he switched his grip from her right wrist to her left hand and said, "Get behind me and hold on to my jacket."

She understood, and did as he said, locking her fingers with the hard length of his and sliding in behind him. Grabbing his jacket with her free hand, she stuck as close as the tail on a kite while, moving fast, he shoved tables and chairs and anything else out of their path.

"Everyone can't fit through the door at once! Form an orderly line!" The man with the torch sounded exasperated. He'd jumped off the stage, and from the motion of the light it appeared he was now wading into the crowd trying to direct everyone toward where another torch seemed to be waving people through the door.

"Don't let go," Schneider warned her as he abandoned the wall to skirt what felt like a large, fixed piece of furniture. Hanging on to him for dear life, Elin shook her head in a fervent promise before she remembered that he couldn't see her, or anything at all. What sounded like a bottle crashed to the floor right in front of her and shattered, and she guessed he'd knocked it off. It was absinthe; she recognized the bittersweet smell even as she sidestepped in an attempt to avoid the broken glass.

"One person at a time through the door!" the man with the torch yelled. The torch's meager light bobbing through the crowd was the only thing providing any illumination at all and that was confined to the few meters in its immediate vicinity. Without it and its position as a point of reference, she would have felt hopelessly disoriented. But Schneider clearly had a goal in mind, and so she left it to him to get them safely out of there and concentrated on staying on her feet while at the same time trying to maintain a radar-like awareness of anyone who might be closing in on them in the dark.

Something the size of a small table hurtled past. From the way Schneider was moving she thought he'd thrown it and the chairs that went with it out of the way. The smell of absinthe lingered; some must have gotten on her shoes. Her shoulder brushed the exposed brick and that's how she knew they were once again beside the wall.

"Whatever you do, don't let go of me," he said, and pulled his hand from hers.

She almost squeaked in protest, but instead she grabbed on to the back of his jacket with both hands. A moment later he stopped abruptly. She bumped into his broad back and stayed pressed up against him, trying to sense where she couldn't see, sending out feelers for anyone coming close, listening to the voices and confusion in the room and the shrieking of the siren and the barking of the flak. At the same time she fought to control her breathing and her heartbeat and all her bodily responses that equaled fear, because the mind was affected by the body. Experiencing fear sensations physically would feed into her emotional reaction to the external stimuli and cloud her ability to use her senses to monitor the space around them. She could feel the flexing of the muscles in his back and the bunching of his arms as he did whatever he was doing even as she focused beyond the two of them.

Was anybody close? Was that sound a footstep coming up behind her? She tensed, instinctively looking back and trying not to panic at the knowledge that even if someone was there and getting ready to, say, plunge a knife into her back she wouldn't know it because she couldn't *see*.

Gooseflesh prickled up and down her arms. Tensing, she was

trying to make herself as small a target as possible when she felt a rush of air that was different in temperature and quality from the rest. Instantly Schneider was on the move again, pulling her with him, through the barrier that was the brick wall. Only the wall was no longer there and she realized they'd gone through, not the wall but a door. They were near the stage door, the one they'd seen Storch emerge from.

He stopped, and she had to stop, too, crowded between his back and another brick wall. A soft whoosh behind her was the sound of the door closing, shutting them off from the crowd in the other room. That made her feel safer from a possible unseen assailant at the same time as it muffled the human-created tumult behind them. Meanwhile, all hell sounded like it was breaking loose in the skies outside.

Kaboom! Louder than the rest, the sound made her jump.

"What was that?" Her voice was even, calm. Far calmer than she felt.

"A bomb. From the sound of it, the airplanes are getting closer. Don't move, you don't want to fall down the stairs," Schneider said, and even as the thought of a bomb dropping somewhere not too far away sent her pulse racing she remembered they were on the third floor and in a stairwell, which was not a good place to be in the pitch dark. She smelled the cigarette before she saw it, saw a red glow and realized that it belonged to a half-smoked butt that he had inexplicably lifted to his mouth, watched it burn brighter as he puffed away. Even as he brought the butt back to life she deduced that he must have snagged it from an ashtray on their way out and frowned.

"What are you *doing*?" she asked, and he pulled the cigarette from his mouth.

"Getting us down the stairs."

Seconds later, all was explained as he held the cigarette tip to the end of something in his hands and it caught fire. She smelled absinthe, saw the wetness that reached halfway up the dangling loop of cloth, and realized he'd grabbed a tablecloth, managed to soak up enough of the spilled absinthe with it to help it burn, then twisted it into a loop so that it would be manageable. The flame as the cloth caught at the apex of the loop was small and blue but cast enough light to reveal that they were standing on a rickety landing at the top of a narrow brick chute with steep wooden steps leading down into utter blackness.

Kaboom!

She shuddered as he dropped the cigarette, ground it under his shoe.

"Grab on. This fire's going to burn itself out quick." With a lightning glance at her, meant, she thought, to determine if she was ready, he headed down the stairs, fast but not suicidally so, holding the burning tablecloth out in front of him to light their way. She followed right behind him, clinging to the tail of his coat and the rail and being careful where she put her feet. Shadows leaped around them. The flames licked away at the cloth and the smell of the burning absinthe filled the air. The chattering flak seemed to have no effect on the louder explosions that were the bombs, which were coming faster and sounding closer, turning her insides to jelly.

"Dammit!" Fiery tendrils shot up the cloth, making his arm jerk and putting his hand holding it at risk, as they reached the tiny vestibule at the foot of the stairs. It was clear that at any second the makeshift torch was going to flame out and they would be left in the dark.

"Hurry," she said as he went for the heavier of the two doors set into the brick walls surrounding them. It clearly led to the outside, probably to a back garden or such. She couldn't wait to go through it and out into the moonlight that would at least allow them to see their surroundings. The thought of being trapped in total darkness at the bottom of the chimneylike stairwell with bombs dropping all around filled her with alarm, but that was mere seconds away from happening, she feared.

"It's locked. Try that one." He sounded tense as, still twisting the knob, he put his shoulder with force to the wood panel. It didn't budge, and she faced the hard truth that there was no escaping that way. And even if they could have gotten outside, Elin realized as she pushed open the second door, the big booms were louder now, ominously loud, thunderclaps amid the chattering flak. She might not be familiar with air raids but common sense told her that meant the bombs were getting closer and what they needed to do right now was take shelter, not escape into the night.

"It's a storage room." She tried to keep any hint of incipient panic out of her voice. As a shelter, this space, basically no more than a closet with, to make it worse, an outside wall, seemed less than ideal, but the only other choice was to go back up the stairs, which really wasn't a choice at all. He swung around to look. The sputtering torchlight lit up a small, windowless room filled with what seemed to be discarded furniture. There was no time to see anything more because the makeshift torch flared bright as a bonfire for a second and then, as he yelped and dropped it, went out. A black and impenetrable darkness engulfed them.

"Inside," he said over a stomping sound that she guessed was him making sure any smoldering remains of cloth were out by pounding them into the floor before wrapping an arm around her waist and sweeping her ahead of him into the room.

"Shouldn't we be underground?" It was impossible to keep the anxiety out of her voice.

"You ever hear the saying about beggars?"

Can't be choosers, she finished it mentally even as she heard the door close and then the snick of a lock.

"You locked the door?"

"We don't want any surprises."

As in a visit from the killer, she knew. They were moving forward, groping their way along the wall. She stumbled into a stack of what felt like wooden chairs and hit her shin and said, *"Ouch."*

A huge explosion, the biggest one of all, shook the building.

Staggering sideways, she sucked in air, pitched up against the inner brick wall—and realized that his arm had dropped away.

"Kurt?"

Another blast almost knocked her off her feet.

She could hear him. He was swearing under his breath.

"You all right?" he asked.

"Where are you?" She was breathing way too fast, but she couldn't help it. Trying to stay calm was one thing but actually doing it was another.

"Here. Give me a minute."

A thud, the scrape of heavy furniture across a wooden floor—he was shoving something big, she thought—and then his hand found her wrist. She grabbed on to him just as another bomb hit.

The blast was enormous. Both of them were knocked off balance by the force of it. As, together, they lurched into the wall, she bit her lip to keep from crying out.

"Get down. Crawl under the table." He pushed her to her knees as he spoke, came down with her, guiding her with a hand on her back as she scrambled beneath what from the size of its legs felt like a substantial table, a trestle table, the kind of big, sturdy table that might be found in a farmhouse kitchen. Something that might protect them if, say, the ceiling were to collapse.

Oh, God, she hoped it wouldn't come to that.

Kaboom. Kaboom. Kaboom. Kaboom.

She started at every blast but managed to sit down with her back against the inner wall. He settled in beside her. The feel of his big body pressed close against her side gave her an anchor in what had become a sightless, nightmare world.

"How long does something like this usually last?" She tried to keep the breathlessness out of her voice.

"Depends. Could be twenty, thirty minutes. Could be longer." A new edge to his voice told her that he was less sanguine than he pretended. Her chest tightened. If *he* was afraid…

"What's that sound?" It was an ominous rumble, a droning, low-pitched roar, audible even over the shrieking sirens and barking flak, and it made the hair rise on the back of her neck.

"Airplanes. A lot of them." He sounded like he was talking through his teeth.

"Coming our way?"

He didn't answer, but he didn't have to. If they were that loud, the answer was *yes*, and they had to be close.

Another bomb hit, and another, and another, in quick succession. The screaming sounds they made as they fell had her biting her lip to keep from screaming in turn. Cringing with every hit, instinctively trying to make herself as small as possible, she pulled her legs up against her chest, wrapped her arms around them, and dropped her head to rest on her knees. Despite her best effort not to, she must have made some small, distressed sound because he hooked an arm around her and pulled her close. She went willingly—no, gladly—abandoning any thought of trying to maintain some semblance of professional distance as the world seemingly blew up around them. Pulse slamming in her ears, she huddled against his side, wrapping her arms around the solid muscles of his waist and burying her face in the broad shelf of his shoulder and closing her eyes, finding comfort in the hard arms wrapped so firmly around her, in his warmth and solid strength, in the very fact of his presence there with her in the dark.

Neither of them spoke. For her part, she couldn't. Her throat was tight with fear. Her heart pounded so hard that, close as they were, she feared he might feel its urgent rhythm. Gritting her teeth, she thought of Niles, tried *not* to think of Niles because all that did was make her more afraid, and prayed that a bomb wouldn't land on top of them.

The explosions came without pause now, deafeningly loud and terrifying. The building shook with every crash. The air pressure changed dramatically, making her ears pop and ring.

An acrid burning smell told her that something—please, God, not the building!—was on fire nearby. The droning overhead grew so loud she could feel it as vibrations in the air, so loud she thought that the wave of airplanes responsible for it must be passing directly overhead.

A tremendous blast hit. Its massive wave of pressure slammed them back against the wall, blew the table sheltering them a good meter up in the air before dropping it back down with a thud in the same position as before. The furniture piled against the outer wall went flying. Tables and chairs crashed all around them with sharp smacks and cracks and the sound of splintering wood. Debris rattled down on the top of the table so fast and hard it sounded like gunfire. The entire building shook, the floor jumped beneath them, and the wall behind them undulated like the surface of the sea.

Ducking, cowering, holding her breath, Elin waited for the building to fall on their heads.

Instead, the man whose arms were wrapped around her, whose head and shoulders had curved protectively above her as the worst of it hit, made a harsh sound under his breath and began to shake.

20

"KURT?" ELIN LIFTED HER HEAD TO LOOK AT HIM, WHICH was useless in the pitch dark.

He didn't answer. But his body had tensed against her, his arms had gone iron hard around her, and his head had fallen back to rest against the wall. She could feel his distress in everything from the rigidity of his muscles to the heavy rasp of his breathing.

"Are you hurt?" Even as she asked it, his arms dropped away from her and he took a deep, harsh breath in what she thought was a vain effort to control the tremors that racked him. Alarmed, she sat upright and turned toward him, unable to see so much as the white of his shirt where her hands had flattened against his broad chest. His shoulder holster was there; she could feel the wide leather strap nudging the side of her hand with his every labored breath. Then her alarm turned to outright fear and she forgot about everything else as without her support he slid sideways and continued to shake violently from head to toe.

"What's happened?" Fright sharpened her voice.

When he didn't answer, her heart turned over at the thought that he might have been hit by a shard of wood sent flying from a piece of broken furniture, or a bomb fragment that had pierced the brick wall. Clambering onto her knees beside him, she conducted a quick examination as best she could. He lay on his side facing her in a semi-fetal position, arms pressed close to his chest, fists clenched, legs bent, trembling like an aspen in the wind. She ran questing hands over his face, his neck, his body without detecting any telltale wetness that might indicate blood, any sign of a projectile or injury. If he felt her hands on him or had any awareness of her or what she was doing, he gave no sign of it.

"Kurt? Can you hear me?"

He didn't answer. His pulse, taken below the ear, was rapid, but with her limited tools of touch and hearing she could detect no sign of a heart attack or other medical emergency. His forehead was damp with sweat. His eyes were closed. His cheeks were warm, rough with stubble, with tense underlying jaw muscles that made her think his teeth might be clenched. His lips were parted and taut rather than soft, and he audibly sucked in air between them. Even as she finished her frantic inspection and fought back panic over the lack of results, she noted with relief that his tremors seemed to be subsiding and his muscles were losing some of their rigidity. His breathing was less stertorous—

Another huge bomb detonated, knocking her off balance with its blast wave and setting the floor to rocking beneath them and every loose item in the room flying and crashing around them. She scrambled back onto her knees beside him even before the sound of the explosion died away. In the few seconds it had taken her to recover, his condition had deteriorated again, she discovered with a fresh upsurge of alarm as she placed a searching hand against his neck. She counted his pulse at well over 120 beats per minute. He was breathing like he was finding it impossible to get enough air and trembling uncontrollably.

"What is wrong with you?" Terror sharpened the question as she hovered over him with no idea what to do or how to help him, because she couldn't *see* and anything she attempted might only make things worse. He didn't reply, but a desperate review of the sequence of events that had led to him being in this state, coupled with some things she knew about him, gave her a glimmer of insight into what might possibly be the answer.

According to Frau Skelton, he'd been sent to the front, which almost certainly meant he'd been heavily involved in the fighting. A raised red scar from a relatively fresh bullet wound still marked his forehead. And he'd only recently returned to the Kripo, which seemed to indicate that he'd only recently recovered enough to work.

What that possibly added up to was combat fatigue. The concept wasn't new. In the Great War it had been called shell shock. Described in medical literature as far back as Hippocrates, it was a soldier's delayed reaction to the horrors of war.

It fit his symptoms.

With that diagnosis, she was able to largely put aside her fear that she was missing some catastrophic physical injury. What she was dealing with was, she thought, an injury to the mind and the soul.

"It's all right." She rested a comforting hand against his cheek. "You're all right. You're safe, and you're not alone. I'm here."

If he heard her, if he was able to make sense of her words, she couldn't tell. She loosened his tie, unfastened his collar. Then she repositioned herself and lifted his head so that instead of quivering against the floor it rested in her lap.

The noise outside continued to be earsplitting, the massive explosions violent and so close together that it was impossible to tell where one ended and another began. Terror quickened her own breathing, made her heart pound and her stomach knot.

Bracing against it, she endured, talking calmly to him all the while, stroking his face, his arm, his back, so he would know he wasn't alone. She was there with him in whatever dark hell he was trapped in, although she had no idea if he was aware enough to register her words or touch.

After what seemed like an eternity, the worst of the bombardment appeared to be ending. The explosions grew more distant until eventually the ground didn't shake at their impact, and she stopped being deathly afraid that the building was going to disintegrate around them at any minute. The flak continued unabated, but it, too, sounded farther away, while the wailing sirens seemed to lose some of their urgency.

She was so intent on keeping track of the position of the falling bombs that she didn't immediately notice that the tenor of his breathing had changed, that he was lying motionless with his head heavy in her lap, that his tremors had stopped.

"My God, I'm sorry," he said in a low, harsh voice, and rolled onto his back. Instantly her focus was all on him.

"You have nothing to be sorry about," she said. "Are you all right?"

He gave an affirmative-sounding grunt.

His head still rested in her lap, and she checked his pulse by placing two fingers along the side of his neck. It still raced but not to the same degree as before. His breathing came fast and shallow, but the muscles in his neck and jaw were no longer rigid, and he was no longer experiencing any tremors as far as she could tell.

"Are you in pain?" She was being cautious in case her tentative diagnosis was wrong.

He replied with a side-to-side movement of his head that she took as a no.

"I'm assuming this has happened to you before?"

"Once or twice." His voice still wasn't his own. It remained thick and hoarse, but also sounded infinitely weary. She inferred from it that he was downplaying the number of times he'd experienced such episodes.

"During air raids?"

"Sometimes. Usually I make sure to be alone."

A touch of wryness had crept in to that last, and from it she deduced that tonight's particular circumstances—he hadn't felt able to leave her to her own devices because of the possible danger posed by the killer—had kept him from isolating himself. And the corollary to that was that he'd been hoping against hope he wouldn't have an attack.

"It's called combat fatigue," she said. "It's extremely common among soldiers who've been in battle, I believe. Particularly those who've been wounded."

He didn't answer. From the quality of his silence, from his posture, from a dozen nonverbal, nonvisual cues, she gleaned that he was deeply embarrassed by what he undoubtedly considered his weakness—and by the fact that she had witnessed it.

"I am a doctor, you know," she said. "And I think you'll find it helps to talk about it. *Have* you talked about it with anyone?"

This time his grunt conveyed a resounding *no*, as if he rejected the idea utterly. She couldn't blame him. Much shame was still attached to a diagnosis of combat fatigue, and prescribed treatments could be brutal. The most modern psychiatric thinking, developed as a result of studies of afflicted Great War veterans, embraced an entirely different approach.

"Maybe you should. Talking can be very therapeutic. And since we're stuck here together—I don't think we can leave yet?" It was more a rhetorical than a real question; the bombs had moved off, but they were still falling not so far away, and the flak was pounding away and the sirens wailed, and from what she'd heard of air raids a second wave was always possible. And given the way he continued to lie there, mostly unmoving with his head still heavy in her lap, she was fairly certain he didn't feel capable of getting up and walking away just yet.

"When the all clear sounds," he said.

"Ah. Well, then, as I was saying, since we're stuck here to-gether, and I'm a doctor, and I've already witnessed the symptoms you exhibit anyway, maybe you should talk about it with *me*."

A profound silence was her answer. His breathing had evened out, and the rise and fall of his chest—her hand still lay flat against his shirtfront, so she knew—felt normal. He was recovering, she could tell. Soon all his internal barriers would be in place again, and he would be back to being his sardonic, closemouthed self. And *this* would once again be shoved into hiding, to eat away at him in secret until conditions inevitably caused it to resurface.

And yet right now they were still caught up together in the strangely intimate bubble that the darkness and the danger and his unexpected vulnerability had created.

I can help him, she thought.

So she tried. Probed a little, asked a leading question.

"I understand you were sent to the front. Which front? Where?"

For a moment she thought he wasn't going to answer. Then she felt his chest move as he took a deeper than normal breath and slowly exhaled.

"The Eastern Front. As part of Operation Barbarossa. I was with the Forty-Sixth Infantry. As a grenadier."

Operation Barbarossa was the bloody, failed invasion of Russia.

"How did you go from being chief of criminal investigations for the Kripo to seeing combat as a grenadier in the Wehrmacht?" Genuine surprise colored her voice. Grenadier was the lowest possible rank, cannon fodder basically. For a man like him to be relegated to such seemed almost inconceivable.

"I got on Heydrich's bad side."

General Reinhard Heydrich, Elin knew, was the former head of the RSHA. Hitler himself had been known to describe him as "the man with the iron heart," and his reputation for excep-tional cruelty to and hatred for all Jews was notorious. His assassination in May of the previous year had been the cause of many a private celebration, including one by Borge and his cronies.

"Some might consider that a badge of honor," she said before she thought.

"Some might," he agreed.

She mulled that over for a moment, unsure of exactly what he'd meant by it. To openly profess a loathing for Heydrich might be construed as criticism of the regime, and to voice any sympathy for the Jews who were his target was enough, if it was overheard or reported, to invite arrest. Intriguing as his response was, she still didn't know him well enough to dare delve any deeper. The risk involved in revealing her own sympathies without being sure of his was simply too great. So she let it lie, and went on.

"You were wounded," she prompted. "How?"

"Mortar," he said. "Shell hit right on top of the two guys next to me. They were blown to smithereens. I took shrapnel to the shoulder, chest, both legs."

That was enough to possibly explain his symptoms. She almost gave herself a figurative pat on the back for drawing it out of him with so little difficulty. But he spoke of it so easily—too easily?

"Were you badly injured?"

"Pretty bad," he agreed.

"Is that when you got the wound to your head?"

The briefest of pauses. "That came later."

Something in his tone, a starkness, an impression of a barrier being raised, told her that this was important.

"Later? When later? Can you tell me what happened?" Her voice was quiet, soothing. With her hand lying flat across the firm muscles just above his sternum, she felt the sudden thump of his heart.

"Later I got the wound to my head."

Ah. There it was. The prickly resistance, the reluctance to go where that memory would take him, told her everything she needed to know. Here was the rabbit hole he didn't want to go down.

"I get the feeling that you don't like revisiting that particular memory."

"I don't."

"And yet you didn't seem to feel a need to avoid revisiting the memory of having a mortar shell explode beside you and being badly wounded as a result."

"That was different."

"How? How was it different?"

She felt the negative jerk of his head and interpreted it as his instinctive rejection of the topic. Through her hand on his chest, she could feel his quickened breathing. She was, instinctively, looking down at him, although she couldn't see a thing. The darkness remained absolute. His silence spoke volumes. *This* was what he needed to talk about; she was almost certain.

"I've seen for myself that it's a bullet wound, you know. Can you tell me how you got it?"

"If you know it's a bullet wound, then you know how I got it. I got shot." His response was abrupt, almost hostile.

"Yes, I understand that. But what I don't understand, and what I'm hoping you'll tell me, are the circumstances. Can you do that, please?" Her tone coaxed him.

He didn't answer. She waited, but the only thing that happened was his breathing evened out and his heartbeat stabilized. Which was what would happen if he was closing himself off from the disturbing memory, locking it away. Perhaps it would be better not to push him, to let it go, but—the longer the trauma remained unaddressed, the more it would damage him.

"You're going to have to talk about what happened sometime, with someone, if you want to stop having these—" she hesitated, searching for the descriptor that was the least stigmatizing "—occurrences. I can help you, I'm almost certain, if you'll let me."

"*Almost* certain? What, are we talking ninety-five percent?"

She took the rasping mockery as an indication that she was aiming in the right direction.

"At least, which is almost as good as one hundred percent," she replied with unruffled composure. "How about we forget the bullet wound for now? Something else I'd really like to know is what happened after you got hit by shrapnel. Who treated you? Was there a field hospital, or...?" She left the question open-ended.

Again she wasn't sure if he was going to answer. Then he made a restless movement and said, "After the battle, the worst of the wounded, including me, were taken to a hospital in Feodosia, near where we'd been fighting. Feodosia's a little town in the Crimea, in case you've never heard of it, that we'd captured earlier. They had doctors, nurses. Equipment."

"Were you there long?"

She felt the negative shake of his head.

"Not long. A few days after we got there, the Russians over-ran our position. It was a hell of a fight, bombs raining down everywhere, mortar fire, hand-to-hand combat in the streets. Of course, those of us tied to a hospital bed couldn't do anything but listen. We didn't even know when our guys retreated. But the Russians took the town and we were left behind. At that point we officially became POWs, but the Russkies didn't see it that way. As far as they were concerned, we were enemy combatants."

He broke off. She felt a rising tension in his body, a kind of heaviness in the air. And she knew she was getting close.

"What happened then?" she asked.

He made another of those restless movements. "God, you don't give up, do you?"

"Only on lost causes. And you're not one."

His answering grunt sounded skeptical, but after a moment he started talking again. "Once the town was theirs, the Russians stormed into the hospital, tossed everybody out of their beds. Unconscious, barely alive, still hooked up to machines, didn't matter. Somebody said they wanted us gone because they needed the hospital for their own wounded. Whatever the reason—if there even was a reason—we were lying there on the floor, 160 men, four wards full, every one of us in a bad way, and this big Ivan came in and started going up and down the rows shooting people point-blank in the head. He would just stop and shoot and go on to the next. Pieces of skull and hair flying everywhere, blood running like rivers, nothing anybody could do. The place was full of Russian soldiers. There was no way to escape, nowhere to go, and most of us, like me, couldn't walk, couldn't stand. With both my legs shot up, I could barely even crawl."

His tone was even, revealing no emotion at all, but that in itself was telling, as was the sharp breath he drew. The horror, the fear, the helplessness he must have felt had been ruthlessly suppressed but it was still there, festering.

"Go on," she said when he didn't. Instinctively, comfortingly, she stroked the firm muscles that she could feel rising and falling with renewed agitation beneath his shirt. A moment later his hand settled over hers, pressing it flat against his body. She felt the warmth and weight of his hand, registered how much bigger it was than hers, and her chest felt tight. Her fingers curled around his so that their hands were entwined.

"Kurt," she said into the silence. Her voice was incredibly gentle. "Please tell me."

She heard him take another of those sharp breaths.

"He started ordering brave soldiers to beg. For their lives. As he stood over them. And they did. They cried and they begged. Most of them he shot anyway, whether they begged or not. Maybe one time out of ten he'd walk on, wouldn't shoot. You could tell it was a game to him. Before he got to me, I swore to myself that I wouldn't. Wouldn't demean myself. Wouldn't beg. But then he's standing over me with this big pistol pointed down at my head and he says in this taunting voice, 'You beg good enough, maybe I let you live.' I was lying on my back, looking straight up into his eyes, and I knew that no matter what I said he was going to shoot me."

His voice went low, ragged. "And you know what I did? I begged for my life anyway. Begged like a baby. I thought of my son and all the things I still had left that I wanted to do and I begged that smirking bastard not to shoot me." He made a sudden, restless movement. "That's what comes back to me when I hear the bombs explode. That's what I have a hard time living with. That he broke me."

21

AT THE PAIN IN HIS VOICE, ELIN'S HEART TURNED OVER.
Leaning above him, she curved a protective arm around his
neck. Her hand tightened on his.

"He didn't break you." Her voice was fierce. "You got through
it. You're still here. You're *alive*. That's what you need to tell yourself, anytime those memories start coming back. You're not broken."

The truncated sound he made might have been a laugh. Laced
with bitterness and self-mockery, but a laugh.

"I think the fact that I'm lying here like this with you says
differently."

"Life breaks all of us, in one way or another," she said, still
fierce. "But that doesn't mean we're broken. We heal, and we go
on. Often we become even stronger than before."

"Is that right?" His free hand slid over her arm that was draped across him and settled there, warm and strong. "So how did life break you, *liebling*?"

With her mother, and Lars, and more. But she couldn't tell him about any of that. They were on opposite sides of an unbreachable divide, and there was too much danger involved in letting her guard down even a little bit. And to make the situation even more impossible, something else was happening that was alarming in a whole different way. Because he'd called her *liebling*, which was probably just a lapse on his part into the way he usually talked to women who *weren't* professional colleagues and thus meant nothing, but still; because she liked the way his hand felt on her arm, liked the heat and weight and slight abrasion of it against the silkiness of her skin; because his fingers laced with hers were unmistakably masculine; because the shoulders she was hugging were wide and the back resting against her thigh was broad and the chest beneath their clasped hands was muscular, she was once again suddenly, acutely aware of him as a man. Her pulse quickened and her blood heated and her body tightened deep inside, and those physical reactions rattled her. To her profound dismay, she faced the unwelcome truth that she was indeed attracted to him, hopelessly attracted to him, in a way she hadn't been to any man for a long time.

That kind of complication could ruin her if she wasn't careful.

"I'm not going to let you change the subject. We're not talking about me, we're talking about you." She was proud of how quickly she recovered enough to make an intelligent, unrevealing response. Even as she spoke she was withdrawing, mentally and physically, reminding herself of where they were and *what he was*, removing her arm from his hold, sitting upright, letting go of his hand.

If he noticed her physical disengagement, he gave no sign of it.

"He didn't just walk on, did he?" she asked gently, remembering the scar.

For a moment she thought he wasn't going to respond. Then she felt the negative shake of his head.

"No, he didn't. He pulled the trigger." His tone was flat, the words matter-of-fact. She wondered what it cost him to make them so. "The next thing I remember is waking up outside on the ground, in a pile of bodies. I knew I'd been shot, my head hurt like you wouldn't believe, I was soaked with blood, but I was conscious and aware. Mostly I was just surprised to be alive. I don't know what happened, whether I turned my head at the last second or the bastard got distracted or what, but the shot didn't kill me. Some of the others in the pile were alive, too. They were whimpering, moaning. Pitiful sounds. I recognized a couple of soldiers who'd been in the ward with me. As far as I could tell, they were dead.

"Bodies kept landing with these big, wet thumps on top of the ones that were already there, shifting the pile, sending me sliding toward the edge. Gradually I realized the Russkies were clearing the wards by throwing the dead and the wounded alike out of the hospital windows. It was dark, and freezing cold, just starting to snow. I didn't have much brainpower left, but it didn't take much to figure out that at some point they were going to come out and make sure we were all dead. Another building was close by, and somebody must have been carrying something in or out because the cellar door had been left open. I managed to get out from under all those bodies, then roll and slither my way into that cellar. The snow was coming down harder, and some combination of it and the dark hid me and what I was doing and covered my trail. I got myself behind some big wooden crates in that cellar and I laid up in there.

"After a bit I heard screaming and crying, which is a terrible sound coming from grown men. I didn't hear any shots, I didn't know how it was happening, but I knew that everybody left alive in that pile of bodies was being killed. Later I learned that the same bastards who'd thrown us out the windows poured water over those men. Hosed them down in that glacial weather until they froze to death. Then the murdering bastards left the bodies there, frozen solid, encased in big sheets of ice. I know this because they were still there when the Wehrmacht retook the town."

"How much later was that?" Horror at the murdered soldiers' fate colored her voice.

"Seventeen, eighteen days. After another ferocious battle."

"You stayed hidden in the cellar all that time?"

"If I hadn't, I wouldn't be here. The Russians had issued orders to kill every German in Feodosia."

"How did you manage? What about water? Food?"

"Water wasn't a problem. Melting snow leaked in, puddled on the floor. As for food, one of the crates was empty of everything except a few tins of beets. Apparently no one who wasn't starving to death in a cellar wanted them." What sounded like the barest hint of humor just touched his voice. "By the time I was rescued I'd lost close to a quarter of my body weight. I was coming in and out of consciousness, burning up with fever, hallucinating, seeing double or triple when I could see at all, untreated bullet wound to the head, suppurating shrapnel wounds, unable to walk, barely able to talk.

"I was in such rough shape I was repatriated—sent back to Germany for treatment. The understanding was that I'd be returning to the front if and when I recovered, but I was still in hospital when Heydrich died. After that, the urgency to send me to my death faded. I'd worked with Nebe before, and the Kripo was short of detectives, so he brought me back once I was well enough to be of use. Then this case came up, and he handed it off to me. Glory to him if I solve it, me as a scapegoat if I don't. Smart man, Nebe."

Elin immediately thought of the conversation she'd had with Kaltenbrunner.

"There's something you should know," she said.

"What's that?"

"When I met with General Kaltenbrunner, he asked if I was satisfied with your work." At the time, telling him what Kaltenbrunner had said had felt too risky, and there was still a degree of risk involved if he should tell anyone that she'd repeated Kaltenbrunner's words and thus warned him and put herself squarely on his side. But by now she was as sure as it was possible to be—and that would be ninety-five percent sure, which was an amazing degree of certitude no matter what he thought of it—that he wouldn't tell. That she could trust him. "He said you could be easily replaced if I wanted."

"*Did* he?" He was silent for a moment, then abruptly his head left her lap. She realized that he was levering himself up and into a sitting position beside her. "I take it you told him I was proving satisfactory?"

"Yes."

"Thank you. For telling him that, and for the warning."

Something in his voice had changed. There was a formality to it that was different from any tone he'd used with her before. Whether he was affronted by Kaltenbrunner's offer to have him replaced, the knowledge that she *could* have him replaced, or the fact that she hadn't told him earlier, or was even driven by something else entirely, she had no way of knowing. And, she decided, she didn't want to know. Formality between them was the route she wanted to take. Keeping their relationship strictly professional was the best way forward for both of them.

"You're welcome." Her reply was coolly impersonal in turn. He was moving. She could hear and feel him as he left her side, she thought, to make his way out from under the table. "What are you doing?"

"Clearing a path out. From the way things were flying around in here, there's going to be a lot of debris between us and the door. The worst seems to be over, and we're not going to wait any longer because we don't want to get caught up in the crowd that'll hit the streets once the all clear sounds." He was worried about encountering the killer, she knew. He continued, "For now, you stay where you are. I'm going to be moving things and I don't want to have to worry about accidentally hitting you."

By the time the all clear sounded, they'd made it out of the building through the back door, which had been blown off its hinges by the blast waves. One of the chimneys had collapsed and bricks were scattered around the back of what turned out to be an open storage area, but otherwise the building seemed to be mostly intact, although it was difficult to be sure in the dark. Nearby buildings seemed to have suffered more serious damage, and debris from them, combined with fallen trees and wires, meant they had to stay to the center of the street as they made their way toward his car.

"Do you think Eden will be up and running again by next Saturday?" Elin asked as he hustled her through the billowing clouds of malodorous yellow smoke that drifted everywhere.

"I don't know."

"If that was his primary hunting ground, he'll be looking for another if it isn't available," she said. "It won't change his timeline, I don't think. He's too far into the cycle to pull out unless he has no other choice."

"We'll just have to see, won't we?"

Streams of people emerging from cellars spilled into the street from both sides, but given the smoke and all the confusion, she thought the chances of them being spotted by the killer, if he was even around, were almost nil. One block over, several buildings appeared to have collapsed, while other buildings in the same general vicinity burned ferociously. Orange flames stretching skyward lit the entire area with a hellish glow. Clanging sirens told of fire vehicles on the way. What looked like giant bonfires dotted the skyline in every direction, and she knew what she was seeing was more buildings on fire from the bombs.

"What about Herr Trott and the others?" she asked.

"They'll have taken shelter. I'll get in touch with them later." They reached his car, and he opened her door. "Get in."

She did, glad to escape the smoke. The sulfurous smell of it did not abate. It clung to her hair, her clothes.

"You're still planning to have that building where I found the children searched tomorrow, aren't you?" she asked. He was frowning out into the darkness while driving with extra care because of all the pedestrians and other impediments in the streets.

"I am."

After that terse reply, they didn't speak for the rest of the drive, which was probably for the best. With the ebbing of the adrenaline rush that had kept her going, she was beyond tired. Anxiety over Niles, and the fact that she'd been targeted by the killer, and all the horrible things happening in the world in general, had her stomach in a knot. She distracted herself by looking out the window. The damage left by the bombs was extensive, with fires and destruction spread out across the city. Fresh craters in the streets and the crush of traffic as emergency vehicles rushed to and from afflicted areas and drivers had to find alternate routes around blockages meant that progress was slow. Unter den Linden seemed to have escaped harm. As they headed toward Grunewald Forest she saw that that area, too, appeared largely untouched.

When they reached the Waldschloss, she expected him to leave her in the lobby as he'd done before, under the disinterested eye of the clerk on duty. But instead, with a clipped "Humor me" when she protested, saying it wasn't necessary, he walked her up to her room. He stood silently as she opened the door to the comfortable bed/sitting combination that had been assigned to her after the first night and hit the light switch, which turned on the small lamp on the table beside the bed.

Elin then stopped dead a few paces inside her room, eyes glued to the bed as the thin white blanket that was the only covering on it in deference to the heat bunched and moved.

A pace or so behind her, Schneider stepped sideways so that she no longer stood between him and who or whatever was beneath the blanket.

Before he could react in any other way, it became obvious that there was no need. Blond hair tousled, face flushed with sleep, wearing her favorite blue pajamas, Pia sat up in the middle of the bed.

"What *time* is it?" She blinked owlishly at Elin.

"About half past three." Elin put her bag down on a chair near the door. "Why are you sleeping in my room instead of yours?"

"I was waiting for you. I was worried. You were attacked earlier. There was an *air raid*. Are you all right?"

"I'm fine. What about you?"

"Apparently no bombs hit around here. Although we did have to hide for about an hour in the cellar." Pia frowned. "What's *he* doing here?"

"He walked me up."

"Pia? Elin? I heard voices. Anything wrong?" Jens appeared in the doorway. His big frame would have been intimidating if he'd looked less like a slightly befuddled polar bear. His fair hair was mussed as if he'd been running his fingers through it in frustration, he wore glasses that were perched halfway down his nose, and he was frowning. He was still dressed in the trousers and shirt he'd worn earlier, although his shirt was unbuttoned at the neck and the sleeves were rolled up to his elbows, and he was in stocking feet. Schneider's presence—she didn't think Jens had spotted him yet—shot to the forefront of Elin's mind. She was jolted by a shaft of fear as she was reminded of how catastrophic it would be if he should notice that Jens was injured.

"Why are you still awake?" Pia asked him.

At the same time Elin, having made a lightning assessment and concluded to her relief that Jens's bandages weren't visible through his shirt, and hoping to get rid of one of the two men before anything could occur that would make the injury apparent, said, "No, nothing's wrong. You can go back to—" bed was obviously the wrong call "—whatever you were doing."

Replying to Pia, Jens said, "I'm still working on those cursed codes," even as Schneider made a movement that attracted his attention. Jens's expression cycled through alarm, suspicion, and distrust, before landing on utter blankness, all in the space of about a second as he saw Schneider and, to Elin's eyes at least, obviously considered the possibility of discovery.

"Making any progress?" Schneider asked Jens, no hint of anything out of the ordinary in his voice. Elin looked at him, really looked at him, for the first time since the lights had gone out in the club. He was grimy from smoke and their time in the storage room, which made her think that she must be, too. A day's worth of stubble darkened his jaw, his collar was open, and his tie hung loose. He looked tough, disreputable, far more crook than cop. Her heart—stupid, heedless organ—stupidly, heedlessly quickened.

He must have felt her looking at him, because his head turned in her direction. Their eyes met. His were impossible to read. She hoped hers were, too.

"You lost your hat," she said without thinking as his bare head registered.

"I have others."

He turned back to Jens, who, in response to whatever look Schneider gave him, said, "Some. Enough to know there's not a single root."

The code. They were talking about solving the code.

"You mind showing me?" Schneider asked.

"It's the middle of the night." Pia's squeaky protest—she'd apparently registered the danger, too—beat out Elin's "Oh, not right now. After everything that's happened, we all need sleep" by a fraction of a second.

"I'm going to be up for a while. From the looks of it, you are, too. Might as well make use of the time," Schneider said to Jens, who, bowing to what he no doubt felt was the inevitability of it, nodded and replied, "My room's right next door, if you want to have a look."

While Elin despaired, and Pia looked like she'd swallowed

an unshelled egg whole, Schneider said to Elin, "I'll be around if you need me. Be down in the lobby at eleven tomorrow. And remember what I said."

That would be, *Until we get this figured out, don't go outside the hotel without an approved escort.*

She nodded. What else could she do? To protest too much now would only invite suspicion.

"Lock the door," Schneider said, stepping into the hall with Jens, and waited while she did so. A moment later Elin heard the sound of Jens's door being opened and closed.

"Oh, my God," Pia whispered as Elin turned to look at her. "What if he notices?"

"I couldn't see the bandages. Let's hope he won't, either."

"Tell me *everything*." Wide-awake now, Pia sat cross-legged in the middle of the bed.

"It's late. I'm filthy. I have to get ready for bed," she protested as she headed for the en suite bathroom, because it was true, and also because she wanted to head off what she knew from long experience would be Pia's relentless interrogation.

"You can talk while you do it, can't you?" Pia called after her.

Sighing inwardly, Elin abandoned all hope of avoiding Pia's questions entirely and instead, in response to relentless prompting, gave her friend a highly edited account of her evening.

Pia fell silent as she finished in the bathroom, and as she walked back into the bedroom Elin saw she was curled up against the pillows sound asleep.

Elin thought about waking her up, but instead she crossed to the room's large, mullioned front window that overlooked the courtyard. Flicking aside the heavy damask curtain, she glanced down. There was enough moonlight to allow her to see that Schneider's car was still parked there.

She was about to turn away from the window when she saw him. He was nothing more than a dark shape moving swiftly through the night, but for her, now, he was impossible to mistake for anyone else. Just as he'd done before, he crossed the road in front of the hotel and disappeared into the inky blackness of the forest.

She sucked in air. What could he possibly be doing in Grunewald Forest in the middle of the night?

Dropping the curtain, Elin turned away from the window. Whatever drew him to the forest she did *not* want to know about, she reminded herself grimly.

And she cursed the stupid quickening of her foolish heart.

22

TO HER SURPRISE AND DESPITE EVERYTHING SHE'D BEEN
through, Elin slept the sleep of the dead, only to wake up not
long after dawn with Niles's name on her lips. She couldn't remember the dream that woke her, but it left her with a panicky
feeling that she knew only talking with her child would ease.
She was afraid to use the telephone in her room in case her calls
were being monitored so she got dressed and went downstairs.
She placed a call from a pay telephone kiosk located in a corner
of the lobby as soon as she felt she could reasonably expect Hilde
or the Rasks to be awake. No one answered her several attempts,
which shook her to her core.

Pia came down the stairs with Jens behind her just as Elin gave
up and stepped out of the kiosk. They were heading to breakfast
in the small restaurant off the lobby, and Elin joined them. Most
of the tables were full, and the restaurant was abuzz, with din-

ers leaning in and talking among themselves about something that was obviously both important and sensitive.

"The Allied invasion of Italy is failing."

"How do you know? It's not in any of the papers."

"Heard it on the BBC." That was said in a hushed whisper.

"*Shh.* Don't say that."

Listening to the BBC was strictly forbidden, as everyone knew. After overhearing that snippet of conversation, Elin, Pia, and Jens exchanged worried glances over their menus. What a collapse of the Allied invasion of Italy would mean for Denmark, for all of them, was instantly on their minds.

"Is this the beginning of the end, do you think?" Pia whispered. Elin and Jens both knew what she meant—the end of the war.

"Oh, please don't let them lose," Elin replied. To hope for an Allied victory was such a dangerous sentiment that her voice was scarcely louder than a breath.

"In the meantime, I'm afraid there'll be massive crackdowns." Jens sounded worried. He'd already told them, as they'd walked into the restaurant, that Schneider had stayed with him for only about twenty minutes last night and seemed to suspect nothing. The entire time, he'd been wondering if he'd have to kill the Kripo detective if he'd found him out. Or if he even could, because the other man, while smaller, was fit *and* armed. The possibility that the two men might end up in a fight to the death had never occurred to Elin, and it filled her with a mixture of horror and dread. Which encapsulated her problem right there: she and Schneider might be working closely together, she might be attracted to him, she might even like him—but they were enemies, firmly entrenched on either side of an unbreachable divide.

"Where did he go after that? Did he leave?" Pia had asked. Elin could have enlightened her about what she'd seen, but she didn't. Instead, she merely shrugged. She wasn't so much preserving his secrets as staying out of anything that might involve them in something they had no need to get involved in, she told herself.

As they ate, taking care to choose her words carefully in case someone should overhear, she told Pia and Jens about her unanswered calls to Smukkeso. After they'd finished what turned out to be a hurried breakfast, Pia placed a call to her mother and Jens telephoned his brother. Neither knew anything of Niles's and Hilde's whereabouts, although Pia's mother said that as far as anyone could tell the Meitners' house was unoccupied. Jens's brother said that Borge and Chancellor Kessel were still being held. And that the atmosphere in Copenhagen was deteriorating fast.

"They might have gone to stay with someone else," Pia said to Elin in an attempt to provide comfort, and Jens pointed out that if Hilde, with or without Niles, had been taken into custody by the authorities his brother would know about it.

"Pieter promised to check with some contacts of his. He should have more information soon," Jens added.

That wasn't enough to calm Elin's fear, but she had to accept it for the moment because there was nothing else any of them could do. She could only trust Hilde to keep Niles safe.

After that, Jens went upstairs to continue working on decoding the letters. He was making some progress, he reported, having reverted to trying the simplest possible method in which he substituted the most commonly used letters in the alphabet for the most commonly appearing figures in the code. It was slow going, involving a lot of guesswork to fill in the gaps, but it seemed to be working so far, and that, he said, had been enough to impress Detective Schneider. That it also required quiet and concentration continued to be true, and additionally served as the perfect excuse to keep him away from the Alex and any too-curious eyes for as long as possible. His wound was healing well, but if suspicion were to fall on him and he were to be subject to a strip search, the jig would be up. And that thought terrified them all.

"I must say, after the way you were attacked last night I think our brave *capitan* is right to insist that you have a police officer follow you around," Pia said as they walked into the lobby. Elin had no doubt that "brave *capitan*," uttered derisively, referred to Schneider. Pia was going into the Alex, too, where she was to meet up with Detective Beckman. Together they were visiting all the victims' families, employers, teachers, classes, anyone who came into regular contact with the victims to inquire about any men who might have been hanging around them shortly before or after their deaths. If anyone of interest was mentioned, Pia was to draw them. If any of the drawings matched, that individual immediately went high on their suspect list. "He might be kind of a jerk, but at least he's trying to keep you safe."

He's not so bad, Elin almost said, but didn't.

As it turned out, it was Trott who was waiting for them in the lobby.

The flutter of disappointment Elin felt upon seeing the older man was a surprise. An unwelcome surprise that she quickly squelched.

To compensate, the smile of greeting she directed at Trott was extra warm.

"Huh, I thought you only smiled like that when you saw the BC. Good to see you're spreading it around," Pia whispered. It took Elin a second to realize that the BC—brave *capitan*—once again referred to Schneider. "What do you suppose happened to *him*?"

Caught by surprise, flustered at her friend's perspicacity, knowing that any denial of smiling warmly at Schneider would only give Pia more interest in exploring the reason behind her denial, Elin studiously ignored the first part of Pia's remark.

"I'm sure *Detective Schneider* had something he needed to do." Her tone was repressive.

"So why not send Officer Lutts?"

"Women police officers don't carry guns." No more needed to be said. After last night, the very real danger had become all too apparent.

She was still trying to figure out why she in particular had been targeted by the killer. The attack had felt so personal— could it have been because of her reputation? Had the thought that "Dr. Murder" with all her vaunted expertise was on his trail motivated the killer to preemptively try to eliminate the threat? Or was there something else?

Before she could come to any kind of solid conclusion, they reached Trott and the topic got pushed to the back of her mind amid the greetings and small talk as they walked outside. The day was sunny but the weather had turned cool, which was only to be expected. Despite the recent heat, it was September, after all.

"I got here about seven. Kurt left shortly after that," Trott said in response to Pia's inquiry as he opened the car door for them. "He said to tell *you*—" he looked at Elin as she slid into the car "—that he'll see you later at the Alex."

"You've known Herr Schneider a long time, haven't you?" Pia asked him curiously as they drove away from the hotel. For once, Elin blessed Pia's uninhibited personality. Even more than Pia, she wanted details on Schneider's background.

"He used to work for me, when he first came on board the Kripo. That would be, oh, about twelve years ago, right about the time the banking crisis hit. He was twenty-seven, fresh out of the army with a wife and a little kid. Things were bad all over, and he was glad to get the job. But he was good at it. He got promoted, I got old, the world went to hell, we both lost everything, and here we are, together again. I keep telling him, we're like Laurel and Hardy. Only most of the time what we do isn't so funny."

He broke off. "Would you look at that? Something's going on at the Tiergarten." He braked, then drove slowly around a line of vehicles parked in the road. His window was down, and he yelled out at the men unloading what looked like large nets from a truck. "What's the trouble?"

"Bomb hit near the zoo. Some of the animals got loose, and they're running free in the park."

"*Heiliger Strohsack!* Good luck to you." He waved and drove on.

From there on in the damage was bad. Whole neighborhoods near the Tempelhof airport were almost entirely wiped out. Fires still smoldered around Potsdamer Platz and east of that area, and smoke from the bombings had left a yellow haze over much of Mitte.

"Kurt told me to take you directly to the Alex." Trott shook his head when Elin asked him to drive by the bombed-out building where she had been attacked and where, presumably, Schneider would be directing a search. "That area got hit again last night. There was a fire, but as soon as it was out Kurt sent men in to search the building you were in and retrieve what they could. There wasn't much, but what there was we had taken to the Alex. Come to think of it, Kurt's probably at the Alex by now, too. Anyway, he told me to take you there and nowhere else. And what he says, I do."

Schneider wasn't there, but to her surprise Officer Lutts was, waiting beside Frau Skelton's desk with orders from Detective Schneider, she said, to stay close to Elin while she was inside the building. A moment's reflection reminded Elin that it was all but certain now that the killer was a policeman or had police connections and would thus presumably have access to the Alex. If she were alone in, say, the evidence room or the lab or the ladies' room, it wouldn't be impossible for the killer to take her unaware, and a murder by stabbing or strangulation could be accomplished quickly and silently. While Officer Lutts wasn't armed, she would serve as a witness as well as another person to shout or fight, and in a busy building such as the Alex that should be enough to deter an attacker. Therefore, Elin didn't

argue as Trott handed her off. Pia left with Detective Beckman, and Elin, with Officer Lutts in tow, headed for the evidence room, where she was told two large cardboard boxes of
items salvaged from the passageways in the bombed-out building waited. They were stacked side by side on the floor at the
back of the room. Elin grabbed a pair of gloves from the supply
closet near the door and headed toward the boxes.

As soon as she lifted the lid off the first box the smell of
smoke wafted out—and she saw the little girl's oversize, flower-
embroidered sweater.

She started to reach for it, then remembered Officer Lutts and
stopped. With no idea what she might find, she was instinctively
wary of having someone watch. Especially someone who might
report everything she saw and learned back to her superiors.

The policewoman sat placidly at the table in the center of the
room, her hands folded on the smooth wooden surface in front
of her, her eyes glued to Elin.

Putting the lid back on the box, Elin turned toward her.

"While I'm busy with this, you can start making an inven-
tory of the supply closet." Elin's manner was brisk. Whether or
not she was technically Officer Lutts's boss, she was going to
behave as if she were. Directing the woman to grab a notebook
and pen, she set her to writing down everything in the supply
closet, which was a walk-in with jam-packed floor-to-ceiling
shelves. With the door open, they were still technically in the
same room, and as the closet was right next to the door to the
hall it would be impossible for anyone to enter without Officer
Lutts hearing them, but the angles were such that Elin would
be able to examine the contents of the boxes in privacy.

This time, when she crouched down and took the lid off the
box, she was prepared for the sweater.

It was a cardigan, she saw as she lifted it out, hand knit from
a beautiful, soft yarn that was originally cream-colored but was
now grubby and stained. The buttons were blue, although sev-

eral were broken. Unfolding it, she spread it across her knees as she admired the riotous display of oversize pink, blue, and yellow flowers scattered across the front of the sweater from shoulders to hem. Someone had put a lot of work into creating an exquisitely embroidered garden. The sweater itself had obviously been made for an adult, and again she found herself hoping that someone like the children's grandmother had knit it. Thrusting a hand into each of the two patch pockets, she found a photograph in the second one. It was of a family group, six people: an old couple, a young couple, two small children.

Nothing was ever one hundred percent certain, but given the ages, genders, and general characteristics of the children, she was almost positive that the photo was of them and their parents and grandparents. Something was written on the back—

As she turned the photo over to get a better look at the writing, the sweater slipped to one side, and the light hit the knit differently. Elin found herself looking at an area on the left front shoulder that was surprisingly clean, as though it had been protected from the elements in a way the rest of the sweater had not. The clean patch was at the top of a green stem where it seemed as though a flower should have been, but—

It was in the shape of a six-pointed star.

Elin froze, staring, as blood began to pound in her ears.

She tucked the photo safely away in her own pocket, then touched the silky wool, tracing the shape.

On the opposite shoulder, the right shoulder, an identical green stem ended in a vibrant pink flower.

The shape on the left side was no flower.

Tiny remnants of thread at points along its edges where something had been snipped away left no possibility for error.

What had once been sewn to the sweater's left shoulder was the Star of David: the bright yellow badge with the word Jew in the center of it that the Nazis had decreed that all Jews over the age of six must wear. From a distance, she had no doubt that it would have looked like just another flower, and that, obviously, had been the sweater maker's intent.

Were the children Jews?

The possibility shook her.

Of course, they could have found the sweater, but everything from how thin and scared and bedraggled they looked, to the fact that two obviously once-beloved young children had been left to survive in the streets, to the policeman chasing them through bombed-out ruins at night, pointed to *yes*.

She suspected that they were two of the U-boats Kurt had been talking about.

The thought with all its implications was staggering.

What should she do?

"This box is full of tweezers, pins, needles—all kinds of things," Officer Lutts called out to her from the closet, making her jump. "Must I list each item separately, or can I write down something like, box of equipment?"

"Separately," Elin pulled herself together enough to call back. Separately, because she needed all the time she could get. Glancing around to make sure that she was still unobserved, she bunched the sweater up and took it over to her bag, which rested on the table.

Quickly she stuffed it inside and closed the bag up again so the sweater couldn't be seen.

Her heart raced. She felt cold all over.

The thought of anyone else knowing that the children might be Jewish was terrifying.

They would be hunted.

They already *were* being hunted, she suspected, by the killer. And if the policeman she'd heard in the ruins was *not* the killer, they were being hunted by him, too.

Why? Was he a catcher? Was he hunting them *because* they were Jews? Or was there something else?

What she knew for sure was that if anyone even suspected they

were Jews, they would be hunted by the most relentless predator of all—the Gestapo with its enormous web of enforcers and
informers.

If they were caught… She couldn't bear to think about what
would happen to them if they were caught.

Goebbels had gloatingly declared Berlin *Judenrein*.

The Gestapo's mission was to make it so.

They were *children*.

She had to find them before anyone else did.

How? And if she did, then what?

How could she protect them? What could she do?

Something, she told herself. *Something.*

Hurrying back to the boxes, she sank to her knees beside them.
If there was anything else damning in them, she wanted to find
it while she was alone, and before anyone else could look. She
dug in, going quickly through the contents of both boxes, then
sank back on her heels with a sigh of relief. Whether any of the
other items belonged to the children she didn't know, but nothing else bore any evidence that whoever owned it was a Jew.

"These things floating in jars—I don't even know what they
are. How should I list them?" Officer Lutts called, before letting out a squeal of disgust. "Oh, this one's an eyeball. There's
a finger! Oh, my—"

"Don't look. Just list them as jars containing body parts," Elin
said before Officer Lutts could finish. She remembered those
formaldehyde-filled jars well.

When she was sure Officer Lutts wasn't going to pop out of
the closet, she pulled the photo from her pocket to take a closer
look at the writing on the back.

"Zur Letzten Instanz." In the last instance.

The phrase meant nothing to her. She was still frowning when
the door from the hall opened without warning. Crouched in
front of the boxes with her back to the door, she was so startled
by the unmistakable sound that she almost tipped over onto her

backside. Instead she caught herself with a steadying hand on the floor even as her head whipped around to identify the intruder.

Schneider. Their eyes met.

"Who is it? Who is there?" Officer Lutts erupted from the closet, notebook in hand, to plant herself squarely between her charge and the newcomer. Recognizing Schneider, she said, "Oh," in a deflated tone and, turning to Elin, added, "Don't worry. It is safe."

"Thank you," Elin said to her. She was on her feet by this time, with the picture tucked away in her pocket again. Switching her attention to Schneider, she said, "Were you looking for me?"

He nodded. Unsmiling. Professional. Cool. "If you're finished in here, I'd like you to come with me. There's something I need you to do."

23

"HE WAS FOUND ABOUT AN HOUR AGO IN THE BUILDING where you were attacked, stepping through the hole where your attacker broke down the wall to get to you," Schneider said.

They were alone in the elevator, heading for the interrogation room. Schneider had told Officer Lutts she was back on regular duty for the rest of the day. The photograph was figuratively burning a hole in Elin's pocket, but she hadn't decided whether she would show it to Schneider. She *was* sure she wasn't going to show him the sweater or tell him that she strongly suspected the children were Jews.

"I never got so much as a look at him. It was too dark, and there was a wall between us most of the time," Elin said. "You should look at his wrists. There should be a bite mark on his wrist. I think probably his right one, but I can't be sure."

The elevator stopped, and they walked out into the wide central corridor. Her heels clicked on the marble floor. The building was much quieter than usual. The offices on either side were practically deserted, because nearly everyone who wasn't racing the clock to find a killer as part of the Special Project Unit had Sundays off.

"I want to check something else, before I decide what to do with him," Schneider said.

They were outside the interrogation room now. The door was ajar. Elin could hear voices inside, but Kurt stopped her from going in by catching her arm.

It dismayed her to discover that she was acutely sensitive to the size and strength of his hand even through her sleeve.

He gave two sharp raps on the partially open door. Gesturing toward the door, he indicated she should listen.

"I want you to read these sentences out loud," a man—she thought it was Detective Albrecht—said, and she heard the rattle of paper. He was inside the interrogation room, speaking to who she presumed was the suspect.

"Drink your coffee. Get in the car," another man replied. He sounded bored as he read the sentences. Elin pictured the two of them sitting across the table from one another. "Stop calling me. Say your prayers."

Elin caught her breath. Her eyes flew to Schneider. He shook his head to warn her to remain silent and again rapped twice on the open door.

On Albrecht's orders, the man read the sentences once more. This time Elin was prepared. *Say your prayers.*

Schneider pulled her a little way down the hallway to ask, "That sound anything like the voice you heard?" His gaze was penetrating.

Elin shook her head. "No, the man who attacked me spoke almost exclusively in a falsetto—an eerie, high-pitched falsetto. He was primed to kill, and the excitement of it was reflected in his voice. This man is reading sentences in an interrogation room."

Schneider grimaced. "In other words, you can't tell."

"No, I can't. But I don't think it's him."

"All right." Still holding on to her arm, he walked her back to the interrogation room and called to Albrecht, "Have him close his eyes." To Elin he whispered, "Don't say anything. Just step inside, look, and shake your head yes or no to let me know if you've seen him before or not."

At the thought of seeing her attacker, a shiver slid down Elin's spine, but a quick look at the small, thin, balding man seated at the interrogation table across from Albrecht reinforced what she'd thought when she'd heard his voice—this wasn't him.

She could see that his sleeves were rolled back and there wasn't a mark on his wrists. Somebody had indeed checked.

She shook her head.

Schneider pulled her out of the room. A moment later, Albrecht followed them out, closing the door behind him.

"So is Herr Frey of railway security to be further detained?" Albrecht asked.

"Finish checking his background, but if nothing turns up you can turn him loose. Make sure we have a good address where he can be found if we want to put hands on him again," Schneider told him.

Albrecht nodded and went back into the interrogation room. Schneider made a gesture inviting her to precede him to the elevator.

"Was there something else?" she asked as the elevator took them down. He'd told Officer Lutts that she would be with him for the rest of the day.

He nodded, still without saying anything.

The look she shot him in reply brimmed with exasperation, and most unexpectedly he smiled. A crooked, slightly wry smile that was so charming it *almost* had her smiling back at him.

But she didn't. She was determined to back away from any

hint of a personal connection with him as fast as she could. Instead she simply raised her eyebrows and waited.

"I need you to do one more thing," he said.

"What?"

"Be patient and you'll see."

Because they were inside the Alex, because she'd totally taken to heart his warning about being wary of unseen people listening in, she didn't say anything else until they were in his car driving away from the building.

"So what's this 'one more thing'?" she asked. They were part of the heavy stream of traffic heading down Unter den Linden and she was looking out through the windshield at the wide boulevard, thankfully undamaged, rather than at him. Throngs of pedestrians shared the sidewalks with bicyclists and even a group on electric scooters. Black-uniformed SS were everywhere, like ants at a picnic. In the distance, the River Spree gleamed brightly blue.

"I'm taking you with me to see Storch. I want you to tell me if—when—you think he's lying. Unless you object, of course."

That got her to look at him. "Do you think he might be our killer?"

"I think he knows everything there is to know about the criminal underworld in Berlin. Further than that I'm not prepared to go, at least not yet. I take it you don't object to coming with me?"

"No, I don't object. Of course I don't object. Anything that helps solve the case."

"That's what I thought you'd say. And I'd appreciate it if you'd keep our little visit to him under your hat. I don't want anybody at the Alex to know that we might be using a known criminal as a resource."

"How did you even find him?" Because ever since she'd seen the sweater in the box she'd been busy thinking about ways in which she, by herself, might be able to find the children and had come up with nothing promising.

"I know where he lives."

She digested that. "What will you tell him?"

"It depends."

"On what?"

But instead of answering the question, he said, "Nobody's been able to locate Erich Frank, by the way. I've got Gunther and Roth out there looking."

"Do you think something's happened to him?"

"I don't know. It's possible he simply decided to go out of town. But Dalsing's not getting out until I do."

There was no time for more, as by then the Brandenburg Gate was in sight, and Kurt was looking for a place to park.

The Baron, as he was deferentially referred to by the staff at the Hotel Adlon, where as it turned out Storch maintained a suite, was already entertaining a *very important* guest, the concierge informed them. He gestured around the huge, wood-paneled lobby with its square marble columns and exquisite Louis XVI furniture. Perhaps they would like to have a seat and wait for a few minutes until his business was concluded? When Schneider, flashing his warrant badge, declined, the man rolled his eyes heavenward, shrugged as if to say that what happened next was out of his hands, and conducted them on what amounted to a deliberately delaying tour of the facilities, pointing out the indoor courtyard with its splashing elephant fountain, the library, the music room, the smoking room, the barber shop, the ladies' lounge, and an array of grand ballrooms before finally coming to a halt in front of closed mahogany double doors.

"Please, I will announce you." Placing himself between Schneider and the door, the concierge gave him a disapproving look when Schneider raised his fist to knock.

The door opened before Schneider could object. A small,

nondescript-looking man in a uniform that indicated his high rank stepped out. His gaze swept Schneider, and he frowned.

"Count Helldorf!" The concierge spoke before anyone else could, and Elin could hear the relief in his voice. "Such an honor to have you in our establishment today, sir! If you will permit me to show you out, there is a private way—"

Count Helldorf's gaze cut to the concierge, and his abrupt answering gesture was one of assent. Without another glance at Schneider and only the most disinterested look at Elin, the man walked away with the concierge bowing and scraping in front of him.

"Give me a nod if you think he's lying. Keep it subtle, we don't want him to catch on." Schneider glanced at Elin as the two men disappeared around a corner. Then, with no more than a peremptory knock on the open door and without waiting for an answer, he gestured to Elin to precede him and then walked behind her into the room.

It smelled of roses from the huge bouquet on the grand piano in the corner.

"Keeping company with Berlin's chief of police now, Storch? How much is he costing you?" Schneider's tone was jovial as he closed the door behind him and strode across the sumptuously appointed sitting room toward the man, who'd been looking out one of the two tall windows toward the French embassy, which was located across the street on Pariser Platz. Storch whipped around to face him. In the harsh light from the window, his skin looked almost unnaturally pale against the white blond of his oiled hair and toothbrush mustache. His pronounced aquiline features reminded Elin of a hawk until they were softened by a broad smile. Other than that, what struck her was the elegance of the black velvet smoking jacket he wore—and the black silk sling cradling his right arm.

"I'd heard you were back with the Kripo. I thought we'd

seen the last of you when you got shipped off to fight," Storch exclaimed.

The two met in the center of the room, and instead of shaking hands—the sling made that awkward—they clapped each other on the shoulder. It was obvious that they knew, or had once known, each other well, which piqued Elin's curiosity.

"You were never that lucky," Schneider said.

"My luck's changed since those old days." He looked Schneider up and down. "So has yours, it seems."

"And not necessarily for the better, hmm?"

"You should have fallen in line with the idea of a perfect Aryan race when you had the chance. You know, blond like Hitler, tall like Goebbels, thin like Göring." Storch chuckled at his own joke.

"We don't all have your ability to bend with the prevailing wind." Schneider's voice was dry.

Storch shrugged philosophically. "If you don't bend, you break."

"You're doing well, I see."

"Are you here to shake me down, my old friend?"

Schneider shook his head. "That would be the guy who just left. I see you've hurt your arm. How did it happen?"

"I went outside too soon after the latest air raid and got hit with a chimney when a late bomb dropped. Broke my arm in two places. It'll be in plaster for weeks."

Having already concluded that an injured arm in a sling provided excellent cover for a possible bite mark, Elin had been suspicious from the moment she'd seen it. But Storch's answer was easy and his demeanor showed no sign of deception. When Schneider glanced her way, she responded with the slightest negative movement of her head. She didn't think he was lying.

Storch looked at Elin, who stood nearby watching their exchange. "And who is this?"

"My associate, Frau Lund."

Storch seemed to accept the introduction on its face value. Nothing in his expression revealed that he knew she was Professor Lund, "Dr. Murder," or that her purpose in Berlin was to find a killer.

Storch looked back at Schneider. "You're fortunate in your associates. She's quite lovely."

"Thank you," Schneider said, while Elin bristled—invisibly, she hoped—at the purely male exchange, conducted as if she weren't right there in front of them.

"Won't you come join us, Frau Lund?" Storch's gesture invited her to sit on the sofa, which was situated across from two gilt-framed armchairs in front of a magnificent marble fireplace.

Elin responded with a polite "Thank you," and crossed the room.

Storch looked back at Schneider. "As I don't flatter myself that this is a social call, why don't you sit down, have some coffee, and tell me what it is you want from me."

Schneider accepted, and as each took a chair Storch picked up the telephone that was on the table beside him and ordered coffee, which was brought almost immediately. When Elin took the first sip and realized it was real coffee, she knew that, whatever else he was, Storch was a high-ranking individual within the hierarchy of the Reich.

At the same time, as he stirred real sugar into his cup, she also saw that Storch's long, thin fingers were bare. If he did indeed possess a silver signet ring with a round stone, he wasn't wearing it.

"So?" Storch asked Schneider when the waiter who served them had gone. "What brings you to my door after all this time?"

Schneider balanced his cup on his knee. "It's come to my attention that you may have a business connection to illegal clubs including Eden on Wilhelmstrasse. Yes or no?"

Storch set his cup down on the table in front of him. "Am

I talking to an officer of the Kripo or my old friend from our days working the factory night shift together?"

"I'm not here to cause you trouble. I'm involved in a case that could result in certain clubs being closed down if it's not solved quickly. I was hoping you could help me. And if you have any financial interest at all in Eden or any similar clubs it would be to your benefit to do so."

Storch gave him a long look. "That turnip winter we shared was a hard one, wasn't it?" To Elin, the question made no sense. Schneider grimaced, and Storch continued, "Two boys—were you only twelve? And I was thirteen—doing the work of grown men in the very dangerous environment of a metalworking plant because all the grown men were off fighting another of our endless wars. It forged a bond, though, as shared hardships do. Despite the way our paths have diverged since, may I trust that bond still stands?"

"You may."

Storch picked up his coffee again and took a sip as he seemed to consider. Then he very deliberately put the cup down and looked at Schneider.

"Very well, then. Yes, I have a significant financial interest in Eden and a number of other underground clubs as well. In fact, I own them, along with a partner. How can I help you?"

In the end, when Schneider pulled the pictures out of an envelope taken from an inner pocket of his jacket and showed them to him, Storch professed not to recognize any of the victims, who Schneider described as having suffered serious assaults without any mention of murder. Storch seemed to accept that— Elin could detect no deception in his reaction—and promised a great deal of valuable information, including offering to take them on a tour, on successive nights, of the clubs he owned. Regular customers at his clubs sometimes ran tabs, and he promised access to those records. In addition, any untoward behavior or violence on the part of customers that was severe enough to come to the attention of management was recorded, and if a customer offended more than once they were banned. He offered up those records, too.

"How many times did he lie?" Schneider asked as, with plans to meet Storch on Tuesday, the next day they were open, for a visit to some of his clubs, they drove away.

Elin shook her head. "As far as I could tell, he didn't. He exhibited almost no signs of deception that I could see."

"In other words, he's not our killer."

"Unless he's a complete psychopath. They feel no guilt or remorse, and thus the behaviors that signify deception are greatly reduced or absent, which means the markers of deceit are also greatly reduced or absent. He also didn't appear to recognize me, and I would have expected at least some small involuntary reaction if he did. But that still doesn't completely rule him out as the killer." She paused for a moment, then added, "His arm troubles me. I didn't pick up on any deception when he talked about it, but that it's injured is certainly a coincidence."

"It is, I agree. Although he didn't have the cast or sling when we saw him at his club."

"No." Elin drew the word out thoughtfully. "But perhaps he hadn't had time to acquire them. Or maybe he hadn't realized then how incriminating a bite mark on his wrist might be. And he wasn't wearing the signet ring you said he owns, which, if he realized it left distinctive marks on at least one of his victims, he wouldn't be."

"Since it's a known symbol of the Ringvereine, it would make sense that he would no longer wear it. I'll see if I can find out what happened to it. And I'll have his alibi checked out for what he was doing before he came to the club last night, and the other nights in question as well. Although I don't think serial murder is much in Storch's line."

"You've known him since you were twelve?"

Schneider nodded. "He was blue-blooded but poor. I was just

poor. We both had mothers and younger siblings to help support while our fathers were off fighting in the Great War. We ended up working in a factory together."

"And sharing a turnip winter? What is that?"

He gave a huff of laughter. "The freezing cold winter of 1916–1917, when there was a famine and everybody everywhere was starving to death and there was nothing to eat but turnips. Sometimes I'd take one or two from my mother's zealously hoarded stash and bring them in, but mostly he would, because there was a communal garden behind his house and he'd sneak in there and dig them up and never mind who they belonged to. We were the youngest two in the plant, and we shared what we brought in to eat and it was almost always turnips, there just wasn't anything else available. We'd roast them in the foundry oven, and we'd mash them and eat them. God, we were hungry, and there was never enough to fill either of us up. We had to be careful about it, too, because the others working there were older and bigger than we were and they were starving just like we were, and they'd take our turnips and eat them in front of us and laugh in our faces if they got the chance."

"That sounds terrible!"

He shrugged. "It was the way things were. We survived."

Looking at him, at the strong features that spoke of steadiness of character, at the reminiscent smile that just touched his mouth as he thought back on his early association with his old friend the criminal with whom he still maintained a bond of trust, at the scar that he'd acquired by getting on the bad side of the depraved murderer Reinhard Heydrich, Elin made up her mind. She'd already concluded that finding the children on her own was going to be difficult, if not impossible.

He was the help she needed.

"I have something to show you," she said, and pulled the photo from her pocket.

24

THE WRITING ON THE BACK OF THE PHOTOGRAPH, *"ZUR
Letzten Instanz,"* was the name of a restaurant. Schneider recognized it at once. Since it was time and past for the evening
meal, he suggested they go there and eat while investigating its
connection to the children, if any.

Elin agreed.

"Nobody knows them." The restaurant manager, who Schneider had entrusted with the photo, handed it back with a regretful shake of her head. "It's possible the owner does, but she's in
Munich until next week."

Kurt thanked her, pocketed the photo, and turned back to
his meal, which he was in the process of consuming with relish.

Not knowing whether to be disappointed or relieved at the
restaurant staff's response to the photo—she'd been on tenter-
hooks for fear someone seeing the picture might confirm that the

children were Jews, a possibility she hadn't shared with Kurt—Elin likewise returned to her meal.

"So you have a mother and younger siblings," she said to him after a moment, picking up on what he'd said earlier. The atmosphere between them as they ate was surprisingly companionable. The food was good, the lighting was low, and they were surrounded by chatter and the clink of glasses and silverware from other tables.

"I do. Actually, one younger sibling, my sister, who works as a teacher. My mother lives with her in Fürstenberg. I visit when I can."

"And your father?"

"Didn't come back from the war." He took another hearty bite of his meal, which was a spicy sausage dish with a rich aroma.

"I'm sorry," she said.

He nodded acknowledgment. "It was a long time ago."

"Still."

"What about you? Siblings?" he asked.

She shook her head and ate another bite of her roast pork. It was very good, but, with one thing and another—worry about Niles, Hilde and Borge, Jens, and the serial murderer who was out there stalking his next victim, and perhaps even stalking *her*, at that very moment—she didn't really have much of an appetite.

"You're an only child?"

"Yes."

"Your mother?"

"Is dead."

"I'm sorry," he said, just as she had to him, and she nodded.

He watched her without saying anything else as she swallowed her suddenly tasteless meat and took a drink of water.

"What?" she asked defensively when he was still looking at her after she'd swallowed that, too.

He shook his head. "Finish your meal. Then we'll talk." He ate another forkful of his, as if to demonstrate how it was done.

"There's no need to wait. I can eat and talk at the same time. Say what you have to say." She cut another small bite of her meat.

"All right." He watched her spear the meat with her fork. "I want to know what happened the last time you were in Berlin, when you came here fifteen years ago to that conference with your parents." He held up a hand to stop her before she could utter the deflection that sprang automatically to her lips. "I've already gathered that you don't want to talk about it, but any files that were kept on it are either missing or destroyed, which means I can't find out what I need to know for myself, so you're going to have to tell me."

She put down her fork, meat still attached. "You *looked* for files on the conference my father attended?"

"I did. There's nothing. No record that Sven Lund or the Lund family was ever in Berlin."

"Why would you do that?"

"Because I need to know." The glint in his eyes was grim. "You're convinced that the man who attacked you is the killer, right?"

She nodded warily.

"And you couldn't figure out why he would attack *you*, specifically, right?"

Again she nodded. Even more warily.

"I've been thinking about that. What if the reason he attacked you was because you encountered him *then*, when you were in Berlin before, and he was afraid you'd remember him now?"

Elin's chest tightened. It was suddenly hard to breathe.

"That's not possible," she said at last.

"Isn't it?" He leaned forward, looking at her intently. They were in a booth in a dark corner, seated on high-backed wooden benches on opposite sides of a small table. The restaurant was full, but all the tables in the wood-paneled room were separated from each other in a way that afforded them almost total privacy. "I think it might be."

"If someone—a man—recognized me from fifteen years ago, don't you think I'd recognize him right back?"

"A man would notice a pretty girl of seventeen a lot quicker than that girl would notice a probably average-looking, older guy. And you're extremely memorable-looking, you know. Especially if said guy had a reason to remember you."

"What kind of reason could he possibly have?"

"Obviously something happened while you were in Berlin all those years ago that upsets you to this day. It might even be the key to this case. *To finding the killer.* I need you to tell me what it was."

Their eyes locked. The intensity of his gaze held her, wouldn't let her look away. What felt like every cell in her body shivered in rejection of what he was asking her to do.

"Something did happen, but it doesn't have anything to do with this case."

"Tell me anyway."

Her pulse began to pound.

"My mother died," she said flatly. Before he could ask *how*, which she knew he would do, just like she knew he would pry the whole terrible memory from her bit by agonizing bit if he had to, she blurted out the rest. "She was hit by a car. She and I were together, we'd just gotten off the Number 41 tram at Rosenthaler Platz. It came out of nowhere. There was so much traffic, so much noise, that we didn't even hear it. She was maybe three steps ahead of me and it just—mowed her down." Her voice dropped to a croaky whisper. Even now, remembering the horror of that moment—the terrible scream, the blood, dropping to her knees on the asphalt beside her mother's lifeless body while strangers crowded around and cars squealed to a stop—made her dizzy. "She was killed instantly. The driver never even slowed down."

She stopped, because she could not, physically, go on. Her throat constricted, her chest squeezed tighter. She reached for her glass of water, determined not to give in to the wave of emotion. Her hand shook, but she managed to lift the glass and drink.

"*Liebling*, my God, I'm sorry. Sorry it happened. Sorry to have had to ask."

That *liebling* undid her. It hit her heart like a tiny, deadly barb and lodged there.

"Don't call me that." She set the glass back down with careful precision. "It's unprofessional."

"Elin, then. Professor Lund. Dr. Murder. Whatever you like." His hand made an abortive movement, like it meant to reach for hers where it rested beside her glass, but then clenched into a fist and stayed where it was instead. "That must have been a nightmare for you."

"It was." She breathed in, deeply, but not so obviously that he would see, she hoped. "I was heartbroken. My father was destroyed. He lived another seven years, but he was never the same. He died of a heart attack. I've always felt that it was really her death that killed him."

That he recognized her pain and was hurting for her showed on his face. She wanted to close her eyes against his sympathy but she didn't, because that would have been to give in to weakness.

One thing she'd learned very early in life was to never give in to weakness. Or at least, not where anyone could see.

"They never found the driver," she said, and resisted the urge to reach for her water again. Forget the rest of her meal. She knew from experience that her stomach would revolt if she tried to put another bite into it.

"Ah," he said.

It was only a single syllable, but she caught the wealth of meaning behind it. Of course she did. As investigators, as she'd previously observed, they were surprisingly attuned.

She shook her head in answer to the thought that he didn't have to put into words. "I never saw him. Not even a glimpse through the windshield. And he couldn't have seen me. I was still standing in the open doorway of the tram. It all happened so fast."

Your life could pass before your eyes in an instant. Time slowed down and speeded up simultaneously. Eternity existed between one heartbeat and the next.

Those were the lessons she'd learned that day, and they flashed through her mind again now. Followed by one more truth, the one that over the years had become her lodestone: *You can't change the past. You can only move on from it.*

"So you see, that can't be it," she concluded, glad that the pressure in her chest was easing and that she could breathe and talk without it requiring a tremendous effort. "That's the terrible thing that happened the last time I was in Berlin that I don't like to talk about, and it can't be the reason I was attacked. And that's because *I never saw the driver and he never saw me.* Not so much as a glimpse. It would have been impossible for me to see him from where I was standing or vice versa. He can't be coming after me now for that."

The waitress appeared to ask if they wanted anything else. Elin had been so caught up in the conversation that she'd never even seen her approach.

"Bring us two brandies, please," Schneider said, and when they arrived he said, "Drink it," to Elin, and she did, or at least sipped at it. While he drank his and watched her and talked of nothing—the weather, the traffic, the food—until she felt normal again. And her brandy was all gone, too, which she realized with some surprise.

Her head might spin a little, but it was worth it. She'd gone where he'd asked her to, told him what he wanted to know, and come out the other side only that little bit the worse for wear.

Then he said, "I'm sorry to keep coming back at you, but I can't let this go. You don't want me to, because you want to catch this guy as much as I do. My gut says there's something there."

She looked at him mutely. From her father, for most of her life, she'd heard ad nauseam about the importance of a detective trusting his gut.

When she didn't say anything, he continued, "You said yourself, these probably weren't his first murders. Fifteen years ago, he would most likely have been somewhere in his twenties. What if he was already killing then? Quite apart from your mother's accident, what if you somehow saw something or learned something that would have put him at risk of being found out? And then your mother died and you went away, but now you're back, and he's still here and still killing, and here you are again, with that same knowledge that could resurface at any time."

"I don't have any knowledge."

"Maybe you don't. But maybe he thinks you do. Tell me about the conference. What was it about? What was your father's part in it?"

Oh, God. Her heart started to thump. But she couldn't call a halt, couldn't refuse, because what if he was right? What if there *was* something there?

"It was a typical law enforcement conference. Sharing investigative techniques, consulting on difficult cases, that sort of thing. I didn't have much to do with it, really. My father was there mainly as a presenter. My mother and I—" she said that with scarcely a wobble "—were there to have fun."

"What was your father's presentation about?"

"Serial murder. He was there to talk about a serial murder case he'd worked on."

His eyes narrowed on her face.

"Interesting," he said. "I can see where you got your career inspiration. What serial murder case?"

She hesitated. People looked at her differently when they knew. The Meitners, for example, hadn't considered her good enough to marry their son.

And yet, if it was going to make a difference to him, she made the unwelcome discovery that she needed to know that, too.

"Dagmar Overbye," she said. One of the few women ever convicted of serial murder, Danish citizen Dagmar Overbye was a notorious killer of at least sixteen infants over a period of four years. Advertising her ability to find adoptive homes for unwanted children—usually infants born out of wedlock whose mothers were too poor/frightened/ashamed to keep them—she accepted a fee from the mothers to care for and place their babies in loving homes. Instead, if she was unable to find a home for the child within a day or so, she killed it, burned the body, and pocketed the fee. She was only caught when a mother changed her mind about giving up her baby and came back for it, only to be told that it was too late: the child had been given away. The mother turned to the police, the police came to investigate, and the horrifying truth was revealed.

Schneider's expression confirmed that he knew exactly who Dagmar Overbye was. That wasn't a surprise. Although it had been twenty-five years since she'd been arrested, the woman and her horrific crimes remained notorious, especially in law enforcement circles.

"Your father was involved in that case?" he asked.

She nodded. "He was the detective who arrested her. He came to the house looking for a baby that had been left there the previous day. The mother wanted her child back. That baby wasn't there, but another baby who'd arrived just a few hours before was, in the arms of a young girl who lived in the house and was looking after the new baby because Dagmar had gone out. My father told me later that the young girl was pale and thin and neglected and seemed scared to death when she saw a policeman on the doorstep. So he came inside and looked around and in the process noticed a strange odor coming from the oven. When he opened the oven door he found the remains of the baby he'd come there looking for. Dagmar had suffocated it."

Schneider was looking at her hard. "Your father told you all that?"

She wet her lips. She could, right now, simply say *yes* and leave it there, she knew. But she didn't. She went on. "He told me some of it. The parts I didn't remember. *I* was the young girl who answered the door. I was six years old. Dagmar Overbye was my biological mother. Or at least, she claimed she was. No one was ever really sure, but the best evidence that she was telling the truth was that I was six years old and still alive."

"Holy hell." Everything from the timbre of his voice to the way he was looking at her changed in an instant. The persona she'd built up over the years, the one she routinely hid behind—education, professional status, fame, even her last name—had been ripped away, leaving her exposed and vulnerable. The shameful truth of her origins was laid bare.

He was looking at her like he'd never seen her before.

Elin squared her shoulders, lifted her chin. "My real mother, the mother of my heart, the one who loved me and raised me, was Amalie Sorensen. *Dr.* Amalie Sorensen, who was a psychiatrist and passed on her passion for her profession to me, her daughter. She and Sven Lund, her husband, the detective who came to Dagmar's door that day, adopted me. Those two wonderful people are my parents, and I will love them and be grateful to them until my dying day."

Their eyes met. Hers, she hoped, revealed none of the cold dread slithering through her veins as she waited for his judgment. His were narrowed. Assessing. Reevaluating everything he thought he knew about her, she could tell.

Her stomach pitted.

To many people, to the Reich itself, her probable genetic connection to one such as Dagmar Overbye made her instantly suspect, instantly undesirable, one of the *untermenschen*. According to the hereditary principle, the tendency to commit mass murder ran in her blood.

"Your parents must have been very proud of you," Schneider said. "What you've made of yourself is a great credit to them and to you, Professor Lund."

All the coldness, all the dread, vanished in the face of the warm little glow that pulsed to life inside her. She was surprised, and dismayed, by how much his reaction mattered to her.

Not that she meant to let it show. Not that she meant to let any of it—the years of insecurity, the lifelong struggle against feeling lesser, the susceptibility to being wounded by what others thought of her, by what, now, *he* thought of her—show.

She had too much pride for that.

"No one at that conference knew I was adopted," she said, perfectly composed. "They didn't know I had any connection whatsoever to the case they were all talking about. Nothing about my father's presentation drew attention to me. So the killer couldn't be coming after me for anything to do with that. Once again, there's just nothing there."

"How sure are you of that?" Schneider asked.

Elin started to answer, then caught herself when his eyes crinkled at the corners with amusement and she realized he was waiting for her standard reply, which she was, indeed, about to deliver.

"Very sure," she said instead, and he laughed.

"Aren't you going to eat any more of that?" He gestured at the meal she'd barely touched. His plate, she saw, was clean. "Do you want something else?"

When she shook her head to both, he signaled for the check.

He paid, and they walked outside. They didn't talk beyond a few commonplace remarks, but the silence between them was easy, comfortable. There was, Elin reflected, a new bond of trust. And more than trust. What that *more* consisted of precisely, she refused to even allow herself to think about.

The temperature had dropped while they were inside. It was now cool bordering on brisk, and she was glad of her long sleeves. In the near distance, the imposing spire of Kaiser Wilhelm Memorial Church was silhouetted against the evening sky. Closer at hand, twilight cast its purple cloak over the cobbled street, and under better conditions the streetlamps at the corners already would have been lit. But instead blackout curtains were being drawn across windows everywhere as the city prepared for its nightly plunge into darkness.

"Sir! Sir!" A timid voice calling behind them had them both looking around. A slight woman wearing the white cap and apron of a kitchen worker ran along the sidewalk after them. A side door in the restaurant was still closing behind her, and Elin realized that she'd come from the restaurant's kitchen.

"What is it?" Schneider turned around. Elin did the same.

"The ones in the picture, the little ones, I've seen them. They come here sometimes." Slightly breathless as she stopped in front of them, the woman gave them a nervous look, her manner making it clear she knew Schneider was a cop. "It's my job to take out the trash late at night, when we're about to close. They'll wait over there—" she pointed to a nearby alley "—until I go back inside and then hunt in our garbage bins for food. They've never done any harm, so I didn't think..." Her voice trailed off, and she seemed to wilt under Schneider's gathering frown. "I didn't see any reason to report them. I... I would have come forward in the restaurant when I saw the picture, but my boss said none of us should get involved."

"What's your name?" Schneider's tone was stern.

"Inez Gorne, sir."

Schneider reached into an inner pocket, pulled out a small leather card case stamped with the Kripo insignia, and handed her one of his cards. "My name and telephone number are on this. If you see them again, Fräulein Gorne, you should call me at once."

Instead of nodding, her whole body bobbed up and down. "Yes, sir, I will. Um..." Schneider had started to turn away. He glanced back at her.

"Is there...is there a reward?" The eagerness in her face was unmistakable.

"There is," Schneider said, and took Elin's arm. They left Fräulein Gorne standing on the sidewalk looking delighted.

Elin, on the other hand, cast a veiled glance at Schneider as she wondered if, perhaps, by involving him in her search for the children she'd done the worst thing imaginable for them instead of something good.

25

NILES AND HILDE WERE STAYING AT ELIN'S HOUSE IN
Copenhagen. That was the oh-so-welcome revelation that
greeted her when Schneider took her back to the hotel later
that night, after several hours spent driving from each victim's
residence to the spot where her body had been found. The purpose was to check distances, routes in and out, and the type of
after-blackout activity surrounding each location in hopes of developing a better understanding of the killer's modus operandi.

Although it was nearly midnight, Pia was waiting in Elin's
room when she got there and barely managed to contain herself until Schneider had gone. He didn't linger, and Elin wondered if it was as apparent to him as it was to her that Pia was
big with news—or if he had more business in the forest that she
wasn't going to think about. In any case, he left her with a quiet
reminder to use the new lock he'd had installed on her door as

well as the old lock, and not to leave the hotel premises alone. With that, and Pia's and Jens's rooms next door, and the carefully vetted policeman he'd placed in the lobby to keep watch on the only staircase in the building, he felt she should be safe during the night. She agreed.

"You two seem to be getting on well," Pia observed after Schneider had gone, giving her a long look from her spot sitting cross-legged in the middle of the bed. But before Elin could respond she burst out with her news. "Never mind that. Jens's brother heard back through one of his contacts. They're safe! Niles and Hilde! I've been dying for you to get back here so I could tell you!"

"Oh, thank God!" Elin's knees went weak. She had to sit on the edge of the bed while Pia told her all about it.

After an exchange of recaps—carefully edited in Elin's case—of how their respective evenings had been spent and many expressions of relief about the discovery of Niles's whereabouts, Pia went to her own room. Elin crossed to the window for a quick peek that confirmed Schneider's car was still there. With that settled, she thrust a sturdy ladder-back chair beneath the doorknob to supplement both new and old locks, just in case. Then, satisfied that she'd prevented any chance of a surreptitious entrance to her room by persons unknown, she fell into bed still utterly refusing to speculate about *why* Schneider's car was still there.

Despite how exhausted she was, she slept poorly. Early the next morning, she called Niles from the pay phone in the lobby.

"I'm really glad to be home, Mama," he said. "But it doesn't feel like home without you. Can't you please come soon?"

"As soon as I can," Elin promised. "I love you."

When Hilde got on the telephone, she didn't say much other than that she'd thought Niles would be more comfortable in his own house, and so that's where she'd taken him. Elin understood Hilde was being cautious. What she read between the lines of Hilde's careful remarks was that her mother-in-law had not wanted to go so far away from Borge, who was still being held although no one knew on what charges, and that she considered both her own home and Smukkeso risky in that the newly emboldened Gestapo, if they decided to raid Borge's properties or even arrest his family, would be likely to target both his known residences. Certainly they would target them first, giving her time to go into hiding with Niles if it became necessary.

Also, she hadn't liked to pull Niles from school, feeling that his absence might draw unwanted attention to him. She was just thankful that Elin had kept her own name and used it for Niles.

Elin was profoundly thankful for that, too.

"Hurry home," Hilde said as they ended the call. Elin heard the distress in her mother-in-law's voice.

The fact that the formidable Hilde was frightened terrified Elin. Just thinking about the possibility that her son and his grandmother might have to go into hiding, or worse, made her sick with fear.

I have to go home. The urgency of it hammered at her. The thought of Niles with only Hilde to protect him was almost enough to take her to her knees.

Panic was useless, she told herself firmly. The only thing she could do for them was recommit every scrap of knowledge and experience she possessed to finding the killer. What would happen if she couldn't find him quickly was something she wasn't prepared to contemplate.

If the killer wasn't found by Saturday night, he would take another life. She was sure of it, and she used the knowledge to give herself even more impetus to get the job done.

Over the next few days she worked tirelessly, getting Trott to take her to question the victims' families in hopes that she might glean something new when Schneider was busy following his own line of investigation, going back over every facet of the case with a figurative magnifying glass, combing through each file for missed facts or new leads or any possible unexplored avenue that might lead to the killer.

She was almost sure that Inge Weber, who was ostensibly the first victim, was not.

"When did he start killing? Where? If it was in Berlin, then who is here now that was here then? And what was happening, in his personal life or the outside world, that might have triggered him to start killing? Because there's always a trigger." She posed those questions to herself, and Schneider, in the same frustrated outburst. "And the first murder doesn't have to be in Berlin. It could have been anytime within about the last twenty years, anywhere in Germany. Or elsewhere. The possibilities are endless."

"You know what I think," Schneider said, and she did. As far as triggers were concerned, he reminded her that beyond anything personal that may have been happening in the life of the killer, there'd been a federal election in 1928, with all its accompanying turmoil. That had been the backdrop to her previous visit to Berlin. Not having a better idea, she agreed that that was as good a place to start looking as any. As a result, he had files from 1927–1928 sent over from the Berlin police. With the help of Officer Lutts—Sonja—with whom she was now on a first-name basis, Elin went through them, looking closely at the sixty-three deaths in Berlin and its environs that were classified as murders in case Kurt's theory about the present murders and the attack on her being linked to a killer already active in that time period was correct.

There were only seven that fit the age/sex profile of the current victims. The manner of death was excluded because that could evolve over time. But when the deaths classified simply as "unnatural" were figured in, the number was much higher. In almost every case, the files were incomplete, and the time-consuming nature of investigating such old cases was beyond daunting. Because *there was no time*, she moved on, desperate to find that one all-important clue that she'd learned from experience would be the thread that unraveled everything.

"The killer had to transport the victims' bodies from the place where they were killed to where they were found," she said to Schneider late Thursday afternoon when he found her in the evidence room, where she and Sonja were going through the artifacts for anything that might provide the piece of evidence she sought. Unfortunately, because the bodies had been found naked, there wasn't a lot. "The very bloody bodies. Yet there wasn't any blood to speak of around the bodies or any trail of blood leading from the street to the bodies. Plus there would be so much blood on his clothes and in his vehicle from the bodies that it would be almost impossible to get rid of all evidence of it. And there were no tire tracks left behind that could be linked together or to the murderer. So what is he doing to hide them? And what is he transporting the body in that solves the problem of all that telltale blood?"

"Maybe he's naked when he kills them," Schneider said.

Elin grimaced. "That would solve the problem of his clothes."

"If you're sure he's acting alone—"

"I am," she said.

"Then he has to be transporting them in something he can load into a vehicle and manage by himself. Could be as simple as a large garbage bin, although that would be awkward to carry and he'd probably end up dragging it and leaving a trail, which we haven't found. My bet's on something like a tarp. Or a mattress cover. Given the weight of those women, he could carry those alone."

"If he's a police officer or a military man, which at this point we assume he is, would he have access to body bags?" she asked. "They don't leak and given the amount of blood it would take something like that to keep it contained."

"He might. But even if he doesn't have official access, there's a black market for everything."

"Maybe he wore a raincoat and wrapped the bodies in a raincoat and tied them up," Sonja said as she emerged from behind the shelves at the back of the room with a bin containing the physical evidence associated with Inge Weber. Elin was going through the bins again looking for any jewelry she might have missed because it had occurred to her that most women almost always wore some jewelry, and if there was none in any of the bins then it was a good bet the killer was taking their jewelry as a trophy.

"That's possible," Elin agreed, while Schneider shot a surprised look at Sonja. From his expression, he'd forgotten she was there. "The problem is, if he transported the body in a raincoat or a tarp or even a body bag, I would expect a significant amount of blood in the area where the body was removed from whatever contained it. And there wasn't any."

"Maybe he used some kind of absorbent padding," Schneider said, as Sonja set the bin down on the table and went back for Astrid Lang's.

"Then there should be fibers from it on the body. They would be readily apparent, because they'd stick to the blood like glue. But there's nothing like that. And what about the tire tracks?" She must have sounded as despairing as she felt because Schneider smiled at her.

"Sooner or later, we'll find the dog hair," he said. She knew he was referencing the Gerd Johansson case and despite her frustration had to smile back at him.

"Did you want me for something?" she asked as an afterthought, as it occurred to her that he'd almost certainly come to the evidence room at this time for a reason.

"A couple of things. First, Dalsing's been released. Order came down from on high. Nothing I could do to stop it." He didn't look happy.

"I don't think he's our guy." Elin's tone was comforting.

"I hope not."

"What else?" she asked.

His expression lightened. "We got an ID on our unknown victim."

Elin felt a rush of excitement. "Really? That's wonderful! Who is she?"

"Her name is Lotte Dietrich. Eighteen years old, from Werder. I'm on my way to talk to her parents now. If you brought a jacket, you might want to grab it. The temperature's dropped considerably since this morning." He slid a look over her burgundy dress. It was long sleeved, but the silklike material was thin.

"I didn't, but never mind." His automatic assumption that she would want to go with him was both correct and a testament to how well their partnership was working. Her bag was by the door. As she picked it up, she called to Sonja to please finish checking all the bins and that she was leaving with Kurt, because the police officers involved in keeping her safe now handed her off like a baton in a relay race and she didn't want Sonja to worry.

On the way out of the building, they spotted General Haupt leaving. He'd shown up at their weekly team meeting earlier that afternoon, for what Elin presumed was an update on the case in advance of her scheduled meeting with General Kaltenbrunner the next morning. He'd stopped by for an update on Monday, too, and had spent about forty minutes with Schneider. But since she and Schneider had agreed not to tell him or anyone about the children, or Storch, or Jens's progress with the code, or anything really that was too sensitive, Haupt hadn't learned much beyond the bare bones of what they were doing. Besides being afraid that Haupt might use what they told him to one-up and thus anger Kaltenbrunner, their working assumption was that their target was close to Amt V and the investigation, and therefore anything they revealed to anyone outside their small group might find its way to the killer.

Upon spotting Haupt, who didn't see them, they ducked out a side entrance to avoid him.

"General Haupt is impressed with your work, by the way," Schneider said as he opened the car door for her. "He thinks you, and you alone, are on the right track."

"How do you know that?" she asked as he got behind the wheel.

"Word from on high again. Other than that, he's disappointed in our progress."

Elin looked at him uncertainly. Schneider was already under unfriendly scrutiny from Kaltenbrunner, and he was the one who would suffer the most immediate consequences if their investigation was judged to be lacking. "Does that worry you?"

Schneider shook his head. "Right now our priority has to be protecting the evidence. Haupt's main complaint is that we seem to have very little of it."

"It's not that we have too little, it's that we have too much. Especially if we're positing the crimes go back fifteen years. It's like looking for a grain of sand on the beach."

"We'll find him," Schneider said.

"But will we find him in time? Before he kills again."

Schneider didn't answer. His silence wasn't encouraging.

"How was the victim identified?" she asked minutes later. By then they were driving out of the city toward Potsdam.

"On Monday her parents reported her missing. The report came to our attention this morning. Her photo was compared to the sketch and postmortem photos of the victim, and there she was."

"Do they know she's…?" Her voice trailed off at the prospect of having to break the news of their daughter's murder to unsuspecting parents.

"Dead? Yes. They didn't take it well."

She shot him a sympathetic look. "Were you the one who had to tell them?"

"It comes with the territory." She could tell from such markers as the tension in his jaw and the increase in his blink rate that the task hadn't been an easy one.

"I'm sorry you had to do it anyway."

He acknowledged that with a nod. "They said she finished school and took a job at a doctor's office in Hellersdorf a couple of months ago. Every Sunday she went home for a visit. When she didn't come home for two Sundays in a row, and she didn't telephone, they came looking for her."

"That fits with the possibility that she was taken at the same time as Greta Neuhaus."

"It does. We need to see if we can place her at Eden that same Saturday night. I'm hoping her parents will be able to tell us if they knew each other."

"Has anyone checked with the doctor's office where she worked?"

"Her parents did, and then I did. The doctor said she's never worked there and neither he nor his office staff had ever heard of her. Also, according to her parents, she had an apartment, and roommates. The address she gave them was a post office box. Walter is checking the address she gave the post office to rent the box as we speak, but given what we've learned so far I don't have high hopes that it will yield anything useful."

"Didn't they have a telephone number for her?"

"She told them they couldn't afford a telephone in their apartment so they all used a nearby pay phone. Unclear if that's true but it's probably not."

"So she lied about her place of employment and possibly her living arrangement as well?"

"It's looking like it."

"Why would she do that? What was she doing?"

"I'm hoping that talking to her parents will help us figure that out."

Werder was a little fishing village just on the other side of

Potsdam. The Dietrichs' house was in Old Town, which was on an island in the middle of the Havel River. Today the river was studded with white caps because of the wind that had come up. As they drove over the bridge to the island Elin watched white-hulled boats scudding across the choppy blue water and found herself wondering how such beautiful sights could coexist with a world so full of suffering.

Old Town itself dated from the fourteenth century, and the Dietrichs' house was a quaint, tile-roofed cottage at the foot of a cobbled lane too narrow to permit cars. Accordingly, they parked at the larger street above it and walked down.

Having been told to expect them, Frau Dietrich, her eyes red and swollen from crying, met them at the door. Not more than fifty, she was an older, plumper version of her deceased daughter. She invited them in, and introduced them to her husband, who, she said, she'd called home from his job as harbormaster upon learning the terrible news. Older than his wife, he sat slumped in a worn leather armchair in the modest front room, looking as pale and lifeless as his wife was red-faced and agitated.

"I'm so sorry about Lotte," Elin said to them, and Schneider echoed the sentiment as Frau Dietrich waved him toward a second armchair near her husband and drew Elin to the sofa and sat beside her.

"Nobody would tell us. How did she die?" Her voice unsteady, Frau Dietrich clasped Elin's hands and addressed the question to her.

"She was stabbed," Elin said, as gently as she could.

"Why would anyone stab our Lotte?" Herr Dietrich's voice was raw with grief. His hands clenched around the arm of his chair. "Was it about—" he exhaled a shaking breath "—sex?"

"She wasn't raped," Schneider said.

"She was such a good girl. So kind and loving," Frau Dietrich said. "What kind of animal would do this?"

"We're going to get whoever it is," Schneider told them. "I give you my word."

"I have to know—did she suffer?" Frau Dietrich's lips trembled.

Elin thought about the terrible wounds the killer had inflicted on Lotte Dietrich. The truthful answer was yes, a great deal. She would never tell the grieving parents that if there was any possible way to avoid it, however. The one saving grace in her mother's death was that she'd been gone in an instant. No time for fear, no time for pain. Elin had never thought she would be able to take comfort in anything about that terrible day, but in the fullness of time she'd come to appreciate that.

"It was all over very fast, and she would have been in shock during the attack," Elin said.

"Shock protects the body from feeling pain," Schneider said. Elin flicked a look at him. It was interesting to discover that he felt the same way she did about shielding the girl's parents from as much of the horrifying reality of their daughter's death as possible.

"Our son was killed in battle in the first month of the war." Frau Dietrich's hands tightened on Elin's. "Lotte, our little Lotte, was all we had left." Her voice broke. Tears brimmed in her eyes. In his chair, Herr Dietrich began to weep with great, noisy sobs.

26

THE VISIT WITH THE DIETRICHS WAS NOTHING SHORT of harrowing. When presented with Greta Neuhaus's photo, neither of the parents recognized her, or had heard their daughter mention her name. While Schneider questioned Herr Dietrich, Frau Dietrich talked to Elin, recounting her daughter's life from the time she was a little girl, pulling out scrapbooks and photo albums, smiling at some memories but at others dissolving into floods of tears. A photo of the family of four brought a lump to Elin's throat. Taken on a sunny day a few years previously, it showed mother, father, son, and daughter standing in front of the house with their arms around each other. They were smiling, clearly happy, with no idea what the future had in store for them.

Night had fallen by the time they said their goodbyes. A few stars were beginning to peep through the clouds, and the wind had risen so that it whistled through the streets with a high-pitched keening sound. Elin had pulled the blackout curtains shut before they left the house and turned on a small lamp near the door because she couldn't bear the idea of leaving the devastated couple sitting there alone in the dark.

Still, hunched and gloomy amid the enveloping shadows, the house looked like it, too, was in mourning as they walked away.

"Here," Schneider said as they headed up the cobbled street, and dropped his jacket around her shoulders. Elin looked at him in mute surprise even as she welcomed the warmth of it and pulled it close.

"You're shivering," he said by way of an explanation.

He was right, she realized, and realized, too, that it was not only because of the cold. Her expertise lay in parsing and interpreting information to find a killer. She'd never been a part of interrogating a newly identified victim's family before.

"Thank you."

"You're welcome."

"That was—" She broke off because there were simply no words.

"Rough," he finished for her, and she nodded.

"Those poor people will never recover from this," she said. Her heart ached for them. The parent-child bond was a universal language that she understood both as a mother and a daughter.

"We're going to catch the bastard."

"I know. But—" *We can't give them their daughter back*, she thought.

"Are you crying?" He was peering down at her.

Her answer was a fierce frown accompanied by a decided shake of her head. She would have added an uncompromising *no*, but she didn't trust her voice.

"My mistake," he said, adding, "It was nice of you to draw their curtains."

She didn't reply, because she couldn't.

They reached the car. Elin was glad to see it, glad of the distraction it offered, glad of the chance to swallow hard and blink away the stinging in her eyes unseen. Without waiting for him to do it, she reached for the passenger door handle. His hand closed around it a fraction of a second before she touched it. She turned toward him in reaction.

He was close, so close that, caught between him and the car, she found herself pressed against him. Her hand, for lack of anywhere else to go, came to rest against the smooth cotton just over his heart. The barely-there starlight made the dark straps of his shoulder holster starkly visible against his white shirt, and his shoulders look very broad.

Their eyes met. Shadowed by the brim of his hat, the dark gleam of his eyes dropped, seeming to search her face. His mouth tightened and his hand came up to cup her jaw. His thumb, very gently, wiped away what she realized from the hot wet feel of it was a tear sliding down her cheek.

"I'm not crying." Her voice was defensive, and way too thick.

"I can see that," he said.

"It's the wind."

"Uh-huh."

Her brows snapped together at his tone, and he smiled a little. Then he bent his head and kissed her.

She was surprised into stillness.

His lips brushed hers in a featherlight caress. They were warm, and firm, and almost tender. And so very male, so unexpectedly arousing, that her breath stopped and her heart leaped and the ground seemed to shift beneath her feet.

He tilted her head back and deepened the kiss, invading her mouth, moving his lips sensuously against hers. Her hand fisted in his shirt. Her toes curled. She didn't quite kiss him back but— she closed her eyes and parted her lips and let him in.

It ended as abruptly as it had begun. He lifted his mouth from hers and for a moment she didn't move. His hand, long-fingered and warm, still cradled her jaw. Her head was tilted up and her back rested against the still-unopened door. For a moment she was almost dizzy. Then her lids flew up to find that he was looking thoughtfully down at her. Her eyes were wide and unblinking as they met his.

She was stunned that he had kissed her, and at how that kiss made her feel.

"Unprofessional, huh?" His voice was a little rueful, a lot husky and low.

She nodded. Emphatically. Then her hand that had been gripping his shirt let go and slid up over his chest and shoulder to settle against the warm nape of his neck. And she went up on tiptoe and closed her eyes and kissed him back.

It was a kiss for the ages, electric, intoxicating, life-altering. Never in a million years would she have thought that this man, this near stranger from a place and culture that were anathema to her own, would have the power to make her head spin and her heart pound and her knees grow weak.

But impossible as it seemed, he did.

A car rattling down the street broke them apart. At the sound of its passing, he lifted his head. Her eyes blinked open just in time to see the boxy shape disappear into the night.

Then she looked at him. His head was turned as he followed the intruder's progress. Strong features, uncompromising jaw, firm lips compressed now in a grim line were silhouetted against the night sky as he looked after the car.

She had the briefest of moments to take stock. Her arms were wrapped around his neck. His were tight around her waist. She was on tiptoe pressed up against him. His jacket had fallen from her shoulders. She could feel it puddled around her feet.

Despite the brisk wind that whistled around them, the last thing she could ever imagine feeling again was cold.

She was melting inside. Her blood had turned to steam. Her pulse raced and her breathing was erratic and her body responded to the heat and hardness of his with a quaking urgency that was so unexpected, so intense, it frightened her.

By the time he looked back at her she was already withdrawing, dropping her arms from around his neck, sinking back down onto her heels.

With a quick, comprehensive look at her face, he let her go.

"We need to get you off the street. Get in the car," he said before she could say anything, and reached for the door handle.

This time he succeeded in opening it and bundled her inside. He got behind the wheel, tossed his jacket into her lap and his hat in the back, and started the car. Taking a fortifying breath as he pulled away, she squared her shoulders. This was where she stomped out every last vestige of the wildfire of desire that still burned inside her by putting them firmly back on a, yes, professional footing.

"Put the jacket on, you look cold," he said. "You're worrying me, by the way."

"What?" Whatever she'd expected from him in the aftermath of that sizzling kiss, that was not it.

"I haven't seen you eat more than a few bites of any meal you've sat down to. It's obvious you're not sleeping. Now you're getting emotional over a victim when you've dealt with any number of similar cases before. If you don't start taking better care of yourself, you're not going to make it through this."

She stared at him fixedly for a moment. Thanks to the blackout, there were no lights behind or ahead of them. Only the stars and dim pale glow of their headlamps on the pavement provided any kind of illumination. They were driving over the bridge, and his attention was on the road. The river was a shiny black ribbon far below. If there were boats on it—she knew there were boats on it—she couldn't see them.

"You kissed me," she said.

"You're changing the subject." He slanted a glance her way, but it was too dark for her to read anything in it.

"That is the subject, and you know it. You're trying to deflect."

"Very insightful, Professor. You might even be right. And you kissed me back, by the way."

"I can't get involved with you."

"Why not? As kisses go, I thought that was a pretty good one."

"It's unprofessional."

"Ah. I knew that was coming."

She frowned at him. "You know it is."

"If you started chasing me around my desk at the Alex, *that* would be unprofessional. If we see each other outside of work, that's our business."

"There is no outside of work. Until we solve this case, we're at work unless we're asleep. And when it's solved, which I hope and pray will be soon, I'll be leaving. I have to go home."

"What you're saying is, you don't think it would be a good idea to get involved with me because you think our time together would be limited."

"Yes," she said, pleased that he understood. Then, because she didn't want him to think that was her only objection, she added cautiously, "Among other reasons."

You are what you are and I am what I am. A Nazi and the mother of a Jewish son. Not that she could tell him that. The danger of doing anything that might turn the beady eyes of the Third Reich toward Niles was too great.

"Nothing in life is certain, you know, especially in times like these. We could have an accident on our way back to town. A bomb could fall on us tonight as we sleep. If Kaltenbrunner gets a little more unhappy with me, I could get sent to the front again. The point I'm trying to make here is, putting things off until the stars align might mean putting them off forever. And this— whatever it is—between you and me, I don't want to miss it."

Her heart thumped. He was right about everything he'd said, and the temptation to give in, to explore where this unlooked-for attraction might lead, was nearly irresistible. She was glad of how dark it was, because she feared what he might read in her eyes. That kiss, that unbelievable kiss, still burned on her lips, pulsed through her body, was maybe even imprinted on her soul. But the chasm between them yawned wide and deep, and more than anything else she had to focus on staying safe and getting home. She had no time, and no room in her life, for him.

"I—" she began.

He held up a hand to stop her. "How about you think about it over dinner? We've got a couple of hours until we're supposed to meet Storch. And I'm hungry, and I wasn't joking about you needing to eat."

She hesitated. Ultimately, her answer had to be no. But she could wait until after dinner.

"I can do that," she said. "Could we eat at the Waldschloss? I'd like to change."

He nodded. "We can."

There wasn't much activity at the Waldschloss when they got there. The policeman assigned to guard the stairs hadn't yet arrived, and, as Elin discovered when she ran upstairs to change, Pia wasn't back from her ongoing assignment of sketching the men who'd been seen around the victims. When she finished changing she tapped on Jens's door to invite him to join her and Schneider, because she was having second thoughts about spending any more un-work-related time in Schneider's company and because Jens, too, needed to eat. He thanked her but turned her down. He was, he said, in the middle of trying a new approach to the code, which he hoped to make enough progress on so that he had something positive to contribute at the team meeting at the Alex the following afternoon. And he thought he should wait for Pia.

Thus Elin was alone when, freshened up and wearing a jade green dress that was one of her favorites, she walked down the wide stairs to the lobby only to discover Schneider waiting for her at the foot. He'd spruced up a bit, too—at least, he had his jacket on and had straightened his tie—and looked big and tough and far too handsome for her peace of mind as he stood there looking up at her.

"You look beautiful," he said as she reached him. The way he said it coupled with memories of that kiss gave her butterflies. She really, really hated that he had the power to give her butterflies.

"Thank you." To her relief, she sounded as composed as she *didn't* feel, and neither of them said anything else as he followed her into the dining room.

It was only about half-full but it was noisy with conversation. Most of the chatter that reached Elin's ears centered on the stunning rescue of Mussolini from his mountain prison by German parachutists. Sentiments seemed to vary between a fierce pride in the derring-do of the commandos who had carried out the rescue, and dashed hopes that the war would end anytime soon.

Once the food came, she and Schneider inevitably started talking about the case.

"We should check to see if any of the other victims had a gap in their life where they disappeared or weren't where they said they were for a few weeks." Elin kept her voice low. Lotte Dietrich's lie to her parents and friends about where she was and what she was doing once she moved to Berlin was mystifying.

"None of the families mentioned something like that."

"Maybe they didn't know," she said.

"We've been through housing records, employment records, the lot. If anything like that's there, nobody caught it. But we can look again."

"We're running out of time," she said. Saturday night was starting to assume monstrous proportions in her mind.

"I've got Gunther and Roth reviewing personnel records for everybody even marginally associated with Amt V. Something happened in the weeks before April 25, when Inge Weber's body was found. Somebody transferred in, somebody lost his job or got demoted or changed jobs, something that triggered this killing spree. If it's there, we'll find it," he said.

Before Elin could reply, another couple was seated at the table next to them, too close to make confidential conversation possible.

By unspoken, mutual agreement they didn't talk about the case, or the war, or anything that could pose a problem if it was overheard. That avoidance also included anything that was too personal or might take the conversation in a direction that neither of them, apparently, was ready for it to go. He told her a funny story about working in the factory and she told him about her horror upon being faced with dissecting her first cadaver. They continued in that light and impersonal vein through the rest of dinner. And then it was time to drive to their prearranged meeting point with Storch, at the Haus Ku'damm Restaurant on the elegant, tree-lined boulevard that was Kurfürstendamm.

It was the third night she'd gone with Kurt to investigate Storch's clubs, and she was starting to panic a little because so far it had not yielded anything of note. Eden was closed until the bomb damage it had suffered in the previous raid could be repaired. No one who worked in the other clubs admitted to recognizing any of the victims, described as runaways who were being desperately searched for by their families when they showed their pictures around. As for Elin's observations of the male clientele, there were dozens who behaved suspiciously and could have been considered potential predators. But with no evidence that any of the victims except Greta Neuhaus had ever visited that kind of illegal establishment, she was losing hope that Storch's clubs would provide the breakthrough they needed. They kept at it because the disheartening truth was they were desperate and the illegal-club angle was the best angle they had.

"I hope you're prepared for a long evening," Storch said as they rode the secret elevator at the back of the establishment down to the cellar. By this time he was aware they were hunting a killer

and had been told the broad parameters of their search. Because
the urgency of the situation called for Storch's wholehearted co-
operation, in Schneider's opinion, only the truth was likely to
get them that. Schneider was relatively certain—"ninety-five
percent?" Elin quizzed him—that Storch wasn't the killer. But
on the slim chance he was wrong and Storch was guilty, keeping him under observation for hours at a time was an excellent away to smoke him out. When Elin responded with a tart
"Unless he kills us while we're doing it," Schneider laughed and
promised he would do his best not to let that happen. To Elin's
concern that Storch might reveal the existence of a serial murderer to the world at large, Schneider said that not only did he
trust Storch to keep his mouth shut, but also that Storch had an
incentive to do so. If word were to get out that a murderer of
young women might be haunting his clubs, it would be bad for
business. Money, Schneider said, was Storch's god, which Elin
had no trouble whatsoever believing. Everything about him was
expensive, from his suite at one of the most exclusive hotels in
Berlin to his clothing. His suit tonight was charcoal pinstripes
with exaggerated shoulders and a nipped waist in the ultramodish
style that he preferred. The cast on his arm was concealed by a
red silk sling—in a time when silk was reserved exclusively for
military uses and thus almost impossible to obtain.

Despite Schneider's faith in his old friend, Elin continued to
be wary of him. Mostly because of the injury to his arm, but
also because of the way he looked at her sometimes when he
thought no one was watching. She wasn't sensing the miasma
of evil that she associated with serial murderers, but still the
glint in his eyes and the way they ran over her made her uneasy.

"What we have here are three clubs that are connected by a
series of tunnels, so if you want to see all of them tonight we're
going to be busy," Storch said.

"We do," Schneider said, and Elin nodded confirmation.

Storch looked Schneider over. "You look like a cop, you know.

You'll fare better down here if you at least unbutton your collar and loosen your tie." Grimacing, Schneider followed Storch's instructions and Storch turned his attention to Elin. "Forgive me for the suggestion, Frau Lund, but you might like to take off your dress. I assume you have a slip or some such beneath? Here our female guests tend toward the—licentious."

27

THE ELEVATOR STOPPED AND THE DOOR OPENED ON
dim lighting, clouds of smoke, throbbing music, and the smell
of beer and sweat.

"Welcome to Club Circus." An attractive young woman appeared out of the gloom to greet them. Enormous false eyelashes
surrounded eyes that looked black because of dilated pupils. Drugs?
An opiate, perhaps? That it was something like that Elin had little
doubt. She was very pale. Her hair, like her lips, was an improb-
able red. She wore a bandeau bra and panties with a garter belt,
stockings, and high heels, all black. Her eyes widened. "Baron
von Storch! We didn't expect to see you tonight! If you'll give me
just a minute, I'll see to it that your special room is made ready."

"No need. You can run along, Margo. I'll take care of my
friends."

"Yes, Baron." She backed away, nodding, as Storch led them

through what, to Elin's bemused eyes, was a kaleidoscope of astonishing sights. A bare-chested man in a turban and harem pants swallowed an enormous sword to her right. To her left, a lithe blonde in a red two-piece swimsuit and high heels did back walkovers in front of tables crowded with drinkers, male and female.

As Storch had warned, the female guests were in various stages of undress. Slips, bras and panties, satiny corselets and garter belts abounded. Having declined to shed her dress, Elin felt conspicuous because of it. A screech overhead brought her eyes up to discover a live monkey in a cage. In the center of the room, scarf dancers performing aerial acrobatics climbed toward the high ceiling.

"Special room?" Schneider cocked an eyebrow at Storch.

That kiss must have sensitized her to his touch, Elin thought, because she became acutely aware of his hand as it came to rest on the small of her back with the obvious intent of keeping her close. He didn't have to worry. She wasn't about to stray far from his side. Given the low lighting, the smoke, the loud music, and frantic activity, she could be stabbed and the attacker could melt away into the crowd in the blink of an eye. If she were on her own, she would be constantly looking over her shoulder. As long as he was with her, though, she trusted him to keep her safe.

"Here at Club Circus we have special rooms for special purposes," Storch said. "Do you really want to know any more?"

"No," Elin and Schneider both said.

"I didn't think so, my straitlaced friends. You want to get a table and some drinks and settle in for a bit, or—"

"How about we get right down to business? I'd like to look around, show these pictures to key members of the staff."

As Schneider finished speaking, Storch nodded, then raised his hand in the air and snapped his fingers. A moment later, Elin spotted a tall, black-haired woman in a sarong skirt swaying toward them on impossibly high heels. She was beautiful, graceful, and wearing no clothes at all above the waist. What she *was* wearing above the waist was an enormous green snake looped multiple times around her neck. Its heavy coils hung to her waist and—just barely—preserved her modesty. It writhed as Elin watched and lifted its head to look around with slanting golden eyes, thus dashing her last hope. The creature was definitely real—and alive.

As the woman reached them, it was all Elin could do not to take a step back.

"Baron! What a lovely surprise! What can I do for you?"

"Helena. And Nadine." With complete disregard for the presence of the snake, which was apparently well-known to him and named Nadine, Storch leaned over and planted a kiss on the woman's cheek. Straightening, he introduced her to Detective Schneider and Frau Lund, and turned to Schneider. "Nothing happens in the Circus that Helena doesn't know about. She's the best person to answer your questions. And you may absolutely trust in her discretion." To Helena he said, "Take him to the office and tell him anything he wants to know." Then he smiled at Elin. "And you, my overdressed Frau Lund, can best serve your purpose by coming with me. We'll get a table, and you may observe to your heart's content."

"She stays with me." Schneider's rejection of Storch's suggestion, uttered before she could reply, was brusque. Elin couldn't see the look he gave his friend, but Storch threw his hands up in a gesture of surrender.

"Of course. Whatever you want. I have some business I should be attending to anyway. When you're finished with Helena, she'll bring you to me." He looked at Helena. "In the billiards room," he said, and she nodded.

Once they were seated on either side of a businesslike desk, Helena efficiently answered Schneider's questions and produced requested records. Elin listened and looked on with as much concentration as she could muster while keeping a wary eye on the snake as it coiled and rippled around Helena's neck. As it turned out, Helena had no useful information to impart. She didn't recognize any of the victims and while customers were occasionally asked to leave or, rarely, physically ejected, and she had the records of all such incidents, which she showed them, the perpetrators weren't identified in any way. It was her view that, with such establishments subject to being raided at any time, they would have no guests if said guests had to worry about their names falling into the hands of the Gestapo.

Finally she took them to the billiards room. It was smoky like the rest of the establishment, but well lit enough that the occupants could see to play on the multiple tables. And Elin could clearly see the bloodied, desperate-looking man being forced at gunpoint out a rear door as Helena, with only a cursory knock, brought them in through a door off the main room.

After a sharp glance over his shoulder identifying them, Storch crossed to their side.

"I'm sorry, I thought you'd be finished by now," Helena murmured to Storch.

He dismissed her with a gesture.

"Probably shouldn't be strong-arming your customers," Schneider said to Storch as Helena, and Nadine, faded away. A group of men who'd been huddled on the far side of the room put their cues down on the nearest table and, with cautious looks in Storch's direction, filed out behind Helena.

"He owes us money. Quite a lot."

"Don't kill him." Schneider's tone made it a stern warning.

"What would be the sense in that? Dead men don't pay up." Storch shepherded them out of the room. "Did you get what you needed from Helena? Are we ready to move on?"

"We're ready to move on," Schneider said. Storch led the way to a door, which he used a key to unlock. They then followed him down two flights of stairs and through another door into a tunnel that stretched away into the distance and was tall enough to stand up in twice over. Yellowish lights were set into concrete walls that were, Elin discovered as she inadvertently touched one, damp with condensation. The air was cold and smelled musty, and the only word she could think of to describe the atmosphere was *creepy*.

"Behold Germania," Storch said, and began to lead the way along the tunnel.

"Germania?" Ellen couldn't help it. She had to ask. Her hand found its way into Schneider's, and his, warm and reassuring, closed around it. She took care that it was his left one, because the knowledge that the three of them were alone in a vast echoing tunnel far underground brought with it the thought that, if Storch were the killer, it would be an easy matter for him to round on them and shoot them dead without anyone being the wiser. For all his vaunted trust in Storch, Schneider clearly was likewise awake to the possibility, because he unbuttoned his jacket and, with a subtle movement, unfastened the leather flap on his holster.

"Speer," Storch said with loathing. "Feathering his nest by feeding a megalomaniac's vision. Their plan was to replace Berlin with Germania, the dazzling new capital of the world. The war put it on hold because the money and manpower were needed elsewhere, but not before a vast underground labyrinth of tunnels and elevators and emergency bunkers and railway lines and canals was built to serve as infrastructure for the new city. Rather than let it go to waste, we make excellent use of our little piece of it. As do others, I'm sure."

"Not as big a fan of our current government as you used to be, I see," Schneider said.

"I was never a fan. I was just smart, unlike you."

"What changed?"

"They're taking us all to ruin, as any but the fools in charge can see. Know what the newest joke making the rounds is? You'll appreciate it. 'What's the difference between Germany and the sun? The sun comes up in the east, while Germany goes down there.'"

Schneider gave a huff of laughter. "Still, I'd be careful where I told that one."

Storch shrugged. "At this point a lot of them agree with me. And I own most of them anyway. If I were to be arrested, they don't get their monthly *nützliche Aufwendungen*. And I tell every secret I know."

Elin thought back to the presence of Berlin's chief of police in Storch's hotel suite. It was now obvious that he'd been there to pick up his *nützliche Aufwendungen*, or bribe.

"I'd worry more about winding up dead," Schneider said.

"Ah, but I have a plan in place to avoid that, too." Storch stopped in front of another door.

"How can you tell where you are? All the doors look alike," Elin said.

"They're marked." He touched a small circlet of what looked like oak leaves carved into the concrete beside the door. It had a number inside it and was barely visible in the dim light. "Each door has a number, and the markings are designed so that you can feel them, and thus find your way, even in the pitch dark."

"Efficient," Elin said.

"That's one thing we Germans are." Storch unlocked the door as he spoke and led the way up a single flight of stairs. "You'll find this place very different," he said as he opened another door to a blast of music. "This is the Delphi."

What they stepped into was a swing club, with a horde of energetic dancers kicking and twirling across the dance floor to the raucous strains of "Sing, Sing, Sing," performed by a live jazz band. Red-and-black posters screaming *"Swing Tanzen Verboten!"*—Swing Is Forbidden, the official stance of the Nazi party—covered the walls. It was smaller than Club Circus, and the patrons—and the music—were louder and livelier. But they learned no more there than they had at Club Circus, and when they left, Elin's stomach was tight with nerves.

"If we don't turn up anything tonight, what's next?" Elin asked in a low voice as they followed Storch through the tunnel to the next club.

"We keep plugging away at it." Schneider's voice was grim. He knew the stakes, and the time frame, as well as she did.

"On Saturday—" she said.

His hand tightened around hers as he said, "I know."

Storch had stopped and was waiting for them in front of the door that, Elin assumed, led to their destination.

"You might remember my manager here from your early days with the Kripo," he said to Schneider as they caught up to him. "Fritz Baer."

Schneider's eyes narrowed. "Jeweler Fritz? You hired a man you know as well as I do should've gone to prison for murder to manage your club?"

"He wasn't convicted." Storch spoke over his shoulder as they climbed the stairs leading to a closed metal door.

"Nobody saw anything. It was too dark." Schneider's reply was pure sarcasm.

"He's smart, and he's honest if you pay him enough. His reputation comes in handy, too. This can be a tough crowd to handle. And if I need him to do something a little extra, well, he hasn't said no yet." As he inserted a key into the lock, he gave a wicked smile over his shoulder. "Far be it from me to tell you how to go about your business, but I would offer him a small inducement to make sure he is really telling you all he knows."

Schneider's sour expression as Storch pushed the door open told Elin what he thought about that.

"Welcome to Paradise," Storch said. "So named because we're about sixteen meters below the cemetery of Kaiser Wilhelm Memorial Church." He lowered his voice as he finished, and Elin saw why as soon as she walked past him into the club. There was a dreamy, otherworldly quality to the place that was apparent in everything from life-size classical statues set into recesses in the stone walls to the bubbling fountain in the center of the dance floor to the music, a torchy "Serenade in Blue" sung by a curvaceous blonde in a silver evening gown.

It was very dark despite the flickering candles on the dozens of small tables. A faint red glow from somewhere overhead tinted everything—the elaborate tapestries hanging on the walls between the statues, the couples swaying dreamily on the dance floor, the tiny sparkling outfits of the waitresses. The thick cloud of smoke that filled the room had a reddish tint, too, and a peculiar sweet smell. As Elin, with Schneider close behind her, followed Storch around the edge of the dance floor, she saw why. Each table had its own hookah pipe with multiple people sucking the smoke in through the attached tubes. Some were soldiers in uniform.

Storch must have seen the surprised look Elin gave them, because he said, "Our brave warriors enjoy getting blitzed on their time off as much as anyone else. While they're here, they're our guests, and when they're not, we're their secret."

"What's in the pipes?" Schneider asked.

"We have a menu, just like with everything else."

"Baron." The man who lumbered toward them was about Elin's height and heavy with muscle that bulged beneath his dark suit. He was bald with a thick neck and squashed-looking features. His eyes, which were smallish anyway, turned positively beady as he looked at Schneider, blinked in surprise, then took a step back and pointed an accusing finger at him.

"What's *he* doing here?" he said to Storch. Elin's gaze was caught by the rings that adorned every finger but his thumb. At least three of them could have been the source of the marks on Lotte Dietrich. "If he's here to arrest me, I'm telling you now there's going to be a hell of a fight."

"Not this time," Schneider responded with a tight smile.

At the same time Storch said, "All that's in the past. He's here to ask some questions about some things that have nothing to do with you. You answer them for him as best you can, and he'll go on about his business."

Storch and his manager exchanged a veiled look: message sent, message received. It lasted less than a second, but it was enough to put Elin on alert. She touched Schneider's arm to get his attention. He glanced around at her, and then his chin tipped up a little and his eyes went wide.

Turning, following his gaze as he continued to look up, Elin's heart leaped. Her breathing suspended. The source of the red light that gave the club its eerie glow hadn't been visible from where they'd stood before. Now it was.

What she was looking at was a ruby-colored stained-glass lozenge about the size of a car. Set into the apex of the arched ceiling, lit from above, its centerpiece was a rich gold, stained-glass insert in the form of a *wolfsangel*.

"Jeweler Fritz stays on the list of suspects," Schneider said in response to Elin's question about whether the absence of a bite mark on the wrists of the Paradise Club's surly manager should preclude him from being the killer. They were on the way back to her hotel. It was after three in the morning, the blackout made the night so dark that they could see almost nothing beyond the pitted pavement a few meters in front of the car, and the shadowy figures and clandestine activity that haunted the busier boroughs of the city were behind them. Elin knew she should have been exhausted. Instead, the burst of adrenaline that came with achieving a real breakthrough in the case had her bubbling with excitement. Schneider was less openly euphoric, but the glint of satisfaction in his eyes told its own story.

"Then what about Storch? We haven't been able to look at his right wrist."

"Storch is on there, too. I may not think it's likely, but I'm not eliminating anybody until I have absolute proof he didn't do it."

"Jeweler Fritz—why do you call him that, anyway?—identified

Inge Weber, Bella Richter, Anna Fromm, and Roswitha Eckard as definitely having been in the club multiple times. The others he said he couldn't say for sure, but they could have been. The killer himself has to have been there. In fact, I'm willing to posit that he met at least some of the victims there and that it's familiar territory for him. That *wolfsangel* on the ceiling can't be a coincidence."

"I don't think it's a coincidence. I think he hunts there. I think he's there a lot. Maybe he's an employee, maybe he's a supplier, maybe he's a regular guest. We're going to look at everyone. And as for Jeweler Fritz, everybody who knew him before the war called him that. He was a jewel thief who ended up stabbing a man to death during a robbery. There were witnesses but when it came to trial no one would testify. They were too afraid."

"Stabbing?"

"Yes. Don't read too much into it. The victim was a man who happened upon the robbery."

Elin's brows knit in an uneasy frown. "Several of those rings of his are the right shape to have made some of the bruises on Lotte Dietrich."

"Would they still have any blood on them or anything else that could tie them to the murder?"

Elin thought about Lotte Dietrich's mutilated body. The bruising had come before the fatal knife attack, which was evident because the blood had covered up the bruises rather than the source of the bruising leaving marks in the blood, but there might be something.

"Possibly," she said.

"I'll have someone collect his rings so they can be checked."

"I think we should consider putting out a public warning to Berlin's women before Saturday night. We don't have to say there's a killer at large. We can say something like there's a rapist abroad in the city, or an escaped convict who's a danger to anyone who crosses his path, so stay home. Anything, just so they're warned. I know we have a solid lead now, and I'm confident we'll catch this guy, but I'm afraid it won't happen in time. And I'm as sure as it's possible to be that he's going to take another victim on Saturday night."

"If we put out a warning, we also warn the killer. If he changes his pattern as a result, a lot of the progress we've made will be lost."

"And the High Command won't like it." There was a tartness to Elin's voice that had him glancing at her with a wry smile.

"That, too." The hotel loomed ahead, its dark shape barely visible as, across the street, the towering pines of Grunewald Forest blocked what little moonlight filtered through the clouds. He pulled into the courtyard. "It's a risk, but with what we know, if we set the trap just right, we've got a fair shot at catching him."

"And if we get it wrong?"

"Then we get it wrong, and we keep working at it. But even if we were to put out a warning, which we can't do, I guarantee you that only a small percentage of the young women in Berlin would be aware of it, and only a small percentage of them would stay at home because of it. If he's out there on Saturday night meaning to kill, he'll find a victim. Unless we can stop him."

"That's taking a huge chance."

"Life's about taking chances."

Elin shivered a little. "I'm not a gambler."

She caught the briefest flash of white teeth through the darkness. "I'm aware."

As he always did, he walked her in. Very circumspect, not really talking, frowning as he cast a sweeping glance around the lobby only to discover that Officer Bruin, the grizzled veteran whose job it was to remain stationed in the lobby at night, had them under narrow-eyed surveillance from an overstuffed chair beside the fireplace. Upon recognizing Schneider, his eyes widened. He jumped to his feet and snapped off a straight-armed salute. "*Heil* Hitler!"

Schneider responded in kind and waved the cop back into his chair. Then he followed Elin upstairs.

"I don't really think I need somebody standing guard downstairs all night, every night," Elin said as they reached her room.

"You may be right, but we're not taking any chances." He sounded slightly grim as he followed her inside. She hit the switch that turned on the lamp beside the bed as he took a quick turn around the room, looking in the closet and the bathroom before heading for the door.

"Walter will be waiting downstairs to take you into the Alex at nine. Come lock this behind me," he said, and left.

A little wistfully, which was stupid because he was doing exactly what she wanted by behaving as if that soul-stirring kiss had never happened, she closed and locked the door. For a moment she stood there and simply looked at it. Then she gave herself a mental shake, kicked off her shoes, walked toward the bathroom, and started taking the pins out of her hair.

Minutes later, she was standing in front of the mirror brushing the heavy gold mass of it out around her shoulders when someone knocked at her door.

Frowning, she padded toward it, hesitated in front of the heavy wooden panel, then asked softly through it, "Who's there?"

"Me."

That was all he said, but then that was all he had to say. She recognized his voice instantly and opened the door to look at him in surprise.

"Did you want something?" Even as she spoke she stepped back to let him in and he walked past her into the room.

"I did."

"What?" She shut the door and turned to see what he was doing. He was right there, facing her, so close she had to look up to meet his eyes. That's what she did, looked up at him, *frowned* up at him actually in a silent question, only to have him answer her with a small wry smile.

"This," he said, and slid a hand around her waist to pull her close and covered her mouth with his.

28

HER LIPS PARTED THE INSTANT HIS TOUCHED THEM. TENTATIVELY
at first, she kissed him back. There it was again, the electricity,
the longing, the need. Urgent and primitive, the sheer physicality of her response overwhelmed every defense. When both arms
went around her waist and he pulled her hard against his body,
she was assaulted by a wave of heat. She arched up against him.
Her arms wrapped around his neck. Her head fell back against
the broad shelf of his shoulder. She loved how big he was, how
solid he felt against her, loved all the muscles and the roughness
of his stubble against her soft skin. He kissed her like he meant
it, like he was starving for the taste of her mouth, like he burned
for her, and she kissed him the same way.

By the time he lifted his head she was dizzy and breathless
and clinging to him like he was the only solid thing left in the
world. Her heart pounded and she felt soft and shivery. It had

been a long time since she'd been with a man, years, and even with Lars, even in the beginning, she'd never felt like this.

Like every cell in her body quaked with desire. Like she wanted him to pick her up and carry her over to the bed that was *right there* and—

She forced her eyes open even as his mouth found the vulnerable spot beneath her ear and lingered there. The slide of his mouth down the side of her throat was hot and sweet and threatened to turn her bones to water. What gave her the strength to resist was the memory of that crisp exchange of "*Heil* Hitler" in the lobby. The harsh reality was he was one thing and she was another.

"Kurt—" The breathlessness of her voice shamed her, as did the fact that she still clung to him as if she feared her knees would buckle if she let go, which she did.

His lips traced the line of her jaw.

"Seize the day, *liebling*. See where it takes you." His hand cupped her breast. Her nipple pebbled against his palm.

"I can't." Two of the hardest words she'd ever spoken.

He lifted his head to look at her. His eyes were dark with passion. His face was hard with it.

"If you're worried about Officer Bruin in the lobby, I can go down and tell him he's off duty, send him home." His voice was husky, low.

She shook her head. "It's not that. It's just—no."

His arm tightened until it was an iron band around her waist. His body was taut with sexual tension. She could feel how much he wanted her, feel the strength of his arousal.

He took a deep breath, and his hand dropped away from her breast. Then slowly, reluctantly, he let her go.

Her heart pounded. Her legs were unsteady. But she stepped away from him, straightened her spine, and tried not to look as shattered as she felt. His jaw was tight and a flush rode high on his cheekbones, but his eyes were opaque as they met hers.

She said nothing. What was there to say? But her eyes—she

had no idea what he might be able to read in her eyes. She was afraid they revealed how much she yearned for him.

"Good night," he said, and turned and walked out the door.

When Elin saw Kurt again the next day, it was as if those heated kisses had been wiped from his mind. On their drive from the Alex to the meeting with Kaltenbrunner he was very much business as usual. Relieved, and also more regretful than she cared to admit even to herself, she, too, clung to her best professional demeanor.

"You know he's going to kill again *tomorrow night*." The urgency she felt was there in her voice. "I accept that we can't put out a warning, but we need to have a solid plan in place to catch him, and at the same time try to safeguard as many women as possible."

"I'm working on something."

"What?"

"Later. Right now, we need to think about what you are and are not going to tell Kaltenbrunner. We need to be careful here."

They went over what she should disclose concerning the investigation, and agreed that, given the near certainty that the killer was affiliated with law enforcement, she wouldn't reveal anything that the killer didn't already know that they knew. That was tricky, because it was difficult to be certain *what* he knew. In practice, it meant she said nothing about Storch and his illegal clubs, or her conviction that the killer would strike again on the following day, or the possibility that her mother had been among the killer's earliest victims. She wouldn't mention the children, the fact that the killer had attacked her, that she had bitten him, or that the blood from that bite had revealed his blood type and his use of Pervitin.

As it turned out, she revealed so little during their meeting that General Haupt, who had arrived minutes after she did and shamelessly sat in on it, much to General Kaltenbrunner's unspoken but obvious displeasure, proclaimed himself disappointed at the lack of progress.

"Sifting through evidence takes time," Elin told him. Having deliberately chosen her outfit with the object of conveying authority and competence, she was sitting in her trim houndstooth suit in the same chair as before, drinking the same kind of coffee, but every bit of pleasure she'd taken in the aromatic brew was gone. She put the still-half-full cup down as she answered, "We *will* find the man responsible. It's a matter of putting the pieces of the puzzle together."

"Please don't think I'm faulting *you*," Haupt said. "You can only work with what you're given. It's those in charge of the investigation who must shoulder the blame. Perhaps a change of leadership—"

Elin's pulse quickened. If it came down to it, Kurt would bear the brunt of the general's dissatisfaction.

"I see no need for that," she said. "It's important to recognize that progress *is* being made. Any change to our team at this point would only hamper the investigation."

"Your track record speaks for itself, Professor Lund," Kaltenbrunner said. "I—and I think General Haupt will agree with me—am certainly prepared to defer to your judgment." *For now*, was what he didn't say, but Elin read the corollary in his manner.

Haupt responded with a brusque nod of agreement.

"Determining the identity of the most recent victim is a step forward, at least," Haupt said. "I'm most intrigued by your methods, Professor Lund. How did you do that?"

"Old-fashioned police work for which I certainly can't claim credit," Elin said. "We made inquiries. We combed through files. We checked the Registry of Persons. Green Cards. Missing persons reports. Eventually we found a match to Lotte Dietrich from Werder."

"Lotte Dietrich from Werder. And what was Lotte Dietrich from Werder doing in Berlin?" Kaltenbrunner asked.

"She told her parents she'd taken a job with a doctor in Hellersdorf. We haven't been able to verify that yet. But we will."

"You've emphasized to Professor Lund how vital it is that no word of this killer and his activities reach the public," Haupt said to Kaltenbrunner. It wasn't a question. It was, rather, a statement laden with warning. Elin thought of Kurt, and the tightrope he'd been walking from the beginning—that they were all walking now—and felt a chill of foreboding. One wrong step, and the iron fist of the Reich could strike down any or all of them.

"I have." Getting to his feet, Kaltenbrunner looked at Elin. "We'll meet again this time next week, Professor Lund, if that is satisfactory?" Elin nodded. "Hopefully you'll have significant progress to report at that time."

There was a warning there as well. She kept her expression pleasant as she, too, stood.

"I'm confident of it, Herr General," she said, and turned to go. Haupt, who'd been seated in the chair beside her, rose when she did and walked her to the door.

"If you're available, I'd like to take you to dinner tonight," he said in a low voice as he opened the door for her. "It would give us a chance to discuss the investigation at greater length."

Elin's stomach dropped even as she stepped into the outer office, which was surprisingly crowded. Offending Haupt was the last thing she wanted to do. Besides being stupid, it was potentially dangerous. Kurt, who'd been waiting for her, got to his feet when he saw her. Careful not to look at him—she didn't want to focus Haupt's attention in that direction—she instead turned to Haupt with a regretful "I wish I could say yes, but I have a full schedule all the way up until bedtime. Until the job is done, I'm working around the clock. I'll be eating at my desk until the killer is caught."

"I understand. Your dedication is commendable." Haupt smiled at her, shot a look at Kurt, who, unaware of her effort to shield him, was looking narrow-eyed at Haupt, and went back inside Kaltenbrunner's office.

As she joined him, Kurt lifted his eyebrows at her. She shook her head and they said nothing until they were in his car.

Then she told him everything, concluding with Haupt's invitation to dinner.

"You don't want to go anywhere alone with him, or anybody else," Kurt said. "Erich Frank's body was found in the Spree this morning. It looks like his throat was slit."

Elin felt cold all over. "Surely you don't suspect General Haupt?"

"At this point, I suspect everybody. You notice I drove you to this meeting when I could easily have assigned someone to do it."

"When did it happen? Frank's death?"

"From the looks of him, the body's been in the water for at least twenty-four hours. So sometime before that."

"You *saw* him? When did you find out?"

"Early this morning, not long after he was fished out of the river. I didn't want to tell you before you talked to Kaltenbrunner. He can't fault you for not telling him something you didn't know."

"Where's the body now? I'd like to see it."

"At the hospital. Dr. Weimann's doing the autopsy sometime this afternoon."

"I want to be there."

"That may pose a problem. You can't go alone, I can't take you and wait around for a couple of hours while the autopsy's being done because I have too much to do, and Walter's out of the office for most of the day. And except for me and Walter, there's nobody else I trust to play bodyguard on an expedition like that. If our guy killed Erich Frank, and my money says he did, then he's cleaning up loose ends. And I'm afraid that you, Professor, just might be a loose end."

A little thrill of horror ran down her spine as she absorbed that.

By midafternoon, Elin had tested Jeweler Fritz's rings, which

Kurt had had collected that morning, and found nothing pertinent to the case. She'd spoken to Dr. Weimann on the telephone, and he'd promised to call her about the results of Erich Frank's autopsy when it was completed. She and Pia had gone through the sketches Pia had made of any suspicious males that had shown up in the vicinity of the victims around the times of their deaths and found two, from two separate victims, that were enough alike that they warranted further investigation.

After that, they all assembled for the team meeting in the Alex's basement conference room. Pia was on her feet, in the process of showing those sketches to everyone seated around the table, when a hurried knock on the door was followed immediately by Frau Skelton opening it without being bidden. Before the secretary could say anything, General Haupt, resplendent in his uniform, walked past her into the room. All talk immediately suspended as the group looked at him in surprise.

"*Heil* Hitler!" Haupt greeted them with a crisp salute. Everyone who was not already standing—that would be everyone except Pia and Kurt, who stood at the rear of the room—scrambled to their feet to respond in kind. Frau Skelton, with an apologetic nod at Kurt, backed away, closing the door behind her. "Sit, sit."

Haupt waved them back into their seats as Kurt said, "Is there something I can do for you, Herr General?"

"I thought I'd listen in. To perhaps get a fuller picture to present to Headquarters when I return there this afternoon. Please, carry on." His voice was perfectly pleasant. The look he gave Elin, who was sitting next to Pia, was warm, but his glance around the table and the look he gave Kurt were steely. To Elin, who assumed that by "Headquarters" he meant the Führer, his words felt like a threat.

"Of course. Please take my seat." Kurt gestured toward the only empty chair at the table, which happened to be beside Elin. Haupt accepted with a nod and sat down. Elin welcomed his close proximity with a small smile, which he returned, while inwardly adrenaline flooded her veins as her fight-or-flight response kicked into gear.

Pia finished in just a few words and sat down on Elin's other side. At Kurt's direction the sketches were passed on to Albrecht, whose new mission it was to identify their subject.

Elin's heart thumped as all eyes turned to Jens, who was seated beside Pia. His wound was healing nicely. The bandage that still covered it was so reduced in size and bulkiness that the possibility that Haupt would detect it under his clothing seemed almost nil. But as Jens stood up and Haupt focused fully on him, Elin had to work hard to keep from visibly tensing. Beside her, Pia's nervous fidgeting with her pencil told her that Pia was as anxious as she was.

But Jens, bless him, was his usual unflappable self. Enormous, ruddy faced, a little clumsy as he fumbled to unroll what turned out to be a large sheet of paper, he said, "I'm sorry to report that I'm not yet having a great deal of success breaking this code. The closest I've come is with this substitution cypher, but as you can see—" he held up the paper, which displayed letters lined up beneath what Elin recognized as symbols from the killer's code "—the result makes no sense. But I'll keep working on it and hopefully something will trigger a breakthrough." Tapping the paper he held, he looked at Kurt. "I'd like to leave this here in case somebody looking at it with a different perspective should see something I'm missing. Maybe we could put it on one of the blackboards."

"Good idea," Kurt said.

"Who is that?" Haupt asked Elin. His low-voiced aside was accompanied by a penetrating look at Jens, and came as Kurt nodded at Detective Vogel to go next.

"Professor Jens Moller. He's part of my team," Elin whispered, quaking, although outwardly she projected ease and confidence. At least, so she hoped. Haupt said nothing else, so she turned her attention to Vogel and prayed that Haupt would think no more about Jens or her team.

They went on around the table until it was her turn. Mindful of all the restrictions she and Kurt had agreed to, she basically repeated what she'd said in Kaltenbrunner's office earlier, much to Haupt's disappointment, she could tell. To give him something he could pass on to Headquarters so that their progress did not seem so inadequate, she added a brief psychological profile of the killer.

"In my opinion, the individual we're looking for is an organized, nonsocial lust murderer motivated by rejection and subsequent hatred of his victims. The location of the bodies, the violence of the attacks, the evidence of torture and mutilation, and the seemingly random, opportunistic selection of the victims all support this hypothesis. In addition, and what might be most helpful to us in identifying him, it's important to note that these lust-motivated attacks do not end in rape. We should search medical records for individuals who, through injury, illness, or any other reason, are unable to perform sexually."

Having finished, she was just sitting down again and looking to Kurt in anticipation of his contribution when a knock shifted everybody's attention to the door. Upon being told to come in, Frau Skelton did so, apologizing for the intrusion even as she looked at Elin.

"Dr. Weimann is on the telephone for you, Professor Lund. He said he's just finished the autopsy and must speak with you about it now, unless you want to wait until Monday, because he's been urgently called away and won't be back until then."

"I can't wait." Elin was already getting to her feet as she spoke. With an apologetic smile at Haupt and an "I'm sorry, I must take this call, please go on" aimed at Kurt and the room in general, she followed Frau Skelton from the room.

"You can talk in here." Frau Skelton pointed her to a closet-like room that held nothing more than a desk, a chair, and a telephone. Elin sat down and Frau Skelton switched the call over to her. With the door left partially open, Elin could see Frau Skelton and vice versa. Kurt and the rest of the crew were only two doors away, so she felt perfectly safe as she spoke to Dr. Weimann.

Cause of death was a cut-throat wound and manner of death was homicide. The weapon was a fixed-blade knife consistent with the one used on the female victims of the killer they were looking for. Time of death was difficult to pinpoint precisely because of the effect of being submerged in water, but Dr. Weimann's best guess was approximately two days previously. In other words, not long before the victim's body was thrown into the Spree.

Elin was still on the telephone when the meeting broke up. Shielded by the partially closed door, she was apparently difficult to see, because no one who passed by appeared to spot her. She watched as Pia and Beckman, as had been previously arranged, went off to interview Jeweler Fritz, who had reluctantly agreed to describe regular customers at the Paradise Club so Pia could sketch them. Conditions governing the interview included Fritz's anonymity, because, he said, he knew better than to give his name to the police, and that the meeting take place at a neutral location, because neither Kurt nor Storch wanted word of what was happening at the club to leak out, and Jeweler Fritz refused point-blank to come to the Alex.

Vogel, Albrecht, Gunther, Roth, and Kurt all crossed her line of vision as they went about their business. Jens appeared, walking with Haupt, and seeing the two of them together almost gave Elin a heart attack. But the conversation seemed friendly enough, and Jens departed while Haupt stopped to talk to Frau Skelton. With her he seemed impatient, tapping her desk with a forefinger, pulling out a silver pocket watch and opening it to show her the time, then wheeling to frown in the direction of the entrance as someone Elin couldn't see arrived.

"Where have you been?" Haupt barked at the unseen newcomer.

"My apologies, Herr General! There was traffic!" The man sounded nervous.

"Don't let it happen again!"

Haupt moved out of her line of vision. From the way Frau Skelton slumped at her desk and dropped her head into her hands Elin presumed he'd gone.

Moments later Dr. Weimann ended their conversation with the promise to send the autopsy file to her as soon as it was complete.

Replacing the receiver, Elin marshaled her resources. Haupt's unexpected appearance at the team meeting had been unsettling enough. Add in the presence of Jens and, to a lesser extent, Pia, and she was thoroughly rattled. But there was much work to be done and little time in which to do it, so she got up, smoothed her hair and skirt, and left the room to find Kurt. The plan was that she would go with him to interview the doctor that Lotte Dietrich had told her parents she worked for in Hellersdorf.

As soon as Frau Skelton saw her, she waved Elin over and told her that Kurt was waiting for her in his car. Gunther and Roth, who were on their way out anyway, had been instructed to escort Elin to him. They were standing by Frau Skelton's desk, looking impatient, but they were polite and the three of them chatted on the way down to the garage.

Kurt had a designated parking space close to the door on the top floor, and Elin spotted him as soon as she entered the garage.

"Thanks, I can take it from here," she said to the two policemen, pointing at Kurt, who stood beside his car talking to someone, and then waving them off as she headed toward him. They went on their way, presumably to their car on a lower floor, and she walked toward Kurt.

The man he was talking to was partially obscured by a concrete support pillar, and Kurt was so engrossed in their conversation that he didn't see her coming toward him.

She'd almost reached the pillar when she distinctly heard Kurt say, "Not a trace?"

"Nothing. We've searched everywhere. *Wertlos kinder*," the other man said.

"Keep looking," Kurt replied as, no more than a step away from rounding the pillar, Elin froze. Her breathing suspended. With a shock of recognition, she absorbed the other man's last words, his voice.

The man they belonged to had been there with her, in that bombed-out building right before she'd been attacked, yelling after the fleeing children, "Halt. This is the police."

29

THE MAN KURT HAD BEEN SPEAKING WITH TURNED TO walk away. As he did, he saw Elin. She'd seen him before, she knew she had, but she couldn't quite place him. He barely broke stride as he passed her, but he said, "Chief," over his shoulder in a warning tone, and that's when Kurt spotted her.

"There you are," he said in greeting.

Recovering her composure enough to move, Elin stepped out of the shelter of the pillar and walked toward him.

Her expression must have set off every internal alarm he possessed. His lips compressed. His eyes narrowed on her face.

"Get in the car," he said in a very different tone than before, and moved to open the passenger-side door for her.

She got in.

She didn't say a word as he got in beside her, started the car, and drove out of the garage.

Kurt shot a sideways glance at her. "Dr. Weimann have any insights I need to know about?" His face had smoothed out. He was being cautious, feeling his way, trying to gauge what she thought, what she knew.

"Who was that?"

"Herr Frey? He works for the railroad. He's been looking into something for me."

All true, all so carefully casual. And as his nonverbal cues told her as clearly as a shout, all designed to mislead.

She was having none of that. "He was the policeman in the passageway. He went chasing after the children, right before the killer attacked me. He might even *be* the killer." As her mind pinged from one unpalatable possibility to the next, her stomach began to churn.

"He's not."

"Not what? Not the killer? Because he's definitely the policeman in the passageway."

"Not the killer."

The terse statement had her turning in her seat to look fully at him. "How do you know?"

"I know."

That was when enlightenment dawned as she remembered exactly where she'd seen Herr Frey before.

"He was the man Detective Albrecht caught climbing through the hole the killer kicked in the wall of the passageway. He was the man you took me to listen to in the Alex's interrogation room."

"So what if he was?"

At least Kurt had the grace—no, the intelligence, because he had to know she'd know he was lying—not to deny it.

"You pretended you didn't know him. You pretended he was a suspect. Why? Because somebody—Detective Albrecht?—caught him, and you couldn't let on that you knew him?"

His jaw went tight. "Has anyone ever told you that you make a lot of assumptions that aren't necessarily correct?"

"Don't even *try*. You know it's the truth." Her eyes widened. "You knew he was in that area that night searching for the children, didn't you? That's why you were there. You didn't just happen to be driving by." Her tone was withering. "You were there to meet him."

"And, let me remind you, I ended up saving your life instead."

She looked at him like she'd never seen him before. "Did Sonja—Officer Lutts—tell you that Pia and I saw the children that morning? Yes, she must have. So you *sent* Herr Frey to look for them. And showed up yourself to meet him. Why? To find them before the killer could? Or—"

She broke off. The possibility that he'd somehow learned the children likely were Jews, that he might be searching for them *because* they were Jews, because he was a Jew catcher or affiliated with Jew catchers, reared its terrifying head.

"What is it you're suspecting me of, I wonder? You want to check my wrists?" His voice was dry. "In case you're forgetting, you already saw Herr Frey's."

"I want you to tell me the truth."

He pulled off the busy road into a grassy, tree-shaded expanse facing the Spree.

"Where are we? What are you doing?"

"We're in a park. I'm parking." As he turned off the engine, she got out of the car. She was too agitated to sit in that confined space with him. The crisp, river-scented breeze and golden late-afternoon sunlight were lost on her, as was the rolling gray expanse of the Spree. Balling her hands into fists and thrusting them into the pockets of her elegant suit jacket, she took to the path beside the parking area and strode toward the river. There were a few cars in the parking lot and a few people at a distance, but no one close by.

Kurt caught up to her. "I thought you *wanted* the children found."

"When you discouraged me from looking for them, when

you took Pia's sketches of the children—all that was a lie. You were looking for them *yourself*. Have you found them? Are you just not telling me? Why? What else aren't you telling me?"

"No, I haven't found them. Yes, I've had people looking. As to why, remember me telling you to keep your focus on the murders so that you can go safely home again? That's why."

"Right from the beginning, your only thought was to protect me." Her words dripped sarcasm.

"Not my only thought, but one of them. Come, Elin, you must know by now that you can trust me."

The look she gave him brimmed with skepticism. "Can I? Then tell me something. Why, when you were choosing a hotel for me, did you choose the Waldschloss?"

He made an impatient sound. "I already told you. To keep you as safe as possible from air raids."

"Really? Then if I were to follow you into Grunewald Forest one dark night—oh, yes, I've watched you—I'd find you doing something completely innocent like searching out truffles by the light of the moon, or communing with owls, or—"

He stopped in his tracks, and stopped her, too, catching her arm and swinging her around to face him.

"Stay out of the forest." His voice was harsh. His face had hardened in an instant.

"Why? What's in there?" She flung the words at him.

"Stay out of the forest." His fingers dug into her arm.

"Then admit it. Admit you're lying. You've been lying to me all along."

"You want to talk about lying all along, what about you? Think I didn't notice the blood on Professor Moller's shoulder the first night you arrived? I did, and—funny thing—the next afternoon I found out the Gestapo were searching your university for a wounded saboteur on the very day you left. With a 'team,' when before that you'd always worked alone. You really think I bought your story that Moller needs peace and quiet to work? You're doing your best to hide him because if he's caught—if you're found out— Well, you don't want to be found out."

Her stomach lurched. Her pulse rocketed. She simply looked at him, silent because her throat was too tight to permit her to speak, and because there was nothing to say.

His face changed. His mouth tightened and his brows snapped together and he gave her arm a little shake.

"How about this, *liebling*? You keep my secrets, and I'll keep yours."

He turned them both around and started back toward the car.

"You're hurting my arm," she said, coldly.

He let go.

Neither of them spoke until they were almost at their destination. There was a huge factory belching smoke, and as they passed it they saw, in its shadow, what looked like an abandoned shantytown of crumbling shacks. A scattering of what once had been personal possessions—broken crockery, a baby carriage tipped onto its side, a mangled bicycle missing both wheels—was strewed over a muddy field.

"What is that?" Despite the hostility that crackled between them, Elin had to ask.

"A *Zigeunerrastplatz*. A forced labor camp for Roma, gypsies. They worked in the factory there. It was cleared out a few months ago."

"What happened to the people?"

"They were deported. To another camp, Auschwitz."

Elin felt the horror of it in her bones.

A few minutes later they arrived at the office of Dr. Helmut Stubler, where Lotte Dietrich had claimed to work. Their appointment was for six o'clock, when the doctor ordinarily would have just finished for the day.

The parking area around the office was jammed with police

vehicles. An ambulance waited near the door, and a growing crowd was gathering.

That an emergency of some sort was in progress was clear.

Kurt got them into the office by flashing his warrant badge at the policemen guarding the door. Once inside, they found themselves confronting a grisly scene. The smell of blood—of recent death—was strong enough to make Elin flinch.

According to the officer in charge, about half an hour previously Dr. Stubler had shot to death his nurse and then turned the gun on himself.

The killer is cleaning up loose ends.

That was the thought that gave Elin chills as she sat beside Kurt in a darkened booth in the Paradise Club looking down through a window at the revelers below. Located directly above Jeweler Fritz's office high among the stone arches, it was accessible only by a narrow flight of stairs from the office itself. Its basic function was to serve as a control room that allowed Storch to monitor the goings-on in his club. One wall was full of equipment—switches that controlled the lights and fountain, a turntable in case, Elin assumed, the live entertainment didn't show up, a microphone and intercom system, and various other items that served she had no idea what function.

For Kurt and her, their position in the control room allowed them to see without being seen. If the killer was down there, the last thing they wanted was for him to spot them and get spooked.

The autopsies were still pending, but preliminary examinations indicated that the deaths of Dr. Stubler and his nurse had happened exactly as they had appeared to: murder/suicide. Probably, the cop in charge opined, a failed romance.

Elin wasn't buying it.

It was a little past two thirty on Saturday—no, Sunday morning now. She and Kurt had been in the club for well over two hours, and the place was hopping. A lot of soldiers in uniform,

a lot of pretty young women, a lot of drink and drugs. With
Pia's sketches in mind, she was doing her best to scan the faces
of the men for a likeness. No luck, largely because she couldn't
really see their faces. They were simply oval shades of pale in
the dark. She was hoping to identify behaviors that might help
narrow down what right now amounted to an entire establishment full of suspects, which was why she was clutching her notebook. Unfortunately, all her vaunted observational powers were
growing more useless by the minute because the smoke, from
cigarettes and hookahs, was so thick it was like trying to see
through a swirling, red-tinged fog. The tiny, flickering candles
on the tables didn't help. They reminded her of a wood full of
feral creatures, their eyes glowing red in the night.

"Stop scowling so, *liebling*. You'll get wrinkles." Leaning back
in his chair, his arms folded over his chest, Kurt was looking at
her through the gloom rather than at the crowd below.

"This is useless. I can't see anything. There's too much smoke."
She, on the other hand, was leaning forward with her face practically pressed to the glass, because *she* was focused on the job
they were there to do. The hostility between them hadn't abated,
although she, at least, was doing her best to keep it civil. He
wasn't. That *liebling* of his had been pure provocation. She chose
to ignore it.

"You want some coffee instead of that bilge you're drinking?
I'm sure Storch—" he nodded at the unmistakable figure, who
was the one person she could clearly track as he made the rounds
of the tables below "—has some around here somewhere."

"No, thank you."

"Did I mention that you're looking particularly beautiful tonight? That shade of black really brings out your eyes."

He was *trying* to get under her skin, she reminded herself. Her
dress—yes, it was black, and long sleeved and belted at the waist
and slim—had been chosen specifically to blend into the shadows. And given that black was pretty much black, no shades or

gradations involved, and her eyes were blue, it definitely did not bring out her eyes.

"Thank you," she said.

"Although you might be a little on the skinny side for some tastes. Not mine, you understand, but some."

She didn't even dignify that with a response.

"Me, I've always gone for the brainy types. And what I've found is that usually the ones with a little more up here—" his typical, obnoxious male gesture indicated a full chest "—have a little less up here." He tapped his forehead.

It was too much. She rounded on him.

He smiled.

Storch walked through the door before she could annihilate Kurt with the ego-crushing reply trembling on the tip of her tongue.

"When is this supposed to happen?" Storch asked Kurt as he closed the door.

"Soon," Kurt answered.

"We got a lot of brass in house tonight." He sounded uneasy. "I'm thinking about pulling my consent."

"Too late." Kurt didn't sound at all perturbed as he slanted a look up at Storch, who'd stopped beside him to peer through the window at the crowd.

With a sharp turn of his head, Storch directed a frown at Kurt. "What the hell does that mean? You told me I could shut it down at any time."

"And you can. But, see, the part I forgot to mention is that I can shut down your club—all your clubs—at any time. Permanently. If I want."

Storch stared at him. "You son of a bitch."

"And here I thought we were friends again."

"You think it's just going to be me taking the flak from this? Think again. From what I've heard, you're not exactly Mr. Popularity in certain circles. And if you go putting some of these officers under arrest—"

"They're not going to be put under arrest. They're going to be detained for patronizing an illegal club until I can get them checked out. Most of them will be free by breakfast tomorrow. And none of them are going to want to publicize the fact that they were out in the middle of the night doing something they shouldn't, probably with somebody they shouldn't. So except for our lucky winner, I don't expect any of the rest of them will have a thing to say."

Before Storch could reply, a voice came out of nowhere.

"Baron, you up there?"

Elin jumped and looked around for the source. With a fulminating look for Kurt, Storch took the two strides needed to reach the wall with all the equipment and pressed a button. The intercom! Of course, the voice—it was Jeweler Fritz; she recognized it now—had come through the intercom.

"What do you want?" Storch said into it.

"I'm getting ready to leave now." Jeweler Fritz had point-blank refused to stay in place during the evening's culmination, because, in his words, he was allergic to police.

"I'm on my way down." Storch let up on the button and turned to Kurt. "You owe me for this. For the rest of your life."

"Next time you need a favor," Kurt said.

"I guarantee you won't be in a position to grant it," Storch answered bitterly, and left.

"That's a nasty habit you have," Elin said after a moment. She was looking out at the crowd again, but no longer held out much hope of seeing anything worthwhile.

"What is?"

"Threatening people."

"In times like these, we all do what we must."

Elin didn't reply. She was restless with nerves. Right at that very moment the killer was out there somewhere hunting, getting ready to take a victim if, please, God, no, he hadn't done so already. She was growing increasingly afraid that he would escape the trap they'd set for him. Because of the *wolfsangel*, because at least half the victims were known to have patronized it, because they had limited resources and secrecy to maintain and this was the best lead they had, Kurt had chosen to focus tonight's operation exclusively on the Paradise Club. Police officers were at that very moment concealed outside, detaining any club-goers who tried to leave before the trap was sprung. As for the trap itself, it would snap shut in the form of a staged police raid that would corral everyone inside at precisely 2:45 a.m. They didn't expect anyone to arrive after that, because the Paradise closed at three.

"If we've calculated this wrong, tonight another girl is going to die." That was the thought Elin couldn't get out of her head. The faces of the victims, of the families, most of whom she'd now met, of Lotte Dietrich's parents, haunted her.

"Everything's in place. If he's here, we'll get him."

"But what if he's not?"

A crash, the shriek of multiple whistles, an explosion of movement as newcomers rushed into the room and the people who were already there jumped to their feet—all that took Elin's breath. She, too, jumped to her feet, eyes riveted on what was happening below.

"Police! Nobody move! *Nobody move!* Hands in the air! Leave those weapons alone, sirs! This is a raid!"

About two dozen cops, approved by Nebe for what was, for public consumption in case word of it should get out, tonight's raid on an illegal club, burst into view from the direction of the official entrance, which was out of sight of the window. Screams, shouts, and futile attempts to run or hide ensued.

Kurt was on his feet, watching beside her as the policemen spread throughout the room, slapping on handcuffs as needed, ordering everyone onto the center dance floor, shoving recalcitrant club-goers in the direction they wanted them to go.

Details were impossible to discern as the smoke swirled and rose toward the ceiling. Squinting down, Elin tried to see through the haze that seemed thicker and redder now as it billowed around the window.

"Holy hell!" Kurt exclaimed.

Elin shot a questioning glance at him just as, from multiple voices below, a bone-chilling cry went up.

"Fire!"

30

STRUCK DUMB, ELIN LOOKED DOWN THROUGH THE
mushrooming cloud of red-tinged smoke as, below, the club
devolved in an instant into a scene of complete pandemonium.
Guests ran screaming in every direction searching for a way
out. Unable to control their erstwhile prisoners, the cops abandoned the effort and shouted and ran, too, some toward the fire
as they snatched up tablecloths and other items with the intent
of battling it. Elin could see no more of it than a fierce red glow
because the window faced away from what was apparently an
outburst of flames near the entrance the cops had used, the official entrance to the Paradise Club through the back door of
a theater on Kurfürstendamm. It was clear from the panicked
movements of everyone below that the scene was one of rapidly escalating danger.

A hand grabbed hers. *"Let's go."*

"Kurt. Oh my God." As the spell that had held her mesmerized broke, she ran with him to the door.

He turned the knob, shoved the door—and nothing happened. It didn't open, didn't budge. Cursing, he twisted the knob some more, kicked at it, put his shoulder to it.

"What's wrong with it? Why won't it open? Is it locked?" The beginnings of panic sent cold tendrils twisting through her. Her heart thumped. Just as they had, Storch had entered the room easily, no unlocking involved. Had he, upon leaving, *locked them in*?

"It's not locked. Something's blocking it." Taking a step back, Kurt gave the door a mighty kick that had no effect on it whatsoever. "Damn it!" He tried again and fell back, cursing.

"We've got to get out of here." She could smell the smoke now, acrid and unpleasant, very different from the sweetish scent given off by the hookahs. The red glow was bright enough that it lit up the control room, bright enough so that she could see thin gray fingers of smoke creeping beneath the door.

"*Kurt.*" She pointed.

His jacket landed on the floor at the bottom of the door. Instantly understanding the purpose—to block the smoke from getting in—she helped him shove it into place against the crack.

"We're not getting out that way. Come on." He whirled back toward the window, and she followed. The approximate size and shape of a car's windshield, the window wasn't made to open. It was thick glass set into the stone wall.

"We're about three stories up." Kurt was already looking down, measuring the distance, when she reached the window. Gazing out, Elin went dizzy with horror. Flames licked the walls, climbed the tapestries, reached for the ceiling. The roiling smoke was bloodred now and so thick that she could barely see through it. The screams, the awful, choking screams, pinpointed the location of the mass of people huddled toward the back of the club. They were fighting and climbing over each other as they fought to escape the flames, to get as far away from them as possible, to get out.

The door she, Kurt, and Storch had entered the Paradise through, the door from the tunnels Storch called Germania, was back there behind the crowd. Had Storch locked it after they'd entered? She couldn't remember, but obviously it was locked or barricaded in some way—or they simply didn't know it was there.

"The door—somebody needs to open the door to the tunnels and let those people out." Elin turned to Kurt and was surprised to find he wasn't beside her any longer.

"*Storch.*" His voice was loud, urgent. He was in front of the control wall, pressing the intercom button. "Are you down there? Can you hear me? We're trapped up here, something's blocking the door. We need you to come up and move it and let us out. *Storch. Anybody. Storch.*"

"Kurt—" Her heart felt like it would beat its way out of her chest.

He looked around at her. "He's not answering," he said grimly, and strode toward her. "No one's answering."

The screams from below reached a crescendo. Muffled as they were, the abject fear in them was enough to send prickles racing over her skin. Throat tightening, Elin looked back through the window.

At what she saw, her stomach dropped.

"Somebody's got to open that door. All those people, they're going to die." Staring down in horror as, having clearly found the door to the tunnels, the crowd below began smashing against it in a mass explosion of panic, Elin placed her open hand against the glass in sympathy. To her shock, it was hot enough to burn her palm. She immediately yanked it back.

We're going to die right along with them. Terror, bitter as bile, rose up in her throat as she faced it, then fiercely rejected it with every bit of her body and soul. *Niles. I can't die. I can't leave Niles.*

"We have to get out. Right now." She turned toward Kurt

in desperation. Tinted red by the fire, his features harsh with dread, his big body braced as if for a fight, he was staring down into the abyss.

Without a word, he turned from the window, strode for the door.

A sound—a whoosh loud enough to startle—jerked her attention back to the floor below. The screaming, struggling mass of people surged forward en masse as if toward salvation. The door—it was open! Had someone unlocked it? Had they broken through? The fire flashed higher as they fled and it fed on fresh oxygen. She could hear the roar, feel the heat of it through the window. A second later, a horrible realization hit her. The oxygen burst had caused the fire to expand exponentially. A leaping, snapping wall of fire now encircled the room below. Anyone who hadn't already made it through the door wasn't getting out.

And neither were they.

"We're trapped." Her heart was in her throat as she looked at Kurt, who was looking out through the window again. The horror of their potential fate left her dizzy.

"Not yet. I'm going to climb down as best I can, and when I'm down I want you to hang from your hands and drop and I'll catch you." He'd retrieved his jacket, she saw as he caught her by the arm. "We don't have long. You have to jump the minute I'm down. If you freeze, you're dead. Understand?"

The thought of jumping into that inferno was paralyzing.

With a great effort of will she pulled herself together.

"Yes."

"Good girl. Get back and get down."

She crouched behind one of the chairs as he pulled his gun from its holster and, with a glance at her to make sure she was safely out of the way, shot out the window.

The almost simultaneous bang of the gunshot and sound of shattering glass was followed by a rush of heat that felt like it came straight from a blast furnace. Without a buffer, the pop and crackle of the fire was terrifying.

"Elin." Low and husky, his voice sounded odd. Had he been hurt?

"Kurt?" Rising cautiously, covering her nose and mouth with her arm as the searing air threatened to crisp her skin, she looked toward where she'd last seen him—beside the window. He wasn't there. She looked all around. The small room was dark, full of smoke—and empty.

"Elin."

Even as she ran toward the window, thinking he might be calling her from below, she realized that the voice wasn't his. Her head swung sharply in the direction from which it had come.

"Say your prayers."

The intercom. Her eyes fixed on it as horror gripped her. The voice had changed in a moment to a high-pitched, sibilant whisper that was coming through the intercom.

Her blood ran cold. The hair rose on the back of her neck.

A wild glance around confirmed she was alone in the room.

"Kurt." She was at the window, fighting panic as she looked down. Fire was everywhere. The walls were engulfed. The heat, the roar, terrified.

The killer was down there, in the office below the control room.

Kurt. He was straightening, looking up, having clearly just hit the ground. Where the fire hadn't yet reached. She tried to call to him, to warn him, but smoke was choking her, making her cough, turning her voice into a croak that didn't reach him.

"Elin!" Coughing, too, he held up his arms to her.

He'd thrown his jacket over the edge of the window to shield against any remaining glass shards. Grabbing that covered edge, she levered herself out the window, hung for the briefest of moments, and dropped straight down into his arms.

He caught her, staggering back a pace as her full weight slammed into him. She grabbed his arms as they wrapped around her waist and hung on.

"He's here, the killer's here. In the office." She coughed, gasped. Even as he set her on her feet she was pulling away, pointing toward the closed office door.

"What?" Wrapping an arm around her, he dragged her toward the office. "Hurry!"

"No! We can't! The killer's in there!"

"It's the only way out."

The heat, the smoke, the crackle and roar as the fire stretched above them eliminated all choice. The *wolfsangel* insert in the ceiling was starting to buckle from the heat. Her eyes widened on it even as a crack snaked across its center.

Kurt's gun was in his hand as they burst through the office door. The electricity still worked in the office, but the overhead light flickered on and off, warning that it could soon go out.

The room appeared empty.

"He's here! He has to be!"

Behind them, the stained-glass lozenge fell with a tremendous crash.

Kurt slammed the door as shards of glass exploded in every direction, peppering the outside of the door with what sounded like bird shot. Elin looked wildly around. Kurt swung the gun in a wide arc.

The smoke and heat were trapped inside with them, but the fire was cut off—for now. The office was small, though, and the fire was growing fast. Soon it would consume the office, too.

"There's nowhere to go." Panic sharpened her voice.

"Trust me." Kurt was checking every possible hiding place. "What makes you think he was in here?"

"He spoke to me over the intercom. He said, *'Say your prayers.'*" Coughing, Elin managed to gasp the words out. "It was *him*. He was *here*."

Kurt was coughing, too, as he grabbed her hand.

"He's not here now. Come on." Gun in hand, he pulled her after him through a door she hadn't noticed before. It opened into a stairwell, steep and narrow, with concrete walls. "Shut the door behind you."

She did. "How did you know this was here?"

"Storch showed me. Earlier today, when I did a dry run."

They were climbing as they spoke, carefully because it was difficult to see.

"He spoke to me over the intercom. After you went out the window. He was in the office."

"I believe you."

"We had him. We had him trapped. He must have started the fire to escape."

"That's what I'm thinking, too."

Judging from the faint threads of moonlight that filtered down, the shaft led outside—and someone else had exited through it before them because the door to the outside was obviously open.

"He must have gone this way. That means he's up ahead of us," Elin whispered in urgent warning as that terrifying truth occurred. The need to cough was uncontrollable, but she muffled the sound with her arm.

"I figured that out." Kurt spoke softly, too. "I'm hoping we can catch up to him."

The thought appalled Elin. Much as she longed to bring the killer to justice, that whispered "Say your prayers," coupled with the fire and their hairbreadth escape, had left her shaken to the core. The prospect that the killer might be hiding somewhere on the stairs, crouched in the dark waiting for them, made her want to jump out of her skin.

Her eyes darted toward every nook and cranny as they approached it. Her heart jumped at each moving shadow.

As they neared the rectangular opening that looked like it might have been cut into flat ground, Kurt's pace slowed. His movements were careful, quiet. Behind him, she was careful and quiet, too, while her heart raced and her insides quivered with fear.

Fresh air, sweet and cool after the hot suffocation of the fire, and a canopy of night sky studded with stars greeted them as they reached the top of the staircase.

Kurt glanced back at her once, in warning, then stepped out into the velvety dark night, his gun at the ready. She was right behind him, her hand clasped in his. He made a gesture to stay low. She did, moving after him in the same kind of semicrouched defensive posture that he adopted.

So many shapes and shadows surrounded them that it was impossible to judge what, if anything, constituted a threat. Sirens in the distance drowned out any telltale sounds.

She shivered as the moon came out from behind a cloud and she saw where they were.

The old cemetery was covered in thick grass with obelisks and statues and grave markers stretching over rolling ground until darkness swallowed up the edges. Behind them to the left, a church spire was silhouetted against the moon.

Storch had said that the reason he'd named it the Paradise Club was because it was located beneath the cemetery of the Kaiser Wilhelm Memorial Church. With that realization, she was oriented, and the cemetery was no longer quite so scary. All they had to do was make it to the street, and the car.

By way of a shadow-filled cemetery with a thousand places to hide.

Was the killer out here waiting for them? He could be behind a grave marker watching them now.

The thought had her looking everywhere, probing every shadow, while her pulse pounded like a drum in her ears.

What if he had a gun as well as a knife?

Her mouth went dry.

Some distance away, a dark shape detached itself from the rest and lurched across the grass. Elin's heart leaped as she spotted it.

"Look." It was a sharp whisper, uttered as she tugged on Kurt's hand. His head swiveled in the direction she pointed just in time to see the figure disappear behind a monument.

He released her hand. That in itself was terrifying, because it meant he thought he might need both hands for whatever ensued.

"Stay close." His whispered warning was scarcely louder than a breath. Moving swiftly, stealthily, toward the monument—it was a giant stone angel with spread wings, Elin saw as she followed in Kurt's wake—he reached it in minutes. Whoever had taken refuge behind the monument hadn't reappeared, which meant he must be still there. Elin's heart was in her throat as Kurt gestured to her to get down. She crouched—and he jumped out in front of the monument, assumed a shooter's two-handed stance, and barked, "Don't move! This is the police!"

"Der Schwarzer Mann! Der Schwarzer Mann!" a little girl shrieked. Elin was shocked as she recognized the words, and the voice.

The children.

"No, it's all right!" Kurt immediately lowered his gun. As he started to approach the monument, the boy yelled, "Go away!" and a rock came hurtling through the darkness to hit Kurt somewhere below the knee.

"Hey!" Kurt jumped back.

Running to join him, motioning to him to stay where he was, Elin didn't immediately see them. It was so dark, and they'd gone silent, and if Kurt hadn't gestured at the base of the monument Elin might never have spotted them. But there they were, hiding in what seemed to be a hollowed-out space that might once have been an animal's den dug deep beneath the slab of granite that was the base. The opening was small, too small for an adult to wriggle through. If the children couldn't be coaxed out, it would take a shovel to reach them. Always supposing there wasn't a tunnel attached with a back exit that would allow them to disappear again.

They were so close. They couldn't lose the children again.

"Christoph, is that you?" As Elin cautiously approached, all she could see of them was a single pale face peering out of the hole through the tufts of tall grass that grew around the slab. She thought it was the boy. "We're your friends, Christoph. We want to help you."

Like an animal gone to earth, he was watching her. She could see the glimmer of his eyes through the darkness. The thought that the killer might be nearby, also watching, with his own motivation for getting hands on the children, stretched her nerves perilously thin. Knowing that Kurt was behind her keeping an eye out was what allowed her to direct all her focus on the task at hand. In the background, sirens screamed as fire trucks and emergency personnel converged on the Paradise. The smell of smoke was just beginning to be noticeable. She was afraid the sounds and smells would further spook the children. If they missed this chance, who knew when, if ever, they would get one again?

"Go away. I'll throw a rock at you," the boy threatened.

"Please don't, Christoph."

No rock was forthcoming, and he didn't duck out of sight, or try to escape. Probably, she thought, because she knew his name.

"Don't be afraid." Elin dropped to her knees in the cool grass in front of the monument.

"He's the police."

The boy was looking beyond her at Kurt, who, as far as she could tell, had not come any closer.

To deny it would be to lie, and she didn't want to do that. "I won't let anything bad happen to you, I promise."

"You're trying to trick me."

What to say? His fear and mistrust were palpable, and he had good reason for it, she knew. Any Jew, even a child, found in Berlin was subject to detention and immediate deportation to a camp. The child might not know exactly what would happen to them if they were taken, but he knew enough to run and hide and be afraid of the police.

"You can trust me, Christoph, I promise." Then inspiration struck. *"Shema, Yisrael, Adonai Eloheinu, Adonai Echad…"*

Elin recited the Shema, the most important of Jewish prayers that every child of that faith knew, which had been taught to her by Lars, who used to say it to Niles every day. She was aware that she was taking a huge risk. By revealing to Kurt that she thought the children were Jews and exposing her own familiarity with the pillars of that religion, she was putting their fate, and her own as well, in his hands. But as she prayed, the boy's face drew close enough to the hole that she could see his fine features, a shock of dark hair.

The child said the final words of the prayer with her.

"I know you're scared, Christoph, and hungry and tired, too. We'll get you food and a bed and make sure you're safe." She could only hope that Kurt had the same good intentions. She was gambling that he did, or that at least he would go along with hers, but there wasn't any way to be sure. He hadn't moved from where she'd left him, but she could feel him watching— and listening. "Please let us help you. Please come out."

Her eyes met Christoph's through the darkness. His were big with fear and shadowed, probably with hunger and exhaustion. He regarded her warily, but also, she thought, with the tiniest flicker of hope.

"I have a little boy about your age," she said. "Your mother would want you to come with me."

"My mama got taken away," the little girl said. Pushing past the boy, she crawled out of the hole. She was skinny, dirty, and ragged, and Elin gathered her up in her arms. "The soldiers arrested her because she was a Jew. Do you know when she's coming back?"

31

"WHERE ARE YOU TAKING US?" CHRISTOPH WALKED nervously down the dark sidewalk. He was as skinny and dirty and ragged as his sister, whose name was Rebekah. Their last name was Cohen, he'd told them, and he was ten years old and she was seven. From the way he stayed a short but wary distance from the rest of them, Elin knew he was poised to run if necessary. What kept him was his sister, who was being carried by Kurt because she had a badly swollen ankle. Elin thought it was probably sprained, which accounted for the lurching gait of the shadowy shape she'd first spotted running across the graveyard.

"Somewhere safe," Elin said firmly. With Rebekah hoisted onto his shoulders and his gun holstered but readily accessible, Kurt strode silently beside her. The little extra emphasis she'd put on the words was for his benefit, because she meant what she said. If he had some other agenda…

The thought made her stomach drop. What would she do if he did? Right now, she was putting all her faith—and possibly staking the children's lives, and her own as well—in the hope that he did not.

"Will there be food? You promised there'd be food," Rebekah said. "I'm hungry."

"Yes," Elin replied, because if there wasn't she would get them something to eat by whatever means necessary. Beyond the car Kurt had not specified a destination, and Elin hadn't wanted to press him in front of the children. She was trying to keep things as calm and unthreatening as possible, which was difficult considering that both she and Kurt were on edge at the knowledge that the killer was still out there, possibly close, possibly watching or following or even targeting them. Added to that was the enormous hullabaloo on Kurfürstendamm as firefighters battled the conflagration that had started in the Paradise Club but had expanded to include the theater that served as its entrance and the shops on either side of it. With screaming sirens, billowing smoke, and people running all over the place, there was a lot to frighten children.

Fortunately, Kurt had parked on a side street that ran perpendicular to Kurfürstendamm so they were not trapped in place by the emergency vehicles that blocked off the area. When they reached his car, Kurt swung the girl off his shoulders and settled her into the back seat. With a long, not entirely trusting look at Elin—"It's going to be all right," she promised him in response—Christoph climbed in beside his sister.

Kurt closed the door on them.

"Where are you taking them?" Elin asked the instant the children could no longer hear them.

"Like you told them, somewhere safe." His face was unreadable in the moonlight.

"Really?" There was a vulnerability to her question that spoke to exactly how much at his mercy she knew she and the children were. Her eyes searched his. He was a Nazi, after all, and a police officer. To aid Jewish children—he would face summary execution if he was found out.

She shivered at the thought.

"Yes, really."

"Where—" She broke off because he was shaking his head.

"You don't need to know, and I'm not going to tell you. You've already told them your first name. Don't tell them your last name, or anything else about yourself." His voice was grim. "If there wasn't a damned murderer out here somewhere with you in his sights, I'd leave you here. As it is—get in the car, Elin."

He turned away as he said it. She hesitated, watching him, but, really, what choice did she have other than to trust him? And deep inside, she felt she could. The man she thought she knew would not turn children over to the Gestapo. Holding on to that, she got in the car, climbing into the back seat with the children. Rebekah immediately scrambled across her brother and scooted close to her side. While Kurt drove, Elin gently examined the little girl's ankle. Bekah, as her brother called her, said she hurt it running away from *Der Schwarzer Mann* two nights ago.

"He almost caught me." The remembered fear was there in her voice. "He's been trying to catch me ever since they took Mama away."

"There's no such thing as *Der Schwarzer Mann*," Christoph said scornfully. "I keep *telling* you. The *Nazis* are chasing us, because they hate us and they want to arrest us like they did Mama."

"Reni said it was the Gestapo who hate us."

"They do, too."

"When was your mother arrested?" Elin asked.

"A long time ago. Before Purim," Christoph said. Elin did a quick calculation. Purim had been in March, so about six months previously. "She went to work and she didn't come home, and our neighbor Reni said she was arrested and they had arrested everyone at her factory. Reni took us to stay in her apartment, but then the Gestapo came for her. We hid in the cupboard and we waited, but she didn't come back and Mama didn't come."

"They didn't come back *ever*. We had to hide all the time and we didn't have any place to live and it was cold and we were hungry. We went with some children who lived in a park but the Gestapo came one night and caught everybody. Christoph and I got away but they shot Christoph and made him fall and he hurt his arm," Bekah said.

"You were shot?" Elin looked at Christoph.

He nodded. "The bullet hit the bottom of my ear and went right on past and hit another boy, Georg. He fell down just like I did, but he didn't get up. I had to get up because of Bekah, and we kept running, but the soldiers chasing us gathered around Georg so that was what saved us. My ear bled and bled, but the worst part was my arm. It hurt for a long time, and now I can't straighten it out." He held it up to show Elin.

Although it was too dark to see much of anything at all, she remembered the ragged edge of his earlobe and the crooked arm. Cautiously feeling his forearm, she determined that he'd suffered a broken ulna that had never been set properly, if at all.

"It can be fixed. Once you're safe." Elin winced inwardly at the thought of the pain the child must have suffered.

Kurt asked, "What happened after that?"

"All the other children were gone, so we went back to our old building and hid in the basement," Christoph said. "I think the Gestapo were looking for us because they kept coming around, but they never found us. Then the building got bombed and we tried to stay there anyway but this policeman came and tried to catch us—"

"It was *Der Schwarzer Mann*," Bekah interrupted. "He tried to catch us and we ran and that's when we had to go live in that hole."

"Do you remember seeing a hurt naked lady lying on the ground not far from your building?" Kurt asked. "It would have been not so long ago in the middle of the night."

Glancing at him, Elin saw that he was looking at the three of them through the rearview mirror. She would have waited a little longer to start questioning the children about what they might have seen regarding Lotte Dietrich's murder, but since she didn't know where they were going she also didn't know how much time remained until they reached their destination. They were headed southwest, she realized, and from the absence of traffic and the shape of the buildings that she could barely see through the darkness she thought that they had entered a residential district.

He wouldn't be driving them across town to a random residential district only to turn the children over to the Gestapo, she told herself stoutly. If he'd wanted to do that, he could have done it right there on Kurfürstendamm.

"Yes," Christoph said. "She wasn't hurt, though. She was dead."

"She was all covered with blood," Bekah added. "The man rolled her out of a bag."

Elin's heart skipped a beat.

"Did you see the man?" she asked.

"Sort of," Christoph answered. "It was really dark."

"Could you describe him, do you think?" Kurt asked.

Christoph shrugged. "It was really dark," he repeated. "We couldn't see his face or anything. He just looked like a normal kind of man."

"Not really tall or fat?"

"Just normal."

"Could you tell what he was wearing? A uniform or anything like that?"

"We were too scared," Bekah said.

"It was too dark." Christoph gave his sister a quelling look.

"What about his car? Did you see a car? Or some other vehicle?"

"No. All we saw was this man, kind of bent down, and he had this big bag on the ground, and then he kind of rolled the naked dead lady out of it."

"Did he see you?" Kurt asked.

"I don't know," Christoph said. "I think maybe he did. He looked up toward where we were and then he stood up fast. But like I said, it was really dark."

"He was scary," Bekah said. "We ran away until he was gone."

"Until he was gone? Did you come back?" Kurt asked.

"When we saw lights. But a policeman shot at us, so we ran away again."

It was clear that the children had not recognized them from that night or associated them with the policeman who'd shot at them, and neither Elin nor Kurt enlightened them.

"When we came back the next time, the dead lady was gone," Christoph said. "Everybody was gone."

"Was that that same night?" Kurt asked.

Christoph nodded.

Realizing that Kurt, whose attention was back on the road, couldn't see, Elin answered for him. "Yes."

"Then what did you do?" Kurt asked.

"We went down where the lady was and looked around. Bekah, show them what you found."

Bekah reached into the pocket of her skirt, pulled something out, and handed it to Elin.

It was a necklace, a small pendant on a delicate gold chain. The darkness made it difficult to see much detail, but Elin's heart started beating faster at the pendant's shape and feel. Moments later, excitement gripped her as they drove through a patch of moonlight bright enough to ascertain that besides being heart shaped, the pendant was gold rimmed and held a tiny yellow flower covered in celluloid.

"Are you sure it's a good idea to leave them?" Elin asked Kurt with concern. "If the killer saw us with them, he might have followed us. As you said, he seems to be cleaning up loose ends. They're loose ends."

"We weren't followed. I made sure of that. And we have to

leave them. They can't stay with us. Too many questions would be asked. They wouldn't be safe. They're not safe anywhere in Berlin. Except possibly here, for a short time."

Elin looked around. The children waited in the back seat, while she and Kurt stood outside the car, which he had just parked at the end of a long driveway beside what appeared to be a carriage house. Even shrouded in darkness, the house it belonged to, three stories tall with pale limestone walls and a red tile roof, looked large and beautiful. The grounds were extensive, with high hedges and lush plantings that provided a maximum of privacy. Unlike in the more densely populated areas of the city, night sounds of insects whirring and small animals rustling in the undergrowth could clearly be heard. The now-brisk night air carried the honey-lemon scent of the linden trees bordering the grounds.

"What is this place?" Elin asked, but before Kurt could answer—if he was even going to answer—a woman appeared out of the darkness, coming from the direction of the house. She was small, with short dark hair, and wore what appeared to be a light-colored satin dressing gown tied hastily around a slim waist.

Kurt stepped away to meet her.

"Maria." His voice was low.

"Who is that?" she asked, equally low. She was looking at Elin. Frowning at Elin.

"A friend."

"You're sure she can be trusted?"

"I wouldn't have brought her if I wasn't."

"Hmmph." She turned her attention back to Kurt. "I didn't expect you. And so late! I have houseguests." There was the faintest scolding note in her voice. Despite how softly she and Kurt were speaking, Elin was just close enough to overhear. Hopefully without appearing to, she hung on every word.

"It's an emergency. Children."

"How many?"

"Two. A boy and a girl."

"I'm housing thirty-four of your U-boats already."

"I know." Kurt sounded apologetic. "I'm finalizing arrangements. It won't be much longer. Can you take them?"

"Children? Of course. Give them to me. I can't linger, I must get back inside. It would never do to have my sister or brother-in-law wake up and start asking questions about what I'm doing outside in the middle of the night."

"I'll get them." Kurt turned back toward the car. Crossing her arms over her chest, glancing all around, Maria stayed where she was.

As Kurt reached Elin, and she realized that separation from the children was imminent, she said urgently, "They need food. And care. Bekah's ankle needs to be soaked in cold water and bandaged. And—"

"They'll get everything they need here. There's even a doctor. They'll be well taken care of, I promise." Kurt opened the car door and leaned into the back seat. When he straightened, Bekah was in his arms. Christoph scrambled out beside him.

"That lady—" Kurt pointed at Maria as he started walking toward her "—is going to take you inside now."

"No!" Bekah held out her arms to Elin as Kurt carried her past. "I want to stay with *you*!"

"You can't, Bekah. You need to go with her." Catching up with Kurt, who stopped to accommodate her, Elin gave Bekah a hug and felt a pang as the thin little arms wrapped around her neck. "It'll be all right," she promised, unwinding Bekah's arms to hold her hand and at the same time ruffling Christoph's hair. "There are people here who will take care of you both, and you'll be safe."

"Will they take us to Mama?" Bekah asked.

Elin's heart broke. She was saved from having to answer by the arrival of Maria.

"Come," Maria said to the child as Kurt set her on the ground. With a scared look at Elin, who nodded encouragement, Bekah

let Maria take her hand. Seen up close, Maria was older than Elin
had at first supposed, closer to Hilde's age than to her own. To
the children Maria added, "We must get you settled," and started
to walk away with Bekah, whose hand she firmly held, beside
her. Christoph trailed a step or two behind.

Bekah's lips trembled as she looked back at Elin. "I'm hungry.
You said there'd be food."

"We have food," Maria said. "You will have some as soon as
we're inside."

As she watched the children disappear into the darkness, Elin's
momentary sense of loss was quickly replaced by a fierce relief
that they'd found an apparent safe harbor. Even if it was for only
a short while.

"This is the best outcome possible for them," Kurt said, his
eyes on her face. "Let's go."

Elin didn't speak as they drove away.

"What will happen to them?" she asked finally.

"If everything goes as planned, they will survive."

The bleakness of that made her feel cold all over.

What a terrible world we live in when the best outcome we can hope
for is that children will survive, she thought.

"Does their survival depend on the arrangements you're finalizing?"

He glanced at her. "Heard that, did you?"

"Every word."

"Remember what I said about keeping your focus on the murders and letting everything else pass you by so that you can safely
go home again?"

"I remember. I think we've crossed the Rubicon on that."

He frowned. "Elin—"

"My husband was Jewish. My son is *mischling*. I can't close my
eyes and pretend I don't see. I can't turn my back and walk away."

His face tightened. He said nothing, just frowned out at the
road unfolding before them.

Everything he'd done since she'd met him combined with what she'd just witnessed to provide a blinding flash of enlightenment.

"The children—those thirty-four U-boats Maria is housing—are you trying to *rescue* them?"

"Leave it alone, Elin."

"I can't leave it alone. I'm part of it now, don't you see? *Tell* me."

32

"WE'RE WORKING TO GET AS MANY OF THE REMAINING
Jews hiding in Berlin to safety outside the country as we can."

Kurt's face was as hard as his answer was terse. Staring at him,
Elin instantly made what felt like a thousand mental connections. His refusal to look for the children that first night, when
he would have known there was a chance they might have seen
the killer. His warning to her to say nothing about them to
Kaltenbrunner. His exclusion of Pia's sketches of them from the
case files. So many clues, and she'd missed them.

Or maybe not, on a subconscious level. Maybe that explained
why she'd allowed this attraction that burned between them to
get as far as it had, why she hadn't shut him down at the first
too-personal touch. Maybe that explained why his kisses melted
her bones, and why he had the power to give her butterflies.

Maybe, somewhere deep inside, she'd recognized the true character of the man all along.

"Does that explain why you've been disappearing into the forest after you drop me off at night?" The question emerged on the heels of a sharp indrawing of her breath as she made one more connection.

His lips compressed. "What I'm doing is dangerous. Knowing about it is dangerous. It's enough to get you arrested. And tortured. And killed. Now that those children you've been so worried about have been taken off the streets, your part in this is *over*. You need to put them, and everything you've learned since we found them, out of your mind. You want to make the world a better place, then concentrate on finding the killer you were brought here to help find." He shot her a narrow-eyed glance. "What did the little girl give you? Anything important?"

It was an effort to shift focus, but she did it.

"Lotte Dietrich's necklace." Everything he'd said was true, and she knew it. Her goal was to stay alive and get back to her son. Blocking the rest out of her mind was the only prudent thing to do. Delving in her pocket, she brought forth the necklace, which she'd wrapped in paper torn from her notebook because, in the absence of her bag, which she'd left in her hotel room, it was the only semisterile thing she had.

"See?" Unwrapping the necklace, she dangled it from her fingers for him to look at.

He frowned at it. Of course, as dark as it was inside the car, telltale details like the tiny yellow flower wouldn't be apparent.

"How sure are you that that was hers?"

"One hundred percent." The faint undertone of defiance in her voice was because she knew how he would react.

"Well, what do you know. I didn't think you ever got to one hundred percent."

"I rarely do, but this matches the earring she was wearing when she died so in this particular case I'm completely sure." She was wrapping the necklace back up as she spoke and returning it to her pocket. "I have to go to the lab, test it for fingerprints—"

"Tomorrow. You realize it's almost dawn? Before we do anything else, we need to grab a few hours' sleep."

"The killer won't sleep. Not tonight." The memory of the fire, coupled with the knowledge that their quarry was still at large in the night, sent cold prickles over her skin. A life was at risk—

"You don't think he'll go to ground?"

"No. He's most likely in a rage. He's been building toward tonight and the ritual was interrupted before the drive to act out his fantasy was satisfied. He won't just give up and go home."

"We know he was there," Kurt said. "We know we almost caught him. Even though he got away, the raid did some good in that it disrupted his plan. The question is, will he try to take another victim tonight? Or do we have some time?"

"I don't know. A lot depends, of course, on the availability of a victim. He could just grab and kill a woman at random, but killing a woman at random won't satisfy him. The choosing, the stalking, the anticipation—those are key elements in his fantasy. But does he know that? If he does, he may do a reset and start the cycle all over again, with either the same or a different victim. And in that case we have some time." She grimaced. "The truth is, we probably won't know whether he's taken another victim or what kind of time frame he's adopted until someone's reported missing or another body is found."

Kurt pulled the car off the road. It was only then, as it drove into the moonlit forecourt, that she realized they'd reached the Waldschloss. Officer Bruin was on duty in the lobby, but he'd obviously been half-asleep until his gaze lit on Kurt and his obligatory, standing *"Heil* Hitler" sounded more like a guilty yelp. Kurt responded in kind and followed Elin up the stairs.

Once they reached her room, instead of leaving after he did his usual check of the premises, Kurt said, "I'm going to stay for the rest of the night. That guy's come for you twice, and he just might try again, especially if he blames you for what happened at the Paradise. Everybody connected with the investigation probably knows where you're staying by now, and if you're the substitute victim he's got in mind I want to make sure he doesn't get the opportunity."

He looked tired and irritable. He was grimy from smoke—she guessed she must be, too—and his shirt had a rip in it. His jacket had been left behind in the club—

When she didn't immediately say anything, he gave her a wry smile. "Don't worry, I plan to sleep on the floor."

He clearly expected an argument. But the truth was, after what she'd been through tonight, she was relieved. Much as she hadn't wanted to face it, the thought of going to sleep alone in her hotel room, even with the theoretical protection of Officer Bruin down below, had been giving her the willies.

"I'm not worried," she said, and smiled at him. "Thank you."

He nodded. Their eyes met. For a moment something—a sizzle of electricity maybe—arced in the air between them.

Then she deliberately broke the connection by crossing to the chest and extracting her nightclothes. When she turned around, he was lifting a pillow from her bed.

"Good night," she said, and went into the bathroom. When she emerged, all washed and brushed and modestly attired in a nightgown plus bathrobe, Kurt was nowhere to be seen. She frowned, looked around again just to make sure, and then heard a rumbling snore. Walking past the end of the bed, she discovered him sound asleep, lying flat on his back on the rug, his hands on his chest, his shoes and tie off and his collar open. His gun was in its holster within arm's reach, and the pillow he'd taken earlier was tucked beneath his head.

She was still looking down at him, trying to ignore the warmth that had pulsed to life somewhere in the region of her heart at the sight of him lying there on her floor for the sole purpose of protecting her, when his lips parted and he let loose with another of those hearty snores. Not exactly the stuff of which romantic dreams were made, she thought, but then again, maybe romantic dreams weren't all they were purported to be. What he was, and what she needed, was a steady, dependable port in the storm. Smiling, she pulled the uppermost quilt from her bed and spread it over him, then climbed into bed and turned off the light.

If he snored all night she didn't hear it because, despite everything, the moment her head touched the pillow she fell fathoms deep asleep.

She awoke the next morning to bright sunlight pouring in around the edge of the curtains and the sound of the shower running in her bathroom. Because it was early and she was still groggy with sleep, it took her a second before she remembered who was in there, but when she did was instantly wide-awake and feeling ridiculously, uncharacteristically shy. Then the full events of the night before came rushing back, and the thought of facing Kurt fresh from the shower dropped to the bottom of her problem list. Relief that they'd found the children before the killer did and that they were now somewhere that was, at least temporarily, safe was tempered by worry for the children's future. Anxiety about what the day might bring—another victim?—was overshadowed by her sudden, acute need to get to the lab and examine the necklace. It was a long shot, but if the killer's prints should be on it all this would be over and—

Sitting up, she was just about to swing her legs over the side of the bed and reach for her robe when the door to the bathroom opened.

Kurt stepped into the room, then stopped when he saw she was awake and looking at him. He'd obviously showered—his hair was damp and the grime was gone—but he wore yesterday's clothes and he badly needed a shave.

"Good morning," she said. Having rejected her first impulse

to scramble back into bed and pull the covers up to her chin, she stood up and pulled on her robe like the adult she was.

He didn't smile. "Pack a bag. The more I think about this guy knowing where you're staying, the more I don't like it. I'm going to move you to another hotel for at least the next couple of nights."

"What about Pia and Jens?"

"The killer's not targeting them," was what he said, but something about his expression—

She gave him a keen look. "You need them to stay because you still need an excuse to come out here, don't you?"

Instead of answering, he turned away. It didn't matter. She knew she was right.

After last night, the knowledge neither alarmed nor infuriated her. She trusted him.

He said, "I'm going downstairs to make some calls. I'll be back."

"Wait." As he looked at her questioningly, she pulled Bekah's sweater from the closet where she'd hidden it among her own things and held it out to him. "This belongs to Bekah—the little girl. When next you visit them, please give it to her."

He took the sweater but shook his head. "I won't be visiting them. Someone could follow me. Someone could stake out the house where they're hiding. I stay far away unless the need is urgent, because there's too much risk for everyone involved. But I'll take your sweater and dispose of it. Keeping it poses a risk to *you*."

After he left, Elin quickly showered, dressed, and was throwing things into her suitcase when Pia, fully dressed and looking as bright-eyed as Elin wasn't feeling, let herself in.

"Was that Schneider I saw leaving your room?" Her friend was agog.

"He slept on the floor." Elin snapped the suitcase shut. "The killer came after me again last night. Kurt thinks he may be targeting me. I'm going to stay at another hotel for the next couple of nights, just in case."

"Tell me everything," Pia ordered, perching on a corner of the bed, but before Elin could give a highly edited version of her evening the door opened and Kurt walked in, minus the sweater. He nodded a greeting at Pia, who wiggled her fingers at him, then turned his attention to Elin.

"The door was unlocked." His tone was censorious.

"My fault," Pia piped up. "Sorry."

He grunted by way of acknowledgment, then said to Elin, "Step into the hall with me for a minute, would you?"

"I'll be right back," she said to Pia, who flopped back on the bed. She followed Kurt out the door and he closed it behind her.

"Storch was arrested last night." He kept his voice low so as not to be overheard. "I have to go see if I can get him released. Walter's here. He'll take you to the Alex when you're ready to go. I've already briefed him, and he's going to be sticking to you like glue. You want to be sure to keep him with you, even inside the Alex. Don't go anywhere, and I mean anywhere, without him."

"What about Sonja?" Elin asked.

"She'll be given other duties for the time being. I'll meet you at the Alex later today and we'll take it from there. For one thing, we'll check you into another hotel, so bring your things."

"We need to get inside the Paradise Club as soon as possible. The killer spoke to me over the intercom. His fingerprints should be on the button in the office. They're probably on the doorknob and other places as well." Sudden hope gave a lilt to her voice.

"Unless he wore gloves. Or wiped the surfaces down after."

"Spoilsport." She frowned at him. "We still need to get in there and check. Anyway, given the fire and how fast everything happened, there's a chance."

He nodded. "I'll see what I can do."

The sound of a door opening behind him had them both

looking around. Jens emerged, stopping on the threshold when he saw Kurt.

"If you're looking for Pia, she's in my room," Elin said.

"I was."

"How's the work on the code coming?" Kurt asked him.

"I thought I'd broken it." Jens sounded disgusted. "Problem is, what the key I came up with left me with was basically a string of random letters. Lots of *l*'s and *s*'s, plus a stray *x* here, a *q* there. Nothing that makes sense. But I'm not giving up."

"Do your best. Last night he targeted Elin again. He's going to keep killing until we stop him, and the only way we're going to stop him is to catch him." He broke off as Trott came into view, trudging up the stairs. "I've got to go." He looked at Elin. "Keep Walter with you. I'll see you later."

She nodded and he left, passing Trott on the stairs.

To Elin's disappointment, the necklace yielded only a single usable fingerprint and it was that of a young girl, almost certainly Bekah. Elin made no record of the discovery. As an additional precaution, after testing the traces of blood that adhered to the necklace—the blood was the same type as Lotte Dietrich's, no surprise—she carefully cleaned the pendant, in total defiance of protocol, in case some other researcher checked it for evidence and found the fingerprint or anything else that might link it to Bekah and went looking for her. A thorough cleaning involved removing the celluloid and swabbing it inside and out with alcohol. In the process, she discovered barely visible words inscribed in white on the white vellum upon which the yellow flower was mounted. The words encircled the flower, and the white on white made them difficult to see. To read them she had to put them under her microscope.

"Heilig soll uns Sein Jede Mutter guten Blutes." Every mother of good German blood should be holy to us.

She had no idea what the significance, if any, of the inscription, or the necklace itself, was. Trott was with her, going through records of Amt V personnel possessing type A blood to check for a history of violence or any kind of anomaly that might serve as a triggering event around the time of the first murder. He could shed no light. Reassembling the necklace, she tucked it into a sterile container and stowed it away. She had moved on to going over the autopsy results for Dr. Stubler and his assistant when Kurt walked in. He'd shaved and changed, and looked surprisingly alert given the amount of sleep deprivation she knew he had to be suffering from, because she was herself.

She greeted him with a quick, spontaneous smile. He smiled back, a slow-dawning smile that did absurd things to her insides.

"You have any problem?" Trott asked him, and Kurt's attention was immediately diverted.

"A few. Luckily Storch has some high-level friends. He didn't help himself by insisting that the Kripo needs to pay for the damage to his club. Because it caught fire as a result of a police operation," he explained in response to Trott's questioning look.

Trott snorted.

"Exactly," Kurt said before turning to Elin. "Ready to go?" When she nodded, he picked up her suitcase from where she'd left it just inside the door and they headed out.

"I don't suppose you've heard anything about a body being found. Or a missing girl," Elin said once they were inside his car. It was late afternoon, and traffic was heavy as they headed toward the Hotel Kaiserhof, where, he told her, he'd booked her a room. It was terrifying to think the killer might have taken another victim and they weren't yet aware of it. It was almost as bad to know that if he hadn't, he was out there somewhere in a carefully masked frenzy planning a fresh kill.

He shook his head. "When I know, you'll know. You make any headway today?"

"According to their autopsy reports, Erich Frank and Dr.

Stubler and his nurse were each killed by a single round from a Walther PPK."

Kurt's expression told her that he recognized the import of what she was saying. "Same weapon?"

"Presumably. The bullet that killed Erich Frank wasn't recovered, so there's no way to be certain."

"Like I said, he's cleaning up loose ends." He sounded so grim that Elin was reminded, once again, that he considered her one of those loose ends. Even with him beside her, the thought was terrifying.

She told him what she'd found inscribed on Lotte Dietrich's necklace. "Does that mean anything to you?"

From the arrested look on his face she knew it did.

"It's the slogan of the Lebensborn Society."

Elin lifted her eyebrows at him in question.

"Himmler instituted a project that encourages the birth of racially pure Aryan children. Young, single women that are verifiably Aryan back through several generations are recruited and matched with selected SS or Wehrmacht officers for the purpose of breeding a secret child for the Fatherland. The conception takes place inside a Lebensborn facility, the expectant mother is cared for inside a Lebensborn facility, and the birth happens inside a Lebensborn facility. After the birth the child is taken from the mother and becomes the property of the state. The mother, having done her patriotic duty, leaves and goes about her life with no one the wiser. The program's existence is a closely guarded secret, but word has spread throughout certain government and military circles." He grimaced. "You can't recruit men to go impregnate attractive young women without some knowledge of it getting out."

Elin's eyes widened. "Do you think Lotte Dietrich was recruited to be part of the Lebensborn program?"

"Given what was written on the necklace, and the fact that she lied to her parents about her whereabouts and what she was doing, it's a strong possibility," he said. "I'll have to pull some high-level strings to find out where to even start to look."

The excitement of possibly having turned up a new lead had Elin shifting in her seat to face him. "Kurt, if Lotte Dietrich never made it to Dr. Stubler's office, why would the killer consider him a loose end? What did Dr. Stubler know about her—or him?"

He gave a slow nod. "Excellent question. How about we go to Dr. Stubler's office and see what we can find? If the killer shot him and his nurse, there's a reason. I've already got a team at the Paradise Club testing for fingerprints and other evidence, and we can swing by there later. Unless you want to check in to the hotel first?"

She shook her head.

"Dr. Stubler's office it is," he said, and they headed toward Hellersdorf.

33

DR. STUBLER'S FILE ON LOTTE DIETRICH INDICATED
that he'd given her a complete physical examination about a
month before she'd moved to Berlin, supposedly to take a job
with him, which they now knew wasn't true. His conclusion,
neatly typed at the end of a list of test results, was that he'd found
her to be a healthy, racially pure young woman with no known
defects or diseases.

That was interesting.

But what was truly exciting was the handwritten notation
beneath it: "To Greta Neuhaus—50 *Reichsmarks*."

"They *were* connected," she said to Kurt as they pulled away
from Stubler's office. Behind them, the policeman who'd let
them in and stayed to supervise was locking up. Questioning the
workers who'd been in the businesses nearby had been useless:
they'd seen, and heard, nothing. The only way that was possible

was if the killer had used a silenced weapon, all the policemen involved, including Kurt, agreed. That pointed to a premeditated, rather than a random, crime, and to someone familiar with weapons as the assailant.

It was well after dark, almost nine in fact, but Elin no longer felt the least bit tired. "What do you suppose the payment was for?"

"At a guess, a recruitment fee."

"You think Greta recruited Lotte for the Lebensborn program?"

"It's looking like it. We'll know more after we follow up on that address."

An address in Wedding had been scrawled on the front of the folder in the same handwriting, presumably Stubler's, as the payment.

"Dr. Stubler lied to Lotte's parents and to the police because he couldn't admit why he'd seen her so it was simply easier to say he'd never seen her at all," Elin concluded. Thinking it over, she frowned.

"But how could the killer have known about Dr. Stubler's connection to Greta and Lotte unless he has a connection to him, too?"

"That's something we're going to have to figure out," Kurt said.

Not long afterward, they were walking in through the badly damaged theater that had been the official front entrance to the Paradise Club. The club, when they reached it, proved to be in even worse shape than the theater. The stone walls were scorched, the few tapestries that still clung to them were blackened, and the stained-glass lozenge with its *wolfsangel* centerpiece lay in ruby-red shards all over the floor. The smell of the fire was strong.

Elin shivered when she looked up at the broken-out window of the control room. She and Kurt could have died in there.

Although she had expected to see him, Storch wasn't there.

Kurt told her that, since his ownership of the club was now an open secret in the wake of his arrest, he was closeted with Pia and Beckman in his suite at the Hotel Adlon while he did his best to describe as many of last night's Paradise Club guests, all of whom had escaped the fire and most of whom had escaped the police because of the fire, as he could remember while Pia drew them. But a quartet of officers from the fire brigade was there, along with Jeweler Fritz, who was supervising a cleanup crew, while Vogel, Albrecht, Gunther, and Roth undertook the collection of evidence potentially left behind by the killer. Unfortunately, the intercom button didn't yield any fingerprints at all, which indicated it had been wiped clean. That wasn't an entirely negative development, because it meant that the killer had not been wearing gloves and left open the possibility that his fingerprints might be found elsewhere, such as on the stepladder that had been wedged against the door to the control room to prevent their escape.

"We did," Albrecht said, when Kurt asked if they'd found any fingerprints on the stepladder.

"Dozens of them," Vogel added gloomily. "All different. Looks like everybody that ever worked here touched that ladder. We'll be trying to match them for weeks."

"Do what you can," Kurt told them, and began questioning Jeweler Fritz about any suspicious activity he might have observed when a distant, vaguely familiar *doo-wop, doo-wop* wail began to sound.

"Air raid," Jeweler Fritz said. "What, you don't think you're far enough underground? Keep working," he barked at his crew, who were making it clear that they were ready to drop everything and run. The firemen, on the other hand, retreated to the tunnels of Germania without hindrance, and as the wails grew louder the policemen elected to go, too.

"Coming, Chief?" Frowning, Albrecht looked back at Kurt, who, having jerked his head at Elin in a silent *You're with me* message, was waiting for her to reach his side.

"Go on without me," Kurt said. Albrecht nodded, and the policemen headed down into the tunnel, where, if the sounds coming from it were any indication, a sizable group seemed to be assembling.

Instead of heading down, Kurt went up, sweeping Elin along with him, back out through the theater entrance where they'd come in, moving swiftly. Once outside, the sirens shrieked like banshees overhead as they hurried through the pitch darkness to Kurt's car.

"Where are we going?" she asked as he drove away into the night at speed. Outwardly she was calm. Inside, growing alarm at the thought of the approaching bombers had her pulse racing. That last raid had been an eye-opening lesson in how deadly and destructive they could be.

"You've seen what happens to me in an air raid." He was tight-lipped and visibly tense. "I can't take the chance of becoming incapacitated and leaving you vulnerable to the killer when he could be anywhere. We're going to my house. We'll wait it out in the cellar."

"That sounds like a good idea. Is it far?"

"Ten minutes."

"Will anyone else be there?"

"No."

He raced down side streets, slowing at intersections for just long enough to make sure the way was clear. By the time he parked beside the curb in front of a narrow, two-story house wedged into a row of what, as best she could tell, appeared to be similar houses, the sirens were so shrill and urgent Elin felt like covering her ears. A low rumble, followed by the first outlying burst of flak as they hurried inside, warned that the airplanes were almost upon the city. Kurt snatched up a torch from a table near the door and turned it on while Elin caught just a glimpse of a front parlor with a fireplace and overflowing bookshelves and a kitchen with an ancient stove that looked like it was rarely used before he hustled her down to the cellar.

Windowless and cold, dark as the inside of a cave, it was home to a boiler and a plethora of pipes and, Elin saw as Kurt switched on a compact battery-powered lantern, an old sofa and chair and a couple of small tables. The lantern's dim glow cast shadows on the walls and barely illuminated the area around the sofa.

"Have you lived here long?" Elin asked as he sank down on the sofa and she settled into the chair. Outside, the flak was going off in earnest. The rapid-fire barrage of antiaircraft fire was a sure warning that the airplanes were getting closer.

"About ten years." He unbuttoned his shirt collar, loosened his tie.

"Alone?" It was a delicate way of asking if he'd once lived there with his wife and son. Keeping him talking, she hoped, might help hold off the onset of symptoms.

The look he gave her told her he knew what she was doing.

"About two years after we moved in, my now-former wife took our son and moved to a much larger house in a much better neighborhood with a much richer man. And one, moreover, who wasn't putting the whole family at risk by refusing to enthusiastically embrace the National Socialist Party. It was probably a wise decision on her part, although I wasn't best pleased about it at the time."

A distant boom as the first bomb hit was followed by another and another, all bracketed by the constant *rat-a-tat-tat* of flak. She shivered a little despite the long sleeves of her blue dress, and he reached for a blanket that had been folded on the back of the sofa and handed it to her.

"Thank you," she said.

"Might as well get comfy. We may be here for a bit." He gave her a sardonic smile. "What else do you want to talk about while you try to distract me?"

She wrapped herself in the blanket, trying not to wince on his behalf as the bombs began dropping in short bursts followed by furious explosions of flak. The booms were growing closer—and louder.

"What did you do to get on Heydrich's bad side?"

He grimaced. "I was working a case when the Gestapo showed up next door and started marching people out of an apartment building and loading them into the back of a van. The new prisoners bolted, knocking the guards down and making a run for it right past me. The officer in charge came barreling out of the building yelling at me to shoot them. I didn't, and he reported me. Word got to Heydrich. He called me in and asked me why. I told him I'm a policeman, not a murderer. He didn't take it well."

She saw one of his hands lightly grip the arm of the sofa. His other, resting beside him on the sofa cushion, appeared relaxed. Outside, the noise continued unabated, but he seemed to be tolerating it well.

"He had you sent to the front," Elin said.

"He did. He would have had me shot, but the Wehrmacht needed warm bodies and he thought it would better serve the Fatherland if he let the Russkies do it. Or so I was told."

"What's going to happen to you once we catch this killer?" Elin looked at him with real worry. The thought of what would become of him after she was gone was beginning to trouble her a great deal.

"Who can say? Life these days is uncertain. Who would have thought that less than two years after Heydrich sent me to my death, as he thought, I'd be back at the Kripo and he'd be dead?"

"Very philosophical."

A huge boom, closer at hand than the rest, interrupted, causing her to jump a little. He didn't, but his hand that was gripping the armrest tightened and the one resting beside him on the couch clenched into a fist. Another boom and the answering flak had his whole body visibly bracing against it.

"Tell me something," he said, and there was a new harshness

to his voice that told her how much the ongoing barrage was beginning to affect him and how hard he was fighting against it. "How did your husband die? He must have been young."

Not so long ago, she would have done everything in her power to keep such damning information from him. But now—

"He—Lars—was twenty-nine. He was one of those who tried to resist, when the Nazis came to Denmark. They caught him and hanged him from a tree." Her throat closed up as the memory squeezed her heart.

Her voice must have gone wobbly, too, because with what seemed to be a real effort of will his hand that had been clenched into a fist relaxed and he reached out for her.

"Come here," he said.

She did, crawling onto the sofa beside him as his arm wrapped around her, and he pulled her close. Resting against him, she took comfort from his warmth, from the solid strength of him beside her, from the mere fact of his presence.

"You loved him," he said.

"I did," she agreed. It still existed, that love, encapsulated in its own special place inside her heart and in its living embodiment in the son she and Lars shared. But she was no longer the person she had been then. Lars had taken the girl who'd loved him with him when he went and left her irrevocably changed.

More blasts hit, several close enough to rattle the house above them. Kurt's breathing deepened, and she slid her arms around his waist and pressed closer against his side. The chattering flak and wailing sirens were so loud now that it was difficult to talk, although she tried, eliciting monosyllabic replies. Beneath everything could be heard the drone of approaching airplanes.

She could feel his growing agitation. His arm around her hardened to iron. His jaw went rigid and the unrest in his eyes as he looked at her spoke of a fierce inner battle being waged.

"Kurt." Tightening her arms around him, she did her best to keep him anchored to the present. "I've got you. It's all right."

A tremendous crash caused the lantern to jump and roll off the table, casting wild shadows that danced across the walls. The following burst of flak was loud enough to hurt her ears. His jaw clenched, his eyes closed, and his head dropped back to rest against the rolled top of the sofa.

Then he began to shake. He shook, and she held him, draping the blanket around him so that they were both wrapped in its warmth, and she murmured any and all words of comfort that came into her head, while bombs fell and flak chattered and sirens screamed. At last the airplanes passed out of range and the air took on the kind of leaden hush that followed in the wake of such disasters.

Finally Kurt stopped shaking. His muscles relaxed, he took a deep, shuddering breath, and opened his eyes. For a moment he stared at the ceiling as if he couldn't quite remember where he was. Then his head swiveled in her direction and their eyes met.

"Elin." His voice was husky. "Oh, hell."

She smiled at him. "We're safe."

His head came up off the back of the sofa. "This can't go on. We've got to do whatever we have to do to get you home. You're not safe here, and as this proves, you can't count on me to keep you safe."

"You've done all right so far," she said, and pulled her knees up beside her and rolled onto them so that she was kneeling on the sofa facing him. Freeing her arms from the entangling blanket, she slid them around his neck.

He frowned at her. "What are you doing?"

"Seizing the day," she said, and kissed him.

And just like that, there they were again, the butterflies.

By the time they left his house, it was morning. And not early, either. Almost ten o'clock, which, Elin pointed out as they drove away, was disgraceful.

"And yet here am I, still sleep-deprived," Kurt said with a touch of wry humor. After taking things upstairs, they'd been awake in his bed until long after dawn, getting to know each other in ways that made her tingle from just thinking about them. Then, after they'd finally fallen asleep and woken up again, he'd joined her in the shower. Later, as she dressed, she'd watched from the bedroom, while, bare-chested and with a face full of foam, he'd shaved.

And those damned butterflies had multiplied by about a thousand, bringing her face-to-face with the sobering truth that this time the Rubicon had been well and truly crossed and where he was concerned, she was a lost cause.

"Sorry about that," she said, meaning to sound flippant but not quite sure she succeeded. Being faced with sobering truths, especially a sobering truth that she'd much rather he didn't discover, was unsettling.

"I'm not." The smile he gave her was crooked and so charming that it left her practically curling her toes in her sensible black pumps, which, courtesy of her suitcase that he'd carried in from the car for her, she was wearing with a deep gold blouse and slim black skirt. Professional to the hilt—that was her. So professional, in fact, that despite being in something of an emotional daze, she was able to register that, while Kurt's block had been spared, the next block over had suffered a direct hit that had leveled one house and taken the roof off its neighbor. Plumes of smoke rising in what was almost a direct line from southeast to northwest spoke of the path the Allied bombers had taken through the city.

Then he braked for an intersection and leaned over to kiss her, and somewhere in the middle of kissing him back her bones melted and her head started to spin and all that professionalism went right out the window.

"No more of that now," he said mock sternly as he straightened and started to drive away. "We're back on the job."

Her brows snapped together and her eyes narrowed and those rampant butterflies got netted and corralled.

"I should probably go check in to the hotel now," she said, commendably cool.

He shook his head. "Too early. I suggest we stop by the Alex and see if any calls have come in about missing women or dead bodies, and then if there's nothing, go on to—" he looked at the address on the folder from Dr. Stubler's office, which lay on the seat between them "—Kösliner Strasse."

"Wouldn't someone have called you at home?" She was not, she discovered, quite ready to go into the Alex, where Frau Skelton and perhaps Trott and no telling who else was likely to be present. She was afraid they'd detect that something had changed between her and Kurt. Besides being embarrassing, any inkling of a personal relationship between them might prove damaging to Kurt especially.

"Telephone line's down. I tried calling in while you were still upstairs." He smiled. "Don't worry, neither one of us has a big scarlet *A* on us. We just keep what's private private and in public go on as we were."

His ability to read her was uncanny.

"General Kaltenbrunner's already made it clear that he doesn't like you very much, and I don't think General Haupt does, either. And I'm sure they still need warm bodies at the front."

"Worried about me, *liebling*?" The smile he gave her then was both teasing and tender.

Everything about the situation scared her. "Maybe I just don't want your blood on my hands," she replied tartly, in pure self-defense, and he laughed.

"Kösliner Strasse it is," he said, and she smiled at him.

Shortly thereafter, they pulled up in front of a large white brick house. Four round pillars supported wide double porches. As they reached the steps, Elin heard the murmur of voices above them, and looked up to discover two young blonde women hanging over the rail of the second-story porch peering down at them. A sign affixed to the wall beside the front door bore the image of a red, three-pronged branch with leaves twining around it.

Kurt's face was hard as he looked at it. "That's the symbol of the Lebensborn Society."

34

A WOMAN WITH NEATLY CURLED GRAY HAIR RELUC-
tantly admitted them. Her name, according to the silver tag
on her white nurse's uniform, was Gertraud Peters, and after
answering Kurt's knock she would have shut the door in their
faces—"No visitors!"—if he hadn't flashed his warrant badge
at her.

"What can I do for you?" she asked after closing and locking the door behind them. Her manner was stiff, and she eyed
the pair of them suspiciously as they stood with her in the wide
entry hall.

"We're here to talk to you about Dr. Stubler," Kurt said, after
introducing Elin as his associate. "I presume you've been informed of his murder."

"Murder!" Frau Peters's jaw dropped and her hand flew to
her heart. Elin's pulse quickened. She and Kurt hadn't been sure

that Dr. Stubler would be known here. "We were told that he had died, but nothing of *murder*."

"I'm sorry to be the bearer of such shocking news," Kurt said. "Is there a place we can go to talk?"

"Yes. This way." Frau Peters turned and started walking away, beckoning them to follow. The faint strains of a radio could be heard from somewhere deep inside the house. Several young women were engaged in various activities in a large living room with tall windows and multiple sofas and chairs, Elin saw, and a couple of them looked curiously at her and Kurt as they passed. Next to the living room was an equally large dining room with four round tables that each appeared to seat a minimum of six, although no one was in it at the time. Elin caught a glimpse of a gleaming kitchen beyond the dining room. The smell of food being prepared filled the air.

"He was just here on Wednesday to check on the girls." Frau Peters turned down another, narrower hall and ushered them into a small office. "Such a good man! What kind of world is this, that such things can happen!"

"Did he check on the girls often?" Kurt asked in a sympathetic tone as Frau Peters, obviously upset, sank into a chair behind a utilitarian wooden desk and motioned them into two chairs opposite.

"Every Wednesday. Every Wednesday without fail. He was so good with them, jollying them along, telling them what they should eat and how much they should exercise, keeping track of their—" she hesitated, then transferred her gaze from Kurt to Elin and dropped her voice into a near whisper "—cycles."

From the corner of her eye, Elin watched as Kurt's unmistakable but fleeting change of expression registered his discomfort with the topic and she had to suppress a smile.

"I'm sure he was wonderful to them throughout their pregnancies, too," Elin said, stepping into the breach.

"Oh, no, he didn't treat them throughout their pregnancies.

The girls only stay until they conceive, and then they're transferred to a maternity home. But he was wonderful to them while
they were with us."

"Did Dr. Stubler have any problems with any of the girls? Or
the men?" Kurt asked. "Arguments, anything?"

"No, nothing like that. Although I don't think he ever in-
teracted with our gentlemen guests, at least not outside of their
initial examinations. He was here for the girls."

"Dr. Stubler conducted initial examinations of the men?" Kurt
asked. Elin knew, as he did, that no records of anything like
that had been found in Stubler's office. But if he had examined
the killer, that might have been enough to qualify Stubler as a
loose end.

"Just to certify that they were free of—" she shot a look at
Kurt, and her voice dropped again as she addressed the rest to
Elin "—communicable diseases." Her tone made it clear what
kind of diseases she was talking about.

"I see," Elin said. From his expression, Kurt clearly did, too.

"Lotte Dietrich was one of your girls, I understand," Kurt said.

"That's right." Frau Peters frowned. "Why do you bring her
up?" Her eyes widened. "Has something happened to her, too?
Oh, no! I hoped she had just gone home."

"She was gone, and you didn't report her missing?" Kurt asked
pointedly without answering Frau Peters's question.

"I did report her missing. Oh, not in the usual way, not to
the police. We operate under a strict secrecy policy, so when
she didn't return when expected I reported that to the personal
staff of the Reichsführer, as I am told to do with any significant
problem that arises. They said I should do nothing more and the
SS would look into it."

"Could you tell us when you saw her last, and under what
circumstances?" Kurt asked.

"She was one of our younger ones, you know, and she was

having trouble adjusting. It—" She looked at Elin again and dropped her voice.

"The physical aspect of it was a bit much for her. More than she'd been expecting, I gathered. She'd been through two cycles, and—well, they weren't successful. Her third one was coming, and she said she wanted to take a break beforehand. So she asked to spend a few days with a friend, which I permitted."

"When was that?" Kurt asked.

Frau Peters opened a drawer, pulled out a ledger, and leafed through it.

"August 27. A Friday. She was to be away Friday and Saturday nights, and then she always went out on Sunday afternoons and came back later Sunday night, so that's when I expected her to return. But—" Frau Peters broke off with an apologetic shrug.

"She didn't come back," Elin concluded for her, and Frau Peters nodded.

"Do you know the name of the friend she went to stay with?" Kurt asked.

"Oh, yes. Greta. Greta Neuhaus. She used to be one of our girls, you know, and she continues to do her duty to the Fatherland by recruiting for us." Frau Peters looked troubled. "May I ask you—we had another girl, Quilla Vormelker, leave us unexpectedly. Without telling me, or anyone. One morning she was just gone. I reported that to the personal staff of the Reichsführer, too, but I've heard nothing. Could you— Would you have any news of her?"

Elin already had her notebook out. "Can you spell that, please?"

Frau Peters did, and as Elin wrote it down, Kurt asked, "When did she leave you?"

Again Frau Peters referred to her ledger. "We last saw her on April 16. A Friday. On Fridays and Saturdays is when our gentlemen guests come to visit with the girls, and she was there on Friday and gone on Saturday. Again, without a word."

Elin's stomach tightened as she wrote down the date. It was a little more than a week before Inge Weber's murder.

"Do you have her home address, or her parents' address, or know of anywhere we could look for her?" Kurt asked.

"I have no contact information for her, or any of the girls. All that is handled by the personal staff of the Reichsführer."

"Would you happen to have a list of the men who were present in the house on that Friday night when Fräulein Vormelker was last known to be here? Or that visited in the weeks right before Lotte Dietrich left?"

Frau Peters shook her head. "Our gentlemen guests are accorded complete anonymity. We aren't allowed to know their names, or anything about them, and they don't tell us. They come in, socialize with the girls, pick one, and—" She broke off, but if there had been any doubt about what she meant her blushing would have abolished it. "This is all arranged through the personal staff of the Reichsführer."

"I could send an artist to draw them, if you or your girls could describe them," Kurt said.

Frau Peters was shaking her head before he finished. "Impossible! One of the promises made to our gentlemen is that their identities will remain secret. I would lose my position at the very least if I were to permit such a thing as you are suggesting. Anything of that nature must be cleared through the personal staff of the Reichsführer."

A knock on the door was followed almost immediately by the entrance of a young woman. Dressed in a simple housedress, she was blonde and attractive, but what caught Elin's attention was her necklace. It was identical to the one that had belonged to Lotte Dietrich.

"Pardon, Frau Peters, but the new girl has arrived. Frau Cook said I should tell you immediately," the girl said.

"Thank you, Anna."

"Excuse me, Anna," Elin said before the girl could withdraw, as she seemed about to do. "Your necklace is lovely. May I ask where you got it?"

"Thank you. We all have one." Anna smiled proudly as she fingered her necklace. Elin could see its heart shape and the tiny yellow flower beneath the celluloid quite clearly. "It's our badge of honor. For our service to the Fatherland."

"All our girls are gifted a set of jewelry when they arrive. A necklace and earrings, as a small thank-you from their country." As Anna left, Frau Peters rose, clearly anxious to attend to the newcomer. Elin and Kurt rose, too. "Oh, dear, I hope the terrible thing that's happened to Dr. Stubler and poor Lotte can be kept from the other girls. They will be in floods of tears." She wrung her hands as she looked at them. "Will it be in the newspapers? Should I prepare them?"

"We don't anticipate any publicity," Kurt said, and he and Elin followed her out the door.

"So Lotte went to stay with Greta on Friday, and Greta as we know went to Eden on Saturday. I'm assuming Lotte was there at Eden with Greta, and the killer lured or abducted them both from the club, or at some point on their way home from the club." Kurt was parking in the garage at the Alex as he spoke. "Taking two girls at the same time would certainly be more of a challenge. Although he could have done something like offer them a ride home."

Elin said, "However it happened, I don't think he meant to take them both. From the way they were killed, it's obvious that Greta was his target, and Lotte was simply in the wrong place at the wrong time. Greta was killed in a fury, a frenzy. Lotte was kept alive for several days afterward, which tells us the killer had to work himself up again."

By then they were out of the car and walking toward the building's door.

"What do you think about the other girl—Quilla whatever her

name is? A victim of the killer, or just a girl who went home?"
Kurt asked. He was walking beside her, not touching her although he was close enough that their arms brushed. She was,
to her dismay, acutely aware of him. He was wearing a jacket
and she had on a long-sleeved blouse and yet, mortifyingly, those
fleeting encounters with what was essentially his elbow were
giving her goose bumps.

"I don't know. Either is possible. But if she was killed, where's
her body? That was months ago. Wouldn't she have been found?"

"Good question. Looks like we're going to be contacting
the office of the personal staff of the Reichsführer—" his tone
turned satiric on that last "—to try to track her down, and to
get information on the men who've been visiting that house."

They'd reached the door to the building. As Kurt opened it
for her and Elin realized they were about to face the scrutiny
she'd been dreading, she squared her shoulders, lifted her chin,
and strode determinedly into the far too brightly lit hallway.

"You look like a general heading into battle," Kurt leaned
forward to whisper as he came up behind her. "Don't worry,
liebling, no one's going to notice the little love bite under this
ear."

He tickled the lobe of the ear in question.

Clapping a hand to the spot, Elin looked back at him in horror only to discover that he was grinning wickedly.

"You're not funny," she said crossly, and his grin widened.
But by the time they reached Frau Skelton's desk she'd recovered her outward professionalism and so had he.

"Here are your telephone calls." Frau Skelton handed Kurt a
list. Her gaze skimmed Elin but only perfunctorily; there was
no sign that she noticed anything amiss. "And Herr Trott has
been—"

"Looking for you," Trott hailed Kurt. He was coming from
the direction of the evidence room. "If the murder weapon is a
close combat knife, we've got our work cut out for us tracking it

down. Every soldier in the Great War, and this one, was issued one, and many of them have been passed on to family and friends. I must have looked at a thousand already. Anyway, I was able to get the things you wanted. I left them on the table in your office."

"Thanks," Kurt said. "I need you to track somebody down for me. A girl, Quilla—what was her name?" He looked at Elin.

"Quilla Vormelker," Elin said.

"Quilla Vormelker," Trott repeated, and wrote the name down as Kurt gave him a quick rundown of what they had discovered.

"You may have to go through the personal staff of the Reichs-führer," Kurt concluded.

Trott grimaced. "This should be fun," he said, and headed toward the exit.

"Come on," Kurt said to Elin as Trott left. She went with him into his office. He closed the door, then pointed her toward a milk-crate-sized box on the table. "I've got to return some of these calls. While I'm doing that, I want you to go through the material Walter brought and see if any of it jogs your memory."

"What kind of material?" Elin moved toward the table.

"An old photo album. Some newspaper clippings." He stepped behind his desk and lifted the sound-deadening box from his telephone. "Walter was a policeman back in 1928, you know. A lot of his friends are old-time cops like him, and some of them attended the same conference your father did. He asked around, and one of the guys had some memorabilia from that confer-ence. That's what's in there."

"Oh my God." Elin froze with her hands on the box lid. In-wardly she recoiled from whatever was inside, and from the as-sessing way Kurt was watching her she had little doubt that he'd been expecting her reaction and was busy gauging how severe it was. "I told you. Nothing happened at that conference. Nothing that relates to this. My mother's death was an accident."

"It can't hurt to look, can it?" His eminently reasonable tone didn't fool her. His gut was still telling him there was something there, and he would follow that instinct until it was proved wrong. No matter how much the dredging up of old memories might distress her.

"No, it can't hurt to look." Her reply was grudging, because she really, truly didn't want to go diving into the past, but she was going to do it anyway. Because, once again, one thing her father had taught her was to never discount a detective's instinct.

She opened the box and sat down.

Kurt was on the telephone as she pulled the items out of the box and started going through them one by one. Ordinarily she would have unashamedly listened to his side of the conversations as she worked, but she was too caught up in the memories dragging her back in time.

None of the newspaper clippings referred to her mother's death. That was what she'd feared the most, so she went through them first and let out a silent sigh of relief when she'd finished. The photo album was different, more intimate, dredging up scenes from the conference. There was one picture of five men, aged perhaps early twenties, standing together on a stage holding small silver trophies topped with Weimar Republic eagles after receiving some type of award—she thought it was something like Heroes of the Republic for saving a life. She remembered the actual scene, because she'd been there at the dinner when the awards were given out. Another was of Dr. Bernard Spilsbury, a celebrity pathologist who was the primary draw of the conference, giving the keynote speech. She'd been in the audience for that, too. Then she turned the page and her breath caught at a picture of her father at a podium delivering his lecture.

Without warning she was whisked back through time and space. Her heart swelled with love and ached with loss. Sven Lund, in his late fifties then, was foursquare and solid, a big, blunt-featured man with a shock of white hair and piercing blue eyes. And, she thought, the gentlest soul and the kindest heart. For a moment she simply looked at him as her throat tightened with emotion. Then the rest of the image came into focus, and she saw that behind him, projected on a screen, was an oversize picture of the subject of his lecture, Dagmar Overbye.

Elin went lightheaded. Her ears rang and her insides shook.

"Elin?" Kurt stood beside her looking down at the album's open page. With a supreme effort of will, Elin managed to push through the worst of it.

"That's my father." Pointing, she concentrated on the beloved image so as not to have to focus on the other. "The woman on the screen behind him is Dagmar Overbye. My presumptive biological mother. And no, I haven't seen anything in any of this stuff that has any bearing on the investigation."

He swore, softly and fluently, clearly not fooled by her outward composure, and his hand came down on her shoulder with silent sympathy. She took comfort from the warm weight of it.

"I'm sorry," he said, but she shook her head.

"My mother and I were outside the room waiting for him. Neither one of them wanted me to listen to his lecture. So we waited, and when he came out we were going to go to dinner and then the theater. But so many people came up to him afterward that we missed dinner and had to wait to eat until the play was over." One of the last, best memories of their life together as a family had been that trip to the theater, and that late dinner.

"All right, enough." He closed the album. "If I'd known that was in there I—"

The rest of what he'd been going to say was lost as, with a sharp knock, Vogel barreled through the door with Albrecht on his heels.

"Chief, you need to come. We've got another body."

35

HER NAME WAS JULIE SMOLSKI, SHE WAS THIRTY-ONE,
which was considerably older than the previous victims, and she'd
been making her way home from her factory job when she'd
been attacked in the small hours of Sunday morning. Her shift
ended at 4:00 a.m., and usually it took her approximately forty
minutes—thirty minutes on the S-Bahn and then a ten-minute
walk from the station—to get home. Her presence at work and
on the train coming home had been verified. Therefore, they
estimated the attack had taken place sometime after 4:30 a.m.

Her family had gone looking for her when they'd awakened
on Sunday to find she hadn't made it home, and the family—a
mother and sister, the victim's husband being a soldier who was
away fighting—were already at the scene when Elin and Kurt
and the rest of the group from the Kripo arrived.

The corpse had been found when debris from the latest air

raid had been removed. Julie Smolski's torn and lacerated nude body had been discovered beneath it. Murder had been obvious at a glance.

Elin shivered as the woman's body was taken away.

"She wasn't his intended target. This was a crime of opportunity. After escaping from the Paradise Club, the killer would have been seething with rage and bloodlust and he went prowling through the night like the predator he is. She was just unlucky enough to cross his path." Elin looked at Kurt. "We saved the intended victim's life at the cost of hers."

The knowledge made her sick.

"If it makes you feel any better, if we'd gone after him that night those children would still be out there, and who knows how much longer they could have survived." They were in his car by this time, driving away from the Friedrichshain neighborhood where the body had been found. Processing the scene had taken time, and it was long past dark. "We're right behind him. The problem is, he knows it. The closer we get, the more dangerous he's going to be."

The worry in his voice was on her behalf, she knew.

"We need to go back to the Alex, to look at Pia's drawings. She didn't only draw the men Storch could remember, she drew the women, too. The killer's original target is still out there, and Pia might have done a picture of her. If we can identify her—" She broke off because his expression told her what a long shot he thought that was. "We have to *try*. He chose her for a reason, and he's not going to stop going after her. We need to get to her before he does. In fact, if we find her and watch her, we might find him." The urgency of it sent adrenaline flowing through her veins.

"Not tonight," Kurt said. "You're pale with exhaustion. You need to eat. You're no good to anyone if you can't think straight."

"I never did check in to that hotel." It was a tacit admission that he was right.

"We can go do that—or we can do it tomorrow and tonight you can come home with me." Kurt looked grim and worried and about as tired as she felt. His eyes were bloodshot, his jaw was dark with stubble, and his shirt was streaked with dirt and, she feared, blood.

As terrible as the last few hours had been, her heart lightened a little just because she was with him. Right now he felt like a safe harbor in a tumultuous sea.

She went home with him. And sat in his kitchen while he made a quick and simple meal of sausage and eggs. After they ate, they went upstairs, took a shower—once he stepped in with her, the previously barely warm water felt like it turned to steam— and went to bed. Eventually, they fell asleep.

The next morning Elin attended Julie Smolski's autopsy. Dr. Weimann confirmed what she already knew in her gut. It appeared to be the work of the same killer who'd murdered Lotte Dietrich and the rest. Trott had been assigned to wait for her outside the autopsy room and drive her back to the Alex. He was with her when Frau Skelton, with an odd look on her face, handed her a letter that had come for her that morning.

As soon as she looked at it, saw the heavy black ink, the scrawled handwriting, Elin felt cold all over. It was addressed to Professor Elin Lund. And the second line read "Dr. Murder."

"Uh, you should probably wait for Kurt to get back before you open that," Trott said uneasily. His gaze shifted between the envelope and her face.

Elin turned the heavy paper envelope over, opened the flap, and drew out the single white sheet.

Her hand was remarkably steady as she unfolded it and read, "Say your prayers."

Kurt called an emergency team meeting for first thing the next morning. Elin was on her feet briefing the group about their visit to the Lebensborn Society house when Jens, who'd already given a brief overview detailing his struggles with the code, abruptly sat up straight.

"What was that name again?" he interrupted Elin unceremoniously. "Of the girl who went missing from the house the week before Inge Weber's murder?"

Looking at him with interest—Jens would never have broken in on her if he hadn't been struck by something momentous—Elin said, "Quilla Vormelker," and at Jens's request spelled it.

"By God." Jens was ruffling through the papers in the file folder in front of him even before she finished. In the few minutes it took him to pull one out, make a series of jottings on the page, and look up again, everyone at the table was staring at him.

"That's it." The excitement in his voice was infectious. The atmosphere in the room was suddenly charged as they all leaned forward with anticipation. Jens looked around at them, his blue eyes sparkling. "I think I've found the key. It was that name. Quilla Vormelker. The *q*, followed by that double *l*. I think it's an inverse substitution cypher interspersed with a pigpen cypher. All the vowels are missing, which in theory should make it harder to crack, but in this case—" he tapped the paper in front of him with the end of his pen with obvious satisfaction "—it may prove his undoing. *Llq* is a very specific combination. And look at what precedes it—*rklmrv*. Once you know what to look for, it's so obvious it jumps off the page. I think—" he bent over the paper, furiously making marks on it as he spoke "—he's talking about some of the women he's killed. Give me a little more time and I'll be able to tell you for sure." He looked at Kurt. "I'm going to need to work on this for a while, but I should have at least a rough translation within the next few hours. With your permission, I'm going to take this and go somewhere private to work."

Kurt nodded. "Take the lab." He looked at Elin. "Unless you have something you need to do in there?"

She shook her head. "No, nothing."

Jens was already on his feet and heading for the door as she spoke.

"We'll reconvene at three," Kurt said to him and the group in general. Jens held up a hand in acknowledgment as he left the room. A short time later, the rest of them, each with specific tasks to go to, followed him out the door.

With a great deal of difficulty, Kurt had managed to obtain permission to view Dr. Stubler's files on the "gentlemen guests" at the Lebensborn Society house. He and Elin went to the Office of the Reichsführer, located in a building on Prinz Albrecht Strasse not far from the RHSA headquarters, because the files could not be taken from the premises. Only about a hundred men had passed through that particular house over the period in question, which should have made looking through the files for the markers Elin sought a manageable exercise. Unfortunately, the files proved useless. No names or identifying characteristics were provided. Not even anything as rudimentary as height, weight—or blood type. All that was there was a declaration of racial purity and a stamp certifying that the examinee was healthy and free of disease.

"This was a waste of time," Kurt said in disgust as they finished looking through the last of the files.

"It does tell us something, though." Elin frowned thoughtfully as she watched Kurt put the file back on the pile with the rest. They were in a small, windowless room with a soldier waiting outside the closed door in case, as they had been informed when they'd been allowed in, they should try to make off with any of the files, which was strictly forbidden. "From the fact that none of the victims were raped, we've been assuming that he's unable to have normal sexual relations. We can further assume that whatever the reason for his disability, it's not apparent visually, or apparent during a physical examination, or Dr. Stubler would have caught it. But he *was* examined by Dr. Stubler, which is evidenced by the fact that he killed him. And Dr. Stubler almost certainly would have examined him only if he was in line to be a 'gentleman guest' at the Lebensborn Society house. Knowing that he is unable to have sexual relations, the killer would not have voluntarily agreed to take part in a breeding program that would expose his disability. Therefore, I think we can posit that he was assigned or ordered to take part. That provides us with near certainty that the killer is himself either military or police, because only a commanding officer of some sort would have the power to order such a thing. And I think we can posit that this happened in early April, because Quilla went missing then. My theory is that our killer felt forced to participate in the breeding program, chose Quilla, was unable to perform, and, frustrated, angry, humiliated, and afraid of having his disability found out, snatched or lured her away and killed her. I'd further posit that this episode was the stressor that led to the other murders. He's venting his fury and shame over his inability to perform sexually on the women he blames for it."

"How sure are you of that?"

"Ninety-five percent." As she pushed back from the table and stood up, Elin gave him a quelling look because she knew what his reaction to her answer would be.

He smiled at her. "That's good enough for me."

Then he walked over to her, tilted her chin up, and kissed her. His lips were warm and firm, the kiss casually possessive. Her response was instant, automatic, the instinctive yin to his yang. It was such a natural gesture, so much the action of a man who considered himself part of a couple that even as her pulse raced and her blood heated she was aware of something more, something deeper, that had blossomed in secret and revealed itself now, in this instant of clarity. A glow of happiness, a sense of rightness, of belonging, as if she were also acknowledging they were a couple.

What shattered her was the knowledge that the connection couldn't last, that the two of them could never have more than this brief interlude. Because no matter how she felt about him, or he about her, she had to go home. As soon as she possibly could.

She'd called home last night, from a random telephone booth with Kurt standing guard outside. "The situation's worsening here," Hilde told her. Her formidable mother-in-law's voice cracked as she added, "They raided our house yesterday. I don't know whether they were looking to arrest me, or for evidence against Borge. I'm praying they don't somehow learn that Niles and I are here."

Niles was more direct. "There are soldiers everywhere now. They make Farmor scared. Come home, Mama, *please.*"

"The moment I can," she'd promised him, and she meant it. Her first priority, always, was her son.

No matter what might be happening between her and Kurt.

Seize the day. That's the course she'd chosen, knowing from the beginning how it had to end.

When Kurt lifted his head, she smiled at him.

Half an hour later, they were back at the Alex when Jens, practically vibrating with excitement, burst into the conference room where they were gathering to announce that he'd solved the code.

Standing at the head of the table, all eyes on him, Jens said, "If you recall, at the bottom of each letter was a line or two of code. I put them together and came up with this." He looked down at the paper in his hand and began to read.

"There is a demon inside me. In this world he goes by the name Xaphan. He is watching even now, as I write this, but he cannot read what I write in code. I pray to God every day not to let the demon surface, but my prayers are in vain. He has killed twenty-seven women and will kill more. He says they are corrupters of men, luring them with their sinful flesh and then destroying them. Therefore they must be destroyed. He seeks them out at the places where they set their traps and takes them to the house of God—"

Jens looked up, glancing around the table. "What's actually there in the code is 'the house of God Equation.' He wrote out the mathematical equation that is known as the God Equation, but I'm translating it as 'the house of God' until I can figure out some other interpretation that makes sense." Having finished his explanation, he looked back down at the paper he held and continued reading.

"—where he returns them to God, who sent them to torment him. There will be more. Please stop him before there are more. He is growing stronger and—"

Jens looked up. "He stops there. In midsentence. As if he were interrupted."

"By Xaphan," Pia said, and shuddered. Elin shuddered, too, inwardly, as a chill ran over her skin. That name—there was something about that name. She'd heard it before…

"He takes them to the house of God where he returns them to God," Albrecht repeated thoughtfully.

"Does that mean he's killing them in a church?" Vogel sounded doubtful.

"'House of God' could be purely metaphorical," Beckman said. "It doesn't have to refer to a church."

"What, exactly, is the God Equation?" Kurt asked.

"It's considered the perfect mathematical equation and is said to prove the existence of God. It's also known as Euler's Identity because it was discovered by the great Swiss mathematician Leonhard Euler," Jens said.

"But how does it help us find the murderer?" Pia asked.

"There's a building not far from where I live," Trott said. "That has a plaque on it dedicated to Leonhard Euler, who apparently lived there in the 1700s."

All conversation stopped as everyone in the room looked at him.

"What's the address?" Kurt was on his feet.

"I couldn't tell you the house number, but it's on Behrenstrasse, in Mitte," Walter said.

The four-story stone building at 21 Behrenstrasse near the Brandenburg Tor had indeed once served as the residence of Leonhard Euler and bore the plaque to prove it. Now it housed multiple offices, including the academy of sciences and several government departments. None of the signatories' names on the various leases had ever come up during the course of the investigation. Dozens of people went in and out throughout the day. Having been granted permission to search the building, Kurt had directed his crew through every nook and cranny of it from the fourth-story attic rooms to the cavernous basement.

They turned up nothing.

"There has to be something here. Nothing else makes sense." Standing in the middle of the basement, Kurt rolled up the building plans, given to him by the property manager, and slapped them against his palm in frustration.

"Remember Germania? Do the tunnels extend this far?" Elin asked in an undertone meant for his ears alone. She was beside him, because after the "say your prayers" letter he was unwilling to let her out of his sight.

"Is there anything beneath this basement?" Kurt asked the property manager, a portly little man named Herr Pichler, who'd followed them around nervously throughout the search. "A sub-basement? A tunnel?"

"There's an old coal cellar. But it hasn't been used for years."

"Show me."

They had to leave the building and walk behind it, where the property manager pointed to an iron hatch set into the ground beneath a half-dead shrub. It was bolted shut. A crowbar had to be found and brought, and the shrub had to be pulled up, but eventually the hatch was pried open, leaving Kurt and Elin and the rest peering into a narrow metal cylinder festooned with cobwebs. The only way down was via a rusty-looking ladder bolted onto the side.

"He couldn't have used this," Elin said in Kurt's ear.

"Doesn't look like it," Kurt agreed, and started down the ladder. At Kurt's direction, Trott went next, just in case something unexpected awaited them at the bottom. Elin went next, leaving the rest to follow.

As she descended rung by careful rung into the cold darkness, a heavy, musty smell overlaid with something bitterly acrid enveloped her.

Stepping into a bunker that was illuminated only by flashlight beams swooping over walls, floor, and ceiling, Elin's mouth went dry. Her heart started to pound. Her stomach cramped.

What she saw left no room for doubt.

They'd found the killer's lair.

36

LANTERNS WERE BROUGHT, ALONG WITH ALL THE EQUIP-
ment needed to collect and preserve evidence.

The killer had burned everything, or tried to, although there
were some things he hadn't been able to destroy. The shackles set
into the wall. The drain in the middle of the floor, which when
pried open yielded a treasure trove of hair, bloodstains, and, Elin
suspected from the rotten-meat smell, bits of decaying flesh, all
of which they would almost certainly be able to tie to his victims. Elin surmised from the stains and smells that adhered to it
that a wheeled iron cart had been used to transport dead bodies.

The walls were scorched, deliberately, probably in an attempt
to destroy any fingerprints. A burn heap in one corner contained scraps of cloth and what looked like parts of a body bag,
which would tie in with what the children had seen, as well
as the charred remains of several notebooks. A spray of dried

blood above the charring on one wall, a dainty silver necklace puddled in a crack in the floor, a ticket to the theater that was the public entrance to the Paradise Club overlooked in a corner, had survived the purge. There was plenty to connect with the victims. Would any of it be enough to identify the killer?

When subjected to the same force that had opened the hatch, a heavily bolted metal door set into the wall opposite the ladder answered the question of how the killer had gotten in and out unseen. It opened into a meticulously constructed concrete tunnel, with the oak leaf circle surrounding a number—43—carved into the wall next to the outside of the door confirming that it was part of the Germania network that ran beneath the city.

"He could have entered from anywhere, and exited, too," Kurt said. "Thus alleviating a multitude of problems, such as getting a live woman down the ladder or a dead woman up, or someone potentially noticing his vehicle regularly parked outside this building in the middle of the night."

"He always seems to be one step ahead of us." Trott frowned into the echoing emptiness of the tunnel. "It's like he knows what we're going to do before we do it."

"He'll make a mistake. They always do," Kurt said as Elin, who was listening to their exchange, carefully bagged the theater ticket. If they were really lucky, the killer's fingerprints might be found on it. Kurt turned to her. "How much of this stuff do we need?"

"Everything," Elin answered. "All of it."

He grimaced, then gestured at the men around him. "You heard her. Pack it up."

By the time they left the bunker, it was well past midnight. As every single member of the team was beyond tired, and a certain amount of sleep was essential if they were to do their best work, a quartet of Orpo officers had been left to stand guard over the entrances—two in the tunnel and two watching the outside hatch—although neither Kurt nor Elin thought the killer would return. Still, it was impossible to be sure.

"How much do you think losing his slaughterhouse will slow him down?" Kurt asked as they walked through his house on their way upstairs. There hadn't been any discussion about where she would spend the night.

"Not at all. He's already chosen his next victim, and I'm sure that, having abandoned this place, he's found a new kill site. His compulsion is too strong and knowing we're so close behind him will only add to the thrill. Is there no way we can get a warning out to the women who were in the Paradise Club on Saturday night? Because she was there then."

"Let me think about it," Kurt said, and since she was too tired to do anything else she chose to do just that and let the subject drop for the night.

Later, with a muffled cry, she jerked awake from a sound sleep in Kurt's arms. Blinking into pitch darkness, still caught up in the mists of the dream that had jolted her awake, she was shivering and breathing way too fast. And frightened. So very, very frightened.

"What?" Like the trained policeman he was, Kurt was instantly alert.

"My mother." As more of the mist started to clear, details came back to her. "The killer's code. Xaphan. I knew I'd heard that name before. My mother was talking to someone about Xaphan."

Her shivering intensified. Kurt stretched a long arm above her to turn on the lamp beside the bed. Propping himself up on one elbow, broad bare shoulders and wide chest blocking her view of the worst of the shadows that stretched eerily across walls and ceiling, he frowned down at her.

"You had a bad dream." He smoothed an errant lock of hair back from her face.

"No." It was all she could do to keep her teeth from chattering. Her eyes were wide and unblinking as they met his. "I mean, yes, I did have a bad dream, but it caused me to remember something real. From when I was here in Berlin with my parents. We were at the conference, and I'd been off doing something, but

I went to find my mother. I came up some stairs and saw her, and she was standing outside one of the seminar rooms talking to a young man. I walked up behind them—they were deep in conversation and didn't see me—and I heard him tell her that there was an evil being living inside him who could take over his body whenever it wanted to. He asked what he could do to get rid of it. I stopped—everyone there knew my mother was a psychiatrist, and they were always asking her odd things. This was clearly one of those situations, so I just stood back and waited for them to be done. My mother gave him some advice—I don't remember what—and then he said, 'Xaphan doesn't like that,' in a much deeper, angrier, grating voice, and turned and walked away. *Stalked* away. He went right past me. I didn't pay much attention to him because I was anxious to go to my mother so we could get on with our plans for the afternoon, but he had to have seen me." She took a breath. "My mother was killed the next day."

The memory was so sharp, and so painful, that she closed her eyes in an effort to block it out. She lay there, unmoving, cold to her bone marrow, silently replaying how it had all unfolded afterward, thinking of a thousand ways it could have been different—and knowing that it was impossible to change a thing.

Kurt tucked the quilt that covered them both more securely around her.

"I think he was the killer," she said, and opened her eyes.

Still propped on an elbow, he loomed above her, his black hair tousled from sleep, the hard planes and angles of his face set in harsh lines, his mouth tight and his eyes narrow with concern for her. He badly needed a shave and, bared to the waist, he looked big and tough and muscular, just the kind of protector anyone would choose. *Her* protector.

The thought made her heart pound.

"He recognized you when you showed up as Dr. Murder in Berlin," Kurt said.

"Yes." She gave a jerky little nod. "He must've thought I'd

overheard what he said to my mother about Xaphan. He must be afraid I'll remember. That's why he's been coming after me."

"What do you remember about him? Can you describe him?" The sudden glint in his eyes told her how vitally important he considered the information.

But already the details of the dream were lost, receded into whatever realm dreams go to when they're done.

"No," she said. "I can't picture him at all. Only that he was a man and seemed young."

If he was disappointed, Kurt didn't show it. "We'll catch him. And in the meantime I've got you safe. Trust me."

"I do." She managed the merest suggestion of a smile for him. Then, because his eyes warmed, and the look in them for her caused her heart to speed up, she backed away from any overt display of emotion with a flat-sounding, "Looks like you were right all along."

"I think you'll find I usually am," he said, and when her slight smile turned into a testy frown because she recognized her own words when they got thrown back at her, *he* smiled. Then he kissed her. Gently and carefully. *Tenderly.* As if he cared.

The thought made her dizzy. It made her scared. It made her stomach clench as every whisper of caution crossing her tired mind about him disappeared. Wrapping her arms around his neck, she kissed him with a fierceness that surprised her. He made a guttural sound and pulled her hard against him. His kisses turned deep and hungry. His hand found her breast, and heat rolled over her in a wave.

Moments later, they were both naked and he was touching her everywhere.

"You're beautiful," he said. His mouth followed his hands and she caught fire and matched his caresses with her own and they both went up in flames.

When it was over, when she was once again wrapped up

soundly in his arms, she almost instantly fell fathoms deep asleep and was, thankfully, far too exhausted to dream.

They were coming downstairs the next morning getting ready to head to the Alex when someone knocked softly on Kurt's back door. Elin started. She checked for a moment and glanced over her shoulder at Kurt, who was a couple of steps behind her. It was early, too early for any ordinary visitor. They'd pulled back the blackout curtains in the bedroom upon arising to discover that the sun was up, but barely. The sky was still awash in the purple-and-pink pinwheels that accompanied the dawn.

Kurt frowned as he looked toward the door but gestured at her to proceed.

"Go in the other room," he said softly as they reached the bottom of the stairs. The fact that his gun was in his hand told her how unusual this kind of early-morning visitation was for him, and her pulse quickened. The knock came again, louder and more urgent, as she whisked away into the front parlor and he walked through the kitchen and pulled open the back door.

"Markus!" Kurt's voice held a note of surprise. Markus, Elin remembered, was his son, and she felt a surge of relief that the visitor wasn't anyone dangerous. Kurt's greeting was followed almost immediately by the sound of someone stepping inside the house and the door being closed again. "What are you doing here? Is everything all right?"

"No. Vater—" The boy hesitated, then came out with the rest in a rush.

From where she now stood, still hidden in the gloom of the dark front parlor but with a clear view of the back door, Elin could see the pair of them. Kurt, clean-shaven and work ready in a white shirt and dark pants, had holstered his gun. Thin in his school uniform, standing no taller than Kurt's shoulder, Markus looked up at his father. His resemblance to Kurt was unmistakable.

"Last night my stepfather played cards with his friends from the Gestapo as he does sometimes, and I heard them talking. They said they are about to launch a roundup of all suspected members of the Black Orchestra because of fears they are plotting against the Führer. My stepfather told them you are one for sure. I came as soon as I could to warn you." The boy's voice held anguish.

Silence spun out for a moment, and Elin caught her breath. Even in Denmark, there'd been rumors for years about the existence of the Black Orchestra, a loose group of high-level Germans determined to bring down the Third Reich. Did it exist? Did it not? No one had ever seemed to know.

Then Kurt laughed and clapped a hand down on Markus's shoulder. "I am truly touched, son, by your loyalty, but you don't have to worry. Your stepfather is mistaken. I have no part in anything like that."

"You don't?" Markus was wide-eyed with relief. "Artur sounded so sure. And the officers wrote down your name."

"As you well know, Artur is not always my biggest fan. And his Gestapo friends can check into my doings however they wish. They'll find nothing."

"I... I shouldn't have suspected you. But—"

Kurt swept him up in an embrace. "You did exactly the right thing to come and tell me." Affectionately thumping Markus on the back, he let him go. The boy stepped back, pink-cheeked but looking pleased. "But listen, you mustn't tell anyone—not Artur or your mother or anyone—that you came here to warn me. They would be very angry, and you would find yourself in a great deal of trouble."

"No, I won't. I wouldn't. Not ever." He sounded so fervent that Elin almost smiled.

"Good. Just put the whole matter out of your head. Are you hungry? Can I give you some breakfast?"

"No. I was on my way to school. I'd better go."

"I can give you a ride."

"My bicycle's here."

"All right then." Kurt opened the back door. Markus started to leave, then hesitated in the doorway to look at him.

"Be careful, Vater."

"I will. You be careful, too."

Then Markus was gone, and Kurt shut and locked the door. Elin walked into the kitchen. Whatever she'd been going to say was lost as she got a good look at his face. His expression was grim. His mouth was tight and his eyes were hard.

And she knew.

"You *are*, aren't you?" she asked, frightened. "One of them. The Black Orchestra."

"If I were to admit anything of the sort, I would be a fool and it would only put you in danger." His voice was as harsh as his face. He walked past her to pluck his jacket and hat from a coatrack near the stairs. "Come on, let's go. We have a busy day ahead."

Hours later, Elin, having been forbidden by Kurt to leave the building until he returned, was working in the lab at the Alex. Fear for Kurt, which to her dismay only underlined how emotionally involved with him she'd become, kept her on edge as she methodically sifted through the mountains of evidence from the night before. When Pia burst into the room with Detective Beckman right behind her she was so startled she almost dropped the sterile tweezers she was using to delicately separate pages of the burned notebooks in hopes of discovering something legible.

Trott, who was her designated bodyguard until Kurt returned from wherever he'd taken himself off to, jumped protectively to his feet.

"What is it?" Elin's eyes were glued to Pia. *Kurt's been arrested*, was her first terrified thought, because she had no doubt at all that he was indeed part of the Black Orchestra and strongly suspected he had gone off today to warn his fellow conspirators.

Despite her racing heart she retained the presence of mind to put her tweezers down in the sterile dish meant to receive them even as Pia rushed toward her.

"It was on the radio." Pia's cheeks were flushed and her eyes were big with alarm as she all but skidded to a stop beside Elin. Behind her, Beckman looked equally perturbed as he closed the door and turned to look at them. "The murders. We were at the Hotel Adlon working with Baron von Storch when we heard it. The broadcaster said the radio station had received a letter from a man claiming to have slashed to death ten women in Berlin over the last five months. The letter said the Kripo couldn't catch him and the famous Dr. Murder had been brought in to help but she couldn't catch him, either. He said he was going to kill again soon and nobody could stop him. The broadcaster said the letter was signed with a *wolfsangel* and the radio station is calling him the Werewolf of Berlin."

Pia ended on such a note of alarm that Elin's nerves, already jangling at the news, sent what felt like shock waves racing over her skin.

Beckman nodded grim confirmation while Trott swore.

"Where's the chief?" Beckman looked at Trott, who shook his head.

"He was following up on something," Elin said, which was not actually a lie. "I have no idea where he is, though."

"There'll be hell to pay over this," Trott said.

"If the killer sent the radio station a letter, that's nothing we could have prevented. It's not our fault." Elin pulled calm around her like a cloak.

"The brass won't see it like that," Trott said.

"How long ago was the broadcast?" Elin asked.

"Maybe thirty minutes," Pia answered.

"It'll be all over the city by now." Trott looked, and sounded, appalled.

"We've got to find the chief," Beckman said. "He's got to know about this *now*."

"There's nothing he can—" Elin began, hoping to ward off a no-holds-barred search for Kurt because of the attention she feared it might attract to him on today of all days.

But before she could finish, a quick knock was followed by Frau Skelton's entrance.

Her expression made it clear that she knew trouble was afoot.

"I just received a call from the Reich Chancellery." Frau Skelton looked at Elin. "Professor Lund, General Haupt wants to see you in his office. Immediately."

37

A SENSE OF COLD DREAD PERMEATED THE BUILDING.
Unlike the old Reich Chancellery next door, which this one was
designed to replace, the New Reich Chancellery was modern
and built to impress. Because the pervading sense of cold dread
matched her own, Elin was supremely conscious of it as she followed the secretary who'd been waiting in the palatial front lobby
to collect her. There hadn't been time to get word to Kurt even
if anyone had known where to reach him. And an urgent summons to meet with General Haupt was impossible to ignore.

If it hadn't been for Trott, whose stolid presence beside her
provided a degree of reassurance, Elin would have been tempted
to turn tail and run.

"Professor Lund, General Haupt," the secretary called out as
she tapped on the office door. The marble-floored reception area
in which they stood was empty despite the multiple chairs lining

the walls, just as the building itself, as far as she was able to see, had been largely empty. Elin found the emptiness chilling. As if whatever happened within these walls could bear no witnesses.

Haupt opened the door himself, so abruptly Elin almost jumped. He was unsmiling. His uniform was immaculate. His fair hair was slicked back from his face. But there was a coldness to his eyes that she found ominous as he looked at her.

"Professor Lund." His gaze swept over her, making her glad that for today she'd chosen to wear the businesslike ensemble of a slim black skirt and white blouse and pin her hair back from her face. He then glanced past her to Trott, who'd greeted him with a smart "*Heil* Hitler" and accompanying salute.

"*Heil,*" he replied, returning the salute without enthusiasm. Then he continued, "There's no need for you to wait. I'll send Professor Lund back to the Alex in my car."

Elin almost choked. Given everything, she wasn't about to part with the protection of this policeman she'd come to trust. She grappled for an excuse, then decided the best way to handle it was to use the small degree of clout her celebrity status gave her and state her position unequivocally.

Never show fear.

"Please wait," she said to Trott, who reassured her with a nod. To Haupt, accompanied by the sweetest smile she could summon, she said, "For security reasons, I prefer to travel with Herr Trott. As I'm sure you're aware, because of this investigation there has been more than one attempt on my life. I know you'll understand."

Haupt's lips compressed, but before he could reply she walked past him into his office, making it clear the arrangement wasn't up for discussion.

Haupt closed the door and crossed the room to his desk without arguing. The room, Elin saw, was immaculately neat. Nothing out of place, not a speck of dust.

"Please sit down." He indicated a chair opposite his desk. Her chair was small and uncomfortable, while his desk and chair were big and impressive. A silent exhibition of power, designed to intimidate—an effective tactic, even though she recognized it.

"Your investigation into the serial murders you were brought here to solve has become public knowledge," Haupt said without preamble. He steepled his hands in front of him: another position meant to convey power. To his left, a large oil painting of Hitler stared at her from above an ornate fireplace. Bookshelves holding a variety of personal mementos as well as books lined the walls. "We can't have that. The women of the city will panic, which will cause their men to panic, which will disrupt the war effort. To prevent such a thing from happening is why secrecy was mandated from the beginning. However, there's no undoing what's been done. The situation must be dealt with as it is."

"We're very close to finding the killer," Elin said. "Once all the evidence we've collected is examined, I anticipate—"

Haupt waved her words away before she could finish. "The news about the murderer they're calling the Werewolf of Berlin was on the radio today. I heard it myself. Tomorrow it will be everywhere. Not just in Berlin, but throughout Germany and even the world. The Führer is angry at this embarrassment to the Reich. Your time is up."

Haupt's own anger pulsed through every word.

She was under no illusion as to how much authority the man wielded. If he wanted to have her arrested, have the whole Kripo team arrested, he could do it with a snap of his fingers. Clasping her hands in her lap, Elin presented what she hoped was a calm and composed front.

"Are you saying I'm being sent back to Denmark?" Her thoughts immediately flew to Kurt. If not for him—leaving him to bear the brunt of what the High Command would clearly consider their failure—such a fate would have been music to her ears.

"Not just yet. The case must be solved, the murderer caught, and the public informed that the situation has been corrected before you go. Fortunately, despite the less than productive combined efforts of you and our Kripo, the case *has* been solved."

"What?" Elin looked at him in astonishment.

He nodded. "You recall a suspect who was held in custody for a few days but eventually released? A certain Orpo officer by the name of Paul Dalsing?"

"I do, yes."

"He killed himself last night. Leaving behind a suicide note in which he confessed to the murders. Which is an extremely fortunate turn of events for your future and that of everyone else involved in this investigation. Tomorrow you and I, General Kaltenbrunner, and the Kripo officer in charge of the investigation will hold a press conference in which we announce that, thanks to the excellent work of the renowned Dr. Murder in collaboration with our own esteemed Kripo, the case has been solved, the murderer caught, and the women of Berlin made safe."

"Herr Dalsing confessed?" To say she was stunned was an understatement.

"Would you care to read the suicide note he left? I have it right here."

"I would, yes." In response to his gesture, she got up and went to stand beside him, while he remained seated: another show of power. The faint sweetish scent of his hair pomade reached her nostrils. The letter, as he had indicated, was there on his desk. She found herself looking at a sheet of ordinary white paper almost completely filled with a spidery, cramped, black ink scrawl that was instantly familiar. And the clincher was, the letter was written in Kurrent.

"Well?" Haupt's face as he looked up at her was hard.

"I can't read it. It's in Kurrent."

With an impatient grunt, Haupt picked up the letter and began to read aloud.

It was, as Haupt had said, a confession, accurate in every respect. Some of the details revealed things only the killer could know. In fact, she had no doubt at all that the killer had written it. But Elin knew, *knew*, from their investigation of Dalsing that he didn't fit the profile of the killer in any number of ways. He had alibis for many of the dates in question, he didn't have type A blood, and as far as they'd been able to determine he'd never been taught Kurrent.

Haupt, however, obviously knew Kurrent well. He was reading the letter to her with no difficulty at all.

With that thought twisting through her mind, Elin looked up and away from Haupt even as he continued to read. She found herself frowning at the bookcase closest to the fireplace. Where, she suddenly realized, a silver trophy topped with a Weimar Republic eagle bookended a row of large binders.

She was as certain as it was possible to be that she'd seen that trophy, or one identical to it, within the last twenty-four hours. In a picture in an old photo album of a group of young men who were each awarded one at the conference her father had brought his family to in Berlin, in fact.

A chill slid over her.

"And there you have it," Haupt said. Caught off guard, Elin had barely enough time to snap her eyes away from the trophy and back to him before he could discover that she'd been focused on anything else.

"A most comprehensive confession," she managed. His eyes, which were on her face now, narrowed. Oh, God, was she looking at him oddly? Heart thumping as the true nature of what just might have been revealed to her snaked its way through the neural connections in her brain, she added, "It's also, as far as I can tell, identical in appearance and composition to previous letters written by the killer."

Did the trophy on the bookshelf belong to him? Did it mean he was there at that conference? She'd seen the photo, and if he'd been one of the young men pictured she was almost positive she would have recognized him in it, fifteen years younger or not. But she had not.

Did he kill my mother? Her mind reeled at the thought. It was all she could do not to physically recoil.

"In my opinion, Dalsing's suicide note conclusively identifies him as the killer. I take it you agree with that." Haupt was looking at her—it was the *way* Haupt was looking at her. As if he could sense the turmoil of her thoughts.

Elin abruptly realized how much danger she was in. Cortisol flooded her body. The cold thick rush of the stress hormone pumping through her system dried her mouth and sent her pulse skyrocketing.

If what she was starting to suspect proved true, her life might hang on how she handled the next few minutes.

"I do." She was proud of—no, profoundly thankful for—how untroubled she sounded, courtesy of the grace of God and a lifetime's worth of training in the art of hiding her feelings.

The tension in his shoulders eased. His frown faded. The ugly glint left his eyes. Subtle signs all, but significant.

She was saying all the right things, telling him what he wanted to hear.

"Then if you will sign this statement I've had prepared attesting to that fact, we can consider this unfortunate matter concluded. Except for the press conference tomorrow in which we hand out copies of your statement, and not incidentally boast of our success."

He pulled another paper, this one typewritten, out of a folder on his desk. Putting it down on the polished wood surface, he handed Elin a pen and tapped the bottom of the page.

"Sign here. And please, include all your degrees. They're quite impressive."

Putting her name to such a lie went against every principle of ethics she'd been taught—but she had no choice.

Elin signed.

Haupt stood up. He was close enough that there was not even an arm's length of space between them. Elin could almost feel the satisfaction he radiated. She could feel something else, too, she realized, and it made the hair stand up on the back of her neck. The icy, soulless aura that she had long ago come to think of as the miasma of evil that marked a killer.

"The press conference is set for nine tomorrow morning. Please come at eight so that we may confer beforehand. And on the morning after, there will be an airplane waiting on the tarmac at Tempelhof to convey you and your team back to Copenhagen, with the Party's thanks for a job well done."

The first thing to do was ascertain if Paul Dalsing was really dead.

Elin had Trott stop at a random telephone kiosk midway between the Chancellery and the Alex and, after looking up the number in the telephone book provided, dropped her *pfennigs* in the slot and called his home. The woman who answered identified herself as Dalsing's sister Mary. His wife was too distraught to come to the telephone, but yes, the news was true. Paul had shot himself in the head with his own service revolver sometime after the family had gone to sleep the night before. No, there'd been no warning signs, and no one had heard a thing. The news was just now reaching the wider circle of his family and friends. How had Professor Lund learned of it?

The more telling question for Elin was, how had Haupt learned of it? And acquired the suicide note Dalsing had supposedly left behind?

Fobbing Dalsing's sister off with a vague reply and extending heartfelt condolences to the family, Elin rang off and turned the kiosk over to Trott with a request that he call his friend who had supplied the album to ask about the photo of the young men holding the trophies. Six young men, one of them the album owner's brother, had received the trophies although only five were pictured, his friend told Trott. Which, if the sixth man was Haupt, Elin thought, would explain why she hadn't spotted him in the photo. No, Trott's friend could not remember the missing man's name—and unfortunately his brother, who might, was dead.

Once back at the Alex, Elin went feverishly to work piecing together bits of various military, personnel, and medical records, and managed to confirm that Haupt's blood type was A. He'd been subject to discipline multiple times for overly violent behavior as a young man before he'd become a Brownshirt and, subsequently, a member of Hitler's personal staff. And he'd returned with Hitler to Berlin in March, mere weeks before the killings started.

Significant evidence, but circumstantial. It wasn't enough.

In hopes of finding definitive proof tying Haupt to the murders, Elin once again started in on the material collected from the murder site. She hit the jackpot with the silver necklace when she was able to recover an almost complete fingerprint from it. The necklace had belonged to Bella Richter. She was wearing it in the photo her family had supplied of her. She just had to compare it to Haupt's fingerprints.

Elin's excitement was dashed when she discovered that, if Haupt's fingerprints were on file, they weren't anywhere she could access. And she didn't want to start looking for them elsewhere for fear of Haupt getting wind of it.

But if they were to charge him, they needed proof. Proof so incontrovertible that no one could argue with it. Haupt was too powerful and had too many powerful friends, including the Führer himself, to attempt to bring him to justice otherwise.

When you strike at a king, you must kill him.

Then she remembered the upcoming press conference. She could try to get Haupt's fingerprints there.

Once one of his fingerprints was proven to match the fingerprint on the necklace, the Kripo would have enough to make an arrest.

By the time Kurt showed up at the Alex, Elin was as certain as it was possible—minus definitive proof—to be that Haupt was the killer, and had, moreover, murdered Dalsing and written the suicide note himself to put an end to the investigation.

The knowledge left her so agitated she could hardly sit still.

Walking into the lab, Kurt took one look at her, pushed his hat to the back of his head, and said, "What's happened?"

She couldn't tell him. Not there. The Alex was alive with eyes to see and ears to hear everything that occurred within its walls.

"She needs to eat," Trott answered for her, rising wearily from a lab stool on the other side of the table. "As far as I know, she hasn't had a bite all day."

"I had breakfast," Elin said, which Kurt knew. A bread roll and coffee, on the way into work. But the need to keep the conversation sounding casual was front and center in her mind.

"Come on, I'll take you to dinner," Kurt said, equally casual, and looked at Trott. "You're welcome to join us."

Trott shook his head. "Over to you. Anyway, I have some things to do."

Kurt nodded in response even as the two men exchanged what Elin perceived to be a speaking glance. A short time later, Elin was beside Kurt in his car. She told him everything in a burst of words so fraught with emotion that she was left feeling drained as she finished. And then, as they stopped at a busy café and he bought her dinner, she had once again to talk of mundane things for fear of being overheard until finally the meal was consumed and they left.

"You know we're going to have to agree with everything Haupt says at that press conference tomorrow, don't you? We have to tell the story the way he wants it told. Put a good face on it for the Reich," Kurt said.

"I know. But once his fingerprint on Bella Richter's necklace is confirmed—"

"You're still not going to say anything. You're going to leave it to me. Once you're safely back in Denmark, I'll take care of it."

She looked at him. "Unless you make a surprise announcement with me—'Dr. Murder'—there to garner publicity, I'm afraid General Haupt and his friends will find a way to shut you up before the truth gets out."

"How about you let me worry about that? Your job was to find the killer, which, if that fingerprint checks out, you've done. Mine is to stop him."

"But—"

"The Party will do everything in its power to prevent anyone from finding out that one of the Führer's closest associates is a serial murderer. They also will do everything in their power to keep the Lebensborn program secret. By everything in their power, I mean they'll kill you if they have to, do you understand?" His voice was grim. "And your friends. And me. And everyone who worked on this case. Whatever it takes to keep their secret."

Elin shuddered as she saw the danger yawning before her. In her zeal to indict Haupt, she'd forgotten that the Nazis would consider any damage to their reputation to be far more important than, say, the lives of murdered young women.

"I understand," Elin said, and she did. Then, for the first time since they'd pulled away from the curb in front of the restaurant, she looked away from him, out through the windows.

"Where are we going?" she asked after a moment. It was late, a little after ten o'clock, and she'd thought he would head for his house. Instead, he'd turned west on Unter den Linden. Because of the blackout, the wide boulevard was nothing short of stygian, but she knew enough landmarks now to tell the difference. Only a few vehicles were out, their headlamps as dim and pale as ghost eyes peering through the veil of night. But on the sidewalks and in the alleys and gardens, dozens of phosphorus pins glowed green and other, more nefarious figures appeared as shadows slinking through shadows.

Behind the cloaked windows, the restaurants, and the cinema, all the forms of legal and illegal entertainment Berlin could offer were in full swing.

"To the Waldschloss. I have something I have to do there."

"You're going into the forest, aren't you?"

"If Haupt is the killer, you should be safe enough at the Waldschloss for a few hours until I can get back," he said, without answering directly. "He wants you at that press conference tomorrow, so no harm will come to you before then. And Officer Bruin will be on duty in the lobby, just in case. I wouldn't leave you if it wasn't necessary, but it has been necessary today and it is tonight."

"I know you're involved in rescuing Jews. I heard what your son told you this morning about the Black Orchestra. If I were arrested and tortured and forced to reveal all I know, those two things are enough to get you killed *and* compromise everything you're doing. So don't you think you might as well tell me the rest?"

The darkness made his expression impossible to read, but his very silence was expressive.

"Kurt?"

He made a sound under his breath. She knew it was capitulation even before he started talking.

"If you must know, my curious *liebling*, there's a train station on the other side of the forest where captured Jews are loaded onto cattle cars and taken away to concentration camps under cover of night. Some of them we help to escape. Some of them we're able to buy back—oh, yes, the guards are susceptible to bribery. We can't save them all, but we save the ones we can, and then I see that they're taken to safe houses until they can be gotten out. It's a slow process because usually we have to wait on the acquisition of false identification papers. Now, given the rumors, I'm working to speed things up so that we can get everyone we currently have in hiding out before some or all of us get arrested."

"If you're caught…"

"They're murdering them, Elin. By the thousands. That's what's happening in those camps. Oh, for public consumption they say what they're doing is 'evacuation' and 'resettlement,' but their real plan is the eradication of every single Jew from the face of the earth. Millions of souls."

"Dear God." That hit home with such force that for a moment it felt like she'd been punched in the stomach. The horror of it was almost impossible to process. Yet somewhere deep inside, she knew it was true. She'd suspected. Borge and his friends had suspected. Hundreds, maybe thousands or even tens of thousands, had suspected. But none of them had wanted to believe.

Now here was truth.

She was shaking as they pulled into the courtyard of the Waldschloss.

Kurt said, "You can't tell anyone—not Pia, or Moller, or anyone—any of this. Just like you can't tell them that you suspect Haupt is the killer. Not a word to anybody. Everyone must act like they don't know about Haupt, or about what's happening in the forest, until everybody, you and your friends included, is safely away. And the best way to make sure they do that is for them *not* to know anything about it. They can't give away what they don't know."

She nodded. "You don't have to worry. I won't tell them."

He parked, then leaned over and kissed her, a brief, hard kiss that made her bones melt and her heart ache in equal measure. Then they got out of the car and went inside.

38

THE PRESS CONFERENCE WAS HELD IN THE NEW REICH
Chancellery's Grande Reception Room. With its glittering pair
of oversize chandeliers and plethora of tall windows, the huge
space was full of light despite the overcast sky outside. Unfortunately, the marble walls and floor threw sound back on itself, so
the shouts of the reporters and sounds of their equipment were
magnified to the point where all was bedlam.

Last night at the Waldschloss, after Kurt had gone, Elin had
talked a little to Pia and Jens, and then, as it grew later, pretended
to go to bed. Instead, unable to sleep as she waited for Kurt to
emerge safely from the forest, she'd packed up her belongings,
keeping out only what she would need until she was at home
again. It was almost dawn before Kurt, using the key she'd given
him, slipped inside her room. At most they'd managed an hour's

sleep, and Kurt, though clean-shaven, was attending the press conference in his clothes from the day before.

"No one will notice," he'd assured her, running an openly admiring glance over her as she slid into her pumps prior to them walking out of the hotel room.

From the moment the press was ushered into the Grande Reception Room, most of the focus had been on Elin.

Professional in her houndstooth suit, her hair left to curl loosely around her shoulders, wearing just enough cosmetics to hide the effects of a near-sleepless night despite the Führer's avowed dislike for women in makeup, Elin stood between Generals Haupt and Kaltenbrunner as cameras flashed and reporters scribbled and microphones recorded their every word. Shunted to the side by both generals, who clearly wanted to be photographed with Elin and Elin only, Kurt managed to look handsome in his dark suit despite the fact that his eyes were slightly bloodshot and said suit was slightly rumpled. Unless asked a direct question, he stayed out of the way and left the talking to the others.

"Dr. Murder, how does it feel to have brought another serial murderer to justice?" one reporter shouted above the din.

"I certainly can't take sole credit," Elin replied, and gestured at the men on either side of her. "General Haupt and General Kaltenbrunner, as well as your Kripo under the direction of Detective Schneider there, were instrumental in solving the case. But it's very satisfactory to know that one more murderer has been stopped."

"Dr. Murder, what was the clue that led you to the Orpo Paul Dalsing?"

General Haupt answered the question before Elin could. "Professor Lund and our detectives had been watching him for some time. They actually arrested him a week ago and then released him to see if he would incriminate himself. That's when it was discovered that he was a Jew, descended from Jewish grandparents, which he had kept hidden. So of course he was watched even more closely, and as a result we found the place where he had committed the atrocious murders. Knowing what we had discovered, he killed himself."

Beside him, Elin gave a corroborating nod as the reporters looked her way even as her stomach knotted at the lie and her skin crawled because Haupt was so near.

There were more questions, more photographs, a quick interview with a radio station. Then a photographer asked if he could get a picture of Dr. Murder alone. Elin, seizing the opportunity she'd been waiting for, said, "Would you mind holding this, please?" to Haupt, who throughout had stayed so close to her that she'd decided his intent was to intimidate. She thrust the small leather handbag she'd brought along for that very purpose into his hands.

Her smile was genuine. The photographer was quick. In no more than a couple of minutes she was reclaiming her handbag with profuse thanks.

"My pleasure," Haupt replied. Though he was smiling, his blue eyes were not as they met hers. Her pulse quickened as she wondered if he suspected what she'd done. But if he did, it would be easy to take the handbag from her, or even to have her arrested. Or maybe not so easy, with the reporters there. "Shall I send a car to take you to the airport in the morning? The flight leaves at noon, so, let us say, at ten? You're staying at the Hotel Waldschloss, I believe?"

"I am, but I wouldn't put you to so much trouble, Herr General. My team and I have made friends during our stay and they are going to drive us to the airport and see us off."

"I see."

A reporter called out, "General Haupt, General Kaltenbrunner, is there anything either of you can tell us about the assassination of Governor Kube in Belarus? Some are saying the assassin was a woman. Is that true?"

Haupt turned toward the reporter. The governor's assassination was a matter of great national concern.

"Yes, I can tell you it is true," he said, and then he and Kaltenbrunner were surrounded by cameras and pelted with questions about that topic and other aspects of the war.

Signaling that their part of the press conference was at an end, an aide showed Elin and Kurt out of the room. Exchanging glances, relieved to have escaped unscathed, they managed to walk at a reasonable pace to Kurt's car. Once they were both inside, Elin sagged with relief as Kurt drove away down Wilhelmstrasse.

"Neat trick." Kurt cast a glance at her handbag, which, wrapped carefully in a handkerchief she'd kept in her pocket, she held on her lap.

"Yes, if it worked." But she could see no reason why the smooth surface should not yield retrievable fingerprints. The bigger question was, did Haupt suspect what she had done, and why?

She said as much to Kurt.

"I think the fact that you're a woman, and beautiful, has its own blinding properties. I doubt General Haupt has any idea what a dogged investigator you are beneath that extremely misleading exterior, Dr. Murder," Kurt said. She smiled at him because he'd called her beautiful and because she suddenly remembered the first time he'd called her Dr. Murder in that sardonic way of his, which had made her bristle, to say the least. She'd been prepared to dislike him intensely then. And now—

She wasn't going to think about now.

She was going to keep the promise she'd made to the victims and do the job she'd been brought in to do.

"Still," Kurt said. "We'll take precautions, in case."

The fingerprint was a match.

We've got him. Elin wanted to cheer. She wanted to jump up and down with glee. But they were in the lab at the Alex. The knowledge that somebody was probably listening in was terrifying under the circumstances, so she didn't say it out loud.

Instead, she beckoned Kurt over to her microscope and showed him the fingerprint from the necklace next to the fingerprint from her handbag. As she pointed out the identical arches and loops and whorls he nodded solemnly.

"So you found the dog hair. I never doubted that you would," he said in her ear. When she beamed at him he laughed, picked her right up off her feet, swung her around in a circle, set her back down, and kissed her. She kissed him back with enthusiasm.

Then he got to sit there and watch while she preserved and stored the evidence, including her handbag, which only contained a hairbrush and a lipstick anyway because she'd known that if her ruse worked and the fingerprints matched, she'd be leaving it behind for use by a prosecutor, and wrote up a detailed report.

"Put it in here," he said, holding out a big brown envelope to her when she was done. She did, and he took it and her to his office. He put the envelope in a secret drawer in his desk, which he then locked.

And with that, her job was done.

She was free to go home. The knowledge made her happy—and sad.

Her mother's love for Niles was, as it had been every moment of every day since his birth, the driving force of her life.

But here in Berlin, in the unlikeliest place under the unlikeliest of circumstances, she'd found another kind of love. A woman's love.

For Kurt.

It was the first time she'd acknowledged having such feelings for him, even to herself. Her very own gift from the universe—with heartbreak attached.

There was no future in it.

She couldn't stay. And he couldn't go.

She squared her shoulders, steeled her heart. Such was life, in this world gone mad with war.

It was harder than she'd expected to say goodbye to Frau Skelton, and Sonja and Roth and Gunther, and the detectives, all of whom were present and in the process of cleaning out their desks. That's when Elin realized that, as far as they knew, Dalsing *was* the serial killer they'd been hunting. Now that he'd been identified and was dead, the case had been officially solved. They'd done what they'd been brought together to do, and the Special Project Unit would be disbanding.

They had no idea the real killer was still out there waiting to be brought to justice.

And able to kill again at will.

There's nothing I can do, she told herself.

For now, like Kurt, she had to play her part in the fiction Haupt had created.

Kurt gave a short speech, congratulating everyone on a job well done.

"Where will you go?" Elin asked them as they opened bottles of beer in celebration.

"To the VA. I've been given a promotion," Sonja said proudly. The VA, Elin had learned over the course of her sojourn at the Alex, was the section of Amt V that included female detectives, so Elin congratulated her with real warmth.

"To the VC," Gunther said with so much loathing that Roth, who claimed a shift to domestic surveillance for himself, was prompted by Elin's expression to explain that Gunther had been assigned to the Canine Unit.

Roth added, "And he hates dogs," to a round of chuckles.

"Back to the Major Crimes Unit," Beckman said, and Albrecht and Vogel nodded agreement.

"We'll have to see," Trott said with a shrug and a glance at Kurt.

Kurt said nothing, and she didn't ask. At least, not until they were alone together in his car. It was raining, big fat droplets pounding down on the windshield as they emerged from the garage. It was too dark to see the sky, but the stars and moon were blotted out and thunder rumbled in the distance.

"What will you do?" she asked him. The words *when I'm gone* hung in the air between them, but so far neither of them had shown any disposition to delve into that.

"I'll see to it that Haupt is dealt with," he said. "And then— murders happen every day in Berlin. There'll be no shortage of work for me at the Kripo."

"Will there be problems for you after you expose General Haupt? General Kaltenbrunner already dislikes you." Elin looked at him anxiously.

"But Nebe likes me. And as long as he has a use for me, I should be fine."

"The Black Orchestra—what if you're arrested?"

"I'm hoping the Gestapo will attribute Pohl's denunciation to our ongoing disagreements. They already have a long list of his complaints against me." He gave her a wry smile. "None of us knows what tomorrow holds, much less anything beyond that. How about we forget our troubles for tonight, and you let me take you to dinner? Someplace fancy."

A goodbye dinner. Elin's heart cracked a little just imagining it. She didn't think she could bear going to a restaurant, talking of nothing in a roomful of people who might be listening in while their time together ticked inexorably away.

"Can we go to your house instead? You could make sausage and eggs."

His eyes were dark and his mouth was tight as he glanced her way. Their eyes met. He knew what she was saying. Electricity arced between them, as wild and hot as the lightning bolt that suddenly split the night sky.

"Sure," he said. "We can do that."

So they went to his house. As soon as they stepped inside, she turned and walked into his arms. He kissed her, and she went up on tiptoe and wrapped her arms around his neck and kissed him back. And then he scooped her clear up off her feet and carried her upstairs. Their passion was steamier than every secret, guilty, erotic dream she'd ever had.

Neither of them even realized they'd forgotten about dinner altogether until they woke up the next morning and it was time to go.

It didn't matter. She wasn't hungry. Neither, it seemed, was he.

The sky was gray. The air smelled of damp. Puddles stood on the pavement as he put her overnight bag and her medical bag, which she'd brought with her from the Alex, into the trunk. They would pick up her other bag at the Waldschloss, along with Pia and Jens and their luggage.

Then Kurt would drive them to the airport and put them all onto an airplane, and they would fly away.

She could hardly bear the thought.

There was so much she wanted to say to him. But what good would it do? Her chest was tight with desolation already. The last thing either of them needed was some big, emotional scene.

During the drive, they barely spoke.

They were on the last stretch of road that would take them to the Waldschloss when Kurt looked over at her.

"Elin. I'm sorry for the reason. But I'm glad you came," he said. His voice was devoid of feeling. His eyes said nothing at all. His face could have been carved from stone.

But now, she knew him. What he expressed the least, meant the most.

"I'm in love with you," she said, although she'd never meant to tell him. And then, the words wrenched out of her. "What are we going to do?"

About this, she meant. *About us*. And he knew, because he knew her, too.

"You're going to go home to your son and leave me to do what I need to do. Copenhagen's not that far, you know. I'm sure I can find a reason to visit. Who knows, you might feel the need to bring someone in to consult on a murder."

Even as she succumbed to a slightly tremulous smile at that, he added softly, "I'm in love with you, too, by the way."

After that, he had to pull over. And he kissed her, and she kissed him back, and even cried a little at the prospect of parting. He made promises, and she vowed to hold him to them.

Finally there was no more time. He let her go, and she slid back into her seat and wiped her eyes and smiled at him.

He drove on to the Waldschloss.

Giddy with happiness, aching with heartbreak, anxious to get home, sad to leave, she got out of the car without daring to look up at him. Their personal relationship was theirs alone. Any hint of it could only be used against one or the other of them. And always, always, there was worry about eyes to see.

Without speaking, they walked through the lobby and went upstairs. It was still early, and except for a few voices coming from the restaurant no one was about. Officer Bruin had been reassigned with the official closing of the case the previous day, and the desk clerk was nowhere to be seen.

Throwing a smiling glance over her shoulder at Kurt, Elin opened the door to her room.

And stopped just over the threshold in shock.

Pia lay sprawled on the floor between the bed and the window. It was obvious at a glance that she was dead.

39

INSTANTLY STEPPING UP BEHIND HER, KURT PUSHED THE DOOR shut and at the same time clapped a hand over her mouth. Big and hard and suffocating, his hand was the only thing that kept Elin from screaming the hotel down. His arm came around her waist, clamping her struggling against him, her back to his front, when she would have run to her friend.

Pia. Not Pia.

"Elin. Don't scream. Elin." His voice was in her ear, low and urgent.

She barely heard him, was barely aware that he was there. Every part of her strained to reach Pia. Sprawled on the floor in her favorite blue pajamas, her face—her face—she had no face. Only a gaping hole where her face had been.

Elin fought to get free.

"Hush. Liebling, *hush.* If you scream, the police will come.

You'll be hauled in for questioning. Moller will be hauled in. They'll find his wound. He'll be arrested, tried, executed—and *so will you*."

She heard him as if from a distance, through the roaring in her ears.

There was so much blood. Pia lay in a lake of thick oily crimson. The carpet was soaked with it. And the smell...that horrible death smell that she knew too well.

Her knees sagged.

No.

Kurt picked her up, carried her into the bathroom, and, his hand still covering her mouth, set her back on her feet on the tile floor.

"*Don't scream*, do you understand?"

She did. She understood. With some distant, still functioning part of her brain, she'd absorbed what he'd said.

Adrenaline rolled through her like rocket fuel. She wanted to scream, to fight, to flee—but with none of those things possible, she began to tremble instead.

"*Elin?*" His arm felt like iron around her. "Did you hear me? You *can't scream*."

She replied with a jerky little nod.

Cautiously, he eased his hand away from her mouth. She sucked in air.

"Pia—" It was a whimper, uttered as he lowered her down until she was sitting on the tile floor with her back against the wall.

"I'm going to go check on her. You sit here. I'll be just a minute."

Her stomach roiled. Her head swam. She retained the presence of mind to drop her head between her knees.

It was the longest minute of her life.

"Elin." Kurt was back, hunkering down beside her. She lifted her head, looked at him in mute distress. "She's dead. Has been for several hours. She took a bullet to the back of the head."

"He's cleaning up loose ends." Her chest felt like it was being crushed. She was only able to breathe in little gasps. "He must have thought she was me."

"You're going to have to pull yourself together." Kurt's voice was harsh, his hands ungentle as they gripped her arms. "We need to get you and Moller out of here. Right now."

"Oh my God, *Jens*. He doesn't know. He'll never leave her."

"He has to. You have to. Or we're all dead."

"He won't. There's nothing we can do. He's going to go insane with grief. Oh my God, *Pia*—" A sudden wave of anguish assaulted her. A sob caught in her throat.

"Elin. We have to go."

She forced the pain away. There was nothing to be done for Pia now. And Kurt was right. They had to get Jens and *go*.

"He won't leave her."

"We're not going to tell him what's happened. Not until we get him away. You're going to stand up and walk down the stairs in front of me—staying within my sight, mind, because we don't know where the hell Haupt is right now—and I'm going to bang on Moller's door and tell him Pia's in the car, you're heading for the car, we're leaving, let's go."

"But as soon as we get to the car, he'll see—"

"All you have to do is stay in front of us, walk to the car, get in, and leave the rest to me. Can you do that?"

Elin thought of Pia. Her dearest friend. Her almost sister—

Then she thought of Niles. And Kurt. And Jens.

And felt a welling up of strength.

She knew what she had to do. What Pia would want her to do. Save the ones who remained.

"Yes," she said with grim determination. "I can."

Kurt helped her up.

Elin hesitated. "What about…her body?"

"She'll be found. The police will come. She'll be taken to Dr.

Weimann, the hospital. And later, I'll make sure she's sent home to Copenhagen. But for now, we've got to get away."

She nodded. She knew everything he'd told her would happen in just that way, and she trusted him for that reassurance.

"Ready?" he asked.

She nodded again. His arm was around her, lending her strength. As they reached the bathroom door it fell away.

Shock was helping her, she knew. What felt like a layer of ice had encased her heart. The horror, the grief—she would feel it all later. But for now, she could play the part she had to play.

Without looking around, she walked out of the hotel room, and down the stairs. Behind her, she heard Kurt bang on Jens's door, heard him yell at him to get moving, that they were all heading for the car and he was last.

Suspecting nothing, Jens emerged from his hotel room, followed them downstairs and across the courtyard, a bag in either hand.

As she slid into the front passenger seat, Elin heard Jens call out, "Pia?" Then, to Kurt, he said, "Where is she?"

She could hear the confusion in his voice. Because he wasn't seeing her anywhere.

From somewhere she found the strength.

"Where do you think? In the back," she called to Jens, and closed her door. A moment later, the rear door opened, Jens looked in—and she heard a sharp thunk, followed by a bigger, heavier thud.

Turning, she watched Kurt heave Jens's limp body into the back seat.

"What did you *do*?"

"Hit him with my gun," Kurt said grimly. "Don't worry, he'll be all right."

He closed the door, threw the bags into the trunk, and got behind the wheel.

Then they drove away from the Waldschloss.

★ ★ ★

Many hours later, dry-eyed and calm even though her heart was shredded, Elin sat huddled in the corner on a hard bench seat on a train chugging its way through Germany to Denmark. At the other end of the bench, Jens, handkerchief in hand, slumped in a tear-soaked puddle. In his grief, his mountainous proportions seemed to have melted. His bulk spilled across three-quarters of the bench. His feet took up over half the floor. His bags, which he had refused to leave behind, took up most of the rest. As he could not bear to be touched or comforted, and Elin wasn't about to leave him alone, the space considerations were what they were.

Kurt was in the locomotive conferring with the engineer. The locomotive was separated from this small passenger compartment, which was basically a single hard bench between two oversize coal bins, by a narrow passage.

Kurt was conferring with the engineer because he knew him, because the engineer was either part of the Black Orchestra or occasionally cooperated with it—Elin wasn't quite clear on that. And, having left Berlin via the Grunewald train station and subsequently passed through Hamburg and Lübeck, they were nearing the most dangerous part of their journey. Flensburg, with its nearby garrison of soldiers, was flashing by outside the windows. And just beyond Flensburg was the bridge connecting Germany to Denmark.

She and Jens were on the train because, given Pia's murder, Kurt had thought it would be nothing short of idiocy for them to show up at Tempelhof to catch the flight that Haupt had arranged for them, where they could easily be arrested or killed, depending on who got to them first. He also thought it would be equally stupid for them to remain in Berlin, for the same reason. He was traveling with them because he'd known about the train, known when it would depart from Grunewald Station and where it was going, because those were the arrangements he'd made when he'd left her at the Waldschloss for his last night-time visit to the forest. And he was also with them because, as he told her, he wasn't about to let Elin, who wasn't thinking clearly, or Jens, who was completely unhinged by grief, travel alone and unprotected.

Behind the locomotive, six freight cars loaded with the furniture and personal effects of the secretary of the Swedish legation in Berlin rattled along. Having been replaced, the secretary had been given permission to have his belongings shipped back to Stockholm. This train was the first leg of that shipment.

Beyond any possible danger to Elin and Jens if they were being sought and were overtaken, the far greater danger to everyone on board lay in those freight cars. The furniture had been carefully packed into large wooden crates so that it might arrive in Stockholm undamaged. At some point before being loaded onto the train, the contents of a number of those crates had been replaced with people: the 143 Jews, thirty of them children, including Christoph and Rebekah Cohen, that Kurt and his associates had rescued in Berlin.

Now they were going to be smuggled through Denmark to safety in Sweden.

Shield and shelter us beneath the shadows of your wings, O God. The Jewish Prayer of Protection rose unbidden in Elin's mind.

"It's all my fault." Lifting his head to look at her, Jens mopped his eyes with the handkerchief. Those were the first words he'd spoken in several hours.

"No." Elin's voice was soft with compassion. She ached, too, with her own loss, although she knew it didn't compare to his.

"She wouldn't have come to this filthy country if it hadn't been for me."

That was true. And it didn't matter. None of them could have foreseen what the outcome would be.

"She loved you."

The sound he made then was pure, raw grief. It tore at Elin's heart.

"We should have been married," he said, and closed his eyes. "I wish we'd been married."

Dawn was breaking, and enough pinkish light crept in through the windows to allow Elin to see the tears streaming down his face.

The train jerked unexpectedly. There was a squeal, long and loud and grating. The brakes—she identified the sound at the same time as she realized the train was slowing down.

A jolt of anxiety brought her head up. She looked out the window but could see nothing except the dark silhouette of trees against a gorgeous pink-and-purple sky.

"We're stopping?" Jens's eyes opened. Red and puffy, they overflowed with tears.

"I'm sure it's nothing. I'll just go see." She stood up and, keeping a hand pressed to the metal wall for balance as the train swayed and squealed and slowed even more, went forward into the cab.

In the cab were Kurt, Herr Frey of railroad security, and an engineer whose name Elin didn't know. Only the engineer was seated, in a high seat that allowed him to look out through the windshield. Although another such seat was empty, Kurt and Herr Frey both stood, hanging on to handles set into the wall as they braced against the movement.

"Elin—" Kurt saw her at once.

"Is something wrong?" she asked.

His face gave her the answer even before the engineer spoke to Kurt. "What do you want me to do?" His voice was gritty with fear.

"If we ram them, could we get through?" Herr Frey was looking out through the windshield, too.

"Oh, sure," the engineer said. "And then we would derail and go over the cliff into the sea."

"Of course we must stop. Whatever this is, we must brazen it out," Kurt said, then looked at Elin again. "You should go back there with Moller. I'll come get you if there's need."

But Elin was already moving to stand beside him. He caught her with an arm around her waist as the train lurched again, and then she was holding on to the same handle he was and looking out through the windshield, too.

The reason for their alarm and the train's braking became instantly clear.

A military truck sat on the track not twenty meters in front of the bridge that loomed behind it. Its headlights shone down the track, only to be dimmed by the powerful searchlight mounted on top of the truck as it was switched on to spear toward them.

Elin's heart leaped into her throat.

The engineer swore. The brakes squealed louder. The train, slowly and painfully, rocked to a stop.

Kurt reached beneath his jacket to free the flap on his holster.

They were close enough to the truck that they could see the shadowy outlines of the soldiers inside. She had no doubt that the soldiers could, equally, see them.

"What do you want?" the engineer leaned out the side window to shout at them. "You will make us late."

A soldier leaned out the truck's passenger window. From his uniform he was an officer of some sort. "We have orders to search the train."

"What? By whose authority?" The engineer was sweating bullets. Elin could see the sudden shine of it on his face, smell the sour scent. But his voice held just the right degree of indignation. "We have a special pass exempting us from search."

"Signed by who?"

"The Minister of the Interior. Reichsführer Himmler himself." The engineer waved a folder out the window, implying that it contained the pass. "And we have a schedule to keep. So if you value your career, you will move your damned truck out of our way."

There was no such pass. Or if there was, it was forged. Knowing that, Elin broke out into her own cold sweat. Behind her, Kurt had tensed. Elin thought of little Bekah and Christoph, of the others sitting in the silent dark in those crates, not knowing what was happening but knowing that the train had stopped. They were undoubtedly terrified as they waited and wondered. Their lives hung in the balance.

So did hers, and Kurt's, and everyone else's on board.

"Let's see that pass. You should know we've had information that there are Jews on that train."

Elin's throat tightened. Her stomach dropped. She could hear Kurt inhale.

"What, do I look like a Jew to you? Do I sound like a Jew?" The engineer's loud indignation was good. Only those in the cab with him could see that where he'd been lobster red in the face before, he had now turned pale.

"I'll take the pass to them." Jens was in the cab, standing behind them. She hadn't heard him enter. He grabbed the folder from the engineer and stepped out of the cab before anyone could stop him, saying to the engineer, "Tell the bastard I'm bringing it."

"Jens—" Elin protested in alarm. There was something in Jens's voice, in his demeanor, that struck her as wrong.

"You can't go out there," Kurt said in her ear. His arm was around her waist, holding her back when she made an abortive movement as if to follow Jens.

"All right then, he's bringing you the pass. And if we miss our ferry because of your actions, then *you* can explain the delay to Reichsführer Himmler," the engineer bawled out the window.

Through the windshield, Elin watched in fear-filled silence as Jens, huge and lumbering, waving the folder in the air for the soldiers to see, approached the truck.

"That piece of paper you've got in there isn't going to keep them from searching this train," Frey said as he pulled a pistol out of his waistband.

"Keep that down where they can't see it." Kurt's voice was grim. "The back of that truck is packed with soldiers. We don't want to get into a firefight unless we have to."

"You, there! What's that you've got in your other hand?" The shout came from the truck. A flashlight beam shot from the window, pinning Jens in its light. "Get your hands in the air! Let me see both of them!"

"This?" Jens yelled back. He raised his hands. The light caught the gleam of a green glass bottle. "A Jäger. Anybody else wants one, I've got more with me."

Elin froze. The Jägermeister—the green bottle. She'd seen Jens with those bottles before. They were his favorites, he'd told her and Pia one day, when they'd teased him about the empty bottles of the foreign drink in his apartment. Later, Pia had told her why he liked them so much. It wasn't the spicy liquor inside. It was the bottle itself, the thick green, almost opaque glass, the large label to further hide the contents, that made it the perfect container to stuff with plastic explosives, turning each innocent-looking Jäger into a powerful bomb.

"No," Elin said piteously, knowing what was about to happen even as Jens reached the truck. The soldier leaned out the window, hand outstretched for the folder Jens held, as the bomb went off. Only Kurt's hold on the handle kept him and Elin upright as the explosion shook the ground, rattled the train. The fireball was bright as the sun, incinerating the truck and the man standing beside it instantly.

There wasn't even time for anyone caught up in it to scream. They were just gone, their lives obliterated between one heartbeat and the next. The roaring inferno that replaced them was their funeral pyre.

"Holy hell." Kurt sounded stunned. "He made bombs. I saw a couple of those damned bottles in his hotel room."

"He did. It was his specialty." Elin couldn't stop staring at the leaping flames. Horror had sunk its claws deep in her chest with Pia's murder. Now it felt like those same claws, having already shredded her heart, were ripping it out completely.

"That man, he is a hero." The engineer sounded awestruck. "He saved us all."

"We've got to *move*." Frey turned from the windshield, clapped Kurt on the shoulder. "You think nobody heard that? We'll have more soldiers on us before we can blink."

"Yes." With a quick squeeze, Kurt's arm dropped away from Elin's waist. He moved toward the door, already focused on what needed to be done. "Let's get those people out of those crates. We're going to have to cross the bridge on foot." Hanging on to the door frame with one hand, already half out the door, he said to the engineer, "Think you can ram that truck so that whoever shows up next will think what they're seeing is a train wreck?"

"I can," the engineer said, and slid off his seat.

Then the men were outside the truck with Elin following. Because there was no helping Jens now, because the need was urgent, because if more soldiers showed up before the people hidden in the crates were out and away, they were all dead, Elin pushed everything else to the back of her mind and worked feverishly with the others to open those crates.

It took maybe ten minutes to get everyone out. For each group that was freed, Kurt's instructions were the same: "Run! Run across the bridge! That's Denmark on the other side! Go into the woods!"

They did. Carrying infants and the infirm elderly, dragging small children by the hand, they ran past the raging inferno of the truck, onto the narrow bridge, and into the purple-tinted mist that blanketed the wide span. Elin saw Bekah and Christoph with other children their age, a family group from the look of them, fleeing with the rest. The pair saw her, too. Despite their obvious terror, Bekah lifted a hand in a tiny wave. Elin waved back.

Finally, they were all out.

"Ram the truck, then jump," was Kurt's last shout to the engineer. The engineer saluted as he climbed back into the cab. That was Elin's final sight of him as Kurt grabbed her hand and they, with Frey, ran for the bridge.

Their feet had barely touched the bridge's wooden planks when a tremendous crash behind them made Elin jump and look around. She was just in time to watch as pieces of the burning truck flew into the sky and the train came barreling through the spot where the truck had been. It roared across grass and rocks toward the cliff and then plunged over, trailing fire as it plummeted like a falling comet to splash with a tremendous sound into the sea.

40

EVEN WITH THE AID OF THE DANISH RESISTANCE, WHO
Frey, having worked with them previously, was able to contact,
it took more than two full days to traverse the relatively short
distance to Copenhagen. They had to be careful, staying away
from major roads and eschewing public transportation. From
the small fishing village of Gilleleje that was their immediate
goal, the Jews were loaded onto private boats. Concealed in the
holds, they were to embark on the perilous crossing to Sweden,
where people were waiting to receive them and they would finally be safe. Before they left, Elin had a chance to hug Bekah
and Christoph and wish them good luck with the family who'd
taken them under their wing at Maria's, and who would be their
new family as they all started over in Sweden.

Word of the crashed train that had hit a military truck, killing fourteen soldiers, dominated the news, and an investigation

had been launched. Divers had been sent down to examine the sunken train, but to all appearances nothing more than a terrible accident had occurred. If anyone had any inkling that 143 Jews had escaped Berlin on that train, there was no public mention of it. Likewise, if anyone was searching for Elin—or Jens—in connection with Pia's death or for any other reason, they heard nothing of it.

Which, Elin reminded herself, didn't mean that nothing was happening behind the scenes.

A terrible rumor had begun circulating among the Resistance over the last twenty-four hours. As the vegetable truck driver who'd brought Elin and Kurt into Copenhagen for the final leg of their journey rendezvoused with the small group of saboteurs who were waiting on the arrival of the weapons hidden beneath the produce, the rumor was confirmed. Eighteen hundred Gestapo agents, sent in specially for the job, would the very next night descend on all of Denmark's Jews in a blitzkrieg-style raid. Upon arrest, they would be sent immediately to concentration camps in Poland. And Denmark would henceforth be proudly Jew-free.

"The concentration camps are charnel houses," the truck driver said starkly, when he heard what was planned. "No one who goes in there will come out alive."

The news struck terror into Elin's soul.

It was the day before Rosh Hashanah, the Jewish New Year. The night of the holiday itself had been chosen deliberately for the roundup because all Jews were expected to be celebrating either at home or at synagogue, making them easy targets.

But the rumors were spreading, whispered from ear to ear, carried from house to house. Fear was spreading, too. Was it true? Was it not? What should they do?

"I must go home." Elin's heart pounded so hard she could feel it knocking against her chest. If the rumors were true, Hilde was at risk, too, and Borge and many friends, but it was the fate of her son that terrified Elin the most.

She was talking to Nikolaj Mikkelsen, a leader of the Resistance, in the office of the warehouse where the trucker had delivered his goods. Mikkelsen had known Jens and, through him, Pia, and expressed profound sadness to learn of their deaths. From Jens, he knew Elin's son had been fathered by a Jew, and when he saw the fear on her face after hearing the rumors, he told her bluntly that he knew.

"Even a little boy won't be safe," he warned. "The orders are that not a drop of Jewish blood is to be left in Denmark."

"I have to get my son away." Elin's voice was utterly calm. Inside she was anything but. Until she'd heard about the looming roundup of Denmark's Jews, she'd thought she had no capacity left to feel emotion. All that had happened over the last few days had left her empty inside.

She discovered now that she was wrong. Every cell in her body awoke to quiver with fear for Niles.

"Be here tonight. A group is meeting at eight. We're working on a plan to evacuate all our Jews and their families—to Sweden. We will get you out."

She looked at him searchingly. She thought he could be trusted, but—

"We are all Danes together," he said. He was tall and fair like most of their countrymen, and his eyes were very blue. "What the Germans are doing will not stand, because we will not stand for it."

She nodded, accepting that what he was telling her was the truth.

"I've found us a car," Kurt said as he walked into the room. He nodded at Mikkelsen, to whom he'd already been introduced, then looked at Elin. "Come on, I'll take you home."

In the car, a dusty Opel that he'd borrowed from one of the warehouse workers, she told him everything.

"To Sweden," Kurt said. "Yes, I suppose that's best."

"You'll come with us."

He gave her that familiar wry smile of his and shook his head. "I can't, *liebling*. I have a son, too. What of Markus? If I were to disappear, and the Party were to learn of some of the things I've done, he would be left to pay the price. They would kill him, and do it gladly." He paused a moment. "And then, there are projects that I'm part of." She understood from his tone that he meant projects similar to the one he'd just completed.

"If you go back and they find out, they'll kill you."

"That's the chance I have to take. It's a clandestine war, but I'm a soldier in it. I can't just walk away. Not even for you."

"So what does that mean? For us?" Her heart was beating very fast. Her eyes clung to his face. He'd managed to acquire a fresh shirt and a shave. To appear unshaven and scruffy in an occupied city like Copenhagen with jackbooted soldiers on every corner and Nazi flags flying from every public building was to invite the kind of scrutiny they both wanted to avoid. But new lines around his eyes and mouth made him look tired and tough and slightly dangerous. A soldier, indeed.

"The same thing it means for any couple forced apart by war. We each do what we have to do, and when it's over I'll come find you."

"Will you?" She looked at him searchingly.

"You can count on it." That smile of his again as he slanted a look at her. "One hundred percent."

That wrung a smile from her, too.

Then they were in Østerbro, her neighborhood. The narrow, colorful houses and the vast green park they bordered were so familiar and so dear that she hurt from looking at them, because she knew that soon she would have to leave again, and this time, maybe, there would be no coming back.

Soldiers patrolled the sidewalks of Østerbro, too.

She frowned at the sight. The soldiers hadn't been there when she'd left. But since then, since the Nazi takeover of the government, so many things had changed.

Scanning the street, with its orderly yards and carefully kept houses, she didn't like the idea of leaving the dusty, battered old car at the curb in front of her house. It would look out of place. It might attract notice. And anyone could be watching. Anyone could see.

She said as much to him. He nodded agreement.

"Let me out on the corner there." She pointed. "Then park the car in the park. There's a spot just inside that entrance—" she pointed again "—where you can leave it." They were approaching her house. "See that blue house? That's where I live. See that door on the side? I'll make sure it's unlocked for you. Just walk across the street and come in."

"I'll be right there."

He stopped at the corner she'd indicated, and she got out. In the simple blue dress that a Resistance member's wife had given her, she assured herself she wasn't conspicuous.

She forced herself to walk—not run—the short distance to her front door. She breathed in the cool autumn air laden with the familiar soft scents of Fælledparken with all its trees and grass and the water beyond. Along with a rush of joy at being home she felt a deep, aching grief for Pia and Jens, who would never come home again.

She was just sending a little prayer for them winging skyward when someone grabbed her arm from behind.

She jumped, looking around at two black-uniformed Gestapo. The one holding her said, "Professor Lund? You will come with us."

Her heart pounded. "What? Why?"

But they didn't answer, and they paid no heed to anything she said. Instead they bundled her into a car that pulled to the curb with another Gestapo behind the wheel.

With a Gestapo on either side, she was escorted into an old

house near the harbor. Elin caught the briefest glimpse of fishing boats coming in loaded with their day's catch, sailboats tying up, and an enormous cargo ship setting off with the tide. It was sunset, a beautiful golden sunset. As the pretty painted door of the house closed behind her she thought how fitting it was that what was probably going to be one of her last sights on earth should be the harbor she loved. The salt smell of the sea drifted in with her, a comforting scent that followed her down the hall into the room at the back of the house.

In a single glance she saw tall windows letting in shafts of evening sun. Dust motes dancing in the air. High-back chairs facing a sofa. In one corner, a massive desk.

A man stepping out from behind the desk.

She wasn't even surprised to see him.

"*Heil* Hitler! Professor Lund, sir," the Gestapo on her left said with a straight-arm salute.

"*Heil* Hitler." General Haupt returned the salute in kind. "You're dismissed for the night, both of you. Close the door behind you as you leave."

Elin's eyes locked on the gun that appeared in Haupt's hand as he moved to the door, locked it, and pocketed the key. She could hear, faintly, the sound of the men's footsteps as they faded away, and then the outside door closing behind them.

She and Haupt were alone. A terrible coldness crept over her.

"It took you long enough to get here, Professor. Did you stop to sightsee along the way? I've had men watching your house for two days." Haupt strolled into the center of the room and stopped, facing her. He was perhaps three meters away, with the gun pointed directly at her.

He was going to kill her, she knew. *Cleaning up loose ends.* Her heart felt like it would beat its way out of her chest.

"Why have you had me brought here, Herr General?" Elin's chin was up. Her voice was even. Her only hope, she knew, was to keep Haupt's murderous alter ego from taking over.

Although she didn't think there was much hope of that at all.

"Let's see. I could choose from a dozen reasons. Shall we start with, you come from a family of Jews. You have a son who's a Jew. Your mother was the notorious child killer Dagmar Overbye, so you come from the blood of criminals. And you lied about all that. You are a stain on our great society, Professor. *Untermenschen.* And a fraud. If that was all, that would be more than enough." He smiled. It was one of the most chilling things she'd ever seen. The underlying structure of his face seemed to undergo a transformation. Jaw, cheeks, mouth—everything was distorted. His eyes were shiny hard, as deadly as a predator's as they met hers.

Even with the distance between them Elin could feel the rising miasma of evil coming off him in waves.

Before it engulfed him completely, she needed to address the man who, she prayed, still existed beneath the demon.

"I'm a doctor. I can help you, Erhard." She kept her eyes on his face and her voice incredibly gentle despite her growing desperation. "*You* are not responsible for the murders of those women. You didn't want to do it, did you? You fought against it. You found it so distressing that you could no longer have sexual relations with any woman. I can fix that. I can fix *you*, make you whole again, if you—"

The hard fury in his eyes seemed to fade. His mouth twitched. "Professor—"

There was a different tone to his voice. Less gloating, more uncertain. The hand holding the gun wavered. Could she get through to him?

Then his face contorted, the gun snapped up, and the evil surged.

"*Say your prayers,*" he said in a harsh, totally different voice.

Elin screamed and dropped to her knees as the gun fired.

Haupt's body smashed to the ground beside her, blood pouring from his head even as the blast reverberated in her ears.

Gasping in horror, Elin could only stare at the spasming corpse for a stunned moment before she fully registered the fact that he was dead.

Then she looked in the direction from which the shot had come to find a shattered window and a man with a gun standing outside.

Elin called Hilde from a telephone booth not far from the park.

"Elin! We've been so worried! Where are you? Are you—"

Elin cut her off ruthlessly.

"Hilde, listen. I want you to grab Niles and walk out the kitchen door—the kitchen door, mind!—to the corner of Blegdamsvej and Østerbrogade. Don't bring anything with you, just come. I'll meet you there."

"Is something wrong? I just got a call from my neighbor telling me I might want to take a trip out of town over the holidays. She sounded like something was wrong. Is this anything to do with that?" Hilde's anxiety rolled down the telephone line.

"I'll explain everything when I see you. Just get Niles and *go*."

"Yes, we're coming. *Niles!*" Hilde was calling to Niles as she hung up.

Elin jumped back in the car. It was almost dark now and the telephone booth had been specifically chosen because there were several large bushes between it and any nearby street, but still the need to get out of Copenhagen was desperate. She didn't know how long it would be before Haupt's body was discovered, but she did know that the Gestapo knew where her house was and they had been watching it.

"They're coming," she said to Kurt as he pulled away from the booth. He'd already explained to her that he'd been parking as instructed when he saw the Gestapo grab her. He'd followed their car, managing to keep them in sight until they stopped. He saw where they took her, parked, and sprinted back, circling the house and spotting her through the window. Haupt was raising his gun to kill her even as he looked in. Kurt had done the only thing there was to do: shoot the man through the window.

Now they had to get her away.

The ten minutes or so it took Hilde and Niles to reach the designated corner felt like hours to Elin.

"There they are!" Elin directed Kurt's attention to the thin, immaculately dressed old woman and the towheaded boy she was holding by the hand. Hilde was looking around as she neared the corner. The blackout was in force in Copenhagen now; the streetlights no longer came on and there was no spillage of light from any windows to light the way. But still enough of the day remained for Hilde to peer very hard into Kurt's car as it stopped beside them and frown at the stranger behind the wheel.

Elin jumped out.

"Mama!" Pulling free of Hilde, Niles bolted into her arms, and she closed them around him like she never meant to let him go.

"Into the car! Into the car!" Kurt swung the rear door open from inside. Elin bundled Niles into the back seat and climbed in beside him while Hilde hurried around to take the front passenger seat.

The doors were hardly closed again before Kurt, who Elin quickly introduced, was driving away with the object of leaving the city behind.

"Mama, what's wrong? Where are we going?" Niles, having been smothered with kisses, was still wrapped in her arms. Snuggled against her, he looked up worriedly.

"Yes, Elin, what is this about?" Hilde looked at her. Her always beautifully coiffed hair was dull and flat and tucked behind her ears, and that, to Elin, said everything she needed to know about how the last few days had gone for Hilde.

"We have to leave Denmark," Elin said. There was no sense in sugarcoating it. "We're going tonight. Kurt is driving us to Gilleleje and we'll take a boat to Sweden from there."

She and Kurt had already decided that it was too dangerous to join the group that would be meeting at the warehouse at

eight. For all they knew, by then Copenhagen might be swarm-
ing with Gestapo agents hunting for Haupt's killer.

"Do we have to? Why?" Niles asked in a small voice.

"To *Sweden*? *Tonight*? But we have no luggage." Hilde sounded
as upset as she had every right to be.

With a sigh, Elin explained, leaving out the more terrifying
details until she could talk without Niles listening in. When,
eventually, he fell asleep, she told Hilde about Pia and Jens and
all the rest.

"They sent Borge and Wilhelm Kessel to Theresienstadt on
Sunday." Hilde's response was flat. Horror swamped Elin. Theresienstadt was a concentration camp in Czechoslovakia.

"Oh, no," Elin said. "On what charge?"

"Beyond the fact that they're Jews? That's all the charge they
need." Hilde slewed around so that she could see Elin more
fully. The interior of the car was darker even than the outside,
which was lit with stars, but even through the shadows the two
women's eyes met. "Sweden is the right choice. I know you
came for Niles, but I thank you for taking me as well."

"Hilde." Elin reached out to clasp the older woman's shoulder. "Of course I came for you. We're family. We'll always be
family, no matter what."

Hilde covered Elin's hand with her own. Even in the dark,
Elin could see how her chin quivered.

By the time they reached Gilleleje, Hilde had fallen asleep
along with Niles. Elin and Kurt had talked sporadically, but so
much lay between them that neither wished to express because
it would only make their parting harder.

He parked at the docks where a boat was waiting for them,
Kurt having stopped along the way to telephone ahead to make
the necessary arrangements.

"Don't wake them yet," he said softly, and got out of the car.

As he came around toward her, she got out, too, and went into his arms.

The butterflies came out in force as they kissed desperately, passionately.

"I love you," he said when he let go of her at last. "I'll come for you when I can."

"I love you, too." She smiled at him, although a smile under such circumstances was hard. "I'll be expecting you."

Then the fisherman whose boat would take them approached. There were others with him, a family group of seven.

"My boat holds ten," the fisherman explained. And with those words it was time to go.

With one last quick kiss for Kurt, Elin woke Niles and Hilde and they joined the others, stepping onto the boat. Finally there was nothing left for it but for Elin to board, too. As she did, she looked back at Kurt, a promise of forever in her eyes.

He lifted a hand in farewell. The boat cast off. The sea was smooth, but Nazi patrol boats were always a threat and could appear at any time. Elin was sent below, to wait out the crossing in the hold with the others.

Before she went, she turned to look at the Swedish coast. She could see cities, all lit up, glowing brightly against the starry sky.

41

THREE YEARS LATER, WHEN THE WAR HAD BEEN OVER for some months, Elin was alone in the kitchen of her own blue house in Østerbro pondering what to make for dinner. She'd returned just weeks before as the Danish Jews had started to come back to Denmark in a trickle that was turning into a flood. To her delight, and gratitude, the house was just as she'd left it. The neighbors had kept it up, as other neighbors had for the other Jews who had fled. It was a warm feeling, to know that their countrymen had kept faith with them. It was an even better feeling to know that because of the efforts of the Danish Resistance to evacuate them in the teeth of the Rosh Hashanah raid, ninety percent of Denmark's Jews had survived the war.

Hilde was in her own house, with Borge, who had been liberated from the concentration camp, as had most of the Danish Jews who had been imprisoned there. Hilde was so thankful to be home and to have her husband back that Niles, who was visiting his grandparents at that moment, had earlier reported she was singing around the house every day. Which, knowing Hilde as she did, Elin found both hilarious and profoundly touching.

When a knock sounded at her front door, Elin abandoned her contemplation of meatballs—Niles's particular favorite—versus smoked herring to answer it.

Pulling the door open, she froze in place.

Kurt stood there on her doorstep, that familiar wry smile on his face.

Her heart began to race.

"You look surprised to see me," he said.

She pulled herself together. "Not at all. You said you'd come. I believed you."

He looked skeptical. "Did you really?"

She began to smile and threw herself into his open arms. "Well, ninety-five percent."

★ ★ ★ ★ ★